She hid—just as Jamie did.

They had that in common.

Holding tight to a tree, she tried and failed to take a few more steps up the mountain. She fell forward, rolled to her back and just lay there, more tears coming as she labored for breath.

Before Jamie could get to her, she tried to stand again. She got upright, then one foot slipped out from under her and her arms floundered in the air—and she fell back. Hard.

In seconds, Jamie reached her. He touched her cheek and knew the fever wasn't that bad. Sick, yes, but not so sick that he had to worry. The bump on her head . . . that worried him. He patted her cheeks, unwilling to speak.

Her eyes opened. As he already knew, they were blue—deep, dark blue, like a sky at midnight. At first vague, her gaze sharpened the moment her eyes met his.

Her reaction surprised him. Her eyes widened, then her lashes sank down and she said, "Jamie Creed. Thank God."

Novels by Lori Foster

TOO MUCH TEMPTATION

NEVER TOO MUCH

SAY NO TO JOE?

UNEXPECTED

THE SECRET LIFE OF BRYAN

WHEN BRUCE MET CYN

JUST A HINT—CLINT

Published by Zebra Books

LORI FOSTER

Jamie

ZEBRA BOOKS
KENSINGTON PUBLISHING CORP.

ZEBRA BOOKS are published by

Kensington Publishing Corp.
850 Third Avenue
New York, NY 10022

Zebra and the Z logo Reg. U.S. Pat. & TM Off.

ISBN 0-7394-5438-2

Printed in the United States of America

To Laurie Damron—
in too many ways to count,
you've become a very respected and admired friend.
I thank you for all you've done,
all you've given,
and the natural generosity of your heart.
Hugs, Lori

Chapter One

The relentless rain came down, accompanied by ground-rattling thunder and great flashes of lightning. Jamie liked storms . . . but not this one. This time he felt more than the turbulence of the weather. The air crackled with electricity—and good intentions. Determination. Resolve.

They hunted him. Well-meaning, but destructive all the same. He had only himself to blame. He'd allowed them to become friendly. He hadn't been aloof enough, had interfered too many times. But God, what other choices did he have? Watch them suffer? Feel their pain?

No, he couldn't. He had enough of his own pain to deal with.

Sitting on the plank floor, his back to a wall, his knees drawn up, he stared out at the darkness. Not a single lamp glowed in his home. The fireplace remained cool and empty; a chill skated up his spine.

He laid his forehead to his knees, trying to

block them out, wanting to pray that they wouldn't find him but unable to summon the right words in the midst of so many feelings bombarding him.

Then it dawned on him. His head shot up, his black eyes seeing beyond his immediate surroundings. *Not just the townsfolk.* No, someone else crept up his mountain. Someone else wanted him.

Without conscious decision, Jamie pushed to his feet and padded barefoot across the icy floor. No locks protected his doors; he didn't need them. At all times, even in sleep, he kept himself open to data from the outside world. As a remote viewer, he could shut down or accept information at will.

But remaining open made him feel more secure. He used his focus on the townsfolk, on the throbbing life around him, as a psychotherapeutic tool, allowing it to tune out other influences. As long as he kept his brain busy accepting information from locals, no one, not even the profs at Farmington Research Institute, could control his intentions with automatic transmissions.

Shoving his raw wooden door open, Jamie moved out to the covered porch. The scent of wet foliage and earth hung heavy in the air. Rain immediately blew in against him, soaking his shirt and jeans, collecting in his beard and long hair until he looked, felt, like a drowned rat.

Something vaguely close to excitement stirred within him, accelerating his heartbeat, making his blood sing. He lifted his nose to the wind, let his heavy eyelids drift shut. He found a target through space and time . . . and he knew.

The first visitor stood alone, a stranger. A woman. Seeking him out. *Needing* him.

Yes, this he could do.

Half-furious and half-thrilled for the distraction, he stepped inside the house and shoved his feet into rubber boots. Forgoing a jacket, sensing the limitations of his time frame, Jamie stepped off the porch and into the pouring rain.

Storms were different deep in the woods, with leaves acting as a canopy, muffling the patter of the rain, absorbing the moisture. Once, long ago, he had hoped they might absorb some of the emotions that assaulted him. But they hadn't. Even from such a distance, high up the mountain in the thick of the trees where no one ever ventured, he had still gotten to know the townsfolk: first the children, then the others.

And they'd gotten to know him.

Despite his efforts to the contrary, they were starting to care. They didn't know about the institute, about the time he'd spent as a guinea pig, learning more about himself than the profs could ever discover with their intrusive mind experiments and illegal testing.

The townsfolk didn't know that their caring could destroy him, could strip away the last piece of self-respect he had.

And he couldn't tell them.

Twice as dark as it'd be in the open, the day looked like night. Jamie made his way cautiously away from his home, down an invisible trail known only to him. He walked and walked, mud caked up to his knees, his clothes so wet they proved useless against the weather.

Pausing beside a large tree that disappeared into the sky, he looked down the hillside.

Clint Evans, the new sheriff who'd listened to Jamie's dire warnings without much disbelief, picked his way tirelessly up the hillside. Jamie narrowed his eyes, knowing this was Julie's doing, that she wanted Clint to get his agreement to attend their wedding.

He would have gone. To make sure everything stayed safe. To keep watch. Julie didn't need to send her hulking new lover after him. He should be pleased it wasn't Joe, because Joe wouldn't give up, no matter what. Worse, it could have been Alyx, Joe's sister, who'd surprised him once when she'd gotten too close for Jamie to send her away. After that she'd come back again. And once more.

She'd actually been in his home, and damn her, she wanted in his heart. She wanted his friendship.

They all did.

Jamie closed his eyes and concentrated on breathing, on blocking destructive sentiment so he could feel the other intruder. His eyes snapped open and he lifted a hand to shield his vision from the downpour. There, farther up the hill from Clint, she shivered and shook, miserable clear to her bones, tears mixing with the rain and mud on her face.

Jamie felt . . . something. He didn't know what. Odd, because normally only those he cared about muddled his perception. His powerful acclaim to telepathy, clairvoyance, and precognition left most people and events as clear to him as an open book.

But when he cared, emotional reactions mixed with his truer senses, leaving him as confused as everyone else.

Maybe *she* didn't know what she felt, so how could *he* know?

Dismissing Clint from his mind, already knowing what Clint would see and what he'd do, Jamie pushed away from the tree. The woman wore no hat, and her hair was plastered to her skull. A redhead, Jamie thought, although with her hair soaked it looked dark enough to be brown. He didn't have to survey her to know of her pale skin barely touched by freckles, or her blue eyes, now bloodshot.

Her face, more plain than otherwise, served as adequate deception to her body, which bordered on sinfully luscious.

With an absorption wrought from years of isolation, Jamie studied her incredible breasts, her small waist, her long, shapely legs. Those legs . . .

Trying to gain better footing on the slick hillside, she turned, showing him her profile. She had a behind that would excite many men. That is, if they noticed. More likely, her quiet demeanor, choice of clothes, and ordinary face put them off. As she intended. She hid, just as Jamie did.

They had that in common.

Holding tight to a skinny tree, she tried and failed to take a few more steps up the mountain. Her feet gained no purchase on the rain-slick ground and she fell forward with a gasp that got her a mouthful of mud. Moaning, she rolled to her back and just lay there, more tears coming, her chest heaving as she coughed and spewed out mud.

Jamie picked his way toward her, and with each step he took, a sense of alarm expanded until her fear and worry and pain became his own. One of the pitfalls of remote viewing was the level of sensory absorption. Sometimes it could be a serious setback.

For most people, time filtered their emotions, unconsciously burying pain, fading loss, and overlooking illness. Only the strongest emotions remained on the surface, powerful enough for others to perceive. For a remote viewer, the more hidden emotions were also clear.

At the moment, the woman's emotional pain and physical discomfort were strong enough that they became Jamie's too.

Exhaustion and a lingering fever robbed her of strength, leaving him weakened as well. Her lungs labored and her eyes burned. . . . Jamie cut her off, breaking contact so he could concentrate on reaching her.

But before he could get to her, before he could warn her not to move, her determination surfaced and she again tried to stand. She got upright, then one foot slipped out from under her and her arms flailed the air—and she fell back. Hard.

She didn't roll down the hill.

The rock kept her from doing so.

In seconds, Jamie reached her. She was so incredibly still. Squatting down, he touched her cheek and knew that her fever wasn't cause for alarm. Sick, yes, but not so feverish as to be life threatening. The bump on her head . . . *that* worried him. He coasted his fingers through her tangled, wet hair, gently prodding, searching, and encountered a considerable swelling behind her right ear, but no blood.

Jamie patted her cheeks, unwilling to speak because Clint drew nearer and he simply couldn't deal with them both right now.

Tipping a leaf to gather the moisture off it, Jamie

wiped some of the mud from her face. Her hair spiked up in front when he pushed it away from her eyes, giving her an appearance that might have been comical in other circumstances. He tapped her cheeks again, smoothed his thumb along her soft, fever-warm cheekbone, and her eyes opened.

As he already knew, they were blue, but unlike any blue he'd ever seen.

Her eyes weren't intense, like Alyx and Joe Winston's. They weren't a gentle blue like Deputy Scott Royal's. They were deep, dark cobalt blue, reminding Jamie of a stormy sky. At first vague, her gaze sharpened the moment it met his.

Jamie half expected hysterics. Absurd, given he should have known exactly what she'd do. But still, her reaction surprised him. Her eyes widened. Then her lashes sank down in relief and she sighed, "Jamie Creed. Thank God I found you."

And just like that she drifted off, as if exhaustion had been hot on her heels and only sheer grit had kept her going until she found him.

Left eye twitching, muscles tensed, Jamie ran through his options before deciding what to do. He wouldn't take chances. He didn't know her, had no idea what she wanted with him. He had to protect himself, because God knew no one else would do it for him.

Mind made up, Jamie stripped her useless jacket from her shoulders and laid it flat on the ground. She wore a thick shirt, and he gripped the front of it in both hands. Drawing a breath, he jerked hard, rending the material from neck to hem. She didn't move. Her body remained boneless. With methodical intent, he stripped her of every shred of clothing, placing each garment atop the jacket so he could easily gather them into one bundle.

When she lay naked in front of him, the proof of her perfect body there for him to see, Jamie took only a moment to absorb the sight of her before hefting her into his arms. She wasn't a petite woman, but then, he wasn't a slouch. He could, *would,* carry her—as far as necessary.

With his right hand, he snatched up her torn pile of clothing. It had been so long since he'd held anyone, since he'd allowed himself the comfort of physical contact, that his heart felt full to bursting, pounding hard and fast. Never mind the mud and rain and whatever ailed her, she still smelled like a woman: soft and feminine and ripe with sex appeal.

He'd missed that smell so much.

First things first. Rather than climb back up to his cabin, Jamie made his way to the west, toward the plunging edge of a cliff. He looked over to a deep ravine cut through the mountain by a fast-moving stream, now swollen from the heavy rains. Tightening his hold on the woman, he reared back and slung her clothes over the side. The ruined garments soared, sank, and hit the creek with a dull splash, separating, dragged along by the current to get dumped a good distance away from him.

Just getting rid of the clothes made Jamie feel better.

She could still have a surveillance device on her body somewhere, and he'd check for that as soon as he got her out of the foul weather. She might not like his thorough inspection—what woman would? But then, he didn't like being hunted, either. Given the howling wind and stinging rain, it looked like they both had to tolerate a few things.

Even burdened with the woman's weight, the climb to his cabin didn't tax him. Whenever he went anywhere, he walked, so his legs were strong and he had an abundance of stamina.

The woman didn't make a peep, didn't open her eyes again, but she must not have been entirely out of it, because her arms went around his neck and she tucked her face in near his chest to avoid the rain. Prodded by a strange yearning, Jamie curled her closer still, even bent over her a bit to afford her more protection. He could feel the rapping of her heartbeat on his chest, her gentle breath on his throat.

Cravings he hadn't suffered in far too long awoke within him. He didn't like it. Or maybe he liked it too much.

He knew the moment Clint spotted them. He felt the sheriff's shock and curiosity slapping against his already heightened senses. Eyes narrowed against the rain, Jamie forged onward, refusing to look back.

Clint called to him, but his words blew away on the storm. Knowing the woods better than even the bears, Jamie easily lost Clint by moving between trees and boulders and across narrow streams.

By the time he reached his cabin, he knew Clint had turned back. What tales he'd tell to the others, Jamie could only guess. But when the rain stopped and the mud dried—tomorrow or the next day—they'd come for him.

He knew it as sure as he knew the woman in his arms would be trouble.

And still, he carried her over the threshold and into his cabin.

When he nudged the door shut with his shoulder, she shifted, making a small, purely feminine sound of discomfort. Charmed, Jamie watched and waited for her to become fully aware.

She lifted her head slightly. Her gaze shied away from his, and she took in her surroundings, then, blinked twice. No smile. No fear. But she had nervousness in spades, almost equal to her tenacity. While Jamie continued to hold her, she licked her lips, hesitated, and finally turned her face up to his.

His awareness on a razor's edge, Jamie assessed her. Mud streaked her pale cheeks. Her long, wet hair tangled around his shoulder. Her lips shivered with the cold.

Taking him off guard, she lifted one small, woman-soft hand to touch the side of his face. "Thank you."

Very slowly, Jamie set her on her feet. Faith tried not to waver, but a hollow weakness invaded her every muscle. At the moment, staying upright seemed pretty impossible.

Showing all the external emotion of a manikin, Jamie caught her upper arms to steady her.

"I'm sorry," she told him in a voice that sounded raspy and thin. She clutched at his shoulders. "I've been sick. I . . . I need to sit down."

"Not until I know you're safe."

A lump of uncertainty lodged in her throat. He didn't mean safe from danger; he meant safe to have her in his home. Carefully keeping her thoughts blank, a practice she'd perfected through necessity, Faith nodded her agreement. She didn't know what he'd do, but she had no choice other than consent. "All right."

With eyes so black and fathomless they should have been frightening, Jamie stared at her. But she recognized those eyes in more ways than she dared to consider, because anything she thought, he'd know. And right now, he couldn't know anything. The timing had to be right.

"I'll help you," he said low and slipped one strong, steady arm around her waist to support her, drawing her cold, limp body flush against his.

Grateful that she wouldn't be falling on her face, Faith leaned into him. Even through his soaked clothes, he radiated heat, and it felt good. He felt good.

Being naked disconcerted her, but complaining would gain her nothing. She understood that much about him. "Go ahead," she said. "Do what you have to."

"You won't like it."

"Neither will you." He smelled of wind and rain and man, strong and mysterious—and more than capable of any number of things, good and bad.

Because she'd allowed those thoughts to ring clear in her mind, Jamie stalled. The sense of danger darkened his eyes even more. "You know me?"

Faith tried to still the trembling of her limbs. "Yes." Naturally seeking his heat and strength, her naked body pressed closer to his. She should give him her name, but not yet.

"Why?" As he asked it, his fingers sifted through her tangled hair, searching her scalp, rough fingertips exploring each ear, along her nape and under her chin.

"You don't trust me."

"I don't trust anyone."

Faith closed her eyes when his warm hand moved down her body, under each arm, beneath the fullness of each breast. Her nipples tightened from the cold, and her skin prickled with goose bumps. She felt ultrasensitive, horribly exposed.

"I don't remember you," Jamie told her, still staring at her face, his voice low and moderate while he touched her. Everywhere.

"That's okay." She swallowed audibly and began to shake more. "I know . . . know you can't, *won't*, take my word for it. But I'm not bugged."

"You could have a device on you and not even know it." His deep voice held no inflection, no emotion. "Who sent you here?"

She shook her head fast, dislodging the thought before it could form. If he knew, all would be ruined. "No one who means you harm."

"You know the people who would harm me?"

"No!" Oh God, she felt sick. Her legs wanted to collapse beneath her. "That is . . . I know people who . . . who care about you."

His expression didn't change, but he might as well have yelled *liar* for all the stock he put in her statement. "You'd never have found my cabin on your own."

"I know." Her heart clapped in time to the raging storm as his palm coasted over her behind, warmly palpating each cheek, slipping under, lifting—going between.

Gripping him tight, she hid her face against his soggy shirt and prayed she wouldn't embarrass herself by crying.

Watching her, soaking up her every reaction, Jamie didn't falter. He caught her right leg and lifted it high against his hip, catching it there with the press of his elbow, making the most intimate parts of her body accessible to him.

The need to plead with him burned in her throat. But more than that, she wanted to beg for his help. She wanted him to care about her—about them.

"Shhh." With his rough hand open on the cool skin of her belly, he whispered, "I'll be quick."

And then his fingers pressed low, moving along the crease of her legs before going inward, sifting through her pubic hair. As unemotional as a doctor, he stroked along her damp cleft. His fingers explored, prodding between her lips, over her, *into her* for a brief but deep and thorough exam that physically burned and robbed her of all modesty, leaving her close to keening in frustration, humiliation, and more.

His fingers felt big and hard, touching her in ways she'd seldom been touched. The idea of fainting to escape the inevitable appealed to her. Unfortunately, she remained cognizant of his every move, the watchful way he took in her every breath, her every shudder, how dispassionately he searched her body.

Her breath chopped, bordering on panic, and her vision blurred. . . .

He withdrew his hand and scooped her up, carrying her to a short, stuffed sofa shoved up against the far wall. Faith didn't meet his gaze when he set her on the edge of the cushions. Cold and desperation had her curling in on herself.

But Jamie wouldn't have that. He crouched in front of her, touched her chin, and brought her face around to his. His long hair hung wet down his back. His silly beard dripped. He'd changed so much. . . .

Faith blanked her mind, wiped it clean and returned his enigmatic gaze with insouciance.

Quirking one ebony eyebrow, he lowered his attention to her mouth, then her legs.

"I-I'm cold."

"I know." His gaze darted up to hers and then away. "I'll be quick." He ran his hands over her thighs, behind her knees, down to each foot. He checked her wet toes, between each one, then straightened and did the same to her hands.

Met with the sight of his tall frame, his lean strength, Faith shook her head. With his disreputable beard and ponytail, he now resembled a hermit more than a highly intuitive genius. If it hadn't been for those eyes, so deep and intelligent, so caring, she might not have recognized him.

Teeth chattering, she stammered in indignation. "What do you p-possibly think I could have h-hidden between my fingers or toes?"

He didn't pause in his inspection. "There are devices invisible to the naked eye, as small as the head of a pin, that can give off a powerful signal."

"Not up here. Not in th-these woods."

He snared her gaze with his. "Depends on how determined the hunter is." He watched her a moment, then smoothed her wet hair back and pressed his palm to her forehead. Scowling, he said, "Don't move. I'll get you some towels so you can dry off." With fluid grace, he rose to his feet and started away.

Faith squeezed her eyes shut. *Damn him, he spoke without feeling, as if he hadn't just touched me more intimately than any man had in—*

Abruptly turning, Jamie narrowed his ebony eyes on her face. Faith gulped; his look was so tactile she felt again the intrusion of his hands on her body. Shocked by her own wayward thoughts, Faith emptied her mind. *Nothingness,* she chanted to herself, *nothingness, nothingness.* She would *not* blow this by thinking things she couldn't think.

After a long, inscrutable silence, Jamie walked away, and Faith slumped, so emotionally and physically depleted she didn't know how much longer she could stay awake. Every muscle ached, every breath hurt. Considering her worry and her strain and the exhaustion of her trip, she didn't have much left in her.

To help keep awake, she looked around Jamie's small cabin. Made of logs and planks of wood, so natural, it seemed grown from the mountain instead of built by men. Square, with a wraparound porch, it boasted several curtainless windows— none with locks. A rustic ladder led to a loft where she could just barely see Jamie moving around the footboard to a full-sized bed.

Beneath the ladder, a door led to a tiny bathroom that appeared to have only a toilet, sink, and minuscule shower. Before too much longer, she'd make use of that shower. But right now, she just wanted to be warm.

She glanced at the large stone fireplace dominating one wall. It appeared to have been cold for a very long time. Not even a hint of ashes remained in the grate. Faith wrapped her arms around herself and prayed Jamie would hurry.

On the opposite side of the room, open kitchen shelves, holding only a few dishes, flanked a double-bowl ceramic sink situated beneath a window. She imagined Jamie there, rinsing a coffee cup while staring out at nature. Contemplative. Alone.

She shook her head again, refusing to get maudlin.

But still, the sight of his neat, tightly situated kitchen made her heart ache. He owned a squat refrigerator, a tiny freezer, a two-burner stove, and a stacked washer and dryer. A single chair rested beneath his round wooden table.

She couldn't imagine eating alone night after night.

Obviously, he had electricity. He also had lamps. But they weren't on. Deep shadows and a dreary chill filled the cabin.

She feared they might fill Jamie's heart, too.

She was just about to give up and lie down, cold or not, when Jamie reappeared with towels, a quilt, some clothes, and a jar of suspicious-looking liquid. Somehow he'd come down the ladder without her hearing him.

Hesitating in front of her, he visually explored her nakedness again, his gaze lingering on her breasts and belly, before reluctantly handing her the towels. "Did you drive here?"

Her hands shook and her lips trembled. "Part of the way." She stood and awkwardly wrapped one towel around herself, but it barely touched the top of her thighs. Never in her life had she flaunted herself in front of anyone, and she disliked doing so now.

"Let me." Jamie set his bundle on a simple square table at the end of the couch, next to a battery-operated radio, and took the second towel from her.

"I can do it."

Lacking sympathy, he said, "No, you can't."

True. Her heavy limbs dragged at her, and her knees wanted to buckle. She pressed her legs together, trying without success to conceal herself.

But as he began drying her with methodical indifference, she gave up. He ran the towel up the insides of her thighs, behind her knees, and she shuddered, feeling very unhinged and out of control.

"You drove . . . ?" he prompted, while easing her back against the couch to save her from collapsing.

Knowing he needed answers, Faith slumped into the deep cushions. "I left my car several hours back and hitchhiked to Visitation."

Jamie paused, then resumed drying her. "You could have been hurt."

"I knew I wouldn't be." As he rubbed the loose towel over her arms, upper chest, and shoulders, she clutched the other towel to keep from losing it. "And I couldn't risk being followed here, though I knew that wouldn't happen either."

His gaze roamed from below her breasts all the way to her feet. He kept looking at her, giving her nudity a lot of attention.

Absently, he pointed out, "You're not psychic."

"No." She'd never demonstrated even the slightest ability, much as she wished it otherwise.

He peered up at her. "Why?"

"Why what?"

Impatience showed briefly in his dark eyes, then disappeared. "Why do you wish you had psychic ability?"

Oh shit.

At her mental curse, he again quirked his eyebrow. Given that he almost never showed reaction of any kind, Faith supposed a raised eyebrow meant a lot. It thrilled her.

But rather than give herself away, she utilized the one talent she did have: blanking her mind. Given the new tightness in his features though, she'd been too conspicuous. Her throat felt scratchy and she cleared it with a rough cough. "It, um, would have been easier if I had some ability."

"Easier how?"

She flapped a hand. "You know, to deal with . . . some people."

"People close to you?"

"Yes."

Accepting her verbal reluctance, Jamie sat down beside her—not touching, but not with obvious distance either. Did he even notice her as a woman? Unless she'd misunderstood, which was entirely possible, he was supposed to . . .

He handed her the second towel, touched her chin, and brought her face around to his. "Who said I would?"

Her eyes flared.

"You may as well tell me."

She worried her bottom lip with her teeth before giving up and admitting with disgust, "I'm usually *much* better at blanking my thoughts."

"An odd talent."

"One I've honed. But for some reason, around you, I'm slipping."

"You're tired." His fingers glided through her wet hair, tunneled in close to her skull and gently massaged.

It felt *too* good. "Jamie . . ."

Following the length of one long tress, he trailed his fingers downward over her bare shoulder, her breast, almost to her nipple. Odd, the way his touch affected her. Her eyelids went heavy, her heartbeat quickened.

And just like that, Jamie released her hair and flattened his hands onto his thighs. "You're also sick. It's no wonder you're having trouble concentrating. So I'll ask again: Who told you I'd notice you as a woman?"

His deep, mellow voice could lull an enraged bull. Faith used the second towel to dry the rain and mud from her hair, and this time she managed to keep her thoughts elusive. "No one that you know."

"How could someone I don't know tell you anything at all about me?"

Careful, Faith. She touched his forearm and became aware of his strength and the tension he hid.

"There are others like you, Jamie. Others who can see and feel things but are also kind."

His lack of belief hung in the air between them, visible in the flat line of his mouth, the enigmatic glimmer of his shadowy eyes as he met her gaze. "You won't give me names?"

Damn, he was pretty good at this elusive, give-nothing-away stuff. "Not yet."

With slow, precise movements, he unbuttoned his flannel shirt. "Then tell me how you found me."

Oh Lord. He couldn't expect her to think while he undressed right next to her. In the closed confines of the small cabin, his scent filled her head, sending sexual lethargy to further weaken her already shaky muscles. Even his bare-bones conversation rang with confidence and unbelievable strength. He was all man, and in every conceivable way they were very much alone. Being unaware of him wasn't an option.

As silky, dark chest hair became exposed, new heat scorched Faith's skin, and it had nothing to do with fever. It wasn't easy, but she directed her attention toward a darkened window. The impenetrable forest muffled the fury of the storm, but every so often the flash of lightning reflected off the wet panes and the echo of thunder rumbled the air.

Faith drew in a deep breath and shook her head. "I'm sorry, I can't tell you that either."

Again, he caught her jaw, his fingers hard, his hot, bottomless gaze boring into hers. She had no choice but to stare him dead in the eyes—and at close range, Jamie Creed's gaze felt lethal. "You'll tell me."

He didn't raise his voice, made no overt threat, but that in no way lessened the impact of his intent. Faith shrank away until she huddled in the corner of the sofa. Her heart pounded a demented beat, leaving her breathless and more shaken than ever.

The slight trace of menace faded from his expression, and he shook his head. "Don't faint."

"No. No, I won't." But she knew she might.

Jamie made a sound of annoyance and, still watching her, shrugged the sopping shirt off his broad, sleek shoulders and let it drop to the floor. His naked chest was . . . the thing of dreams, at least her dreams.

Her mouth went dry and her belly constricted. *Wow, oh wow.*

"Then again . . ." With the sight of his partial nudity, fainting seemed a real possibility. He wasn't a thick man but ripcord lean, as if he lived off the bare necessities and his frame had room only for muscle, not fat. Naturally dark, smooth, firm flesh stretched taut over bone and sinew, all male angles and innate strength.

She needed food. And sleep. And a shower sounded better and better. Even so, she'd be happy sitting there for about . . . oh, an hour or so, just looking at him. Or maybe touching him. Or maybe even—

Jamie tapped her forehead. "You wanna block those thoughts a little?"

Startled, Faith jerked her gaze up to his. Lo and behold, he looked amused. He didn't actually smile, no, never that. And he was still tense. But somehow she just knew he wanted to laugh at her.

Well, hell. Making a fool of herself was not part of the plan.

Taking a drastic mood swing, Jamie pressed the heels of his hands against his eye sockets. "What," he asked, "*is* the plan?"

Did she cause him pain with her strategy? She'd never intended that. He'd had more than enough pain in his life already. Faith touched his shoulder and relished his warmth and tensile strength. "I'm so sorry, Jamie, but there's a natural order for things. You'll understand, I swear. When it's time."

He dropped his hands, staring at her with drugging force. "I don't have time."

Tears gathered, and Faith hated herself for them. But in the past weeks, exhaustion had become her constant companion. Because of her illness, she had few reserves left.

Trying a smile that almost hurt, she said, "Jamie," and even to her own ears, her voice sounded gentle, scolding, and so very sad. "All you have is time."

Chapter Two

All you have is time.

Jamie couldn't argue with that. His life consisted of endless days and even longer nights. But he wouldn't admit it to her. She couldn't read his mind, but she knew things about him. That meant she'd gotten her information from somewhere, from *someone*, and since few people knew of him, he had to assume she'd been in contact with the institute.

Just thinking it made him edgy with destructive emotions, emotions the profs had tried to strip from him. They'd been ruthless but unsuccessful. Still, the lessons were impossible to forget.

Normally, underhanded tactics never occurred to Jamie. With his abilities, he didn't need subterfuge or guile to get what he needed. More often than not, information bombarded him even when he didn't want it to.

But with this woman . . .

He handed her the dry flannel shirt he'd retrieved from his loft, deliberately removing any inflection from his tone. "Put it on."

"Thank you." She hugged the shirt to her breasts with anticipation.

Jamie wanted to watch her dress, to again see her fascinating body with her pale skin and intriguing curves, her pink nipples . . .

He wasn't an idiot, and he wouldn't start acting like one now. Being this close to her could be dangerous. Touching her would heighten that danger, leaving him vulnerable. He'd let a woman do that to him once; no way in hell would he let it happen a second time.

Turning, he gave her his back and stripped off his wet jeans.

Her attention burned over him with the severity of a live flame. Awareness, fascination, *yearning* . . . Jamie glanced over his shoulder to see her eyes glazed, her lips slightly parted. She liked his body. She wanted him. He didn't need psychic ability to know it. Being a man was enough.

It had been a hell of a long time since a woman had looked at him like that. Sure, he'd grown used to the infatuations of the town women. They romanticized his life and made him out as an ethereal Romeo. Some of them twittered when he got near. Some of them fantasized so blatantly that he felt naked in front of them.

Some of them greeted him with smothering compassion, hoping to befriend him.

He squeezed his eyes shut, unable to think about them right now. He had his hands full. They'd come, he knew it. Alyx would lead the pack, damn her. And Cyn . . . so big-hearted and so determined to save him from himself. Julie would be all practicality; Shay and Luna would be bull-headed and stubborn despite what the men had to say about it.

They were warm and loving, and Jamie liked them all, when he knew liking had no place in his life.

But he'd deal with them when he had to. Not yet.

For right now, he had a bigger problem: the carnal temptation of a red-haired, chatty woman who kept some secrets yet divulged things he'd be better off not knowing.

As a man, Jamie watched her—and wondered if he could use her sexual interest to his advantage.

Even as he considered it, guilt surfaced. She was sick. She was female.

But she plotted against him, and he had to find out what those plots entailed. "Put on the shirt."

"Oh." She inhaled sharply, suffered a coughing fit, and twisted slightly away from him. The graceful line of her back intrigued him. The voluptuous swell of her hips warmed him. Her legs . . . God, she had killer legs that would wrap around a man and hold him tight.

As Jamie watched her pull on the shirt, he stepped into warm, dry jeans and carefully tugged up the zipper. He hadn't even thought about underwear or a shirt for himself, but then, given the unique situation, clothes weren't a priority.

He didn't look at her now, but he heard shifting and rustling and had no problem at all imagining her every move.

"Okay," she whispered. "Coast is clear."

Jamie faced her. Her efforts to towel dry her hair had left it more disheveled than ever. Long tresses curled and twisted, springing in different directions. Without really thinking about it, Jamie reached out and ran his fingers along one corkscrew curl that fell to her shoulder, tugging it out straight, examining the texture, then watching it spring back as he released it.

Totally female, she smoothed her hair and rushed into flustered explanations. "It's a mess. I haven't washed it in three days because of traveling, and with the wind and the mud . . ."

Realizing what he'd done, Jamie took a step backward, away from her allure. The shirt covered her better than the towel had, leaving only her legs bare. But what legs . . . She probably stood five-six or five-seven, not petite but not exactly tall either. She'd rolled up the sleeves to free her hands.

As he studied her legs, she slowly snagged the quilt and pulled it over her lap.

Deprived of that splendid view, Jamie picked up the jar of liquid and settled beside her. "This'll make you feel better."

She stared in horror at the Mason jar of wild peaches and dirty moonshine. "What is it?"

"Homemade liquor. Some locals brew it."

"Moonshine!" Damp curls bounced as she shook her head. "Oh, no. I'm not a drinker. One sip and I'm smashed. I can't even drink a social glass of wine without getting tipsy. It's embarrassing really, because everyone should be able to drink one lousy glass."

Damn, she talked a lot.

"But I can't. There was this one time—"

"I insist." Jamie unscrewed the metal lid. Careful not to touch her injury, he cupped the back of her head and held the jar to her mouth.

"But I don't want—"

"You don't want to get drunk," he said for her. "You don't want to accidentally tell me things that you don't want me to know."

Sadness softened her blue eyes. "I'm sorry."

He hardened his heart, giving her a stare that meant business. "Drink it or leave."

Pink lips parted. Color left her face. "You don't mean that."

Unflinching, he watched her indecision, the desperation that flickered over her features.

"But where would I go? It's storming and I'm sick and you brought me here. . . ."

Jamie didn't relent. His survival instincts were too ingrained to allow any advantage.

For only a single moment, she closed her eyes and her shoulders slumped in defeat. "All right." Her chin lifted and she returned his stare. "But . . . will you please trust me? Just a little. I swear to you, I don't mean you any harm." Her small cool palm flattened on the front of his chest, right over his heart—which immediately began to thump at the contact. Her fingers curled the tiniest bit, biting into his flesh, turning him on more.

Face tipped up to his, she leaned closer. "I'm open to you, Jamie. You can feel my intent. You know I mean what I say."

For one startling heartbeat, her desperation became his, causing him pain, making his brain throb and his heart ache. He didn't know why she was desperate, or what he could do to help her, but she believed he could.

She trusted and needed him.

His pulse quickened as something oddly sweet expanded in his chest, conflicting with his suspicions. He gave a slow nod. "All right. I'll trust you, but only until you give me reason not to."

Body going limp, she whispered, "Thank you." Her hand left his chest and curled over his where he held the jar. She wrinkled her nose and brought the potent liquor to her mouth. Apparently unfamiliar with moonshine, she made the mistake of trying to gulp and nearly choked herself.

While she sputtered and wheezed and tried to suck in air, Jamie set the jar aside and rubbed between her shoulder blades. Touching her was nice, which made it dangerous.

Finally, after nearly a minute, she drew in a startled, strangled gasp of air.

"Ohmigod," she rasped, her eyes watering and her cheeks hot. "That's *awful.*"

Jamie's mood lightened. A feeling that could have been humor wormed through his cynicism. "Sip it this time."

"This time?" Her eyes flared comically in horror. "I have to drink more?"

He nodded and again carried the jar to her mouth.

Holding her nose, she dutifully sipped and made a face each time.

When he lowered the jar, she explained, "I'm a teetotaler." A small burp purled past her compressed lips. "Oops, sorry. I told you I didn't have the knack for drinking."

Mesmerized, Jamie noted how her eyes had lightened, her cheeks darkened. "Just a little more." Enough to loosen her up and free her of reserve.

She licked her lips, already becoming foggy. "The peaches help, huh?"

"If you say so." But he still felt guilty, damn it. "It's all I have for ailments. I've been meaning to get to town. . . . Actually, I've been to town. But not to shop."

"Just to help people?" She voluntarily took another swig, surprising Jamie. This time it went down her throat smooth as silk.

Probably not a good sign.

He relinquished the jar into her hands. "My supplies are low, but I can find you something simple to eat."

"Anything would be good. It's been hours and hours and hours since I ate anything."

"Hours and hours, huh?" He watched her, appreciating the new flush to her skin, the fading caution in her eyes, the restless way she shifted on the couch.

Moonshine made for some heady liquor, guaranteed to give a quick kick. Jamie did more business with the reclusive moonshiners than with any reputable businessman. Anything he needed, they could get. So he dealt with them often.

She tipped the jar to her mouth once again.

"That's enough." Jamie pulled it away from her, capped it, and went to the fireplace. "I'll warm things up in here first, then get you the food."

Flopping back onto his couch, she stretched her legs straight out, folded her hands on her belly.

The quilt fell away, exposing her legs again. She gave a lusty sigh. "I'm not that cold now, but thanks."

Jamie kept getting distracted with her, the sound of her voice, how she moved, her air of femininity. "Stay put."

She waved a hand. "I'm not about to move, trust me. My legs are mush."

Her legs were sexy. Hell, everything about her was sexy. But given how long he'd been celibate, likely any woman alone in his cabin would affect him the same way.

Then he remembered Alyx Winston barging in, *more than once,* and he shook his head. He liked Alyx, even if she was a major pain in the ass. He'd noticed her long legs and her behind and . . . everything about her. He wasn't dead. But he didn't want Alyx sexually. He'd leave her to Deputy Royal. God knew, that man would have his hands full.

After opening the flue on the fireplace, Jamie went outside to fetch wood from the farthest corner of the porch, where he kept it in a covered bin. Chopping wood kept him busy, helped to exhaust him sufficiently so that he could doze. He had enough to last him three winters.

The fading daylight couldn't penetrate the combination of black clouds and thick forest, allowing darkness to descend on the mountain earlier than usual. The wind whistled through branches, tossing fallen leaves and twigs onto the wooden planks of the porch floor and swirling a bone-deep chill around Jamie's bare feet.

When he walked back into the cabin, his arms laden with chunks of wood, his gaze went immediately to the woman. She'd sprawled onto her back, one leg on the couch, one over the side, her foot on the floor. In a vague and inadequate attempt at modesty, she'd draped one corner of the quilt over her thighs.

Staring at the ceiling, she smiled and hummed . . . definitely drunk.

She looked so appealing, in an inebriated, easy way, that Jamie almost missed the relevance of her carefree thoughts, complete with visions of a little girl, laughing one moment, so very serious the next. Jamie saw the child holding up her arms, being lifted and hugged.

The little girl's eyes twinkled, and in a tiny, childlike voice, she squeaked, "Mommy."

The wood fell from Jamie's arms with a terrible clatter.

Luckily, the logs missed his toes, but that damn vision hit him square in the lungs, knocking the wind out of him. He'd connected too strongly with her, felt the warmth of the child, smelled her powder scent, her carefree happiness, the . . . love.

Damn.

In a snap, her memories turned to vapor, disappearing in the air with a poof. She bolted upright, held her head with a moan, then struggled to her feet. They stared at each other, Jamie flabbergasted, the woman alarmed.

Weaving on her feet, she whispered, "Jamie? Are you all right?"

He hadn't been all right in years. But now . . . a *mother* had invaded his cabin? Jamie searched her mind, seeking out that elusive comfort he'd felt for only a flash. He failed. Her thoughts now centered on him, soft, caring thoughts that battered against his better sense.

"I'm fine." He stepped over the fallen wood, giving himself a moment by loading the fireplace with wadded paper and twigs from a bucket on the hearth. He felt her coming toward him even as the air stirred with the female scent of her body. Before her hand settled on his shoulder, he'd already grown rigid.

She stroked him, knelt behind him. "Your hands are shaking," she whispered. "I can take care of the fire if you want."

Jamie glanced at his hands, saw it was true, and curled his fingers into tight fists. Moderating his voice and actions had never been quite so difficult. "Go back to the couch."

She leaned against him, her breasts flattening against his shoulder blades, her breath on the side of his throat. He could feel her stiffened nipples and the brush of her lips on his shoulder as she spoke. "I don't want to."

No, he knew what she wanted. And God help him, he wanted to give in.

Tossing a quick look over his shoulder, he said to himself as much as her, "You're drunk."

Her lips curled in a teasing smile. "You got me drunk."

For a reason. He should remember that. "Tell me about your daughter."

She dropped back on her behind. "My . . . ?"

His gaze fell to the junction of her thighs, and belatedly she pulled the shirt closed to cover herself.

Sweat dampened Jamie's skin. *Damn.* "You have a daughter."

Saying it made her think of the little girl, and more images danced in front of him, so clear and crisp he could almost feel the springy texture of the girl's wildly curling hair, the puny strength in her skinny arms as she gave a tight hug.

He saw her as a tiny infant, making mewling sounds, clutching at the woman's finger. A toddler taking first steps. Crying with illness, laughing at a bird.

Held safe and secure.

Hiding.

And finally, a young child staring at the world with an acute perception few ever possessed and others never believed.

Horror-struck, Jamie grabbed the woman's shoulders, inadvertently squeezing. "Your daughter is psychic?" *Christ.* Had her daughter sent her here?

She pressed back, her fear palpable. "Jamie?" she whispered. "You sound angry."

Enraged was more like it, but not for the reasons she assumed. Thanks to his *gift*, his life had been a never-ending hell. To wish that on a kid . . .

He shoved himself away from the woman and rose to his feet, pacing several steps, then storming back. But words didn't come to him. Even through the mind-muddling moonshine, he felt her need, a mother's need for her daughter, and he accepted in that moment that he couldn't send her away, not until he knew it all.

Not until he helped.

He caught her arm above the elbow and hauled her to her feet, then had to hang on to her to keep her from falling on her face. She'd gotten too drunk too quick.

To rid her of her fear, Jamie regulated his voice into a bland drone. "Sit on the couch. The floor is cold, and you're already sick."

"I want you to sit with me. I don't want to be alone."

Was she a torture device meant to break him down? "I will. In a few minutes."

"You promise?"

Because he couldn't make promises, Jamie led her to the couch and forcibly seated her. He tucked the quilt around her. "Stay here."

Mulish obstinacy had her bottom lip sticking out and her eyes sparking. "You can be so grumpy. I wasn't expecting that. Mysterious, yeah. Private, sure. But not grumpy."

Jamie tuned her out and instead focused on the townsfolk. It'd rain throughout the night, and tomorrow the hillside would be slick and impenetrable, layered in fog, ripe with mosquitoes and other nasty bugs that enjoyed the humidity. That meant he'd have at least until the day after before they came calling.

He resolved to have things figured out by then.

Feeling better now that he had a bare-bones plan, he put the wood in the grate and struck a match. As bluish flames licked upward, Jamie became aware of the trouble brewing in town. He concentrated, and almost groaned aloud as a few details became clear to him.

Trouble with a capital *T*.

But this time, maybe he'd stay uninvolved. He didn't sense any dire physical threat, at least not right off. And emotionally . . . well, these weren't weak people. In fact, he thought strength might be the biggest problem. Visitation, North Carolina, now had its fair share of macho men and determined women, and the result was sometimes the same as penning too many bulls together.

But perhaps, just perhaps, the resulting confusion would serve as an impetus to set things right, to resolve issues so that one and all could be happy.

"Jamie?"

He rose from the hearth and glanced at the woman. Okay, so *he* wouldn't be happy. But then, he never expected to be. Not anymore. "What?"

Smiling like a sap, she sat cross-legged on the couch, the quilt again pushed aside but the tails of the flannel shirt tucked into her lap. A high-priced hooker couldn't be more provocative. Eve herself couldn't have tempted Adam more than Jamie now felt tempted just looking at her.

Her long hair tumbled around her shoulders and back, half hiding her plain face. The flannel opened in a V over her cleavage, and her nipples, still hard, pressed against the soft material.

She gave a shrug that almost toppled her from the couch. "You looked lost in thought. You okay?"

He wished she'd quit asking him that. "I'll get you something to eat."

To his consternation, she left the couch and tottered toward him. "I'll help."

Jamie backed up a step before he caught himself. "I told you to sit on the couch."

She flapped a hand. "But you're not my boss. You're just Jamie Creed, psychic extraordinaire, rebel with a lot of causes, hermit in hiding." And that made her giggle.

Jamie gave up and used the excuse of rummaging through his small refrigerator to put distance between them. "I have cheese and bologna and not much else that I can get ready in a hurry."

"Sounds delish. I'm a simple woman with simple needs. Feed me and I'm yours."

Please make her shut up. Never again would Jamie give her alcohol. . . . What was he saying? He wouldn't know her long enough to worry about her drinking habits or lack thereof.

While he assembled a sandwich and put it on a plate, she hovered close, right at his elbow. Used to being alone, Jamie repeatedly bumped into her until he glared her back a few steps.

Brazen to the core, she went to his fridge and peered inside. "Could I have some mayo with that?"

Jamie stepped around her and retrieved the mayonnaise. "Anything else?"

"Something to drink? My throat is scratchy."

Probably more from yakking her head off than from illness. "I've got water, tea, or moonshine."

She opened her mouth, and Jamie said, "You'll have tea."

"But I'm sorta starting to like the—"

"No. No more moonshine for you." *Ever.*

She laughed. "Okay. Tea it is. I actually like tea anyway. Especially raspberry tea with lemon in it. But I don't suppose you have that. Oh God. You do have coffee, don't you? I mean, I can't function in the morning without coffee. I'll be half-asleep all day. Even Cory knows I need my coffee."

His senses prickled. Very slowly, he faced her. "Cory?"

"My daughter. You saw her already, remember?"

Something about the child reached out to him.

Jamie doubted he'd ever forget her. Patiently he explained, "I saw a girl. You didn't tell me her name."

"Cory."

In an aberrant show of frustration, Jamie rolled his eyes. "Thank you."

"She's beautiful, isn't she? And smart. And sweet. And I love her more than anything else in the whole world."

Christ. Not only gabby, but a drama queen, too. "Come on." Jamie caught her arm and led her a few steps to the single chair at his table. He put the plate of food in front of her and fetched a glass of tea.

"So do you?"

"Do I what?" Jamie leaned back against the counter and crossed his arms over his chest. The novelty of company put him off balance. Even before moving to Visitation, he couldn't recall entertaining anyone.

He sure as hell didn't remember anyone talking to him so much.

"Have coffee? Please say you do. Otherwise I'm going to have to go back out, and that mountain is a real bitch, especially in this rain. But I'd brave it for coffee—"

"You don't have any clothes."

That stymied her, but only for a moment. She snapped her fingers—or at least she tried to. "I guess that means *you'd* have to go, huh? But for coffee—"

"I have coffee."

"Shew." She relaxed. "Of course you do. Everyone has coffee." After biting into her sandwich, she closed her eyes in bliss, then popped them open again.

Mouth full, she asked, "What about sugar? I can't choke down black coffee without sugar. I'm not a trucker, you know."

"I have sugar and powdered creamer."

"Great. Crisis averted." She grinned and took another hefty bite.

Jamie watched her eat, awestruck by her hearty appetite. She wasn't indelicate, but she ate like a starving man instead of one medium-sized female. Then again, her body wasn't exactly on the slim side. Not that she carried extra weight. He'd describe her as . . . robust.

A substantial woman with soft curves and sleek muscles.

"Where is your daughter?"

"Safe."

"Meaning?"

She waved a hand. "I have her with people I trust." And with a sly, exaggerated tip of her head, she said, "That's all I'm saying."

Or so she thought. But Jamie didn't say so aloud.

In record time, all the while chatting about nothing and everything, she finished off the food and drank all the tea.

Sheepish, she glanced at him and confessed, "I gotta go."

Startled from his perusal of her physical features, Jamie asked, "Go where?"

She crossed her legs and jiggled. "You know. *Go.*"

Oh. Another novelty for him. He picked up her empty plate and glass, then gestured with a tilt of his head. "Bathroom's right there."

"Wanna shower with me?"

He damn near dropped her plate, but quickly recovered. Face as deadpan as he could make it, Jamie said, "You should sleep."

"I don't want to sleep. It's so funny because I was really exhausted before." She held her arms out to her sides—which hiked up the damn shirt. "But now I'm wide awake."

Great. She would have to be that kind of drunk. "I'm not showering with you."

Sighing, she wrapped her arms around herself and turned a wobbly circle. "Cory loves showers, which is strange because most little girls love baths. Bubble baths to be exact. But not Cory. She said there's something about the shower that helps to define her thoughts."

Jamie narrowed his eyes. "Just how old is this child?"

"She's almost eight." Then, a little startled, she asked, "You didn't already know that?"

"I saw her around that age, but—"

"But she has a vocabulary that'll blow your mind." Laughing, she nodded. "Believe me, I know. Most people think she's older than she is. With the way she talks and accesses everything, and being tall for her age, Cory gives the illusion of being older."

Seeing that she couldn't hold her liquor worth a damn, Jamie tuned out her chatter and tried springing a question on her. "What's your name?"

"Faith." Her hand slapped over her mouth and her eyes went round.

"Faith, huh?" Should he take her on faith? Trust her sudden appearance in his life? *Hell, no.*

"Oops. Slip of the tongue there."

"Tell me your last name."

"I shouldn't."

"What does it matter if I know your name?"

Her mouth opened, then snapped shut. "I'm not sure."

Because she was drunk. "So tell me."

She chewed her lips, then shrugged. "Owen. Faith Owen."

The name meant nothing to him, and Jamie wondered why she'd been reticent in the first place.

"There." Clear disgruntlement marred her brow. "I answered your questions. Now come shower with me."

She'd be the death of him, yet. Gently, Jamie said, "No."

"But we're supposed to . . . you know." Faith bobbed her eyebrows.

Everything masculine in Jamie came to attention. He slowly straightened. "What?"

"You know, get friendly." She sighed dramatically. "I know that's probably not the kind of friendly I'm supposed to be after. But still, showering together sounds fun, doncha think?"

Jamie had to get her on a different track before he self-combusted. He took two long strides toward her, meaning to urge her into the bathroom, but when he reached her, she flung her arms around him and didn't want to let go.

"Faith . . ."

"I like hearing you say my name." She rubbed her nose into his chest and made little needy sounds of pleasure. "God, you smell *so* good, but I smell like mud. Maybe sweat too, but that's too gross to even consider. I have to shower."

He realized that instead of prying her loose, his hands were smoothing her back, stroking. Savoring the feel of her. Teeth locked, Jamie caught her shoulders and edged her away. "I thought you had to use the bathroom."

She winced. "Oh, I do. Thanks for reminding me."

"No problem."

Smiling, she said, "I knew you were different."

"Yeah. Different." And now rigid with arousal. "Shower while you're in there. Then you can get some sleep." He led her into his minuscule bathroom and left her standing behind him while he adjusted the water temperature. Unfortunately, when he turned back around, he found her too close again. She kept creeping up on him, crowding him.

He should set her straight about that right now.

Her smile turned dreamy. "Cory's different too. She's always been homeschooled because it was too risky to send her to a public school. I didn't want anyone to figure out what she can do."

Lust retreated behind somber reality. "Because someone might want to hurt her."

Faith swallowed hard, her smile slipping away to be replaced by sympathy. "Like they hurt you."

She said that as if she had firsthand knowledge of his pain. But she couldn't, not unless she'd been involved. Stony and cold, Jamie asked, "What do you know of that, Faith?"

"You're angry again." She started to turn away.

In a lightning-fast move, Jamie snatched her wrist in his hand and jerked her against him. She squealed, startled, then leaned into him.

In a momentary loss of control, Jamie shook her. "What do you know of it?"

Rather than retreat from his rough treatment, she put her free arm around his neck, her fingers twining in his long hair. "I'm sorry, but I was there."

Dread, regret, and blazing anger clawed through him. "At the institute?"

"Yes."

She stepped away, and he let her, too shocked to do more than stare at her. He felt her memories, how they hurt her—just not as much as they hurt him. He felt her concern, her caring.

And he saw that little girl again, almost reaching out to him, dredging up an unslaked hunger to be accepted, to maybe be loved. . . .

The disturbing image and emotions disappeared when Faith spoke. "They won't ever hurt you again, Jamie. I promise."

He couldn't even blink. How the hell could she make such an asinine pledge? He knew what they were capable of, and he had an awful suspicion that she did, too. Were she and her daughter on the run from them? Did Faith want him to hide them on the mountain? To protect them?

Faith stood by the toilet, her knees pressed together. "Don't worry about it right now. It'll be okay."

Incredulous, Jamie glared at her.

She gave a little jiggle. "I'm sorry, but now I really do have to go."

Jamie finally recovered enough to leave the bathroom. She knew about the institute.

She knew about *him.*

For one of the few times in his life, he had absolutely no idea what to do.

Chapter Three

The rain aided in the plan, offering camouflage and keeping almost everyone indoors and out of sight. With the country roads all but empty, following Lamar Knute, a pathetic local drunk, home from the bar proved to be a piece of cake. Too smashed to pay attention to anything other than keeping his car on the road, Knute hadn't even glanced in his rearview mirror. He'd be the perfect pawn, as long as things worked out.

Word about town was that the local sheriff and deputy were watching Knute, hoping to catch him in unlawful activity so they could lock him up. But putting Knute in a cell wouldn't have the desired effect.

It wouldn't keep the lawmen busy.

And it wouldn't bring Jamie Creed out of hiding.

Waiting in the bushes wasn't fun, not soaked to the knees with only the ridiculous disguise for protection. But if it'd bring Creed out . . .

The dog cried, cold and scared, the noise annoying. Hopefully it wouldn't be too much longer.

Ah-ha. Finally Knute left his car and headed for his house, red-eyed and mean drunk. But that didn't matter.

Yesterday the dog had gotten loose and wandered through town. One and all had seen the signs of neglect, the burs and ticks, the lack of flesh. *Stupid bastard.*

Yes indeed, Lamar Knute would serve perfectly as the first target.

When he neared the dog, it barked, startling him so that he almost tripped. He cursed, raised his hand—and that was all the distraction needed. With speed, training, and experience, the body erupted from the bushes, kicking out fast and hard. Well before Knute could touch the poor dog, a steel-toed boot connected squarely in his chest, sending him backward into a puddle of mud.

"Son of a bitch!" Knute roared, then clutched his chest in pain.

A thick stick, collected earlier from the side of the road, hit him next, connecting with his hip, his thigh, his shoulder. *Thwack, thwack, thwack.* Too fast to be deflected, too hard for a quick recovery. Once more, not as hard, against his jaw, and Knute screamed out.

God, it felt good to dominate, to take ultimate control.

"Stop! Stop it, please." The bastard curled in on himself, sniveling, cowering.

The dog served as a good excuse for the attack, which would keep others from guessing at identities. "You aren't very good to your dog."

"It's a fucking animal."

"Animals need care. When was the last time you brushed him? Or took him to see a vet?"

Knute obviously lacked good sense, to provoke an attacker. "A vet! That costs money. And I ain't wasting good money on a worthless hound—"

Perfect. *Thwack, thwack.*

"Stop! Why are you doing this?"

Thwack.

"Ow, stop!"

Thwack. "You're a slimeball, Knute, you know that?" *Thwack, thwack.* The stick landed again and again with satisfying force. With each strike, the sense of power grew.

"For the love of God, *stop!*"

One breath, then another, and calm settled in. "You won't ever mistreat the dog again."

"Fine, fine! I won't. Jus' quit beatin' on me."

"You better not change your mind." The thick stick lifted into the air with credible menace. Holding back the blow took Herculean effort. "You won't know when, and you won't know where. But trust me, next time, I won't stop until your black heart does."

"Jesus." The man stared hard through the pouring rain, petrified, his ugly face pale and twisted in pain. "Who the hell are you?"

Beneath the silly black mask, white teeth flashed in a cocky grin. "I'm your worst nightmare. Remember that."

"I ain't likely to forget." Knute pushed to his feet and stumbled. "I think you crippled me." And still grumbling, he headed for his house in a haphazard, awkward trot, constantly looking over his shoulder in fear. Seconds later, he disappeared into his house and slammed the door.

No more time to waste. Getting caught now would ruin well-laid plans.

The dog whined, unaware of its improved future. "Sorry dog. You're on your own now." Rain dripped off the dog's snout, its stooped back. Pitiful. But surely someone else's problem.

A twig snapped, and bushes rustled.

It couldn't be that easy.

Filled with anticipation, the stranger jerked around and searched the surrounding area. Nothing. Not a single sign of Creed. Must have been an animal, or maybe the wind.

Disappointment set in, but not for long.

Sooner or later, Jamie would come out of hiding. He couldn't help himself. His do-gooder nature dictated that he try to protect everyone, more than he protected himself. That was the key.

The plan would work. If not today—then tomorrow or the day after. Eventually, all the pieces would fall into place. Patience. That's all it took. Patience . . . and planning.

Within minutes, the hidden car pulled out of the bushes and drove away.

Half an hour later, bushes at the back of a sprawling, well-maintained farmhouse provided cover. Knute's old dog went straight to the door, scratched once, and seconds later it opened. A girl of about fifteen looked at the shivering mutt huddled on her stoop. She promptly yelled for her daddy while stepping out into the rain, trying to shield the dog's body with her own.

A very tall man appeared, scanned the area, then went to one knee. His gentle voice carried on the wind. Seconds later, a woman appeared with an old blanket, cooing and tsking, and the dog went inside with a lot of attention.

Swallowing around a melon-sized lump of emotion proved impossible. Cold, wet, but pleased with the end result . . . yep, it was time to call it a night.

There were a lot of unanswered questions, but tomorrow would bring more time to investigate. Patience, that's all it took.

A laugh bubbled out. *Yeah, right. Patience? Ha. Anticipation beat patience any day of the week.*

Jamie's head hurt with questions.

Why would the mother of a young girl be in his cabin? Where was her daughter? What did she want from him?

Faith knew him from the Farmington Research Institute. But how?

Worse than the awful confusion, he kept thinking about her naked body, her open *sexual* invitation. And he kept thinking about that elusive comfort he'd felt for only a heartbeat, the comfort that had reached out to him from her daughter.

He wanted to trust Faith, no two ways about that. But what would she do to him?

The shower shut off and he heard humming. *Humming.*

Like a caged animal, Jamie prowled around his cabin—which didn't feel like his cabin anymore. Not only did it smell different with a woman flitting about, but things were out of place. The cushions on his couch. The jar of moonshine. The few dishes in the sink.

The fire shone bright, and the room had already warmed.

But damn, he'd become more accustomed to his cold shadows.

Prodded by anger and uncertainty, Jamie went to the couch and straightened the cushions. He picked up the damp towels and tossed them in the dryer, then put his wet jeans in the laundry basket. He stored things away, cleaned dishes, added more wood to the fire, and then . . . he had nothing left to do.

The fire snapped and crackled, and with it his apprehension expanded, his pulse accelerated. By the time Faith finally opened the door and stepped out, Jamie felt ready to jump out of his skin.

Speaking as she left the bathroom, she said, "I used some of your toothpaste and a corner of a washcloth to clean my teeth. Oh, and your lotion. Hope that's okay."

Jamie saw that she'd also taken his comb from the medicine cabinet to tackle the tangles in her hair. Head bent to the task, she wobbled forward, no less drunk but now pink and fresh and . . .

She looked up and found him just standing there in the middle of the floor, watching her. Her open happiness assailed him. She swayed, dropped the comb, and regained her balance. "Hi."

It was a miracle she'd managed her shower without drowning herself, given her state of inebriation. Jamie swallowed. "Hi." He cleared his throat. "I meant to ask, how's your head? You hit it pretty hard."

"Oh, yeah." She gingerly prodded the injury and winced. "Sore, but the moonshine helped. It's something of a cure-all, huh?"

"That's why I keep it on hand."

"And it's easier to get than real supplies?"

Shrugging, he said, "The men who make it want me to know as little about them as I want them to know of me."

"Unlike your friends in town."

He started to deny having friends, but ended up with another shrug.

He hadn't even thought to put on a shirt. Or maybe, to be honest, he hadn't wanted to. And now her admiring gaze moved over him with drunken appreciation.

She swaggered toward him to touch his beard, her expression absorbed, wondrous. "You are so shaggy," she breathed, making it sound like a damned compliment. "I remembered you being clean-cut and well groomed. If it hadn't been for your eyes, I might not have recognized you."

Defensiveness burned to the surface, but he didn't allow it to sound in his reasonable reply. "Why should I bother shaving?"

Her fingers continued to stroke him, down his throat and back up to his jawline, making him nuts. "Because all this facial hair hides your handsome face."

"Yeah?" He held himself rigid. "Maybe that's the point."

Weaving unsteadily, she touched the end of his nose. "You think certain people are still after you, don't you?" She smiled in a *you're-so-silly* way.

Jamie had had enough. Too much. He'd grown used to dealing with other people's problems, their chaos and disappointments. He had none of that in his life, because he had no one in his life.

That's the way it had to be, and damned if he'd let a chatty, pushy, *stacked* redhead disrupt what he'd so carefully built.

Jamie curved his hands around her throat and held her still. "I have reason to be concerned, Faith." Menace lacing his tone, he growled, "After all, *you're* here, aren't you?"

Through the night, Jamie sat in a chair, watching Faith sleep. Too restless to give in to sleep himself, he'd been sitting there since she dozed off, trying to understand her.

And trying to understand himself.

Faith wasn't the least bit afraid of him. Just the opposite, she seemed to trust him implicitly.

He didn't have a clock up by his bed, but he didn't need one to know dawn approached. She would wake up soon.

Drawing his feet up to the hard wooden seat of the chair and wrapping his arms around his knees, Jamie studied her. Contrary to his expectations, she hadn't shied away from his veiled accusation, hadn't paled in the face of his fury.

Instead, she'd gone on tiptoe, hugged him tight, and told him not to worry so much. Her scent intoxicated him. The feel of her soft body stirred him.

And her hug had been . . . reassuring.

While he'd mentally floundered for a response, she'd yawned and announced that she needed to sleep.

Getting her up the ladder had been a trick. Because she wore only a shirt, he went up first and then half pulled her up behind him. He'd figured that with her stuck in his bed, he'd sleep on the couch and have privacy in the rest of his cabin. He'd even carried a glass of water up to her since she had a sore throat.

But then he couldn't make himself walk away.

Shit.

Jamie didn't want privacy. Not from her. Not right now.

He wanted to crawl into that bed with her and feel her all along the length of his body. He wanted—

She shifted the tiniest bit, and Jamie went on alert, as fascinated with her as with the wild animals that often crept around outside his cabin. He shouldn't be.

Now that she'd eaten and had some sleep, he should probably get her out of his home and away from his life. If he took her down the mountain to Clint, or to Joe or Bryan, or hell, even Alyx, they'd help him.

If he told them to run her out of town, they would.

But Jamie sat there in the chair, his feet and chest bare, his heart beating a slow, steady rhythm.

Curled on her side, facing him, Faith exuded peace.

Jamie tipped his head, studying the shapely line of her body: the dip in her waist, the rise of her full hips, and the slope of her long thighs. He considered the way his shirt hung on her narrower shoulders, the way her breasts filled out the front. Thinking about the warmth of her body, he wondered if the shirt might carry her delicious scent when he got it back.

His eyes narrowed a little at the rise and fall of her chest, the flutter of her eyelashes as she dreamed. He could have given her some sort of bottoms—sweatpants, maybe—but he hadn't wanted to, and she hadn't insisted.

Her slight fever, combined with the trapped heat from the fireplace, made her too warm. Minutes ago, she'd kicked the sheet away, leaving herself displayed, one leg stretched out, the other drawn up closer to her body.

Jamie's blood thrummed through his veins, thick and hot. He hadn't touched a woman sexually in years upon years, and this woman would let him. She'd as much as said so, and it plagued him, made his guts clench and his lungs burn with each steady, deep breath.

Damn it, he knew a few things about her, so why couldn't he know her reasons for being here, offering herself? Even when tanked the night before, and now sound asleep, her thoughts eluded him, staying just out of reach. How could she deliberately hide them from him when no stranger had ever been able to do that? Not in Visitation, not even at the institute.

Well . . . except for those people he'd cared about. They had confused him. Jamie shook his head. No, he wouldn't think about that or he'd never get this situation figured out.

His thoughts parried back and forth, diffused by a mostly naked woman in his bed. Even knowing that she had hidden motives, his awareness grew more acute with each passing second.

Rather than concentrating on reading her to know how to deflect whatever she might try, he just . . . wanted her.

Sexually.

She could be here to expose him, but still he couldn't stop the hot need from flooding his body. He had an erection. He felt primed.

Damn it.

Her hair, now clean and dry, wasn't just red but a deep, shiny titian streaked with gold and brown, brighter than her brownish eyebrows, eyelashes, and pubic hair. Jamie had known she'd be a redhead, but not that her hair would turn him on almost as much as her nudity.

In twisted ropes, her hair hung past her shoulders, one length. Long enough for a ponytail, which he instinctively recognized to be her preferred style. He wanted to touch her hair again, to run his fingers through it. The sensory pleasure a man derived from a woman's hair, sweet and warm and silky, resurged from long-ago memories. He could almost feel it sliding over his chest, tangling in his fingers, brushing his cheek.

She slept like a baby, but still guarded her thoughts. Why? *How?*

Right now, with lust as a focus, she seemed harmless enough. But how long would it be before things turned hellish?

Faith made a soft, sleepy sound, and Jamie tensed, struggling with himself—but it was no use.

No matter how he'd lived his life in recent years, he was still a man.

With all the same weaknesses.

Surrendering to the inevitable, he pushed out of his chair and stalked on silent feet to the end of the bed. Again, this time from a much different vantage point, he studied Faith.

Breathing hard and fast, he took in the sight of her naked bottom and exposed vulva. Pink and warm. His hands curled into fists, his heart punched hard.

How would it feel to slide inside her, deep and slow, to have her squeezing him, to hear her soft moans and sharp cries of pleasure?

His jaw ached as he ground his teeth together, remembering how she'd felt on his fingers, the tightness of her, the scalding heat.

Standing there, Jamie tortured himself with the sight of her, wanting her but at the same time . . . more than a little afraid of her.

As he acknowledged that awful reality, she turned onto her back. The shirt bunched around her waist and he could see her from her navel down to her toes.

God. Without even realizing it, he pressed a hand to his crotch, trying to ease the painful throb of desire. His vision narrowed and blurred.

She shifted again, sighed—and her sleepy eyes opened. For barely a moment, she stared at the ceiling, acclimating herself to her surroundings before bolting upright.

A moan shimmered from her lips, and she grabbed her head, then swallowed convulsively.

Only embers remained in the fireplace, lending

pale light to the dark room. Jamie dropped his hand but didn't move away. He couldn't. "There's water on the nightstand."

Her gaze clapped onto his. For one startling moment, Jamie thought she might scream. Instead, she visibly collected herself, nodded, and slowly, all the while watching him, pulled the sheet up to cover herself.

"Jamie?" Her voice shivered, not with fear but with uncertainty and embarrassment. She reached for the water glass and drank half before inquiring, "What time is it?"

He shrugged. "Close to morning."

"I see." She took another drink and cleared her throat. "Um . . . what are you doing?"

"Who are you, Faith?" He hated the near panic in his tone, but couldn't erase it. "Why are you here?"

Tucking her hair behind her ears, she looked away, thinking hard. Then she set the glass aside and scooted up in the bed. Jamie tried to decipher her intentions, tried to glean even a hint of her purpose. But she'd erased her thoughts like a chalkboard, leaving only the dust of ideas behind.

She patted the mattress beside her.

Oh, no. Hell, no. Jamie didn't move. If he got that close to her—on a damn bed—he'd touch her and he wouldn't be able to stop.

"Please?" Smiling, Faith patted the mattress again. "I'm a friend—"

"I don't have friends."

Chastising him with a look, she whispered, "Yes, you do, even if they're friends you don't really want." She tried a smile that felt like a warm lick.

"Now come here, Jamie. I'm finally sober again, and after all that sleep, I feel so much better. Let me talk with you. Don't be nervous."

The masculine side of him rebelled at such a stupid accusation. Nervous? Why the hell should he be nervous?

Because she already had him doing things he normally wouldn't do.

But now he felt challenged. Faith watched him with a big-eyed innocent look that he didn't buy for a single second. He'd learned at Farmington that innocent looks meant nothing. He'd learned that feigned innocence could mask the most reprehensible plans.

And since Faith wouldn't let him read her . . .

She huffed out a breath. "Honest to God, Jamie. I'm harmless."

"I have great instincts, Faith, as you can imagine."

She laughed, a light, happy sound that sank into Jamie. "Of course you do. And even though you're not privy to my thoughts, you know you want to sit with me." Her lashes lowered in coy persuasion. "Trust yourself, if you don't trust me."

He'd already learned *not* to trust himself, especially with appealing women who pretended to want him.

Another lusty sigh, then: "It's so darn hard to tell, what with your poker face and flat replies, but you sort of seem angry again." She puckered her lips. "I think I know why."

And here he'd meant to hide all emotion. But he admitted, in the same deadpan tone, "Because you infuriate me."

Hopeful, she asked, "And maybe turn you on?"

"No."

"Jamie," she cajoled, all playful and singsong. "Not even a little?"

His brows snapped down. "No, damn it." *Pushy woman.*

Faith arched a brow and looked at his crotch, and he actually felt her attention like a gentle stroke on his boner. His breath caught.

"You don't lie well, Jamie, not with the proof there for me to see." She again patted the bed. "So come on. Let's talk about . . . it."

It? She had to be kidding. But Jamie found himself stepping toward her. Stiff-legged, overwrought with caution, he lowered himself beside her.

"Relax," Faith teased. "Put your legs up. Lean back and get cozy."

Cozy? Strangling on an absurd need for physical contact, sexual or otherwise, Jamie swung his legs up onto the bed. But hell, he felt cold and stiff as a corpse, as far from cozy as a body could get.

Faith twisted to face him, treated him to another gentle smile, and put both hands on his shoulders, pressing him back until he rested against the headboard. "There. Isn't that better?"

Better than what? Jamie just watched her, waiting for . . . he didn't know.

Tucking her legs beneath her, she angled toward him and put a hand to her forehead. "Am I feverish, do you think? Or is it just warm in here?"

He didn't touch her. "Both."

Exasperated, she took his hand and pressed his palm to her forehead. "What do you think?"

He thought he wanted to fuck her long and

hard. His fingers opened, sliding into her hair. Just as he'd suspected: warm silk, woman soft. His thighs stiffened. He struggled for control. "You might have a slight fever."

She turned her cheek into his palm. "You like my hair? Because I never did. Guys make fun of redheads."

Rather than admit to any of his current obsessions, he speculated aloud. "I don't remember any redheads at the institute."

"I was a blonde, then. Bleached blond actually, but not like a platinum blond, not Marilyn Monroe blond. More of a golden blond. But I hated messing with it, always touching up my roots and that other stuff women have to do when they dye their hair. And then my situation changed, so like you and your beard, I decided to—"

Jamie smashed his fingers over her mouth. Jesus, God Almighty, she chattered a lot. It wasn't something familiar to him. She made his head spin. "Did I know you as Faith?"

She shook her head, mumbled against his fingers, and he released her mouth. But she pinched her lips together and stayed silent.

Jamie felt his left eye twitching. He quelled the impulse to try another threat, sensing it wouldn't work any better now than it had before. But instead of chattering too, he just waited, staring her down.

She flushed. "All right. But I know this is going to take us down a slippery slope that I'd hoped to put off until later."

"Later when?"

"I don't know. A day or two?"

A day or . . . ? He glared at her.

"All right, already. I just . . . I don't want you to jump to conclusions, okay?"

Too late. His brain had already been leaping around like an Olympic sprinter. "Let's start with the truth, why don't we?"

"Sure." Scooting a few inches closer until her knee touched his side, Faith brought her breasts perilously close to his shoulder. That distracted Jamie, until she said, "You didn't know my name. There was no reason for you to. I was just a worker bee."

"Worker bee?"

"You know, fetch and carry, take notes, record findings . . . stuff like that."

Record findings? Awful possibilities occurred to Jamie, sending acid to churn in his stomach. "A mere worker bee, yet you met me, when I was kept away from everyone else?"

The isolation had been almost unbearable at times. Once they'd moved him to the parapsychology lab, only Professor Kline and his personal assistant—his paramour—had visited Jamie. Of course, Jamie should have known that Delayna was involved with Kline. And he would have, if they hadn't starved him for company to the point that he ignored his own misgivings, the truths that had pounded against his brain. He'd wanted someone to care for him, someone he could give emotion to, and he'd fallen right into their trap.

Kline made sure that he admired Delayna, and what man wouldn't? Especially when she catered to him, sympathized with him, comforted him. They'd deliberately set him up to go through hell, all in the name of science.

Breaking out in a sweat, Jamie still recalled the exact wording of the institute's mission statement: *Striving to improve human conditions through studied and scientific perception of abilities that surpass average restrictions of the human mind.*

He'd surpassed restrictions, all right. And barely survived to tell about it.

"*Almost* everyone else."

Jumping at the intrusion of Faith's voice when he'd been so lost in sick memories, Jamie shook his head and faced her. "What did you say?"

"Not everyone was kept away from you." Faith nervously twisted her hands together. "The things that happened there . . . the different tests to validate the extent of remote-viewing accuracy, had to be recorded."

A strange foreboding unfurled. Before Jamie had left the institute, he'd been the number one remote viewer, with other psychic talents thrown in for devastating scores in every test.

Faith curled her fingers around his arm, and her tension transferred to him through her quivering apprehension. "In your case, there were only a few people who were trusted enough to be privy to the details of the tests run and the end results achieved. You were top secret, Jamie. What they did to you was top secret. But it all still had to be put into a file."

A layer of ice froze around his heart, settled in his lungs. Shrugging off her hand, Jamie struggled to contain the queasy sense of betrayal. "And you were one of those people?"

"Yes. I was the only other person."

Ripe with disdain, his gaze roamed over her.

"I'm not buying it, Faith." *He didn't want to buy it.* "You're too young to have any formal training or background that'd make you trustworthy to a cynic like Kline."

"I'm twenty-seven. A few years younger than you."

Jamie didn't recall exactly how long ago he'd left Farmington. Too many days and nights had melded together in loneliness, and a man with no agenda, no schedule to keep, never bothered with a calendar. But he knew it had been years upon years. Faith couldn't have been more than nineteen, twenty at most, when she worked for them—and when she'd had a baby.

Jesus, around the time he'd run away, desperate to save his sanity, she'd been pregnant.

But what did it matter? In light of what she'd just told him, he didn't care about her age or what she might have gone through as a young mother alone.

He didn't care, damn it.

"So who are you, Faith?" There'd been days when he'd cursed his ability to know the inside of other people's brains, when he'd had no choice but to feel their pain, their fears and worries. Now, when he most wished for it, he couldn't fathom a single thought in Faith's head.

The unknown conjured many possibilities and had him simmering with rage. He straightened away from the headboard, his stomach in knots, his heart glacial. "Are you Kline's daughter?"

"No." A visible strain etched Faith's features. Her breath accelerated and she chewed her bottom lip before inching closer. "Kline's daughter disappeared years ago, some say to carry on his

work, others say to hide from the disgrace her father caused."

"I never met her," Jamie mused aloud. "So I wouldn't recognize her. But I know Kline was proud of her. I know he shared things with her." His hands fisted. "I know she would have been about your age."

"I'm no relationship to any of them, Jamie, I swear. And I didn't work directly for any of the professors." Her chest rose and fell in desperation. "But . . . I . . ."

Jamie felt more alone by the moment. "You what?"

Trembling, Faith whispered, "I worked for . . . Delayna."

Just hearing the name caused Jamie to jerk hard, all his muscles contracting in reaction. His breath left him in one frantic whoosh.

Of all the things Faith might have said, of all the possible betrayals, he hadn't expected that. Unwanted memories of Delayna flooded into his system. How she'd pretended to care for him, making love to him, toying with him—and allowing Kline, her lover, to tape every second of it so they could examine him like a fucking mouse in mating season.

All in the name of understanding the anomalous mental phenomena of his ability—and how personal feelings of affection, love, and finally rejection might affect that ability.

They'd wanted to know the way his brain worked, why he made a better remote viewer than all the others. And they'd wanted to see how he'd do under stress, if he could adequately sift emotion from truth.

On that, he'd failed. Oh, yeah, he'd failed miserably. His pathetic need for Delayna had left him as helpless as an abandoned newborn. She'd plotted against him, yet he'd been deaf, dumb, and blind to her deception. He hadn't wanted to believe her capable of such callous manipulation.

Just as he didn't want to believe it of Faith.

Unable to keep the memories at bay, Jamie sucked air into his lungs. They'd made him an unwilling participant, a man forced through one repugnant experiment after another. He'd wanted to leave, but they wouldn't let him. Until his escape, he'd been as much a prisoner as any jailed convict.

And Delayna had watched it all in controlled scientific curiosity—as had Faith.

Crushing pain exploded in Jamie's head, in his heart. He shoved away from Faith, heaving in his rage.

"Get out." He meant to shout, but the words came out a mere whisper.

"Wait!" Faith scrambled off the mattress after him.

Jamie ducked back from her outreached hand. If she touched him, he'd lose it, and he'd lose himself. At that moment, volatile fury ruled his mind. He couldn't be trusted.

Through his teeth, Jamie rasped, "Be smart, Faith." His muscles bunched and flexed with the need to retaliate. "Get the fuck out of my cabin and don't come back."

Full of persuasion and a hint of desperation, her voice gentled. "Jamie, please. Just let me explain—"

"No." He struggled with himself, but it was no use. "You've said enough. Your association with Delayna tells me all I need to hear."

"No, it doesn't—"

So bitter and cold his breath should have frosted, Jamie said, "I hate that bitch, and I hate anyone associated with her."

As if he'd struck her, Faith flinched away. "Oh, Jamie, *no*. You don't mean that."

"I mean it."

"You can't."

His jaw damn near dropped. How dare she argue with a man in a killing rage? Was she too simple to realize the peril? Too blind to see his fury? And why the hell wouldn't she believe him, anyway? She looked stubborn and determined and . . . devastated.

That knocked the wind out of him. What did Faith have to be devastated about? She was the intruder, the one hiding behind deception.

But it wasn't in Jamie's nature to hurt others. He was a man compelled to help, to make things right for anyone within his realm.

Jesus, he needed to be alone. He needed to collect his thoughts and bury the pain.

Snatching Faith's arm into a tight grip, Jamie dragged her to the ladder. "Get out. Now."

Her chin shot up. "I won't. I *can't*."

Incredulous, Jamie stared at her. "You . . ." He didn't know what to say. In his present mood, he scared himself.

But she didn't look afraid. Worried, yes, but not really fearful.

If only he could detect her thoughts.

She'd blindsided him, gigged him good, and he hated it that he hadn't seen it coming, had never suspected it. Why had his ability failed him when he needed it most?

And now she refused to leave?

Jamie couldn't take it in. Confusion left him floundering.

But one thing was for sure: Faith knew about the single time in his entire life that he'd fully trusted someone. He'd allowed Delayna to get close, to crawl into his heart. He'd loved her and thought she loved him. But Delayna had turned out to be a backstabbing bitch with ulterior motives no better than the so-called scientists who wanted to dissect his brain in the name of research.

And Faith had worked for her, with her. She knew what they'd done, how foolish he'd been, how pitiful and useless. She'd *seen* him.

He couldn't bear it.

"Fine," Jamie said, too blown to fight her. "Then I'll go." Jerking around, desperate to get away, Jamie stormed across the floor. He refused to call the churning anguish in his chest anything other than anger.

But he'd taken no more than three steps when Faith crashed into his back, causing him to stagger forward. "Jamie, please!"

"What the—" After he regained his balance, Jamie tried to shake her off. Arms and legs wrapped around him, Faith clung monkey-style, crying hard, crawling up his back. He felt like a clown in a circus, or an unwilling actor thrust into a play.

"You promised you wouldn't overreact," she wailed.

Of all the . . . The woman could define over-reaction! Case in point, she had her legs tight around his waist, her face squeezed in close on top of his shoulder, while she hung from his neck.

Reaching back, Jamie gripped her upper arm in a hard fist and, twisting toward her, sent her away with a shove made brutal from fury and hurt and a dangerous need for distance. Faith fell to the floor, scrambled to her knees, and crawled right back at him. "Damn you, Jamie Creed, *you will let me explain.*"

Cleansing breath finally filled Jamie's lungs, rushing in too fast, making his head spin and his vision blur. No way in hell could he discuss this with Faith. He didn't discuss it with anyone. He didn't even think about it except in the occasional nightmare.

Jaw aching, Jamie loomed over her. "I said to get out."

"And I refused." Faith grabbed him again, this time around his knees. Her face pressed against his thighs, and with his legs hobbled, he nearly tripped.

Christ, he couldn't believe this, couldn't believe her audacity or his sudden weak-brained urge to grab her up close and beg her to tell him he'd misunderstood. But there was no misunderstanding. She was no different from Delayna, and he'd be a fool to spend another second with her.

Looking down at her, Jamie couldn't remain immune to the sexual supplication of her pose. Her face rested just below his crotch, her long, silky hair clinging to the denim of his pants, her arms holding him as if she'd never let him go.

Regardless of his justified fury, his body stirred, and he wished he'd fucked her before finding out the truth. If he had, maybe the truth wouldn't hurt so much. Maybe the consolation of physical relief, the knowledge that he'd used her as much as she wanted to use him, would temper the razor-sharp slice of betrayal.

Faith turned her face up to him, treating him to the full force of her entreaty.

It reminded him of Delayna, of how deceitful some women could be.

Regaining a tiny measure of control, Jamie squeezed her shoulders and pried her loose, lifting her up so that her feet dangled off the floor. "Do. Not. Touch me."

Her full bottom lip quivered, and big tears filled her eyes. "I *have* to touch you," she explained in a tormented whisper. "Don't you see? You're hurting, and I'm here to make you feel better."

The words were, in part, true enough to cut deep. Sure, he hurt. Pain had become a part of his life: the pain of solitude, of want and need. But the crushing blow she'd delivered, made more so by her sincerity and the compassion in her expression, couldn't compare to the accustomed ache Jamie lived with day in and day out.

This pain could finish him off.

In an act of self-preservation, Jamie separated himself from her, literally lifting and tossing her onto the bed. Before she'd finished bouncing, he reached the ladder. He'd go outside. He'd vanish into the woods. God knew he excelled at vanishing.

He'd leave Faith no choice but to vacate his cabin, to get out of his head and out of his life.

Hell, maybe he'd go to Alyx and tell her that Faith . . . No, Alyx would tear her up—and screw it, he didn't want Alyx's help.

He wanted no one's help.

He trusted no one. *He didn't.*

Six rungs down, the ladder shook and Faith yelled to him. "Jamie Creed, don't you dare leave without me!"

He looked up—and wished like hell he hadn't.

God Almighty, Faith had both feet on the ladder rungs, scurrying down after him too fast, and she wore only a shirt.

No panties.

A rush of sexual hunger fused with resentment, and the result wasn't pretty. Jamie felt primitive, savage. He felt capable of things that no man should ever feel.

Frozen in place, Jamie stared up, half hearing her continued pleas and orders while an inferno of carnal imagery sparked and then combusted inside him. His palms began to sweat, jeopardizing his grip on the ladder.

And then the unthinkable happened.

In her haste, Faith's bare foot slipped off a rung. She cried out, floundering and grasping for the ladder, clunking down two more rungs while awkwardly trying to regain purchase.

Jamie leapt the final few feet to the floor just as she lost her hold and fell back with a shriek that made his ears ring. She twisted in midair, trying to land on her feet. Instinct brought his arms up, and he half caught her in a tangle of thrashing limbs and accelerated breathing. It wasn't a secure hold by any means.

Grunting, Jamie bore her weight as they both hit the wooden floor, fast and hard. Pain flashed through his hip, his shoulder. His head smacked the floor, sending stars to dance before his eyes. *Good God.*

Sprawled out diagonally over him, Faith lay unmoving, one hand clenched on his shoulder, the other on his waist. Her face was practically in his armpit. He could feel her fast breaths, the pounding of her heart. Her legs straddling one of his.

For several moments, Jamie couldn't take it in. He queried his body, wondering if he'd broken anything, trying to get air back into his traumatized lungs.

Faith shifted—and moaned. He almost moaned too, because her naked sex pressed against his hip. He could feel the heat of her.

Jamie decided that he must be a glutton for punishment, given how swiftly his body reacted. How he could go from blind fury to arousal after a bone-jarring fall, he didn't know.

Pain evident in her voice, Faith whispered, "Jamie . . . my leg."

Her fear brought him around. First sickness, then a bump on the head, and now a hurt leg? The woman was a walking catastrophe, and if he weren't careful, she'd take him down with her. Jamie stared at the ceiling, wondering what to do.

"Jamie?"

He closed his eyes. "Well, shit."

Chapter Four

Careful not to jar Faith, Jamie lifted his head. His brains didn't spill out, so he assumed he'd be okay. Maybe.

The flannel shirt, which he now wanted to burn, bunched up around her waist, leaving her lush bottom completely bare. A long red welt traveled from her left hip down the length of her thigh to just below her knee. Already the flesh of her thigh looked discolored and swollen.

He couldn't freaking believe this. Being cursed with psychic ability was one thing. Being cursed with Faith was overkill.

Striving for a calm that remained just out of reach, Jamie asked, "How bad are you hurt?"

She said, "I . . . I don't know. My leg . . . I'm afraid to move it."

Her thoughts were blessedly free, and Jamie registered her alarm, her very real pain. And her relief.

It was the relief that got to him and sparked his

temper back into an inferno. If she hadn't injured herself, he'd give that upturned bottom a sound . . . *No, don't go there.* His hand and her butt should never make contact, no matter how appealing the idea might be.

Jamie carefully inhaled and exhaled until he could speak without giving away his level of frustration and desperation. Injecting just the right amount of disdain, he pointed out, "There's no reason to get too happy with yourself, Faith. Injury or not, I can still carry you off the mountain."

She said nothing to that.

"It'll be light out very soon. The rain is letting up some. I know these woods like the back of my hand. There are plenty of passable trails, plenty of ways—"

"Please don't make me leave, Jamie. Please."

Jamie wasn't a man given to theatrics, not since that awful day when Delayna had turned his world upside down and revealed him for less than he'd always believed himself to be. Not since the day he'd almost torn the lab apart, acting more the animal than a civilized man.

He felt every bit as volatile now. He wanted to snarl. He wanted to punch a hole in the wall, and he wanted to stroke Faith's ass, to spread her legs and look at her again, kiss her, do a number of sensual, intimate things to her.

If he didn't get it together, he'd end up hyperventilating on all his deep breaths.

Squeezing his eyes shut, Jamie counted to ten, then opened them again. "We can't stay like this." *With you laying on top of me and turning me on and making me forget everything but my desire to fuck you.* "I'm going to move you."

Filled with trepidation, Faith nodded. "Okay."

Jamie slid one hand around her upper arm and curved the other over the top of her thigh, just beneath a soft, pale cheek. He gave in to one slow, easy caress, then got himself together again. "Easy now."

As gentle as he could be, Jamie rolled Faith to her back. Discomfort washed the color from her cheeks. Her shoulders rested on the floor perpendicular to him, but one of his legs was still under hers, which raised her pelvis like an offering.

Jamie stared at the sexy curve of her belly, the tight curls covering her mound, and wondered if any man anywhere had ever found himself in such an untenable position.

Then his gaze came back to her belly. Smooth, firm, and almost concave between her sharp hipbones. His brows came down, and more suspicions crowded in.

The hard, cold floor did not make a comfortable place for conversing. But Faith accepted the reprieve without complaint. She'd stay on a bed of nails if it'd keep Jamie from throwing her out.

Watching the conflicting emotions in his beautiful dark eyes, she said a prayer of thanks that, for whatever reason, her body appealed to him.

He stared at her belly so long, his face a mask, that Faith held her breath. Good grief, he unnerved her. If only she could know his thoughts as easily as he knew hers.

His hand hovered over her abdomen until, with slow precision, he tugged the hem of the flannel shirt down to cover her. Faith couldn't look away from his face, and she didn't care if he read her mind. None of that mattered now. Not with him so wounded.

Black eyes flashed at her, narrow and mean. But all he said was, "You're okay?"

"I think so." But for good measure, she tacked on, "It probably isn't broken, but it hurts."

Jamie gave his attention back to her legs. "You deserve it for coming down the ladder like that. You should have left when I told you to. You shouldn't have followed me, dogging my heels, giving me orders. You shouldn't have—"

"Cared?"

His jaw flexed. "Don't expect any sympathy from me. As soon as possible, you're leaving here." The dark scowl and growled words contrasted with the careful way he touched her leg, prodding, checking for damage.

Faith hissed in pain.

Mouth going flat, Jamie demanded, "Can you wiggle your toes?"

She closed her eyes . . . and wiggled.

"Good. How about flexing your knee?"

He helped, wrapping his long, hard fingers around her ankle and lifting her leg. Even as Faith managed it, pain sank in and she curled her fingers tight in resistance.

Jamie winced, lowered her leg, and pried her hand from his forearm. Her short nails left deep grooves in his skin, and shame struck her.

"Oh God, Jamie, I'm so sorry. I didn't realize—"

"Forget it." He ignored her apology, refusing to look at her. "I don't think it's broken."

"It hurts really bad."

Jamie shrugged.

Determined to get through to him, Faith insisted, "No way can I walk on it."

Palpable frustration rose off him. Even through his contained expression, Faith could see his blistering ire. She wouldn't be surprised if his beard caught on fire.

So much heat, she decided, was preferable to his icy distance any day.

"We need to get you off the damn floor. Can you stand?"

So he could toss her out? In a rush, Faith reached for him, wrapping her arms around his neck and holding on tight when he would have pushed her back. She'd break both her legs if it'd give her a chance to fulfill her purpose.

Jamie caught a fistful of her hair and pried her head back. The gentleness, apparently, was long gone.

"Oww!"

Fierceness shone from the depths of his obsidian eyes. "Did you do it on purpose, then?"

Blank-brained, Faith blinked at him. She wasn't afraid of Jamie, but she didn't like his antagonism at all. "What are you talking about?"

"Did you throw yourself off the ladder on purpose?"

Of all the harebrained . . . That deserved a slap, and she landed one on his hard, sleek shoulder. Not that he seemed to notice. "Don't be such an ass."

Surprise at her waspish tone replaced the animosity.

Nose to nose with him, Faith pointed out, "I could have broken my damn neck, you know."

"From an eight-foot drop?"

"I had no way of knowing you'd catch me after you just threatened to throw me down the mountain." Perturbed, she tossed her hair and glared at him. "For all I knew, you might have let me land on my head."

"I probably should have." Jamie's eyes narrowed again. "Who'd ever know, Faith? I could claim I never saw you."

But Faith knew most of the anger had drained out of him and she now had to deal with weary cynicism. She didn't know which was worse. "You're not going to hurt me, Jamie, and we both know it." She stroked his neck, the shoulder she'd just smacked. "You're a caregiver. A healer and a helper."

"You must not have been around when I left the institute."

"I was there." She cupped her hand over his jaw, the feel of his beard warm and rough on her palm. "You tore the lab apart, and you almost tore Professor Kline apart. But you were justified."

"I wanted to find the files they'd kept on me. I wanted them destroyed."

Faith hugged herself close to him. "I had them." She leaned back and gave him what reassurance she could. "But you don't have to worry. They're gone now."

After a long, frustrated stare, Jamie pinched the bridge of his nose and muttered something low.

"Jamie." Faith pulled his hand down and held it between her own. She left herself mostly open to him. "I want to stay here. I *need* to stay here, as much for you as for me."

For long, quiet moments, Jamie peered at her, until realization dawned. "You're afraid."

"Very. But not just for me. For you, too."

"Bullshit. You said no one was after me."

"I know, but—"

Malicious satisfaction changed his expression. "Then there's no reason to fear for me, is there?"

"It's not that simple, Jamie." Her head started to pound. "I told you that *certain* people aren't after you. The people you've always suspected—like Kline or Delayna. But something's wrong."

"So someone sent *you* here to look out for me?" He glanced at her various bruises. "That's a joke."

His disbelief brought a blush to her cheeks. All she could hope was that the details would remain sketchy for a while longer. "Yes. Sort of. But I wanted to come anyway."

Faith risked another rejection and stroked her hand through his long hair. It was tangled and unruly but clean and soft. Cool in comparison to the heat of his skin.

"Ever since that day when Delayna took part in that wretched experiment, I've wanted to come to you. I've thought about it, about you, a million times. I hated her and I hated Professor Kline." Hoping he'd understand, Faith said, "I quit."

"Just like that?"

"I waited to make sure you didn't come back. Kline swore you would, because he said you had nowhere else to go, no one else to go to. I heard him and Delayna talking about you, how he found you living in foster homes. He said you had no family or friends. After you left, he searched for you, but I knew when a week went by and they hadn't found you, you were gone for good."

And knowing that had just about killed her. Faith swallowed. "So I quit."

"Kline let you leave?"

"He wasn't happy about it." An understatement, for sure. "For months, he threatened me."

"Because he assumed you'd expose the institute?"

"Yes. And . . . because I destroyed the files on you."

With that one statement, Faith regained Jamie's attention in a big way. His concentrated stare unnerved her, but at least he wasn't telling her to leave.

"Why would you do that?"

"I'm not psychic, Jamie, but I knew that the existence of those files hurt you. You didn't want anyone to know what they'd done to you." Remembering that awful time, how hurt Jamie had been, hurt Faith now. Whenever she recalled the wild, nearly crazed look on Jamie's face when he'd searched the lab, she wanted to weep. "I made certain they disappeared."

"Kline might have killed you for that."

Faith shook her head. "He didn't know I was responsible. He thought *you'd* found them."

Jamie's brows shot up. "A logical assumption. God knows, I looked everywhere and destroyed what I could."

"Yes. But the files were in my office, and like I said, you never noticed me, so how could you have known to check my office?" Not that the small room she'd had could really be termed an office. Maybe a broom closet. "Kline knew I was privy to the tests, and he assumed that since I'd documented them, I could help reconstruct them, maybe be a witness to the results."

"Was he right?"

"Yes."

"But you refused?"

Her chin lifted. "Yes."

Gradually, the ferocity faded from Jamie's gaze. "You never said a word to anyone about what happened at Farmington, about what happened with me, did you?"

Faith shook her head. "The institute is still there, but changed. Very changed."

She could tell that Jamie didn't believe her. Given his experiences at Farmington, his personal demons wouldn't let him accept that things might be different.

As he continued to scrutinize her, Faith knew, just as she might read a book, Jamie read her.

"Can I please tell you about the changes?"

Glancing around the floor, at the way they were still half stacked on each other, Jamie shrugged. "Sure, why not? It's not like we've got anything more important to do."

Faith smiled at his sardonic reply but quickly sobered. "Professor Kline passed away. He's gone, Jamie. Dead."

Brutal satisfaction brought an unholy light to his incredible eyes. He said one word. *"Good."*

Faith agreed. "His death brought about an investigation. The lab, the entire institute came under government scrutiny. Investigators exposed the more secretive experiments and shut them down. Even the CIA's involvement got brought out in the open."

"It was never secret." Jamie shrugged. "I was used to recover one of their top men."

"Yes. But you agreed to that assignment. There were other assignments involving stranger stuff, things that weren't sanctioned and that pushed the edge of morality, that were recorded as well." Faith forgot about her leg as she sought convincing words. "Jamie, you weren't the only one they used—you were just the most successful."

"And my success was limited."

His modesty—or perhaps denial—surprised her. "Oh, no, you have no idea how important you were to Professor Kline. You were the measuring stick for every experiment after you left. He compared every other volunteer to you. But during the investigation, files were uncovered. Not *your* files, but others with enough information to give Kline away."

"And that started a chain reaction," Jamie guessed.

"Yes. Given how unethical and illegal the experiments were that Kline supervised, he became a pariah. Senators who had once backed him no longer wanted to be associated with him, either as a man or a scientist. Society condemned him. His wife divorced him and has since remarried. I haven't heard anything more about his daughter."

"So Kline lost everything?"

Faith shrugged. "His labs, his funding, his family, and his money."

Appearing thoughtful, Jamie murmured, "That wouldn't stop Kline."

"No, unfortunately, it didn't." It saddened Faith

still to remember the turn of events. "He took his experiments to the private sector."

Jamie closed his eyes. "Bastard."

Beneath her legs, Faith could feel the rippling of Jamie's muscles, the tension radiating from him. Knowing how others had likely been hurt caused him pain, too.

Without looking at her, as if it didn't matter to him all that much, Jamie asked, "Whatever happened to Delayna?"

Glad that his eyes weren't on her, Faith whispered, "Not long after I left, she left, too. No one knows where she went. She just . . . disappeared."

Other than the hardening of Jamie's jaw, he showed no emotion at all.

Curling close, Faith stroked his neck, his disreputable beard. He was astute enough to guess at what had transpired after all the investigations and the splitting up of teams, but still, she spelled it out.

"Professor Kline caused his own demise. He drew in unsuspecting citizens with the lure of tapping into their hidden telepathy. He promised to assist them in finding lost loved ones. He offered a chance to contribute to noble causes, like cancer cures. He gave them all the promise of better odds on winning the lottery. You name a vulnerability, a need, and Kline profited from it."

"I'm not surprised." Jamie stared past her shoulder. "But I don't imagine Kline's more visible supporters of the past were happy to see him setting up shop again."

"That was a problem. It kept him in the public eye and under scrutiny."

Jamie nodded. "So someone killed him to keep things quiet."

"I don't know for sure, but I think it's possible. The CIA didn't want Professor Kline taking what he'd learned anywhere except the military. And continuing the experiments, in any way, ran the risk of bringing down everyone who'd ever been associated with the project." She took a deep breath and shook her head sadly. "It's said that he died of a heart attack, though he had no history of health problems. Still, the whole thing was so hush-hush, no one is sure."

"You said you destroyed every record concerning me."

"Yes."

"You're sure there weren't duplicates somewhere?"

"At one point, yes, there were duplicates that I didn't have access to." Weighing her odds of reaching him, against pushing him too hard, Faith decided to tell Jamie one small truth. "Delayna gave me all the files before I quit. This might be hard for you to believe, Jamie, but I think she knew I'd destroy them. She regretted her role in your life. She said that what had been done to you was inhumane and should never be done to another soul."

Raw emotion flashed across Jamie's features before he deliberately changed the subject. "How did the papers find out about Kline? I know it wasn't you."

"No. That was Delayna, too." Faith half laughed at herself and admitted her awful cowardice—a cowardice that she couldn't yet explain to him. "As you already guessed, I was too afraid to say anything."

His gaze connected with hers, touching her in ways that surpassed the physical. "By not speaking up, you let others suffer."

"Yes." But she'd had little choice. She couldn't trade one life to save another—and because Kline truly was a monster, that's what speaking up would have cost.

"I'm not judging you on that, Faith. I can't. I didn't say anything either."

"Don't think that way, Jamie." Faith wanted to offer him comfort any way she could. "We both did what we had to at the time. And we both lost things we valued."

At her desperate words, his gaze sharpened, invading her, sifting through the layers of her mind. Some things she had to keep private, but other things Jamie deserved to know.

"You lost your family."

"Yes." There'd been so much confusion then— and so much hope. "But only for a while. To protect them, I had to isolate myself. I cut ties with everyone I knew so that the professor couldn't use them against me."

Jamie nodded in approval. "Smart move. Kline is . . . *was* more than capable of doing anything to get what he wanted."

With a grim smile, Faith agreed. "We both know that, don't we?"

For several heartbeats, Jamie connected with her, until Faith looked away. In a whisper, she confessed some of the threats that had come fast and furious on the heels of her resignation.

"He said if one word of what I knew became public, my younger brother would have a fatal car accident. He was a new driver. Kline said it would be easy to make it look like an accident."

This time Jamie's fingers curled around hers, and the sign of understanding, the show of comfort, nearly did Faith in. After everything he'd been through, including her present intrusion into his life, Jamie still had so much compassion. But she'd been holding on by a thread, and she needed Jamie's strength, not his comfort.

"He said my dad would lose his job, and my mother would run into men who enjoyed . . . redheads."

Jamie eyed her hair. "Your mother's hair is like yours?" He fingered one long curl. "The same different shades of red?"

What did that have to do with anything? Faith shook her head. "Yes. My brother has brown hair."

"What about your father?"

She looked away. "He had brown hair, too."

"Had?"

"He passed away a few years ago. It wasn't Kline," Faith assured him. "He had a stroke and never recovered."

"I'm sorry." Jamie hesitated, then gave her hair a tug. "Go on."

Faith swallowed down the uneasiness that always came with the memories. "It was horrible. My family didn't understand why I walked out of their lives, and naturally, I couldn't explain. They were so hurt, but I didn't know what else I could do. I couldn't involve them in something that was my problem because of choices I'd made."

"You made those choices before knowing Kline was a monster. Once you knew, you left."

"Not soon enough." And that's what haunted Faith the most. "Maybe if I'd done something sooner, you would have been spared."

Jamie stiffened, but not in anger. Not anymore. Did that mean he believed her? Faith hoped so.

"Don't fool yourself, Faith. Kline had a lot of important people in his pocket." Leaning closer, Jamie dipped his head down to see her face. "You were just one small redheaded woman. What is it you called yourself? A worker bee. You didn't have enough clout to stop him."

"Maybe not, but—"

Jamie easily stole her thoughts. "After you quit, you were financially strapped."

"Sad but true." Faith made a face. "They owed me two paychecks that they wouldn't give me, and I was too afraid to press them about it."

"And since Farmington carried your scholarship, you had to quit college."

She'd known how Jamie would get inside her head, but still it unsettled her. He knew her thoughts the same as if she'd spoken them aloud. "I found a job as a waitress and made it on my own."

Now he frowned in apparent confusion. "You were already pregnant, right?"

Before a reply could form, Faith slammed the door shut on her thoughts, and that annoyed Jamie no end.

With his temper banked, Jamie asked, "Why did you do that, Faith?"

Being edgy put a snap in her tone. "Would you like it if I was in your head?"

"I don't even like having you in my house—but here you are."

Heat ran up Faith's neck to settle in her cheeks. Jamie sounded very sincere in saying that, but she had to believe it was only bluster.

She tried to reason with him. "That was a painful time for me, more painful than you can know. I was afraid of so many things and so heartsick over what they'd done to you. It was cruel. And what they learned couldn't possibly apply to anything useful."

"You're wrong." Jamie dropped her hand, then rested back against the floor, stacking his hands behind his head in a pose of negligent disinterest. "They learned that when I'm emotionally charged, when my feelings come into play, I'm useless as a remote channel. I can't decipher shit."

"That's not true." Faith knew that she had to convince him.

"Yeah, it is. Concern and caring distort the facts, hope alters the reality. Kline figured out that he could twist my thoughts into being what he wanted them to be—and then use me to justify things that were . . . unjustifiable."

Jamie's new distance pained her, so Faith leaned over him, resting a hand on his muscular chest, her head on his shoulder. He kept his arms behind his head, but the position was still cozy and made her aches and pains disappear. "That's why you avoid friends now, isn't it? It's why you isolate yourself here and refuse to get too involved."

"Wrong again, Faith. I'm so damned involved with so many people now that I . . ."

She raised her head and smiled at him. "Worry even more?" God, he was so wonderful, and he didn't even realize it. Beneath her palm, she felt the steady thump of his heartbeat, a heart with more capacity for love than ten men combined.

Her fingers curled the tiniest bit. "You're human, Jamie, and you're allowed to experience human emotions."

"It muddles things." Again he closed his eyes, as if he couldn't quite figure it all out and he needed the quiet in his own brain to work on it. "It makes it impossible for me to be able to help."

"No." Faith stroked his hot skin, unsure whether or not it relaxed him, but knowing it made her feel better. "Don't you see, Jamie? It doesn't matter what ability you have, or how you fight it, you're still a man."

Rather than reassure him, her statement seemed to annoy him more. He shoved up to one elbow, eyes narrowed, shoulders squared.

He looked at her body with lascivious interest. "Yeah, I'm a man, Faith." His gaze lingered on her hand, open against his bare chest, then came back up to hers. "And you figure you can use that against me?"

Faith licked her lips and again opened her mind so Jamie would know that she spoke the truth. "I can use that to *help* you, Jamie. I can use it to convince you of what I already know—that you're capable of caring for someone and still seeing the truth in all situations."

"You want me to care for you?"

He looked so appalled by such a possibility, Faith almost blushed. "Yes." And she reiterated again, "So I can help you."

"Why would you even want to?"

Her leg started throbbing. She needed coffee, and she was starting to get cold again. But this was too important to mess up, so she gave Jamie the truth rather than screw up a lie.

Because she was open to him, he smirked. "The truth would be nice for a change."

"All right." Faith brought her hand up to his shoulder, awed at the silky texture and the awesome heat that radiated from his skin. "Once I help you, then you can help my daughter. Because, Jamie, she needs you."

"Right." His jaw worked, his eyes blazed. "To do *what?*"

"I plan to tell you everything. Believe me, I will. But it has to be in the right order. If I try to explain now, before you understand just how far-reaching your abilities are, then things might not work out."

Jamie removed her hand from his body, scooped his muscular arms beneath her legs and back, and rolled to his feet in one fluid movement that amazed Faith.

She wasn't a lightweight. She weighed easily one-forty, yet Jamie treated her weight as negligible. He carried her without jarring her leg, without causing her any additional pain.

Trying for a spot of vagrant humor, Faith leaned away from him to see his face. "You're not going to dump me outside, are you?"

"I should." There was no real anger to his tone now. "But no, I'm taking you to the couch."

Thank God. "I'm sorry I'm such a burden. I hadn't planned to be sick or to hit my head or to tumble down a ladder. I hadn't planned on passing out last night and sleeping so long. I swear." She laid her head on his shoulder and sighed. "But I'm glad if being hurt convinces you to give me another chance."

"Don't push it, Faith." Taking long strides toward the couch, Jamie glanced down at her. "I haven't ruled out getting rid of you. But for now . . . you have me curious."

"About?"

He snorted. "Hell, everything. But especially how you manage to compartmentalize your thoughts, hiding some things while revealing others. It's like . . . in deliberate layers, and some are buried beneath others. I've never known anyone who could do that."

Shew. That she could explain. "You have me curious, too. Can we talk for just a while?"

"Do you do anything except talk?" Gently, Jamie lowered her to the couch and pulled her to rest on her side. He crouched in front of her and, with a sound of frustration, touched the ragged welt on her leg. "You're going to have more bruises and bumps than a drunk in a brawl."

"I'm sorry. I'd blame it on nervousness, but that'd be a lie and you said you want the truth."

Jamie continued to examine her thigh, tracing the bruises with a fingertip. "So you're just clumsy and gabby by nature, huh? Is that what you're telling me?"

"I'm afraid so. But I like to listen too, so will you tell me about this cabin and how you found it? And about your friends in Visitation." He seemed resigned to her interrogation until she added, "And can you tell me why you haven't been with a woman in so long?"

Jamie's head shot up, his gaze clapping onto hers in red-hot male resentment. "Who says I haven't?"

"Ummm—"

"You can't tell me." Brows coming together, Jamie growled, "You've got some nerve, lady."

"I'm sorry! I just know that you've kept yourself alone, which I assumed meant celibate, too. But if you tell me otherwise—"

He interrupted her. "I'm not telling you a damn thing."

"All right." Faith tried a conciliatory smile. "Then what about the cabin? Where'd you get it?"

Visibly tamping down his anger, Jamie worked his jaw and finally found a reasonable tone. "It used to belong to a wealthy, eccentric hunter." He stood and on his way to the kitchen area, said, "He paid through the nose to have it built to his specifications. Then he died in a fall down the mountain, and his heirs didn't want any part of it. Too isolated and probably too many memories about the man who'd owned it."

Faith blinked in surprise. She hadn't expected such a detailed accounting. "How'd you find out about it?"

While pulling ice from the freezer, Jamie glanced at her, and his expression went flat. "Dumb question, Faith. The same way I find out about everything. I just know."

"Oh, yeah." Her shoulder lifted in an apologetic shrug. "You had enough money to buy it outright?"

"The institute paid me well before I left."

"Not that good. Remember, I was involved there."

He dumped the ice into a hand towel, then stepped over to a utility cabinet. "Trust me." After locating a hammer, he began pounding the ice into fragments. "Your involvement with Kline is not something I'm ever going to forget."

Faith didn't want to give him too much time to get angry again, so she asked more questions. Speaking over the rap of the hammer, she asked, "So where'd you get the money?"

"Hoping to learn all my secrets?"

"Yes." He glared at her over his shoulder, and Faith sighed. "But not to use them against you."

He didn't appear convinced, but he let it go. "I know things, Faith. Gambling to make money is a cinch. Betting on horses is easy. Stocks are a piece of cake."

Fascinated and taken by surprise, Faith pushed up into a sitting position. "That's . . ."

"Illegal?"

"I was going to say ingenious. I never even thought of it."

"Kline did." Jamie began bundling the small towel together to make a compress of the crushed ice. "He said I had to stay at the institute, where I could be controlled, or the government would have me hunted down and eliminated. He said I was a security threat to the nation, given my mental abilities."

"That bastard!"

Dismissing her outrage, Jamie agreed. "He was that."

It took Faith a moment to get her temper under control. More than ever, she was glad Kline had found a bad end to his evilness. "When did you finally realize that he lied to you just to keep you around?"

"I never knew for sure." Jamie turned to face her, resting back on the counter. "But I finally decided I didn't care. I figured if they hunted me down, I'd be ready."

Faith's heart wanted to break as she realized the terror he must have lived with. It explained a lot about his cautious nature and the way he'd isolated himself.

"I hid, and I covered my trail. But someone really determined could have found me. So after a few years, when no one came, it dawned on me that Kline could have been lying to serve his own purposes."

Kline's influence on Jamie had been worse than Faith expected. Sympathy welled up, enough to choke her. But she hid it, instinctively knowing Jamie wouldn't want her pity. "I guess there's a lot about you that I don't know. I'm sorry."

One brow lifted. "So you don't know that I have a comfortable savings? I'm shocked. I thought you'd dug up every little scrap of my life."

"I wouldn't even know where to look. No, I only know what my . . . Never mind." If Faith told Jamie where she'd gotten her information, it wouldn't take him long to learn the rest.

Jamie's shoulders tightened, but he said nothing. He turned back to the cabinet and quickly and efficiently prepared the coffeemaker, which set her mouth to watering. More than ever before, she needed her morning kick of caffeine.

But when Jamie set the moonshine on the counter too, Faith bit back a groan. Next to the moonshine, he stacked a clean cloth and some ointment.

"I don't want to drink any more of that, Jamie."

"It's for your leg, not your mouth." He snorted. "You get too damn amorous when you drink."

Remembering some of what she'd said and done the night before, Faith blushed. "Should I apologize again, then?"

Jamie shrugged, and she said, "No, I don't think I will. The truth is, you'd interest me whether I was drunk or not. And you already know it, because I'm not blocking my thoughts."

"Wrong." With the ice pack in hand, Jamie started toward her. "The fact that you can hide your thoughts at will means I can't trust anything you say. You distort things, picking and choosing what I glean and what you keep well buried."

"What you read is real, Jamie."

"But taken out of context, anything can be misconstrued."

Accepting that he had a point, Faith felt compelled to explain. "I had to learn to do it for Cory."

"Is that right?"

"She's a child, Jamie. Whenever I was upset or sad, she took on the emotion. She used to cry, and I wouldn't know why. I thought she had colic. Or worse. Even though the doctors couldn't find anything wrong with her, it scared me to death. But the more afraid I got, the more upset she got. It was . . . heartbreaking."

Jamie sat close to her and moved the hem of the flannel shirt out of his way so he could see her thigh. "It bothers you so much when she cries?"

"If you've never loved a child, then you can't know."

Jamie gave her an unreadable look. "No, I've never loved a kid."

Baring her soul, Faith pressed a hand to her heart and said, "It's devastating. I'd sooner take a beating than see Cory hurt or afraid."

Jamie's expression changed, but Faith had no clue to his thoughts. As usual, he didn't let her see any more than he wanted her to see. "How did you figure out that she reacted to your feelings?"

"Purely by accident. I'd been paying—or rather, *trying* to pay—the monthly bills. I was stressed, and Cory kept crying even though I did everything in my power to get her to stop. She wasn't even six months old yet, and I was so worn out that I thought I'd just die. Then a song came on the radio and I started singing to her, dancing. My brain sort of relaxed. *I relaxed.* And then . . . Cory relaxed."

Gently placing the ice pack against her leg, Jamie asked, "Don't most moms sing to their kids?"

Wow. Faith caught her breath as the cold about stopped her heart. Luckily, his question gave her something else to focus on.

"Sure. I sang to her all the time. But this was the first time that I deliberately lightened my own mood. And it worked."

"So she felt all this as an infant?"

"Absolutely. From then on, I paid attention to her mood swings, and they often reflected my own. Whenever something bothered me, rather than dwell on those emotions, I'd think about how much I loved her, how precious she is to me. I counted my blessings instead of looking at the problems."

"But the problems were still there."

"Of course. I just didn't let them interfere between my daughter and me. I watched the birds
out the window, looked at photographs of loved
ones. I'd sing and dance, watch cartoons, or read
an amusing book. And eventually I figured out how
to put one emotion aside to concentrate on another."

With one hand, Jamie held the ice pack in place.
With the other, he tipped up Faith's chin. His eyes
were dark, probing her thoughts even before he
said, "What about lust?"

The question surprised her so, that Faith blinked
twice before croaking, *"What?"*

"You're a grown woman, Faith. I know you've
felt it. When you dated, when men visited." He
dropped his hand and leaned away from her. "If
your daughter knows your feelings, how did she
react to that?"

Faith shook her head. She couldn't tell Jamie
that other than family and the occasional friend,
men didn't visit her. Before finding Jamie again,
she couldn't remember the last time she'd felt
lust.

"She's an innocent child. Her concept of feelings doesn't extend to something like . . . desire.
It's not in her understanding. She would interpret
it another way, maybe as . . . I don't know. An intensity of caring or something."

"Like wanting coffee?" Jamie asked, and Faith
considered smacking him.

"Yes, like that. She'd equate it with wanting, but
not in a sexual way. Hate, lust, fury, and most other
strong, adult emotions aren't in her repertoire.
She's a child, so the way she interprets things will
always be slanted with what she knows."

Appearing very dissatisfied with her explanation, Jamie pushed to his feet. "So this special ability of yours is self-taught out of necessity, as part of an altruistic mother's love?"

Coming out of nowhere, his sarcasm lashed against Faith. She glared at him. "Yes."

"It's not just a means to dupe me?"

Throwing up her hands, Faith stressed, "I don't *want* to dupe you. I want to help you."

"So I can help your daughter in return—but naturally you can't give me details?"

Because she couldn't, Faith shrugged. "That's about it."

Jamie stepped away. "And I'm supposed to take your word on . . . faith?"

"Don't be nasty. This situation is hard enough on us both as it is."

"Fine."

Faith thought he let that go too easily, but she wasn't sure what to say. He went to the counter, poured a cup of coffee, and returned with it, the moonshine, the cloth, and the ointment.

It was an odd mix, and Faith eyed his approach, asking hopefully, "Is the coffee for me?"

Jamie glanced at her as he seated himself. "Sure. If you want to explain. Otherwise, it's for me." And just to be despicable, she was sure, he took a savoring sip of the coffee.

"Dirty pool, Jamie."

"So sue me." He set the mug of coffee out of her reach, then dabbed the cloth in the moonshine and settled close to her on the couch. "This is going to hurt like hell."

"And won't that just make your day?"

He stroked his thumb over her jaw. Staring first at her mouth, then into her eyes, he said, "I don't want you here, Faith, and if I could send you away right now, believe me, I would. But I've never taken pleasure in someone else's pain."

His justified censure made her feel like a heel, and she winced. "I know that. I'm sorry."

Jamie's touch lingered a second more before he gave his attention back to her leg. "The scratch isn't deep."

"Then . . ."

"There's no reason to take chances, Faith. Especially high up on this mountain."

Darn. "Okay." Covering her face with her hands, Faith held her breath . . . and still she gasped in pain when the alcohol hit her abraded skin. It burned like fire, kept on burning and burning, even as Jamie blew against the scratch in an effort to ease the sting.

"Quit complaining," he finally said, surprising her with the grumpy words when his touch was so tender. He put a clean cloth over her leg before again easing the ice pack into place. "You brought it on yourself, and I'll be damned if I want your leg to get infected and fall off."

"Gee, your concern warms me."

Jamie glanced up. "I'll never get rid of you if that happens."

If he meant to help her forget the sting, his tactic worked. Faith smacked his shoulder. "Don't exaggerate. It's not that bad."

He settled into the couch with his coffee—the brat—and shrugged. "You never know." As he again sipped, he took in the sight of her scrunched-up face. "It's still burning?"

"Yeah, and if you won't give me coffee, at least distract me." She flapped a hand to hurry him. "Tell me about your friends."

"Not much to tell. Joe moved here with Luna and took over running the lake. He's an original badass, complete with earring and tattoo and enough muscle to put off most grown men. He'd never planned to be a husband or father, but inheriting Willow and Austin proved he could do both as good as he does everything else."

"I take it Willow and Austin are the kids?"

"Yeah." He looked off in the distance at nothing in particular. Almost to himself, he said, "Amazing how resilient kids are." He shook his head. "They had it rough for a while there, but now they're happy. And secure."

Faith knew just how important feeling safe and secure could be. She felt both with Jamie. "You like Joe?"

"I respect him. He's an odd family guy, big and mean, with a visage that usually guarantees compliance with any orders he might give. But once you get to know him—"

"The way you've gotten to know him?"

Jamie ran a hand through his hair. Instead of answering, he went on with his recount of Visitation's citizens. "Bryan tailed Joe here. Back then, Bryan was a bounty hunter after the man who was after Joe."

"Okay." Faith thought her eyes might cross trying to follow that one.

With no consideration to her confusion, Jamie said, "Bryan married Shay and came back to settle here, and then his twin, Bruce, who's a preacher, also moved here." He paused, his eyes lighting as he added softly, "Bruce fell head over heels in love with Cyn, and now they're married, too."

Faith eased closer to Jamie. "You're smiling."

At her gently spoken words, Jamie's eyes widened in incredulity, then narrowed with annoyance. "I am not."

She took great pleasure in saying, "Are too."

He stared at her.

Faith tilted her head, studying him with a smile of her own. "Is it Cyn? You like her?"

After blinking twice, Jamie muttered a foul word under his breath. "Yeah, I guess I do. She's . . . pushy as hell, and her life was a nightmare—that is, until she met Bruce. She's . . ."

"Special?"

Jamie glared at her. "Do you always finish other people's sentences?"

Faith had to bite back her grin. "Yeah, I do. It's yet another of my many faults, like clumsiness and gabbing too much. I'm sorry."

Skeptical, he studied her face. "You don't look sorry. You look amused."

A laugh bubbled out, and she shrugged helplessly. "Sorry again."

Jamie rolled his eyes—which for Jamie, was pretty demonstrative.

Proud of herself, Faith asked, "So who else do you know in Visitation?

"There's Alyx Winston, Joe's sister and a real hell-raiser. Poor Scott, the deputy, has his hands full with her. But it's easier for him now that Clint is here, because Clint rightfully took the position of sheriff, which freed up some of Scott's time and allowed Clint to stay close to Julie."

She'd never be able to keep so many names straight. "For a recluse, you know an awful lot of people. Do they all care about you?"

Jamie set his mug of coffee on the table and stood to pace. Head down, hands on his hips, he nodded. "They do. I don't know how to stop them."

Faith moved to the very edge of the couch. "Why would you want to stop them? You care about them, too. That's how friendship works."

His shoulders hunched in a posture of self-defense. "No."

"Yes."

He jerked around to face her. "Damn it, Faith . . ."

Ignoring the pain in her leg, she set the ice pack aside and left the couch. Raising her voice to match his, she said, "Denying it doesn't make it less true."

Jamie looked ready for more arguments.

In two hobbling steps, Faith reached him. She put her hands on his shoulders and leaned into him, using him to help support her weight rather than stress her throbbing leg. "Don't you see, Jamie?"

"See what?"

She tried to shake him, but he didn't budge an inch. "You care about them, all of them, but you can still read their thoughts and intents. You can still see future problems, can't you?"

Jamie's gaze locked on hers like a lifeline. Appearing very uncertain, yet at the same time astonished, he nodded. "Sometimes."

"Whenever necessary," Faith insisted. "And I'm betting you could do it anytime you wanted." She had to believe that. "You just respect their privacy too much to tune into them when there's nothing wrong. But despite your feelings, the moment something *is* wrong, you know it."

Jamie worked his jaw, considering what she said, and then suddenly he lifted his head in alarm. He seemed to see beyond Faith.

Pulled from the moment of revelation, Jamie cursed.

Faith's heart shot into her throat. "What is it?"

Groaning long and low, Jamie muttered, "Alyx Winston."

Oh. Not a tragedy? "What about Alyx?"

"She's coming here."

"Now?" New panic settled on Faith. Good grief. She hadn't even been to the bathroom yet, hadn't had a single cup of coffee or cleaned her teeth or her face, or combed her hair. . . .

Jamie shook his head. "Calm down. You have time to do everything. She won't be here till later."

"But . . . you looked so put-upon. I expected her to burst in on us any moment."

"You haven't met Alyx. She's like a small tornado, determined to be my damn pal, dropping in for visits uninvited because she thinks she can force some kind of closeness."

Faith softened. "She cares about you."

Jamie nearly fried her with a hot glare, but when Faith just grinned, pleased with any show of emotion from him—even frustrated emotion—he gave up with a long huff. "Go use the john, do whatever prettying-up you think you have to do, but make it quick. I want you sitting down so you can ice that leg. It'll help with the swelling."

"Thank you."

Jamie leveled his brows. "The quicker it mends, the quicker you can leave."

But Faith, still smiling, said, "La la la. I'm not listening, Jamie Creed, so save your insults. You're just being mean to be mean." She hobbled toward the bathroom with her fingers in her ears, still singing, and even the pain in her thigh couldn't dampen her mood.

"Faith?"

He spoke so quietly that she winced before pulling one finger from her ear and peering at him. "Hmm?"

The seconds ticked by, and finally Jamie's dark frown relaxed. "I'll get you some coffee, then put on breakfast. I trust you like bacon and eggs?"

Coffee. "Oh, bless you, Jamie, bless you. And truly, I swear, you won't regret this."

"I better not."

He turned away, so he didn't see the way Faith clasped her hands together and swallowed a squeal of pure joy. Things were moving right along. She just had to keep to her course and everything would be okay.

Jamie would see to it.

Chapter Five

Alyx cursed as her foot slipped across slick, wet leaves and sank into a soft, muddy crevice on the mountain. Her ankle boot filled with sludge. "Great. Just great." She jerked her foot loose and shook off the excess mud. "Stupid never-ending rain."

Holding up a hand to shield her face, she tried to gauge how much farther she had to go. Finding Jamie's cabin the first time, when she hadn't even known the way, wasn't much harder than slogging blindly through this storm. Of course, the other times Jamie had known she was coming and met her partway. He'd tried to talk her into going back, but her stubbornness had won out.

Groaning at her own audacity and buried in guilt, Alyx kept going.

She'd known that Jamie didn't want his whereabouts uncovered. He wanted to maintain a distance from everyone, appearing only when it suited him, helping only when he deemed necessary.

Yet she'd opened her big mouth and spilled the beans, in part to ensure Jamie didn't get company without warning. But also . . . to tweak Scott.

Alyx had known how he'd react to her news . . . and yeah, it had gotten his attention big-time.

When would Scott realize he loved her and wanted to marry her and be with her forever? Better be soon, because she was fed up with waiting.

Never in her life had she met anyone as inflexible and controlling as Scott. Well, except maybe her brother Joe, but on Joe she found it amusing. Scott's controlled nature challenged her, made her proud, and turned her on. He was just so strong, in body strength and in strength of will. He made a fabulous deputy. He'd make an even better husband.

Pushing forward, Alyx mentally checked off the markers she'd memorized: the giant split boulder with a tree growing out of the middle, the rushing stream to the west, the dead fir tree, the . . . ah-ha. Way up ahead, just barely visible, she could see smoke. Heaven knew it was cold enough up in the mountain on this dreary day to need a fire in the grate. Alyx had goose bumps on her goose bumps, and she couldn't wait to get inside and soak up some warmth.

When she'd first planned this odyssey, she had expected to reach Jamie by late morning and hopefully convince him to come to town before the town came to him. But then one thing after another had come up.

Joe asked her to run by the store to pick up some necessities, and since she was staying with him and Luna, how could she refuse? And then Luna, delayed at the hairdresser's, had asked her to stay with Austin until she got home. And she and Willow, who was now sixteen, had done some online shopping for new clothes. . . .

Hearing a loud crack of thunder, Alyx wondered if she should have cancelled her visit, but it wasn't in her nature to alter plans just because of nasty weather. She wasn't made of sugar, and she wouldn't melt.

So what if the mountain got darker early, or if the storm worsened?

Tucking her package tighter beneath her arm and giving her big floppy-brimmed hat a tug to keep it secure, Alyx forged onward.

Would Jamie be happy to see her? Right. Like Jamie ever showed happiness. Last time he'd looked more annoyed than anything else. Not that Jamie showed any emotion much. It just sort of shone from his dark, mysterious eyes, eyes that made a body feel as if he could see clean down to her soul.

Alyx shivered, more from nervousness—which she'd never admit to anyone—than from the whistling wind and freezing rain.

Jamie would probably—

"I should *probably* refuse to let you come any closer."

With a startled yelp, Alyx backpedaled in the wet leaves and mud. She would have fallen on her butt if Jamie hadn't shot out a hand and grabbed her upper arm. He yanked her upright, and the package beneath her arm dropped.

With his free hand, he caught that too, impressing the hell out of Alyx. Next to Joe and Scott, Jamie had the best reflexes of any man she knew.

"Great," Jamie complained. "Third in line. What a boost to the old ego."

Alyx blinked several times, trying to clear the rain from her vision. Jamie, *joking*? She scrubbed a hand over her face and gave him a toothy grin. "Well, Joe's my brother, and you know what a badass he is."

Hauling her along, Jamie continued up the hill.

Alyx hustled rather than be dragged through the mud. Clearing her throat, she added, "And you know I have a thing for Scott."

"A thing, huh? You're in love with a capital *L*. You should tell him so."

What an appalling thought. "No way. He has never, not once, mentioned love to me. Why should I be first?"

"Why should he?"

Alyx bristled. "I'm always the one having to chase him." Besides, what if she told him and he said . . . nothing in return?

Jamie shook his head. "You don't give him much of a chance to make the first move. You taunt him, provoke him, and then jump him. All he can do is react."

Alyx dug in her heels. "You're saying I'm too forward? Is that it? Just because I'm a woman, I shouldn't go after what I want? Is that it, Jamie?"

He let her go but kept walking. Well, damn. Alyx scampered after him, slipped twice, lost her hat once, and finally got next to him again. "Why are you in such a rush? I've never seen you rush."

"I have company—as you already know."

The change of subject brightened her. "That's right! A naked lady." She gouged her elbow into Jamie's ribs. "What's up with that anyway? Did you invite her here?"

The question no sooner left her mouth than Jamie's shoulders stiffened and his bearded jaw started flexing.

He said flatly, "No."

Hackles rising at this unusual sign of his distress, Alyx knotted her hands into fists and evil thoughts crowded her mind. "Want me to get rid of her for you?"

Jamie stopped, dropped his head forward, shook it. "Unbelievable." Then he started on his way again. "I don't need you to defend me, Alyx. Scott doesn't need you to defend him."

"What does Scott have to do with this?"

"You attempt to emasculate him. Publicly. All the time."

"I do not!"

Jamie glanced at her. "He cares for you, you know."

Just peachy. Except she wanted more than caring. She wanted love. Full-blown. No holds barred. The forever kind. "Yeah . . . like, how much?"

Jamie, not exactly a ray of sunshine today, shook his head.

The cabin finally came into view, and Alyx hurried her step, anxious to get out of the rain. "Jamie? Okay, come on, explain that stupid comment."

"I don't make stupid comments." He kept walking.

"Explain it anyway. How could I possibly emasculate Scott?" She snorted. "The man is so macho, it's unnerving."

"Doesn't unnerve you."

"And he's got an ego the size of this mountain."

"Now that's the pot calling the kettle black."

Scowling, Alyx charged forward, filled with indignation. "He takes charge in every situation—"

"Except around you, because you never give him a chance. As a deputy, maintaining a cool head at all times is important to him. But you make him lose his temper. On purpose. Over and over again."

Remembering some of the times Scott had lost control, Alyx fought a grin. "It's funny when he blusters and clomps around and carries on."

On a rock path that led to his porch, Jamie stomped some of the mud from his boots. At the porch, he pulled the boots off and set them aside out of the rain, then removed his jacket and hung it on a peg.

With a shrug, Alyx kicked out of her boots, curling her sock-covered toes against the cold.

When Jamie faced her, she looked up and raised a brow at his severe stare. "What is it?"

"Her name is Faith."

Eyes widening, Alyx looked past Jamie to the uncovered window. Her voice dropped to a whisper. "She's in there now?"

"Did you think I threw her off the cliff?"

"I don't know what you'd do, Jamie." She stepped forward and put a hand to his forearm, as serious and sincere as a nun. "But whatever you'd choose to do, I'd back you on it. I know you're hiding from someone or something, and I only want to help. Whatever you need done, you can count on me. You can trust me."

To her surprise, hot color stained Jamie's cheekbones. Before she could decide if it was embarrassment or something else, he shook off her hand and pushed the front door open.

Even hermits had gallant tendencies, Alyx decided, when Jamie stood aside and allowed her to enter first.

Feeling unusually reserved, Alyx dropped her package, pulled off her sodden hat, and stripped off her jacket. As she crept forward into the small cabin, her curious gaze flitted around, going over the chair at the table, the ladder to the upstairs, the couch, the—

Her eyes shot back to the couch. *Well, well, well.* Sitting prim and proper, wearing a flannel shirt with a quilt draped over her lap, the woman watched her.

Alyx drew back. Huh. She was . . . well, pretty darn plain. Her features were mostly nondescript: an average nose, average eyes with brown lashes and brows, an oval face and flushed cheeks. For some reason, Alyx had expected a femme fatale, or at the very least someone especially cute or adorable—a woman to wiggle her way around Jamie Creed's barriers.

But this woman just sat there, long reddish-brown hair twisted around her shoulders, her hands clasped together over her thighs.

A polite, cautious smile appeared, and she said, "Hello, Alyx. We were expecting you."

"You were?"

"Jamie said you were coming."

"Oh. Yeah." Wondering just what Jamie had said about her, Alyx sauntered forward. "That's our Jamie. Always on the ball. Nothing gets past him."

"I know." Her head tipped. "I'm Faith. I'd get up to greet you, but—"

"You don't have any clothes." Alyx stopped right in front of her, her hands on her hips, her feet braced apart. "So, Faith, what are you doing here? And naked at that. What are you up to?"

Faith almost laughed, and her dark blue eyes sought out Jamie as she said, "I wasn't naked when I got here. Jamie took my clothes and threw them away."

Alyx blinked, not a single retort coming to mind. Jamie had stripped her? "Um . . ."

"Jamie?" Faith asked. "Aren't you going to strip Alyx, too?"

Alyx went military straight, and her chin tucked in. What kind of craziness had she walked into? "No, he's not."

"But Jamie insisted it was necessary."

"If he even tried, I'd—"

"Put away your fists, Alyx." And to Faith, Jamie said, "She wouldn't let anyone trail her up here. I trust her."

Alyx said, "You do?" But realizing how surprised she sounded, she frowned. "Of course you do. I already told you, if anyone bothers you, just let me know and I'll take care of it."

As droll as ever, Jamie nodded. "Yeah, I'll be sure to do that."

With a nod, Alyx said, "Okay then. Just know, Jamie, I always have your best interests at heart."

"Uh-huh."

By way of explanation, Faith leaned forward and whispered in confidence, "Jamie is very cautious, and he was afraid I might have some sort of tracking device or something on me. Of course, I didn't. Like you, I want to protect him. But Jamie doesn't take chances. So he took off all my clothes and pitched them. I don't really know where. I have a cold and getting here wasn't easy, and I admit I was a little disoriented when he carried me in."

"I see." Alyx didn't see a blessed thing. *Jamie had stripped her?* She turned to Jamie—and jumped to find him right behind her with the kitchen chair. He plunked it down, caught her shoulders, and all but pressed her into the seat.

Faith scowled at him. "Jamie, where are your manners? Don't you want to offer Alyx something to drink?"

In his bland, monotone voice, Jamie explained, "She's not staying."

Faith said, "She's not?"

Alyx asked, "Why not?"

Jamie's piercing gaze bored into her. "Because you have to get back."

"Oh."

Faith prodded at him. "Well, at least get her a towel so she can dry off."

Never had Alyx seen anyone boss Jamie around. She didn't think anyone, especially not anyone female, would dare.

Fascinated, she looked from Jamie to Faith and back again. Jamie stared down at Faith, his arms crossed over his chest, his pose reeking of intimidation.

Faith huffed out a breath. "Never mind. I'll do it." She pushed aside the quilt and started to stand.

A sound reminiscent of a growl rumbled out of Jamie, but by the time Alyx got twisted around in her chair to see the phenomenon for herself, he'd turned away, saying, "Stay put, Faith. I'll get the damn towel."

Faith smiled. "Thank you." She leaned toward Alyx again. "He doesn't want me up and about since I hurt my leg." She lifted the flannel and stuck out her leg. Dark purpling bruises and a painful scratch ran the length of one thigh.

"Ouch." Alyx didn't know what to think. First Faith had teased Jamie, then ordered him around. Very weird. She nodded at Faith's leg. "How'd you do that?"

"It was an accident—not that Jamie wants to believe it. But he was trying to throw me out, and naturally, I didn't want to go. Not that I'd injure my leg on purpose just to get to stay. And who's to say Jamie wouldn't make me leave with a broken leg if that's what he wanted to do? He can be very pigheaded. But—"

"Here." Jamie thrust the towel at Alyx, breaking into Faith's tale. "Dry off."

"Gee, thanks." Alyx pulled the towel out of her face and stared at Jamie. Never, ever, had she expected to see him flustered. Whatever Faith's purpose for her visit, she had Jamie on pins and needles.

As if that wasn't revelation enough, to Alyx's astonishment, Jamie crouched in front of Faith and touched her leg.

"Is it feeling better?"

Alyx's mouth fell open at the husky timbre in his voice.

"The ice helped." Faith confided to Alyx, "He's had me putting ice on it all day to take down the swelling. Other than leaving the couch for breakfast and lunch, he's made me sit. He even complained when I wanted to fix my hair before you got here."

"Your hair looks fine," Jamie said.

Alyx tucked in her chin. How, exactly, did Jamie think stroking Faith's leg would help the situation any? But that's what he did. Very gently. And Faith let him. In fact, her face went all soft and adoring and she touched the top of Jamie's head, threading her fingers through his hair.

Oh, wow.

As Alyx absently dried off her face and throat, she took in the set of Jamie's shoulders. He feigned a casual, relaxed pose, but those shoulders were rock hard in the way that Scott's got whenever he was aroused.

Feeling like a voyeur, and amazed that Jamie hadn't already called her on it, Alyx cleared her throat. "Hey, you know . . . Should I be seeing this?"

In one abrupt movement, Jamie came to his feet and rounded on Alyx. The switch from seducer of Faith to confronter of Alyx startled her enough that she pressed back in her chair.

Just as quickly, Jamie's familiar blank mask fell into place. "What are you doing here, Alyx?"

Wasn't that her question for Faith?

"That," Jamie said, "is none of your business."

Her mouth fell open again, not because he'd snatched her thoughts right out of her head, but because of how he'd replied to them. "That's never stopped you from butting in."

"Fine." Jamie's heated gaze felt like a laser cutting into her. "I won't tell you what Scott is going to do."

Dirty pool! Jamie knew that little dig would drive her crazy.

"Yeah, I did."

Alyx squashed her hands over her ears. Sometimes having her every unspoken thought heard loud and clear really rattled her. "All right, Jamie, don't get mean." Not one to get intimidated, Alyx smoothed out her damp sweater. "I'm not used to seeing you mean. Hell, I'm not used to seeing you . . . anything. Except sort of vacant."

"Alyx," he warned.

"I had some lame idea about warning you of a future visit—"

"Which I'm already aware of."

"Yeah, well . . ." Her guilt surfaced again, and she held up her hands in a placating gesture. "I also thought to apologize because, Jamie, I'm the one who offered to lead the others here."

"I know."

" 'Course you did." Defeated, Alyx drooped in her seat. He probably knew everything. But she wouldn't let that stop her.

Jamie sighed. "No, Alyx, I didn't think it would."

"Hey." Faith frowned at them both. "It's impolite to leave me out of the conversation."

Reminded of Faith's presence, Alyx turned her face up to Jamie. "So other than interrupting some hanky-panky, I guess this is a wasted trip, huh?"

Jamie crossed his arms, and Alyx watched his eyes narrow with burning gratification. Uh-oh.

He took a step closer, looming over her. "Scott's going to be waiting for you, Alyx."

She almost slid off her chair. "What? Where?"

"At the bottom of the mountain. When you go back."

"No way! You're just saying that to get rid of me. Scott doesn't even know I came here today. He's still working." And still peeved about the other visits she'd made to see Jamie.

"He'll find your car. He'll wait for you. And Alyx?" Jamie leaned closer, his entire countenance one of deep victory. "He's not going to be happy."

Alyx shot out of her seat. Indignation and independence battled apprehension. "So what? Big deal. Scott's not my husband. He's only a boyfriend. He has no rights over me. He . . ." She gulped, then flared anew. "He better not even *think* about yelling at me."

Suddenly Jamie looked at her closer, and Alyx had the odd sensation of being analyzed. She took a step back, but Jamie followed.

"Stop that," she breathed.

He drew nearer, his gaze so fierce and speculative it almost stopped her heart. He caught her hand before she even knew he'd reached for it. Imprisoning it against his chest, Jamie scrutinized her, and no matter how she tried, Alyx couldn't look away.

"Jamie," she whispered with a nervous twitter, "you're spooking me."

He dropped her hand and retreated. But with

another strange look, he gave a slow, chastising shake of his head.

"Good God." Alyx's heart beat so fast, she wondered how it stayed contained in her chest. "What the heck is the matter with you?"

Jamie locked his hands behind his back and paced away.

So Alyx turned to Faith, hoping for enlightenment.

The other woman gave a helpless shrug. "You can't keep secrets from Jamie." And she smiled at Jamie's back, raising her voice an octave. "Even though he *cares* about you."

Jamie promptly went rigid and swung around to face Faith with haunted eyes.

Alyx decided she should be on her way. "Yeah, well, who'd want to keep secrets from Jamie, anyway?"

Jamie jerked back to her, and his expression altered to one of disapproval.

Heading for the door where she'd dropped her package, Alyx said, "Before I hit the road, I have something for you."

Jamie began prowling the small interior of the cabin, so Alyx, anxious to get on her way with that prediction of Scott waiting, just carried the contents to Faith. "It's not much. Some stuff I thought you might need so that you could leave."

In long strides, Jamie crossed the room. "She's not going anywhere."

Whoa. Alyx pulled back. Man, he was jumpy today. "Down, boy. I might not be a mind reader, but I figured that much out for myself. Still, she could use a few clothes, don't you think? Does she even have anything on under that shirt?"

Biting her lip, Faith glanced up at Jamie.

With heated intensity, Jamie stared down at Faith.

"Here we go again." Once more feeling like a fifth wheel, Alyx sighed dramatically. Faith and Jamie did a great job of dismissing her existence.

Catching Faith's chin on the edge of his fist, Jamie lifted her face. "You might as well accept them, Faith. Wearing clothes or not isn't going to make a difference."

Eyes widening, Alyx wondered, *a difference to what?*

With a demure smile, Faith purred, "Meaning you'll still want me even if I'm fully clothed?"

Drugging testosterone pulsed off Jamie in waves. Alyx thought she might swoon, except that this was all too interesting to miss.

"Meaning," Jamie growled, "that regardless of what you do or don't wear, I'm not touching you."

Faith pointed out, "You're touching me now," which caused Jamie to retreat as if his hand had caught on fire.

Alyx decided the volatile situation needed a little lighthearted humor. "Hey, before you jump each other's bones, how about letting me give her the rest of this stuff so I can leave? I think I'm too young to witness all this chemistry."

Beaming at her, Faith said, "There is a lot of chemistry, isn't there? I thought so right off."

Mumbling something about impossible, irrational women, Jamie put both hands in his over-long hair and plopped down on the couch next to Faith.

Faith leaned into him.

And Jamie, still grumbling, didn't move away.

Jamie has a girlfriend. Jamie has a girlfriend—

"Knock it off, Alyx."

Oops. She'd momentarily forgotten the way Jamie nosed around her brain. "Mea culpa." To keep from irritating him further, Alyx delved into her bag and unloaded it item by item.

"Here you go, Faith. A nightgown, a couple pair of socks, a sweatshirt, and a pair of jeans."

Faith lifted up the gown to better see it. "Lovely."

Alyx shrugged. "It was a gift from Sophie, my cousin, Cole's wife. Sophie owns a lingerie boutique, so what does she get me? A long white cotton gown. I think that was Cole's doing, though."

"You don't like cotton?" Faith asked.

"In panties or T-shirts, sure. But this"—she fingered the long sleeve of the gown—"looks like something for a sacrificial virgin."

Laughing, Faith asked, "Which you're not?"

"Uh, no. But my male relatives still think of me as a tomboy virgin, so I suppose it fits their image, even if it is humiliating."

Jamie started to look dazed, so Alyx moved on. "The gown should fit fine. But I'm thinking my jeans might be too tight and way too long."

Without rancor, Faith agreed. "You've got such long legs, and you're so slim."

Alyx stretched out her legs in agreement. "Yeah, and those jeans are too short on me now, so feel free to cut them off if you want."

"Okay. Thank you."

"I also brought you some scented lotion because I just couldn't see Jamie owning anything but the most basic stuff."

Faith wrinkled her nose. "His lotion doesn't have a smell."

"I figured." Alyx dug further in the bag. "Oh, and a hairbrush." She pulled that out with a flourish and presented it to Faith. "Sorry, but that's it."

Everything got piled in Faith's lap. Somewhat overwhelmed, Faith said, "This is so kind of you."

"I wish I could have figured out what else to bring, but having never met you, I had no idea what you'd want."

Faith smiled up at her. "Thank you. It was very brave of you to venture out in the storm."

Jamie coughed, but when Alyx eyed him, he merely raised a brow and asked, "All done? Good. I'll see you out."

Alyx tried to keep her butt in the chair, but with Jamie latched onto her arm, literally lifting her to her feet, she had no choice but to stand. For a shadowy, lurking hermit of a guy, Jamie had incredible strength. Why had she never noticed that before?

Probably because he always vanished before anyone could really observe him much. Even her trips to his cabin hadn't been eventful. He'd tolerated her, assisted her, and then seen her on her way.

Just as he intended to do now.

"So, Faith," Alyx said over her shoulder as Jamie steered her to the door. "I know why I visited. But what are you doing here?"

Jamie didn't give Faith a chance to answer. He

lowered his head so that he stared Alyx right in the eyes, and the impact was enough that she damn near swallowed her tongue.

When Jamie turned on the mysticism, it was pretty potent stuff.

"Time for you to go, Alyx. Right now." His voice was as lacking in inflection as ever, but still Alyx felt his urgency. He wanted her gone. In a big way.

The rascal.

Of course, Jamie read her thoughts. "Listen to me, Alyx. If you wait any longer, Scott's going to bring out the search party, and you really don't want to cause that kind of fuss, do you?"

"Search party!"

"He'll find your car on the side of the road, in a storm, well away from town. But you're nowhere in sight. You know what he'll think."

Shoot. "I can take care of myself. Scott should know that."

Jamie gave her a pitying look. "First thing he'll do is call your brother."

Groaning, Alyx collapsed back against the closed door.

"When Joe tells him that he hasn't seen you in hours, Scott will call everyone else, just in case a friend picked you up. Clint will know. And Bryan and Bruce and—"

"All right, already. You've made your point." With appropriate haste, Alyx shoved her arms into her jacket, zipped it up, and squashed the big hat onto her head. "You'd think a grown woman could come and go as she pleases without causing a panic."

"People care about you, Alyx."

Maybe this was her chance to pry some info out of Jamie. "You mean Scott?"

Jamie opened the door. "That's a question you can put to him yourself."

"Oh, yeah, sure. Snoop in my brain all you want but don't tell me something useful." Peeved at his evasive tactics, Alyx stepped out onto the porch and realized that the rain had stopped. "Well, hallelujah."

"It's dark already," Jamie told her. He reached beneath a wooden bench and withdrew a heavy-duty flashlight. "Take this with you."

"Will that leave you without?"

"I live in the woods. I have more than one flashlight."

"Okay, thanks." While Alyx yanked on her ankle boots—which were now ruined—she began to worry. "So, smarty-pants. If I hurry, am I going to make it back to my car in time to avert a call to the National Guard?"

"If you don't waste time getting down the mountain—maybe."

Alyx rolled her eyes. She had no doubt that Jamie knew exactly what would happen; the rat just didn't want to tell her. She started off in a rush, but at the last minute, she turned back. "Jamie? You said people care about me."

"You know they do."

She nodded. "Yeah, well, they care about you, too, bud. Even if I hadn't offered to show them the way here, they'd have come. Julie, Cyn, Shay, and Luna. They're professional fretters."

"And you're not?"

Alyx shrugged. "Not like they are. The guys

might have let it go, but with the women prodding them . . . they were all too willing to check up on you. I'll try to hold them off as long as I can, but I'd say you have two days, tops, before we all converge on you."

"I know." Jamie looked up at the treetops, pensive and as withdrawn as ever. "It'll be okay."

With him distracted, Alyx decided *what the hell* and put her arms around his lean waist. Jamie Creed felt as warm and hard and sturdy as any other living, breathing man.

She gave him a tight hug. When he stiffened, she laughed, pulled back, and punched him in the arm. "Get used to it, Jamie, because there's going to be a lot more of that in your future."

Given the look on his face, the idea didn't please him one bit.

Chuckling, Alyx walked off into the woods. She didn't want to linger any longer, not with Jamie's dire warning about Scott. The good deputy already had this thing about trying to curtail her every move, as if she were the typical helpless little woman. Surely that wasn't the type of woman that Scott preferred? Alyx hoped not, because she was more than capable of taking care of herself, and Scott should appreciate that.

Before much longer, she'd make sure that he did.

Chapter Six

Jamie hesitated, not yet ready to go back inside. He watched Alyx until he couldn't see her anymore, already knowing what Scott would have to say, already knowing what Alyx would do.

What would happen when Scott found out the extent of Alyx's antics? No man, definitely not a deputy, would just smile and say, "Have fun."

At the same time, Jamie knew Alyx grew restless. Being an impatient, full-steam-ahead kind of woman, she wanted Scott to commit. Yet Scott hesitated. Maybe he should . . . *No.* He'd keep his nose out of it. Alyx was right—he butted in too often.

If anyone was threatened, or the situation became dangerous, he'd interfere in a heartbeat. But for now, they could work it out on their own.

Already anticipating the fireworks, Jamie shook his head. Those two would put on more of a show than the last Fourth of July display. But it was a good match. Scott wouldn't be content with a woman who stood in his shadow. And Alyx . . . she measured all men against her brother, and considering Joe's personality and capability, not a lot of them passed muster.

But Scott did. In part because Joe respected him so much.

"Jamie?"

Shit.

Jamie twisted to see Faith standing in the doorway, backlit by all the lamps she'd turned on in his cabin. No shadows for Faith. She liked everything bright and cheery—which suited her but clashed with him in a big way.

Looking her over from her fiery hair to her curled toes, Jamie saw that she'd pulled on the long white gown and socks that Alyx had brought her and wore the flannel shirt like a housecoat. She should have looked comical in such a get-up, but instead she looked . . . virginal, just as Alyx had claimed. She also looked appealing.

The humid breeze lifted her coppery curls and sent them dancing past her face.

Alyx thought Faith plain.

Jamie thought it too, at least in the face.

So with her delectable body well hidden, why did he feel so drawn to her?

Tipping her head at him, she asked, "Is everything okay?"

Jamie struggled for breath. "You should be resting that leg."

"I've rested it all day. It's sore, but it doesn't hurt that much more to stand." Wrapping her arms around herself, she came a few more steps out, until she stood next to him. "Aren't you cold?"

"No." Before leaving to meet Alyx, he'd donned

a T-shirt and jacket. He was so used to the mountain weather that even without the jacket, he
barely felt the chill in the air.

Faith smoothed her palm over his back,
stroking the soft cotton of his well-worn shirt—and
his already elevated temperature went up another
notch.

"Are you impervious to all that plagues mortal
man, then?"

Leaning back against the porch rail, Jamie absorbed the novelty of having a woman so close, not
just physically close, but . . . emotionally. Throughout the long day, Faith had talked up a storm,
telling him so many things. Nothing important, at
least not the important things he'd wanted to
know.

But he now knew her favorite foods, that she
cried over Hallmark commercials and couldn't
stand slapstick comedy. She enjoyed simple things
like a picnic or a good book. She couldn't draw a
stick figure, but in her opinion, her daughter had
incredible artistic talent.

And she loved being a mother.

Belatedly, Jamie answered her question. "No. If
I were impervious, you wouldn't bother me so
much."

Dimples showed in her cheeks as she grinned.
"Am I bothering you?"

Damn. He'd been celibate far too long. Everything about her seemed designed to fire his blood.
It made him naturally defensive. "No reason to
look so pleased, Faith. It wasn't a compliment."

With a familiarity that shouldn't have existed,
she nudged her shoulder into his ribs. "I can take

my satisfaction where I find it, Creed. Knowing
that I have any effect on you, other than outright
anger, encourages me."

The urge to slip his arm around her nearly got
him, but Jamie resisted. He watched her while she
watched the trees swaying.

Her soft sigh sounded serene. "It's really beautiful here."

Jamie glanced out at the sheltering darkness of
tall trees and enormous rocks. He listened to the
comforting sounds of whispering wind and the
rustle of leaves. Beautiful, yes, but no longer quite
so secure, not with Faith's intrusion.

"What's that sound I hear?" Faith asked, cocking her head to listen. "Like . . . the sound of water
moving?"

"There's a creek close by. With all this rain, it's
moving faster than usual. Down the mountain a
bit, it turns into a small fall. Pretty."

"I bet. I'd love to see it sometime."

Jamie barely registered her words. Having been
alone so long, his senses were finely honed and he
could distinguish the scents of Faith's hair, her
skin, against the earthier scents of the surrounding forest. Her light fragrance carried on the air so
that he inhaled her essence with every breath.

At the moment, she looked so relaxed, and her
thoughts were so carefree, that he half hated to
disturb her. But having been duped by a woman
once before, he refused to leave anything to chance.
"I have some questions for you, Faith."

Caution brought a stillness to her, and her gaze
crept up to his. "You do?"

He'd thought about it all day, during her chatter, while watching her eat. Because he hadn't slept the night before, exhaustion pulled at him. But he wouldn't sleep until he had a few truths. "About your child. About Cory."

Her thoughts slammed shut with all the echoing clatter of a heavy steel door. Jamie wanted to trust her. Hell, he wanted to take her, to strip her naked again and touch her everywhere. But how could he when she kept closing him out?

Grim, Jamie nodded. "Yeah, that's what I thought."

Eyes wide and wary, she hunched her shoulders. "What?"

He took her arm and turned her toward the cabin. "Whatever's going on here, it somehow involves Cory in ways you don't want me to know."

"How many times do I have to tell you—"

"To wait? Forget that." Jamie sensed that Cory might be in trouble. Waiting surely wouldn't help, not if the child needed him—as Faith kept insisting. "I want answers now."

Without even thinking about it, Jamie gave her support and kept his steps slow to accommodate her injured leg.

Once inside, he closed the door behind him, then bent to scoop Faith into his arms. Again, it was an automatic gesture meant to spare her leg— or so he told himself. But now that he held her, he didn't want to put her down.

"It's nearing bedtime," he explained, answering her unasked question. That delicious fragrance of woman filled his head and cramped his muscles. She felt soft and warm, and he liked holding her.

With her face only inches from his, Faith whispered, "And?"

Jamie lowered her to the couch, but continued to loom over her, one hand on the seat by her hip, the other on the couch back, caging her in.

She looked apprehensive and anxious. He shook his head, already knowing what she hoped would happen, but ready to disappoint her.

Slowly, he forced himself to straighten away. Folding his arms over his chest and giving her his most nerve-wracking stare, Jamie said, "I'm not going to sleep with you in my cabin without knowing what I'm getting into."

"Oh." She licked her lips, and damn, he wanted to lick them, too.

Taking another step back, Jamie studied her and realized she was far too uneasy to give much away. He shouldn't have warned her. She laced her fingers together and held herself in a guarded position, blanking her mind against him.

To throw her off, Jamie said, "Do you want some tea? And I think I have some cheese crackers somewhere."

It took her a moment to assimilate his words with what she'd expected to hear. "Oh. Yes. Thank you." Wariness stilted the words. "I am starting to get hungry."

Jamie raised his brows. "Again?"

Her mental barriers slipped, and Jamie felt her embarrassment mingle with her confusion over his attitude. "It's been hours since lunch. Surely you could eat again?"

Jamie shrugged. Generally, he had two meals a day, but only when his hunger registered. With

Faith, he didn't have a chance to get hungry. The woman was a bottomless pit.

When he didn't agree, she blushed. "I'm sorry. I eat when I'm nervous. I don't mean to be a bother, but—"

"Enough with the apologies, Faith. Given that you refuse to leave or level with me, they don't exactly ring true."

She said, "Ouch," to give him his due, then tracked him with wide eyes as he went to the kitchen. "You don't really want me to leave, Jamie."

"No?"

"Today has been wonderful." She fretted with the hem of the flannel shirt. "I just don't want to ruin it."

"Then tell me why you're here."

"Okay." Jamie gave her a sharp look, and she said, "I-I'll try to tell you as much as I can."

You'll tell me more than that, Jamie silently vowed as he strode to the kitchen and got out two glasses. He didn't bother with ice. He just poured the tea, grabbed a canister of crackers, and went back to the couch. "Here you go."

She accepted the glass with a smile. "May I at least say 'thank you'?"

Lifting her sock-covered feet, Jamie seated himself on the cushion next to her. "You may."

Once again holding herself still, Faith swallowed, licked her lips, and whispered, "Thank you."

Satisfied with her reaction, Jamie sipped his tea, then set it aside. Cocking his head at her, he asked, "My nearness makes you nervous?"

"Ha." Faith slapped a hand over her mouth.

"Sorry. But yes. Everything about you makes me nervous. You have such a poker face. I've babbled to you all day, spilling my guts, and it's almost impossible to tell what you're thinking."

"I'm thinking that you look damn cute in that gown."

Her chin tucked in, and she frowned warily. "You are not."

Feeling in control for a change, Jamie lounged back, at his leisure. But he kept one hand curled around Faith's ankle, his thumb stroking absently against her arch.

"You hide, Faith, just as I hide. But I still see you."

"Um . . . I don't know what you mean."

"You know exactly what I mean, so don't lie to me."

Her hands shook, and Jamie took her tea to set beside his. Casually, he looked her over, taking in the thrust of her breasts, her narrow waist, the flare of her hips. "You don't want anyone to know that you're stacked."

Her lips parted, and a blush ran up her neck. "Not too many guys ever look past my face."

"Because you downplay your features." With his free hand, Jamie reached out and ran his fingers over several springy curls. "You wear your hair in a ponytail and don't bother with makeup. Your clothes are usually plain, without shape, meant to hide all your curves." His brows lifted, and he murmured, "Meant to hide your breasts and waist and ass."

A pulse danced wildly in her throat. Jamie

brushed it with the backs of his fingers—and got hit with the melting sensation of her naked desire.

Pausing, he watched her face, seeing how her eyes grew heavy and her lips parted. She looked . . . ripe. Ready.

With his attention on her, Faith's breath accelerated, drawing his gaze to her breasts. Her nipples pressed against the fabric of the nightgown.

Hello.

Jamie knew she wasn't cold, not now. So . . .

Faith wanted him?

Not as part of a put-on to use him, but out of sincere sexual interest? He couldn't quite fathom that, not with his beard and shaggy hair and . . . less-than-welcoming attitude so far.

Forcing his rapt notice away from her breasts, he voiced his most immediate question. "Why do you want me, Faith? Explain it to me."

As if coming out of a daze, Faith floundered. "I, what, that is . . ."

Maybe he shouldn't have just blurted that out. And in fact, he was supposed to be picking her brain about more important things. And he would. In a second.

"You want me. Sexually. Why?"

More color rushed into her face, and her lost expression turned mutinous. She appeared ready to clout him. "That's really unfair how you do that, drawing out a woman's most intimate thoughts when you weren't invited in."

"When I wasn't . . ." Jamie could hardly credit her accusation. "You forced your way into my home, Faith. You refuse to leave. All I did was glean a few thoughts—which you weren't hiding worth a damn anyway. It wouldn't take intuition to figure them out."

"Baloney. I might not have a stone face like you, but I'm not altogether transparent."

Jamie's temper sparked. He leaned closer to her. "You're staring at me like I'm your next meal. Your face is flushed. Hell, even your nipples are puckered."

Faith gasped so hard she nearly choked herself, and her arms wound around her chest, squeezing tight. She started to scramble off the couch, but Jamie easily subdued her.

"Oh, no, you don't."

"Let me go!"

"I don't think so." He trapped her hands when she started swatting at him.

Straining away from him, Faith muttered, "Damn it, Jamie, I'm embarrassed."

"Well, get over it." He caught her shoulders and pressed her onto her back in the cushions. But that meant he sprawled over her, and the suggestive position threatened his newly claimed control.

Especially when she stared at his mouth while breathing hard.

"Faith," he growled, resisting the urge to kiss her, "tell me why you want me."

All the fight went out of her. Instead of shoving against his chest, Faith used her hands to hide her face. "All right."

Jamie braced himself.

"You're sexy."

If he hadn't already been flat against her, he would have collapsed.

"There." She dropped her hands to glare at him. "I said it. Are you happy?"

He wasn't quite sure. Confused, yeah. But happy? It'd been so long since Jamie had experienced true happiness, he might not recognize it anymore.

But triumph, satisfaction, interest, he had those in spades.

Rather than tell her so, Jamie shrugged. "Could be your idea of sexy is a little warped."

"Are you kidding?" Faith curled her hands around his biceps and gave a little hum of appreciation. "Do you ever look in a mirror? You're a superstud, Jamie Creed."

Guarded, Jamie asked, "Did you get into my moonshine again?"

Rather than take offense, Faith laughed. "Trust me, it's true. You're dark and brooding, full of mystery, and God knows you have a fabulous body, all lean strength and long bones—"

Brows shooting up, Jamie repeated, "Long bones?"

Faith sputtered. "I don't mean *that.*" Giving him a shove that Jamie disregarded, she ordered, "Get your mind out of the gutter."

That'd be a little hard to do with her smaller body conforming to his in some pretty enticing ways. Seeing her stiffened nipples by no means compared with actually feeling them against his chest. His palms itched with the need to cup her breasts in his hands, caress her, stroke her. She looked soft, smelled soft, felt soft.

Shit.

On very unfamiliar ground, Jamie kept his face blank and asked, "You really think so? Even with the beard and . . . everything else?"

She cupped his jaw in trembling hands, which sent an answering shiver through Jamie's limbs. Stroking his beard with her thumbs, she said, "Sure, you'd be sexier without all the fur, but your eyes . . . Man, Jamie, you have very compelling eyes." Her sigh drifted against his lips, warm and gentle. "Then there's your kindness, the way you care so much about people. And the wounded way you protect yourself." Loaded with sincerity, she vowed, "No red-blooded woman could ever resist you."

Jamie didn't know if he should be insulted or turned on. Wounded? Jesus, he didn't want people seeing him like that. But he couldn't think clearly, not when Faith left herself open to him, and he had not only his own sexual need to deal with, but hers, too.

Talk about potent.

Feeling her excitement added to his; her heat made him hotter; her desire pushed his right over the edge.

Right now, if he touched her between her legs, she'd be damp and warm, ready for him. He knew it, and it made him nuts.

In survival mode, Jamie closed his eyes and focused on his purpose. Then Faith shifted one of her legs and Jamie just naturally settled between her thighs, and damn it, that felt right in too many ways to count.

Until Faith gasped, and pain stiffened her spine. That brought him a moment of sanity.

Levering himself up and away from her, Jamie cursed. "Your leg—"

"No!" Her arms wound tight around his neck.

"Don't go. Please. My leg is fine." She tucked her face against his chest. "I've been so alone and so scared and it feels good just to be held. By you. Please, Jamie."

Jamie hesitated, but he wanted to do more than hold her. And with that thought in mind, he tamped down on his lust and steered them back on track. "Did you breast-feed?"

That odd stillness claimed her, before Faith pushed back to see his face. "What?"

"With Cory. Was she a breast-fed baby or bottle fed?"

Panic ran through Faith. Her eyes darted over Jamie's face and her back pressed into the couch. But Jamie wasn't about to let her retreat again. As she pulled away, he settled more closely to her, reminding her she had nowhere to go—not until he allowed it.

"It's not a tough question, Faith."

Her eyes were big and sad when she looked up at him. "Cory was . . . was bottle fed."

"You didn't want to nurse her?"

She let out a shuddering breath. "I did. I wanted to so badly. But I couldn't."

"Why?"

Appearing more pained by the moment, she shook her head but said nothing. She closed herself off from him, taking every part of herself that she could and hiding it away in a secret place in her mind where Jamie couldn't see, couldn't know. After the incredible sensation of having her openly want him, sharing herself so completely, her distance felt icy cold.

Fine, Jamie thought, seeing it as another sign

that her intentions were suspect at best, threatening at worst. Under the circumstances, it wasn't easy, but he hardened his heart against her.

He would not be influenced by his base desires.

So he had a boner? Big deal. Wasn't the first time, sure as hell wouldn't be the last. Regardless of what many men tried to claim, no guy had ever died from unrequited lust.

With that thought in mind, Jamie pushed her with his questions. "What about her birth, Faith?"

When her lashes lifted, big tears swam in her eyes. "What about it?"

"Was it a difficult labor?"

"No. Cory was a big baby, eight pounds and fourteen ounces. But there were no problems."

Damn near nine pounds. For some reason, that intrigued Jamie. "You said she's tall for her age?"

"And mature."

"Did you need drugs?"

"For what?"

"The birth." Impatient, Jamie scowled. "Or did you go natural?"

Faith stalled, turning her face away from him.

Jamie brought it right back. "Answer me, Faith."

"I . . . I hate drugs."

Which was a non-answer if he'd ever heard one. Deciding he'd had enough of her evasiveness and his own warped guessing game, Jamie gave her all his weight, pressing into her until her frantic breaths mingled with his own and her heartbeat started a drumroll. "You have a sexy belly, Faith."

Whatever she'd been expecting, he'd taken her by surprise. She blinked at him, no words coming to her.

"I've seen it," Jamie reminded her. "I've seen all of you."

She nodded. "Because you took my clothes."

He lifted himself a few inches, pressed his hand between their bodies, over her navel. Watching her closely for any signs of deception, Jamie pointed out the obvious. "You don't have the belly of a woman who's carried a big baby."

Her mouth opened and closed without uttering a single sound.

His fingers caressed her, and he said, "You don't have the body of a woman who's been pregnant. Ever."

Eyes narrowing, her bravado back, Faith faced off with him. "And you've seen a lot of pregnant ladies, I take it?"

"I'm not an idiot, Faith." Jamie caressed her again, angling his fingers downward and pressing in. She sucked in a startled, excited breath. "You like that? Well, I'd like the truth. Tell me about Cory."

He knew Cory existed, because he'd seen her, and he knew Faith cared about the child. Her thoughts were too clear and pure whenever Faith focused on her. But she hadn't birthed Cory. So who was the little girl?

Jamie expected Faith's barriers to stay in place. He expected her to impede his efforts at reading her while she sought believable excuses.

Instead, she opened herself to him, presenting him with a flood of carnal sensations that devastated his intentions, throwing him off guard. It was like getting full-blown drunk in a heartbeat. Or having an orgasm with no foreplay.

It was like being loved without knowing why.

Lust was there, hot and ripe, stirring his blood and sending his heart on a frantic gallop. But Faith also shared her neediness, her tenderness, her mother's love and worry for her child, her hope for understanding.

Her caring for Jamie.

His head spun, leaving him unable to concentrate on any one single sentiment. Other than the time Delayna had used him as a lab rat, he'd never suffered such a tumultuous emotional inferno. But with Delayna, it had been his feelings alone, because that bitch hadn't felt a thing.

Now, Faith's feelings, combined with his own, left him utterly lost.

"Don't, Jamie," she begged, grabbing his face and pulling him down to her. Her lips pressed a damp kiss onto his cheekbone, the bridge of his nose. "Don't think, just feel me. Accept me." Her lips moved over his, frenzied but light, a whisper of sensation—and Jamie gave up.

She'd rocked his foundation, and he didn't have it in him to fight. Not right now.

To anchor himself, Jamie tangled his fingers in her hair and held her still so his mouth could settle onto hers, rocking, sucking, taking, and giving.

He groaned at the mind-blowing taste and feel of her, the resiliency of her lips, and her reciprocal hunger as she opened her mouth, accepting his tongue and giving him her own.

She arched into him, trying to get closer, trying to crawl inside him.

He must have forgotten how wonderful kissing could be, Jamie thought, because he didn't remember anything like this. And he'd be damned before he let it go.

Mindless, Jamie ran a hand down Faith's side, pausing at the nip in her waist, the voluptuous flair of her hip, before clasping her thigh to spread her legs wider.

The moment his strong fingers curled around her, Faith twisted away with a gasp.

Her leg, damn it. He'd hurt her. He'd totally forgotten . . . *everything*.

The paleness of Faith's face, the way she bit her bottom lip and squeezed her eyes shut, showed plain enough the hurt she suffered. But she remained open to him, too, and Jamie felt it, her regret, her frustration, and the stinging in her leg.

Struggling to get his lust under control, Jamie put his forehead to hers. His chest worked like a bellows and his hands shook. "Christ, I'm sorry."

"It's . . . it's okay."

Agony twisted inside Jamie, and he shook his head. "No, Faith. It's not."

"Jamie, don't do this." Her eyes pleaded with him. "I'll be fine."

Untangling her hands from his shirt, Jamie slowly lifted himself away from her to stand beside the sofa. Faith immediately turned on her side, curling her leg toward her body, visibly struggling to subdue the ache. She reached out a hand to him. "Jamie?"

He didn't know what to do. Never in his life, not even with Delayna, had he felt so disoriented and alone, so . . . desperate. He took a step back.

Faith struggled into a partial upright position. "Jamie."

Again, he shook his head, still backing up— away from her. "Eat your crackers, Faith. Then rest."

"Please, *please* don't go."

Jamie reached the door and, feeling behind himself, he turned the knob. If he didn't leave now, he'd be all over her. He knew it. *She knew it—* and wanted it.

But they hadn't settled a thing. There were so many unanswered questions, so many dubious intents, that only a blind idiot would stay.

And still . . . he wanted to. And for that reason more than any other, Jamie ignored the anxiety on her face, the physical discomfort she felt, the neediness.

"You can sleep in my bed. It'll be more comfortable for you. Don't . . . don't wait up for me." He stepped onto the porch and into the soothing hush of the surrounding woods, closing the door softly behind him.

Chapter Seven

Flicking the flashlight around the area, mud clear to her knees, Alyx finally reached her sporty red Mazda. Thankfully, she saw no sign of Scott.

Mentally thanking Jamie for both the flashlight and the warning, Alyx dug her keys out of her pocket and unlocked the driver's door. Not only had the woods quickly darkened to an eerie pitch black that might have frightened a lesser woman, the damp cold had penetrated her clothes and left her shivering like a wet pup.

Pathetic.

Even out of the woods, the dark, cloud-filled sky gave the illusion of midnight instead of early evening.

Alyx turned on the ignition and kicked on the heat. Ridiculous to need the heater this time of year. Usually late July in Visitation was sweltering hot. But the storm had brought with it an unseasonable cold front, and mixed with the wind and lack of sun, it was truly miserable weather. Alyx couldn't wait for summer weather to return. She liked swimming in the lake, wallowing in the sunshine. She did not like wearing more clothes than necessary.

Anxious to get home and shower, she tossed her hat onto the passenger's seat, put the car in gear, stepped on the gas . . . and went nowhere.

The rainfall had left the ground soupy, and her tires spun without gaining purchase. *Great.*

Alyx reached for her cell phone, then thought better of it. No matter whom she called, Scott would find out. Unless she could reach one of the ladies . . . but no, she couldn't see any of them pushing her car out of the mud.

Dropping her head forward to rest it on the steering wheel, Alyx moaned. A split second later, headlights flashed in her rearview mirror and the moan turned into a curse. Jamie had warned her, so she knew without looking that it had to be Scott. If her stupid car hadn't been stuck, she'd be ahead of him right now.

A flashing blue light danced around the darkened, heavily wooded area, telling Alyx that Scott had spotted the car. But the moment he realized it was *her* car, the colored lights went off again and he pulled up behind her. Damn.

Putting on a brave face, Alyx stepped back out of the car to greet him. Caught in his headlights, she knew he'd already seen her wet clothes and muddy jeans. He opened his door and emerged so slowly, Alyx had a moment's trepidation.

Naturally, she hid it. "Hey, Scott. Fancy meeting you here."

"Alyx?" His tone of voice told her it was worry,

not anger, that had him scowling. He reached her in a few long strides. Big hands clasping her shoulders, turning her this way and that, he checked her over for signs of injury. "What's happened? Are you okay?"

Her heart melted. Even though she knew she could take care of herself, it still thrilled her that Scott could be so sweet and concerned. "I'm great." Alyx gave him her best cocky smile. "I was just about to head home, but my stupid car is stuck. Are you done for the night?"

He eyed her car, then eyed her. She saw the suspicion, followed by condemnation, enter his gentle blue eyes. "What were you doing here, Alyx?"

She shrugged. Not telling him something was acceptable. But she'd never outright lie to him. "I wanted to see Jamie."

His hands fell away from her, and he took a quick step back. Denying her words, he shook his head. "No. Not even you would be foolish enough to . . . What am I saying? Of course you would."

Sheepish, because she realized now that it had been somewhat foolish, Alyx nodded. "Yeah, I would."

His mouth set in a hard line. He yanked off his hat to slap against his leg. "Damn it, woman. It's dark—"

"It wasn't dark when I left, and it really only got dark a few minutes ago."

Unappeased, Scott jammed the hat back on his head, then bent so that his nose almost butted into hers. "Do you have any idea how irresponsible you've been?"

Alyx missed the insult in his words because his

mulish mouth looked oh-so-kissable. She scoped the surrounding area, but didn't see a spot suitable to seduction. Hmm. Maybe Scott's car . . . but no, he wouldn't like her getting mud everywhere.

"Alyx, are you listening to me? Do you have any idea what could happen to a woman alone in the woods, with this damn storm—"

She waved away his concerns. "A little rain and mud isn't going to kill me, Scott."

His eyes looked ready to pop out of his head. "There are *bears* in those woods. And bobcats and coyotes and mountain lions—"

"Seriously?" Alyx looked behind her at the wall of tall trees and enormous rocks and impenetrable darkness. "I didn't see any ferocious animals. Just a few squirrels and some little critters rustling around in the fallen leaves. I couldn't make out what they were."

Scott pulled back, his spine ramrod straight, his shoulders taut. Outraged, he just stared at her, then muttered, "Jesus, Joseph, and Mary." Hands on his hips, he paced away, raged back. "Why, Alyx? You knew we all planned to go up together when the rain let up. Why sneak off alone? Why not wait—"

Affronted, Alyx glared at him. "I didn't sneak."

"No? Then what would you call it? You didn't tell a blessed soul you were going, did you?"

"What makes you so sure I didn't?"

In a near roar, Scott shouted, "Because everyone else has enough sense to stop you."

That got her temper sparking. "Stop me *how?* I'm a big girl, Scott."

He eyed her up and down. "Compared to what?"

Okay, so compared to him she seemed small. That wasn't the point. "I'm an adult. I'm allowed to come and go as I please. No one said a peep when Clint went up there snooping around."

"Dear God, don't tell me you're comparing yourself to a grown man who outweighs you by damn near a hundred pounds and stands half a foot taller."

"Size isn't everything, you know. In fact, in the scheme of things, it counts for very little." The sound of Scott's teeth grinding seemed especially eerie on the deserted road.

"In case you've forgotten, Clint is a trained fighter, lethal in his own right."

"Has he ever fought a bear?"

"He was *armed.*"

Alyx gasped. "You're saying he would have *shot* the poor bear?"

Scott literally vibrated with anger. "Damn it, woman, *we all knew where he was.*"

Hmmm. Alyx had to admit Scott had a point. Reasoning that aloud, she said, "So if he'd gone missing, you'd have known where to look for him, right?" She nodded, willing to admit when she was wrong. "Okay, I see what you mean. And I'm sorry I worried you."

Hoping to soothe him, Alyx put her hand on Scott's chest, which was rock hard with tension.

"It is worry, right? That's why you're so fired up?"

He looked wary at her sudden turnaround. "Yeah . . ."

Hey, she could be reasonable. Especially when she had better things to do than fight.

Like . . . make love.

"If it makes you feel any better, Jamie knew I was coming. He met me partway. And he told me to hurry back or you'd be here and cause a scene, only I did hurry, and still, here you are." She tried another smile. "And really, we are causing a scene. I bet with all our shouting, we've scared off any bears that might have been lurking around. What do you think?"

Scott removed his hat again, slapped it twice against his leg, glared at her, and took another stomping turn around the area. His frustration was palpable, but he didn't scare Alyx. She trusted Scott implicitly.

"Hey." Alyx followed on his heels. "Do you think Jamie knew that even if I did hurry, I was still going to run into you? I do. I think that rat knew all along, and he just threw me to the wolf anyway."

"Wolf?" Scott slowly turned to face her. Now he looked . . . insulted. "Is that what I am? A wolf?"

"Figure of speech." Alyx grinned. "You know, because of the way you bluster and carry on."

His head snapped back and his big shoulders went stiff. *"Bluster?"*

"Scott." Dragging his name out to three syllables, Alyx scooted up close to him and put her hands on his shoulders. She smiled up at him. "I *am* sorry. You're right. I should have told someone what I was doing."

"Not just someone, Alyx." His thumb met his chest. "Me."

It was odd, but she kind of liked it when he acted territorial. Prodding him, she asked, "Because you're the deputy?"

"Because we're involved."

Well, that wasn't quite the declaration she'd hoped for, and disappointment settled around her. She was so sick in love with him—a first for her—that she *needed* him to feel the same.

Scott clasped her waist and pulled her up close against him. In a gentler, slightly affected voice, Scott said, "You're giving me gray hairs, Alyx Winston. I can't take it."

That alarmed her. Alyx went on tiptoe to kiss him, once, hard and fast. "But you're a big, strong man of the law. A little fretting here and there isn't going to hurt you much, right?"

He stared at her mouth until she kissed him again, lingering this time, then he hugged her right off her feet. "Yeah, I suppose for you, I can tolerate it."

Tolerate? She wanted him to accept her, not tolerate her, because Alyx knew, even if she tried, she couldn't become a different woman. She *was* headstrong and capable and adventurous. She loved Scott's qualities—and she wanted him to love hers.

When Alyx frowned, Scott held her away from him. "Will you promise not to go see Jamie again without me?"

Alyx bit her lip. "How about I promise I won't go without telling you first?"

"What's the difference?"

"I might want to see him without you, or maybe when you're too busy to go with me. Or maybe Jamie will eventually move to town, like he should, and then it won't even matter to you if I go see him."

Scott lifted her to her toes, his gaze burning, and stated unequivocally, "It'll matter."

"Oh." So, Alyx thought, it wasn't just the danger of the woods, but a touch of jealousy as well. Jealousy indicated more than tolerance, didn't it? She gave Scott a fat smile.

Scott dropped his hands so fast, Alyx almost fell. He rubbed his face, muttering to himself, then drew a calming breath. "So tell me, Alyx, when are you going home again?"

That question came out of nowhere, startling Alyx. "Trying to get rid of me?"

"Not at all."

"Then why ask?"

He pulled her back up to him and kissed her silly. When his mouth was on hers, Scott could make her forget her own name.

His forehead to hers, Scott said, "You seldom stay in Visitation for more than a few days before hightailing it back home."

"You miss me?" she teased.

"Damn right." Another kiss, a cuddle on her butt, then he said, "Now that Clint's on as a full-time sheriff, I thought I'd take a vacation."

"A vacation? Really?"

"Once the rain lets up, yeah. I haven't had time off in a helluva long time." His hand cupped her face, his thumb brushing the edge of her mouth while his voice dropped and became intimate. "It'd be nice if you were around."

"Then I promise to be here."

With something resembling an evil light to his normally gentle eyes, Scott added, "Not that I'd mind spending some time just fishing and kicking back."

"I can fish."

"Maybe." Scott half grinned. "But I've yet to see you kick back."

With Scott, she'd be more than happy to become a couch potato, especially if she could get him naked on said couch.

And speaking of naked . . . Alyx trailed a fingertip along the buttons to his uniform shirt, beneath his jacket. "How about we discuss this back at your place?"

He looked more than a little tempted, then shook his head. "Sorry, baby, I can't. I have one more trip yet tonight. And we can't just leave your car here."

"It's stuck in the mud."

"I can push it out."

Of course he could, but she didn't want it pushed out. Not now. She wanted to climb into Scott's cruiser with him and . . . visit. "You're too good at resisting me."

He wrapped his long fingers around the back of her neck, caressing her before giving in to another kiss. In a husky rumble that Alyx felt deep inside herself, Scott said, "You probably have no idea just how irresistible you are to me."

Mmmm. Now that sounded nice. "If I'm so irresistible, then maybe I should come with you tonight."

Scott ran his hand along his jaw and considered her car. "How about I push you free and follow you to Joe's? Then maybe we can get together in the morning?"

Alyx frowned at him in suspicion.

Raising a brow, he asked, "What? You don't want to see me tomorrow?"

"You know I do, but . . . Are you going to tell Joe that I visited Jamie?"

That soured Scott's mood real quick. "Hell, no. It's bad enough that I know. I don't want the whole town hearing about it." Then he shrugged. "Besides, you're right. You're damn near twenty-eight, Alyx. Like you said, you don't have to answer to him."

That surprised her. "No, I don't. But that doesn't stop Joe from griping at me."

"You're staying in his house." Scott folded his arms over his chest and stared down at her with grim resolve. "Maybe that gives him a few rights to dictate."

Inching closer, Alyx licked her lips and decided the timing was as right as it was ever likely to get. "You know, I was thinking about that."

"Yeah?"

"Staying with Joe so often isn't such a good idea. He's a newlywed after all, and their house is already full with the four of them."

Scott went still. "You're not going to visit anymore?"

"I didn't mean that!" She gave him a small push. "Don't go putting words in my mouth."

Perplexed, Scott said, "Sorry."

"I meant that when I visit, maybe I shouldn't stay with Joe."

Rife with visible tension, Scott said, "You aren't here long enough or often enough to warrant getting your own place."

That summed up the problem in a nutshell. Alyx was happiest when in Visitation, near Scott— and that made her feel vulnerable. Never before had her happiness depended on a man. She'd spent years playing the field, going her own way, doing her own thing.

But lately, the urge to nest had churned inside her. She wanted to settle down, to belong. She wanted to be with Scott . . . on a permanent basis.

A solution seemed obvious to her. "I could be."

Dark shadows masked Scott's expression. "What does that mean, Alyx?"

"Well, you know web design is pretty much a mobile business. Have computer, can travel." Her smile felt forced, so she let it go. "The thing is, I just finished a really big job. So I have an extra influx of cash. And with the fees from all the permanent sites I maintain now, I could easily finance a move and set myself up down here."

"When are you planning to do this?"

Alyx studied Scott's expression and decided he didn't look worried about the forced proximity. "In a week or so. I'm hanging out till this stuff gets settled with Jamie, then I'll go home and close up my apartment there, pack up, and . . ." She shrugged. "Move here."

It was so quiet Alyx could hear the crickets chirping in the woods. Gravel crunched under her restless feet. She crossed her arms, uncrossed them.

Blast the man, she did not like being left on pins and needles. "Well?"

Still inscrutable, Scott asked, "You find a place to stay yet?"

"No. I haven't even really looked." Why the hell was she so nervous? She could have faced the stupid bear without being so jumpy. Of course, she didn't love the bear. "But I'm sure I can find something."

Scott tucked a fist under her chin, tipped her face up, then rubbed her bottom lip with his thumb. He seemed undecided, then determined. "My house is big enough for two."

Her heart soared, then took a dizzying turn around her stomach, making her jittery and jubilant enough to float. So he hadn't exactly proposed, so what? Living together would lead to all kinds of new commitments, she was sure of it. All she had to do was show him how great it'd be.

It wasn't easy, but Alyx kept her voice blasé. "That could work, I suppose."

A brief flash of relief showed on his face.

"I've never lived with anyone before." Alyx bobbed her eyebrows. "It sounds . . . lascivious. And *fun.*"

The relief disappeared behind a blank mask. Scott hesitated, then abruptly stepped around her. "It's getting late. If you want to get behind the wheel, I'll give you a push."

The thought of kicking him in his very sexy butt appealed, but Alyx stifled the urge. How could he be so unaffected by such a life-altering decision? Sure, she'd acted blasé, but that's because she was crazy nuts in love with him and didn't want to throw her heart at his feet without knowing how he felt. But they'd be *living* together. Didn't that mean anything to him?

Miffed, Alyx waltzed past him to the driver's side door. "What are you going to tell Joe about me staying with you?"

Scott stiffened, opened his mouth—and headlights flashed in the distance. Surprised that anyone else was on the long, lonely road that time of night, Alyx shielded her eyes and stared, but Scott said, "Get in your car and lock the doors."

"Why? Who is it?"

"I don't know. And until I find out, I want you inside." He was beside her in an instant, and somehow, though she resisted, Alyx found herself back in the car.

"Hey! I can take care of myself, Scott. I don't—"

"Lock the doors." When she only frowned at him, he growled, "*Alyx . . . ,*" in a warning tone.

"This is dumb," she complained through the closed car, but obediently pushed the power-lock button.

Scott said, "Thank you," before moving to stand by his cruiser.

A sporty Porsche in some dark color that Alyx couldn't identify drew close, slowed, and finally stopped. The engine continued to purr, but the tinted driver's window lowered and a beautiful woman with pale blond hair leaned out to smile at Scott.

Alyx narrowed her eyes, studied the woman, and realized that she'd seen her earlier in town while doing errands for her brother.

"Well, hello there," Blondie cooed. "Just what I need—a man of authority."

Smiling like a sap, Scott approached the car. "Deputy Scott Royal, at your service. What can I do for you, ma'am?"

Gritting her teeth, Alyx lowered the window enough to hear their every word.

"For starters, you can call me Becky."

Scott grinned. "All right, Becky. What's the problem?"

"I got into Visitation yesterday for a nice long vacation. But today I had errands to run and they took longer than I'd expected. Now that it's dark . . . I'm not sure I'm heading in the right direction. Everything looks different at night, doesn't it? Especially in the rain."

Bracing one hand on the roof of her car, Scott leaned closer. Still smiling, he remarked, "I hope our lousy weather won't ruin your trip."

The woman gave him an *eat-you-up* once-over, and Alyx had to fight the urge to explode from her car.

"Actually, my vacation is looking better and better by the minute."

Scott laughed, and Alyx decided enough was enough. She threw open her door and climbed out of the car. "Scott?" Her voice sounded girly shrill, and she nearly choked. She would not make an ass out of herself just because a bleached bimbo in a nice ride could fool Scott with her sugary tone.

Alyx cleared her throat, and in something closer to a baritone, demanded, "Are we leaving or what?"

The woman took in Alyx's wind-tangled hair, her dirty jeans, and blinked. "I'm sorry," she said, turning back to Scott, "I'm holding you up."

"Not at all. Helping lost ladies is part of the job description." Scott didn't even glance at Alyx, which made her want to rip that silly grin right off his handsome face.

He showered the hussy with his most engaging manner while straightening and pointing down the road. "You're headed the right way. A few more miles, you'll see a sharp bend in the road. You'll go downhill a little and to the left. You can't miss it."

"Thank you so much." Becky hesitated. "When I saw two cars here, I thought maybe I was closer to town than I recalled. I mean, this is a deserted road, isn't it?"

"Nothing but trees and more trees."

"So . . . you're just assisting"—the blonde's gaze swung toward Alyx again, then dismissed her—"yet another lady in distress?"

"It's this damn rain combined with the winding roads. There've been more mishaps today than we usually see in a year." He rapped the roof of her car. "So you be careful driving now, you hear?"

"You have my word." Becky reached out and touched his arm. "I'll see you around town?"

Tapping his badge, Scott said, "You won't be able to avoid me."

The woman released him, gave a three-finger wave and another sickly sweet "Thank you," and finally, the Porsche drove away.

Hands on his hips, Scott stood on the side of the roadway and watched until the car disappeared out of sight. He had a very speculative look in his eyes.

Infuriated, Alyx stomped through puddles and squishy mud until she got close enough, and then slugged him in the biceps.

"*Ow.*" Jumping as if a snake had bit him, Scott scowled down at her. He flexed his arm. "What the hell was that for?"

Alyx was not a woman prone to the silent treatment. When irritated, she vented. "You were flirting with her!"

His expression turned impassive. "Of course I wasn't."

The dismissive tone irritated Alyx even more. "Scott Royal, we *just* agreed to live together."

"So?" He said it like a taunt, confusing Alyx. Especially when he added, "It's not like we're getting married or anything." The question hung in the air, and Scott prodded, "Right?"

First hurt, then angry, Alyx sucked in a breath. "We have a relationship," she said, almost choking on the words, "which means you have no business coming on to other women."

Appearing oh-so-calm, Scott claimed, "It's called being polite, Alyx. You could have tried it instead of screeching at me in front of her."

Alyx punched him again, this time in the ribs. "That was *not* mere politeness, you . . . you . . ."

Scott flinched, but he also laughed, and Alyx wanted to throttle him. He had more mood swings than a menopausal woman. She drew back her fist, and Scott caught her hands, deftly pinning them behind her back.

Unwilling to actually hurt him, she gave a half-hearted struggle. "Let me go."

"No." In one quick move, he snugged her up close so that her hips fit tight to his and her upper body arched awkwardly, pressing her breasts forward. Giving her a warm smile while studying her chest, Scott murmured, "Settle down, Alyx."

Her eyes nearly crossed. "How dare you—"

Cutting her off in mid-tirade, Scott kissed her. She opened her mouth to complain—and his tongue licked in, first teasing, then boldly claiming, and her toes curled in her wet boots. Warmth spread, heating her from the inside out.

Wow, she did love Scott's mouth. The fight went right out of her.

Against her lips, Scott whispered, "I wasn't flirting, honey, I swear. Why would I even want to when I've got you close at hand?"

Too muddled to think straight, Alyx just listened.

"Strangers make me curious, that's all. And what better way to get to know a stranger than to play along?"

Blinking fast to regain her wits, Alyx asked, "What do you mean?"

He nuzzled her neck. "I guess I'm the cautious sort. Comes with the job." Then he raised his head, all intent and annoyed again. "Which is why I asked you to stay in the car. This time it was a woman alone, but it could just as easily have been someone dangerous."

Alyx studied him. "So you don't think one woman can be a threat?"

"I didn't . . ." He wisely chose to retrench. "I don't know. I don't think *she's* a threat."

"Hmm. I saw her in town earlier today. All primped up and dressed nice, just standing around, sort of checking things out."

Scott grinned. "Ah. Very suspicious."

New fury surfaced. "I don't like her." And before he could accuse her of jealousy, Alyx added, "I don't trust her, either."

"Why?"

"Because she's too slick. She's exactly the type of woman a man would never suspect."

Scratching his ear, Scott asked, "Suspect her of what, exactly?"

"I don't know."

He fought a smile. "Alyx, honey, you're over-reacting. I didn't see any prison tattoos. No bulging muscles. Hell, she appears to be a slight woman."

"She's as tall as me. And she probably weighs close to the same." Alyx pushed forward another step. "You don't think I can be lethal?"

Scott barely stifled his laugh. "This is ridiculous. She didn't make any threats. All she did was ask for directions."

Alyx snorted. "Right. Because the rain confused her."

"Don't sneer." Gripping her shoulders, Scott bent to look her in the eyes. "We should be talking about you, not Becky. You didn't stay in the car like I asked you to."

"Why should I? You just said she wasn't danger-ous."

"True. But she could have had someone with her, a drunk or abusive boyfriend."

"It wouldn't have mattered." Alyx lifted her chin. "There's no way I'd sit idle if you were in danger."

Back to being irritated, Scott growled, "Alyx—"

"I'm not made that way." She knotted her hands in his shirt and tried to shake him, hoping he'd understand. "I'm not helpless, and I'm not a cow-ard."

"I never said you were a coward."

"Then don't treat me like one." And Alyx shook him again for an entirely different reason. "Besides, I think a drunk would have been preferable to that hussy anyway. Did you see how she looked at you?

If she tries that again, I'll show her what a woman can do. I'll show her that I don't need rippling muscle to—"

Scott cut off that awful threat with another hard smooch. "I do love how fiery you get, babe." He nuzzled his nose against hers. "Let's save it for when we're alone—preferably with a bed close by."

And Alyx, wearing her own sappy smile, said, "Okay."

Jamie didn't go down the mountain. He went up. Not so far that he couldn't see his cabin and the lights shining from it, but far enough away that he wouldn't, couldn't, touch Faith.

He knew the path by rote; too many times, he'd wandered the mountain just because he had nothing else to do. Jamie felt at peace among the tall trees and wild animals.

He felt alone—just as he should.

Locating his favorite boulder, he sat down, his hands flattened out on either side on the hard, cold surface. The scents of damp earth and moss and evergreens filled his lungs with each deep breath. Wind blew his hair in his face, and he hunched his shoulders against the chill.

That's when the warning hit him.

Jamie stilled, sifting through the battle of emotions to grasp the darkest, the one most menacing. As it drifted in and out, too unclear for him to perceive, he tried to absorb it. Confusing bits and pieces came to him, but they didn't meld together for an adequate view of the threat.

Jamie concentrated harder, focusing. Images of a woman flitted by, haloed by doubt, the face indistinguishable. Faith? Or someone else?

He saw Scott and Alyx, and with impatience he pushed their images aside. Those two would forever clash wills, and Jamie wasn't about to be enmeshed in their scorching romance. In the end, just knowing what he did of human nature, Jamie trusted that they'd work things out with no interference from him.

Narrowing his focus, Jamie contemplated the face he'd seen—and to his surprise, Cory intruded.

The little girl just popped in, not the threat, but instead the exact opposite. Darkness faded away, replaced by soft lights and powder scents and an aura of gentleness.

Without knowing why, Jamie held his breath, going immobile. Even his heart seemed to stutter to a standstill. The image of the child shone as crisp and clear as reality. Big, solemn eyes stared at him from a small, sweet face surrounded by dark curls. Her hand reached out, so tiny, so soft—and Jamie could almost swear she touched him.

Suddenly his heart began to punch with near violence, but not from dread. Some tremendous, choking sentiment swelled inside his chest. He couldn't call it pain, but considered it far from comfortable—and yet, he didn't want it to go away. He clung to it, to her, soaking in the sensation, embracing it with all his might.

His hands shook and his throat closed up and his vision blurred, making him blink hard.

Something wet and warm tickled his face, sliding down his cheekbone to the corner of his mouth. He tasted salt.

A tear?

Jerking hard, appalled, confused, and humiliated, Jamie swiped at his face with both hands. Jesus. He had no reason to get sappy. He stared out at the dark, surrounding woods, dripping with rain, crawling with nocturnal activity. He was as alone as ever.

But . . . the little girl was there too, still somehow a part of him. She *saw* him, just as he saw her.

And her rosebud mouth lifted in a gentle smile of amusement.

Because she'd surprised him? Or because she'd seen his reaction?

Jamie's face burned, his jaw clenched, and that made her laugh, a slight, giggling sound that sank into him and chased away the embarrassment. Bemused by such a strange turn, he shook his head. *Unbelievable.*

Then it struck Jamie: he'd often told people things, first Joe and Luna, then the others. Incredible, *unbelievable* things—that he'd nonetheless expected them to believe.

On faith.

A brief chuckle took Jamie by surprise. It was rusty and surreal, echoing down the mountain with an eerie resonance. Because the sound had come from him, he froze in shock, clamping his mouth shut to guard against any other outbursts. At the same time, his mind buzzed with possibilities.

Cory had sent him his own Faith. That sounded

ridiculously poetic, but Jamie believed it as surely as he believed the little girl wanted him to understand, to trust. The same way he'd expected others to trust.

While considering the ramifications of that, the most profound thing occurred to him.

It was possible that the closer he got to a person, the better he understood them. When emotionally connected, reading thoughts became as easy as snapping his fingers.

Could it be that caring for someone didn't disable his ability? Could it be that it . . . *enhanced it?*

Jamie thought back on the various occasions when he'd known things about Joe, Bryan, Bruce, even Clint. He thought about the women, how he'd always been aware of what they wanted and needed. He thought of Alyx and how easily he'd deciphered her every thought during her visit.

Even though he cared greatly for her.

Or was he mixing the natural ability of an astute man with his extraordinary ability to filter the thoughts of others? He'd often seen Joe intuitively know what would happen in certain circumstances. Scott did the same, except around Alyx. Scott was too emotionally involved with Alyx to make sound judgments every time.

Could the same be true for him?

Jesus, it was all confusing.

Slowly reclining onto the boulder and stacking his hands behind his head, Jamie stared up at the blackness that went on forever. He forgot about the cold, damp air, about the chill seeping into his spine and the possibility of more rain.

Going back in time, he sorted through old truths to make better sense of them.

Sex had never been just sex for Jamie. His awareness of a woman, of her every thought and sensation, had made it impossible to remain detached during physical contact. For that reason, he hadn't gotten physically involved very often.

With Delayna . . . She had claimed genuine affection for him. He'd *felt* her caring, especially when making love to her, when her heartbeat matched his own and her nails stung his shoulders. She'd been open and honest, holding him tight, finding her pleasure in an explosive orgasm that triggered his own. Her feelings, both physical and emotional, had been like a warm blanket around him.

Yet supposedly she'd lied—or had she? Professor Kline had wanted him confused and hurt, disoriented. How else could he study the impact of those reactions on Jamie's psychic ability?

What if Kline had lied, instead of Delayna? What if Delayna had just gone along with the ruse for some reason? Maybe Kline had even forced her to play along.

God knew, Kline had enjoyed manipulating people.

Jamie chewed that over, his head pounding with the conflicting ideas, not happy with any conclusion except that he needed the truth for the same reasons Kline had: the truth would shed light on the extent of his skill and anything that hindered it.

One thing was certain—he did care about

everyone in Visitation. It pained him greatly when he thought they were in danger. He'd do just about anything to keep them safe.

But did he need to isolate himself to ensure he could help?

Oddly enough, when Jamie thought of Delayna now, he felt only regret. Days, hours, even minutes ago, memories of her would have sliced into him with the savagery of a butcher knife. But that had changed.

Everything had changed.

What hurt now was the idea of his own gullibility. His own foolishness. Like any other man, Jamie had his pride, and allowing Delayna or Kline—or both—to use him struck deep at the core of his masculine ego.

Could he possibly have let the professor dupe him with words, with emotion, to the point that he believed a bastard like Kline instead of trusting himself?

It'd mean he had to accept his own weaknesses, and that wasn't easy for Jamie. He'd always considered himself strong enough to go it alone, to close himself off from everyone. Strong enough that he didn't need anyone else in his life.

He honestly didn't know if he had it within him to reverse everything now, to open himself to a normal existence.

As he thought it, Cory materialized again, reprimanding him with a teasing look far too old for her years. Jamie took in the twinkle in her dark eyes, the dimple in her pale cheek, and the way her small pink mouth fought a grin.

He forgot about his pride and loneliness.

The little imp was pleased with herself, and for whatever reason, that pleased Jamie.

He searched for any threat toward Cory, but found none. He wasn't sure what to make of that. Did Cory have some odd notion of protecting him? Did she worry for him because Faith worried?

That idea didn't sit right. He'd already decided to guard himself against Faith until he figured out what impact she'd have on him.

But Cory . . . she was different, in some way familiar, and strangely connected. They shared an ability that few could ever claim, which provided unique possibilities. While Jamie viewed her, she viewed him, as if they stood face-to-face. He'd never encountered that before. It was almost the same as having her next to him.

Closing his eyes, Jamie gave her a message. Support. Understanding. And reassurance.

If she would only trust him with the details, he'd do anything necessary to keep her safe.

In return, he got a hug, a child's hug so real, so warm and tight and precious, that he couldn't swallow past the lump in his throat, and his eyes burned with moisture again.

Then Cory began fading away.

Confident that she'd return, knowing he'd eventually meet her face-to-face, Jamie watched her go. Someday they would share experiences; he would teach her all that he'd learned through the years, things that didn't apply to anyone else he knew. Maybe that's all Cory really wanted or needed from him. Maybe the threat he'd sensed in town had nothing to do with her or with him.

The mournful howl of a coyote lulled Jamie, and he relaxed, soaking in the night and the new sensation of hopefulness after so many years of desolation.

He'd return to Faith. Later.

For now, he wanted to consider things. He needed time to acclimate himself to his newfound realities, to plan his next move. To anticipate all the things he might be free to do.

Like smiling.

Chapter Eight

Becky drove close to a mile before pulling her Porsche to the side of the road and turning off the headlights. Again, she tried her cell phone—and finally got a signal.

"Cursed mountains." She waited while the phone rang, keeping her gaze on the rearview mirror, knowing the deputy would be along soon. "Answer, damn you."

"Yeah?" came Doug's sleepy voice.

"About time." Rushing so she wouldn't be caught, Becky said, "Listen up. I think we finally got a lucky break."

"You think?"

"Hey, I'm not psychic, but I don't believe in co-incidence either." Laughing at the inside joke, Becky took another cautious peek in the rearview mirror. "I saw a woman pulled over on the side of the road. She had mud clear up to her knees, and her clothes were soaked."

"Faith Owen?"

"No, someone else. But she'd been poking around up the mountains."

Bewildered, Doug said, "So?"

Sighing, Becky rubbed her forehead. Doug could be such an idiot. "It's been raining like hell. Why else would a woman be climbing up a mountain, unless it was to visit someone?"

Awe colored his tone. "You're talking about Creed?"

If she didn't need Doug for backup, she'd have dumped his sorry ass long ago. "Yes, I'm talking about Creed."

"But . . . he's supposed to be a loner, right? Why would he be having visitors?"

"I have no idea why a woman would visit him. But where else would a loner live in this stupid Podunk town, than up in the mountains somewhere? That'd make sense. He sure as hell isn't anywhere else in Visitation. I know because I've been checking. But I lost Faith's trail here, and I know she was going to him."

"No, you assume she was going to him."

Becky shook her head. "We missed her by mere hours. She left in a hurry. Where else would she be going?"

"I don't know."

Ignoring him, Becky continued to think out loud. "She'll want Creed to help her protect the kid." Anger burned in her throat, and she murmured, "This is going to work out even better."

"If Creed's as good as you say, he'll be on to us before we even have a chance to act."

"Leave Creed to me."

But still, Doug fretted. "He's probably not going to be too fond of gaining the limelight again."

Spineless wimp. "Listen up, Doug. This is my big chance. It's *your* big chance. And you promised to help."

"But—"

"But nothing. You're in too deep to pull back now. We're close. So damn close to having it all. For once, show some guts, will you?"

Her insult angered him. Becky heard the chill in his voice when he said, "Did you happen to ask the woman why she was there? Maybe she has nothing to do with Creed."

"Of course I didn't ask. That might've tipped my hand. Right now, they just think I'm a tourist here on vacation."

"They?" he asked with rising alarm.

With a mental shrug, Becky admitted, "She had a rather hunky deputy with her."

"Oh God." He started breathing hard. "This keeps getting worse and worse. Hell, before you know it, the whole damn town will be involved."

His cowardice set her temper on edge. "Not likely. As you said, he's a loner. No one will even know we're near him."

"Except the deputy, who's already seen you poking around."

"I didn't poke around, I asked for directions. Don't worry about the deputy. I'll handle him."

"Yeah, I just bet you will."

Becky smiled, confident that Scott Royal would be no problem whatsoever. She'd always had stunning success with men. "This is going to be a piece of cake."

"I don't know—"

"I know." She laughed, then decided it was time to go. "Get yourself down here. I've got everything planned out." She gave directions, telling him where they'd meet, reminding him to be discreet so no one would notice him. "Creed will be off that mountain by the end of the week, Faith and the kid with him. Then we'll finally get everything we need. No one will even know what's going on—until it's too late."

Faith woke with a start that had her gasping aloud. Even before she sat upright in bed, her mind centered on Jamie. Had he ever come back in?

A glance at the window showed the gray tinge of approaching dawn. Damn, she'd slept through the night when she'd only meant to close her eyes a few minutes.

Tossing back the covers, she climbed out of Jamie's warm bed with barely a squeak of the mattress. Shivers raced up her spine, and she wrapped her arms around herself. For hours and hours, she'd lain awake, waiting for him, worrying, wishing she had even a modicum of psychic ability so she could connect with him, somehow bring him home where he belonged. With her. And with Cory.

But she'd had only the empty cabin and the sounds of the surrounding mountain to fill the void he'd left. The radio annoyed her, she wasn't hungry anymore, and with nothing else to do, she'd gone to Jamie's bed and curled up with her own misery.

Why had she rushed things? Just because she'd always cared for Jamie didn't mean he'd return that sentiment in less than two days' time.

Praying she'd find him below, Faith hurried to the ladder and peered down. Too many shadows lurked in the room below for her to see clearly. Taking care this time so she wouldn't fall and cause herself yet more injuries, she climbed down.

Just as she got both feet on the solid floor, the sound of even breathing reached her ears, and she froze, staring wide-eyed toward the couch. Yep, a body was there—a tall, lean body—stretched out end to end.

Thank you, God.

As Faith crept closer, her eyes adjusted so that she could see more than just indistinct forms. On his back, one muscled arm over his head, the other resting over his abdomen, Jamie slept. He wore unsnapped jeans, a dark T-shirt, and socks.

He looked so . . . beautiful to her. So incredible. Yet even in sleep, he wasn't entirely at peace. There was a tense set to him, an air of readiness—

Eyes still closed, he murmured, "Your idea of beauty is questionable."

"Ack!"

Faith lurched back so fast, she almost fell on her butt. In a flash, Jamie reached out and snagged her wrist, helping her to regain her balance.

Heart pounding wildly, Faith accused, "You're playing possum!"

Very slowly, still holding her arm, Jamie sat up.

"And you're as clumsy as ever." His eyes glittered with no sign of sleepiness. "Don't you have enough bruises already?"

"Yes, I do." Faith snatched her arm away from him and every awful, worried, sympathetic, and tearful thing she'd suffered the night before vanished. Propping her hands on her hips, she glared at him. "Just where the hell were you all night, Jamie Creed?"

Jamie cocked a brow, but ruined the effect by saying around a wide yawn, "I was out."

Out? That was it? What kind of explanation was that?

"I don't owe you any explanations, Faith." As he spoke, he stretched elaborately. Muscles flexed and contracted, and a funny tingle started in the pit of Faith's belly.

Crossing her arms under her breasts, she centered her mind and tried not to stare. "Do you have any idea how worried I was?"

"Worried enough to pass out in my bed and not stir so much as an eyelash when I came in?"

Her mouth opened, but nothing came out. She snapped it shut and glowered, thankful that the dark room kept him from seeing her blush. "I can't help it that I'm a sound sleeper. But *before* I fell asleep, believe me, Jamie, I was plenty worried."

"You have no reason to act like a betrayed wife."

Faith gasped, and more heat rushed to her face.

As if he hadn't just insulted her, he tipped his head. "Did you know you snore?"

Her mouth fell open again.

"Not that I mind so much." Jamie rose to his feet, towering over her, smelling warm and male, and so damn sexy.

Faith forgot to breathe when he stepped close and, with one finger, eased her jaw closed. "It was actually kind of cute."

He tapped the tip of her nose, then gave her his back as he walked into the bathroom and shut the door.

Faith stared after him, dumbfounded over all the ways he seemed different this morning. More relaxed. Even good-humored.

It was so *un*-Jamielike.

Just what the heck had gone on in those woods last night?

Turning, she dropped onto the couch—and the scented warmth left behind from his body immediately surrounded her. Oh God. The man was a walking furnace. Realizing how cool the cabin had gotten during the night, Faith drew up her feet and snuggled into the couch cushions, trying to decide what to do next.

The toilet flushed, water ran, and a few minutes later Jamie reappeared. "It's all yours," he said on his way to the kitchen. "I'll put on the coffee."

Dumbfounded by his laid-back manner, Faith watched him, squinting a little when he flipped on the kitchen light. He opened the canister of coffee, and the delicious aroma of fresh-ground beans wafted to her.

Inhaling, Faith said, "You sure know the way to a woman's heart."

Jamie stilled before glancing at her over his broad

shoulder. His bold gaze moved over her, turning her insides to mush. "That's good to know, Faith." Then he went back to making coffee.

Good to know? Slapping both hands to her cheeks, Faith tried to think, but after that look, all she could do was shiver. Deciding retreat might be the better option, she tottered into the bathroom. She took her time, washing her face, cleaning her teeth, combing her hair. It didn't help. A year wouldn't help her to figure out Jamie Creed and his odd mood swings.

By the time she emerged, the coffee had finished brewing. Jamie had already poured her a steaming cup and had fetched his flannel shirt for her to use as a housecoat again. He set the coffee on the table and looked at her, waiting.

When she just stood outside the bathroom door, staring at him in indecision, he pulled out the chair at the kitchen table. "Come here, Faith."

Her eyes nearly crossed. How did Jamie make such a simple, polite, even considerate request sound so . . . sexual?

His eyes never leaving her face, Jamie patted the chair with encouragement. "Sit. Give your leg a rest."

Or had he? Maybe she had herself and her lack of sexual experience to blame. Maybe she heard innuendos that didn't exist. Maybe—

"Does your leg hurt?" Jamie dropped his compelling gaze to her lower body, and slowly tracked it back up to her face. Lifting a brow, he asked, "Do you need me to carry you?"

Lord help her. Forcing her feet into motion, Faith said, "No. I'm fine now." She hurried to the table.

Like a true gentleman, Jamie helped her to slip on the flannel shirt and then held her chair as she seated herself.

Her butt had just settled on the wooden seat when Jamie said, "Let me see."

She paused with the coffee cup halfway to her mouth. "See what?"

"Your leg."

"Oh. Oh, no, really. It's fine." Faith continued to protest, but it did her no good.

Kneeling down, Jamie tossed up the hem of her gown as if he had the right, as if seeing her leg meant nothing, as if—

"I'm concerned?" Jamie shook his head, and his warm fingers curled around her ankle so she couldn't bolt away. "Relax, Faith. I won't strip you naked." Their gazes met, and he murmured, "Again."

Faith gulped at the visual suggestion and the heated look in his eyes. Lord help her, Jamie was in a strange mood.

He shoved the gown all the way up to her hip, but she slapped it back down until only her thigh showed. Determined not to complain, she sat rigid in the chair.

"Don't be a martyr, Faith. Silence doesn't suit you." His rough fingertips glided gently over her skin. "How bad does it hurt?"

She drew a steadying breath that didn't help one iota. Everything they'd done the night before remained fresh in her mind, and being touched by Jamie now erased the time they'd spent apart.

"I . . . I should confess that I bruise easily."

"Is that right?" Jamie still touched her, so she could only nod an affirmative.

His hands fell away and he stood, but stayed close to her chair. The fly of his rumpled jeans was eye level, which meant Faith kept her gaze glued to her coffee cup so her thoughts wouldn't shatter.

"The slightest bumps bruise me. It did hurt when I fell," she assured him. "I wasn't lying about that. And I didn't know how badly it might be injured. But today it's only a little sore and stiff. No big deal."

Jamie's hand cupped the back of her head, and he smoothed her hair. "I suppose I'll have to take your word for it, won't I?"

Now why did *that* sound so momentous, as if it held secret meaning?

His hand moved around to her chin, and he turned her face up to his. Snared in his gaze, Faith was unable to look away.

"I have to take off for a while today."

Her heart rocketed into her throat. "No!"

"Shhh." Again, he smoothed over her hair, then tunneled his fingers in close to her scalp, gently massaging. "I'm going into town, Faith. It'll be okay. I should be back before dinnertime."

"Jamie, no." Faith tried to stand, but Jamie pressed her shoulders, keeping her in the chair.

He bent low to look her in the eyes. His voice was firm, his expression inexorable. "I'm going."

In a whisper, Faith begged, *"No."*

Both hands cupped her face. "I don't want you to worry about anything. I'm coming back, and you'll be fine here without me. I promise. I wouldn't leave you otherwise."

"But I don't want to be here without you."

"Do you know how to cook?"

He caught her off guard with that ridiculous question and, feeling insulted, Faith snapped, "Of course I do."

"Then you can fix yourself some breakfast. And why don't you put on something for dinner? I'll be hungry by the time I return, and God knows, you're always hungry."

Faith glared at him. "Ha-ha. Very funny."

But Jamie didn't take the bait. He squeezed her shoulders. "I have roasts and chops in the freezer. Canned vegetables on the shelf. Use whatever you need."

Faith curled her hands into fists, resisting the urge to cry. She didn't want to be a burden to him, but the prospect of spending the day alone left her empty. She wanted to be with Jamie. She wanted him to *want* to be with her.

Jamie softened. "Why don't you take a nice long shower?"

"Yeah, that'll take, oh, ten minutes."

"That's about as long as the hot water lasts anyway. Maybe you can try on the jeans Alyx brought you. Go through my clothes if you want and see if you can find anything else to wear. Make yourself at home, okay?"

None of this made sense. Why was he so determined to leave her? Keeping her tone as lacking in inflection as his, Faith inquired, "What's happened, Jamie? Why are you so different?"

His thumb moved over her cheek, and for one heart-stopping moment, Faith thought he'd kiss her.

"No." He touched her mouth, and said in a whisper, "If I kissed you, I wouldn't want to stop."

Faith started to speak, to tell him she wouldn't want him to stop either, but he shook his head.

"I need to get some things done." With palpable reluctance, Jamie straightened away. "If you want to make a list, I'll pick up whatever you need. Just don't have me shopping all day."

She had no idea what to say to him. She knew he'd go, even though she didn't want him to.

He took a sip of coffee, watching her over the rim. "When I get back, we'll talk about things."

"What things?"

"Cory. Life. Men"—his eyes twinkled with mischief, confounding Faith, until he said—"and how women affect them."

As Luna instructed, Scott walked to the back room of the old house, the room that had once served as Joe's bedroom before he and Luna had married. Adjacent to the kitchen, it made a perfect television room where the kids could relax with a snack. On the kitchen table sat a box of cold cereal, beside it, a little spilled milk. He stepped around the table to enter the other room, but paused when he heard Alyx's teasing voice.

"So Clay is getting frisky with you, huh?"

Sixteen-year-old Willow sounded hesitant as she replied. "Sort of. But . . . he always stops, ya know?"

Voice firm, Alyx said, "Of course he does, because he respects you."

"He stops even when I don't ask him to."

"Oh." Alyx cleared her throat. "But . . . you would ask him to, right? I mean, Willow, honey, you're too young to—"

"*Please* don't lecture me like Joe does."

There was a pause, then Alyx drawled, "God forbid I should sound like Big Brother." She laughed. "Is Joe driving you crazy, then?"

"No. It's just that he's not very good at talking about kissing and boys and stuff. His advice is just *don't*. He says all teenage boys are wild animals and I should avoid them."

Scott rolled his eyes. So Joe-the-stud-turned-parent was uncomfortable talking about sex with his new daughter? What a hoot. That ought to be good for a month's worth of insults.

Alyx sighed. "I remember. Do you know when I was your age, Joe would run off all the guys who liked me? It got so embarrassing that I decided to just run them off myself instead."

Scott had never heard that before, but it explained a lot about Alyx. She had a tendency to bulldoze with no finesse, and it had damn near sent him packing. But Alyx was just so . . . exciting. And big hearted. And so turn-him-inside-out sexy that he not only refused to walk away—he wanted to be with her forever. He wanted to know that she was his and his alone.

He wanted to marry the woman.

She, however, seemed more than happy just to share his bed, and perhaps, out of convenience, his house.

Alyx mused aloud, "Maybe that's why I haven't really gotten hooked on any guys, ya know? I'm too used to keeping things flirty and fun. As long as they don't get serious, I don't have to chase them away."

Scott ground his teeth together, until he heard

Willow ask, "Do you want to chase away Deputy Royal?"

"No." Alyx's voice softened. "I meant other than Scott."

A warm feeling of contentment cloaked Scott. Alyx might be averse to marriage, but at least he was special to her.

"That's how I feel about Clay."

Peeking around the corner, Scott saw both Willow and Alyx on the floor, their chins propped on folded hands, their feet in the air. Empty cereal bowls sat in front of them. Willow wore a cute T-shirt and jeans, Alyx an enormous rumpled football jersey and loose gray shorts. They were both barefoot.

"Clay's a great guy. I like him."

Willow rolled to her back with a groan. "I really, *really* like him. But I don't understand him."

"Guys are tough to figure out."

Scott did a double take. As far as he was concerned, Alyx had that backward. Guys were easy— it was women who remained a mystery.

"Sometimes," Willow whispered, "we'll be kissing and stuff . . . " She peeked at Alyx, who nodded encouragement, then went on. "And suddenly Clay says he has to stop. Even when I still want to kiss him."

"Ah. Has he told you why?"

"No." Willow draped an arm over her eyes and gave another dramatic sigh. "He just shoves my head on his shoulder and hugs me real tight and tells me to be quiet. Isn't that rude? I mean, when he tells me that, I'm usually not even talking."

Alyx smothered a grin. "I think Clay is a very honorable young man who cares about you and doesn't want to rush you."

The way Alyx had rushed him? Scott thought with wry humor.

"So it doesn't matter what I want? Clay doesn't even ask me. And when I try to tell him that, he looks like he's in pain. It annoys me. *You* wouldn't let a guy tell you what you should or shouldn't do. And you wouldn't let a guy tell you to be quiet."

"Sometimes I might." Alyx's feet rocked in the air and, looking pensive, she drew circles in the carpet with a fingertip. "Under the right circumstances, you understand. If I knew he had good reasons."

Lifting her arm away, Willow said, "But I've told Clay how much I like kissing him."

"Kissing is great," Alyx agreed. "But Clay's a little older than you, right?"

"A little."

"He probably doesn't want to stop at just kissing, if you know what I mean."

Willow gave her a long look. "Of course I know what you mean. I'm not dumb." Lifting the chain from around her neck, she showed Alyx the class ring she wore. "We're going together."

Leaning close, Alyx admired the ring. "I never got a ring from a guy."

"Never?"

"Nope." She released the chain and let her long legs drop to the floor. "By the time Joe stopped ruining my dates, I dunno, I just decided I kind of preferred variety."

Scowling again, Scott decided he'd find a way to put an end to Alyx's preferences.

Suddenly Willow sat up. "See, that's just it. I could talk about all this with Luna, but she's not like you."

"Like me how?"

"You know. You're sort of wild and crazy and stuff."

Scott watched Alyx closely and saw her frown. "You think I'm wild and crazy?"

"And independent, too."

"Yeah, well—"

"The thing is, I really do like Clay a lot." Willow fidgeted with the chain, then burst out, "Do you think it's dumb for me to not be dating other guys? He asked me that once. If I wanted to, I mean."

"What did you say?"

"I sort of panicked. I thought that maybe *he* wanted to date other girls. But he said no. He said he's not his dad and he cares about me and he hates the idea of me with anyone else, but that if I wanted to, he wouldn't stand in my way."

Ducking back behind the wall, Scott nodded. He knew Clay well, and more than ever before, he respected the young man.

Willow made another female sound of frustration. "I felt so stupid. And Clay got really smug and grinned about it and he kept hugging me like he thought my reaction was cute or something."

Sympathetic to Willow's plight, Alyx sneered, *"Cute,"* as if it were an insult.

"Exactly. I thought about smacking him."

"Naw. Violence isn't the answer. Clay was probably just really happy to know you cared so much."

"Maybe." Willow heaved out a long breath. "But I can't imagine *you* doing that, panicking over the idea of Deputy Royal with someone else."

Alyx said in the meanest voice Scott had ever

heard from her, "I better not catch Scott with another woman."

A shocked silence lingered for several seconds before Willow exclaimed, "You'd be *jealous?*"

"What?" Alyx scoffed, laughed a little too hard, scoffed again. "Jealous? *No.* Where'd you get that idea? I just wouldn't like it, that's all. Scott's dating me. He doesn't need to date anyone else."

No, he didn't, Scott thought with a grin. Alyx was about as much as any one man could handle. But if she held him to exclusivity, then he damn well had the right to do the same with her.

"You see?" Willow said with approval. "That's *exactly* how I feel about Clay."

Alyx whispered, "How?"

And in the same whisper, Willow confessed, "I think I might be in love with him."

Their voices lowered even more, and Alyx choked out, "You're in love with Clay?"

"Isn't that what you feel for Deputy Royal?"

Fearing what he might—or might not—hear, Scott decided he'd done enough eavesdropping for one day. He cleared his throat, then tapped on the doorframe. "Good morning, ladies."

Two heads swiveled in his direction, both blank with surprise. Willow scrambled to her feet, her cheeks bright pink.

Alyx narrowed her eyes in suspicion. "What are you doing here?"

"What kind of greeting is that?" But even as he spoke, Scott kept wondering how it would look to Willow if Alyx moved in with him. She was an impressionable young girl dealing with some serious issues. As a deputy, a leading citizen of Visitation, he had to set a good example, right?

Would Alyx buy that argument?

Scott cleared his throat again. "I told you I'd come by this morning. I thought you might want to have breakfast with me."

"Oh, yeah," Alyx said, rising from the floor and dusting herself off. "Sorry. I guess I got . . . distracted."

No kidding. He felt pretty damn distracted right about now, too. "Luna told me you two lazy bums were back here watching morning cartoons, but she didn't tell me you'd already eaten." He indicated the cereal bowls with a tilt of his head.

"You call that breakfast?" Alyx snorted. "That was just a morning snack."

Willow glanced from Scott to Alyx and back again. "Joe's making a trip to town, Austin spent the night with a friend, and Luna said she had bills to pay." She rolled one slim shoulder. "So Alyx and I were just gabbing."

"Alyx excels at gabbing, so you picked the right gal."

That brought a smile to Alyx's mouth. She sauntered toward him with a saucy sway to her hips. "Actually, I excel at everything I do."

Unfair, to flirt with him in front of a kid. Scott kept his expression impassive as he stared down at her. "Is that right?"

Dancing her fingers up his chest, Alyx said, "I can be ready in fifteen minutes. Do you mind waiting?"

A little uneasy at the idea of being left alone

with Willow after what he'd heard, Scott glanced at his watch. "Make it ten and you've got a deal."

"Done."

Alyx scooped up the cereal bowls and headed for the kitchen. In one minute flat she'd put every-thing away and wiped off the table. The second she left the kitchen, an uncomfortable lull fell be-tween him and Willow. Damn, he felt awkward, when he never had before. But then, he'd never heard Willow having one of *those* talks before. And with Alyx no less.

"She's something else, isn't she?" Willow sud-denly asked, and Scott jumped.

"What's that?"

Willow grinned. "Alyx. She's pretty cool, huh?"

Hot was a better description, but Scott nodded. "In a unique, one-of-a-kind way, yeah."

"I like her."

"Me, too." Hell, he more than liked her, and it made him nuts because he didn't know if Alyx felt the same.

Whenever he tried to nail her down on their fu-ture, she managed to throw him for a loop. Last night, on the heels of knowing she'd been to see Jamie—again—he'd thrown out the bait for a more permanent arrangement.

But typical of Alyx, she'd taken his start of a pro-posal and turned it into a casual living arrange-ment. Scott consoled himself with the knowledge that, if she lived with him, he'd at least be able to keep her from running after Jamie.

The two of them seemed to have a special friendship, and while Scott adamantly refused to acknowledge any sign of jealousy, the risks Alyx took made his blood run cold. Knowing she'd gone off in the woods alone, so close to nightfall, amplified his need to protect her. Keeping her close seemed a good way to do that.

Not that Alyx would ever admit to needing his protection. And that was something of a rub, because he wasn't just a natural-born protector, he'd made protection his career as well. Hell, as deputy, he made it his business to look out for everyone.

"Deputy Royal?"

With a start, Scott realized Willow had spoken to him and he hadn't heard a single word. "I'm sorry, Willow. What did you say?"

Willow grinned in a knowing way. "Nothing important."

"You sure?"

Alyx came into the room and asked, "Sure about what?"

Willow laughed and headed for the doorway. "I'll see you both later. Clay and I are going to the matinee movies."

Now dressed in trim white shorts and a beige halter that showed off every sleek, sexy curve of her tall body, Alyx hugged herself up to Scott's arm. "Have fun, honey," she called to Willow. "And remember, Clay has your best interests at heart."

Scott waited until Willow was out of sight before he gave in to the consuming urge to once again stake a claim.

"Alyx?"

When she looked up at him, still smiling, Scott lowered his mouth to hers, kissing her first gently, then with fast-growing hunger. Lately, he couldn't be around her without wanting her.

Right. Who was he kidding? He'd never been able to get close to Alyx without thinking of rumpled sheets, warm damp bodies, and frenzied sex.

Familiarity had only made it worse, sharpening the razor's edge of lust. The more time he spent with her, the more he wanted her. Living with her would be the next best thing to marriage.

Except Scott hated to be a bad influence on Joe's kids. And he could just imagine what Joe would have to say about it. Shit.

He lifted away, and Alyx sighed dreamily. Damn, she was so beautiful. And so smart and sexy and . . .

He had it bad.

Scott teased the warm velvet texture of her cheek with his fingertips, then put his forehead to hers. "Alyx, you know I have your best interests at heart too, right?"

Typical of Alyx, she laughed, gave his butt a squeeze, and said, "I don't need anyone to take care of me, Scott."

His guts clenched. "Maybe not. But what if I want to do it anyway?"

Her smile dazzled him. "I appreciate the sentiment." Catching his hand, Alyx dragged him out of the room. "Now let's go. I'm hoping you'll get a chance to arrest someone on the way to breakfast."

"That's not likely."

"You never know." She bobbed her eyebrows at him. "I think Visitation may be due for a little excitement."

Scott eyed the enticing sway of her hips in her snug shorts and prayed she was wrong. Because Alyx Winston was just about as much excitement as he could take.

Chapter Nine

Jamie sat on a fallen tree trunk, his elbows on his knees, his eyes narrowed, while he waited for Joe. He knew he'd be along soon, which was why he couldn't stay and have breakfast with Faith. But he'd hated leaving her. And wasn't that a stitch?

He could barely remember the last time he'd actually enjoyed company. More often than not, his thoughts focused on separating himself rather than taking pleasure in small talk or the sheer presence of another person.

Impatient, Jamie pushed his long hair back from his face and squinted up at the sky. The clouds had finally cleared enough to let skinny rays of sunshine penetrate. The day would get warm by midafternoon. After all the rain, it'd probably feel like a sauna.

The rumble of Joe's truck finally disturbed the quiet drone of the surrounding woods. Jamie stood, brushed off his well-worn, tattered jeans, and moved to stand in the middle of the road.

Joe rounded the bend, spotted Jamie, and slammed on his brakes. Gravel kicked from the rear tires as Joe steered the truck to the curb. Even from the slight distance, Jamie could hear him cursing.

He hid it on the outside, but on the inside, Jamie grinned.

And damn, it felt good.

Joe slammed his door and stomped toward Jamie with a lot of bluster and fanfare. His dark hair practically stood on end, and his hands were fisted. "Why the *hell* do you have to do that?"

All innocence, Jamie asked, "What?" on his way to the passenger-side door.

Joe's eyes sparked blue fire. "Stand in the middle of the goddamn road! One of these days someone is going to run over your sorry ass."

Jamie opened the truck door, climbed in, and raised a brow at Joe, who had followed hot on his heels. "You coming?"

For two heartbeats, Joe looked ready to implode. Then he threw up his hands, rounded the hood of the truck while muttering under his breath, and jerked his door open. "You're certifiable, you know that?"

"Nah." Jamie settled into the leather seat and admired Joe's truck. "Maybe I used to be, but not anymore."

Joe went so utterly and comically still that Jamie had a hard time wearing a mask of indifference. "What did you say?"

After snapping on his seatbelt, Jamie faced Joe. "Do you think you could drive while we talk? I'm in sort of a rush to get back."

"The hell you say!" But Joe put the truck in gear and accelerated back to the roadway. After a minute, his voice gruff, Joe asked, "Where are you going, anyway?"

"To town with you."

"Jamie—"

"I need to buy some things." Jamie waited, anticipating Joe's reaction, and then added, "And I need a haircut and a shave."

"*A haircut and a . . .*" Slanting him a look ripe with incredulity, Joe growled, "You want to tell me what the hell is going on here, Jamie?"

"Actually, yeah, I do. Because I might need your help."

Another wave of shock went through Joe. "Are you serious?"

Jamie settled back in his seat and stretched out his legs. He really liked Joe's truck a lot and always enjoyed riding in it. It was roomy and comfortable and had plenty of power. Maybe if things worked out, and he found out he didn't have to hide anymore, he could see about getting his license. Then he'd buy a truck just like Joe's. "I've got a woman in my cabin."

"A naked woman, I know." Joe tugged at his earring. "It's all the wives are talking about."

Nodding, Jamie said, "Clint told you. Her name is Faith. She used to work at the institute."

It was fascinating, seeing Joe go on the alert. Jamie wasn't even reading him, just observing him, man to man, and he noticed the changes. Joe was plenty big enough to intimidate most anyone, but when he straightened in that protective way, when his muscles bunched and his gaze went cold and hard, he looked all but invincible.

Odd that Joe got that way now for Jamie. Odd but nice.

Jamie wondered how many other reactions he'd observed that he'd attributed to psychic ability.

"Institute?"

Enjoying the cautious way Joe said that, Jamie clarified. "Not a mental institute, so relax."

"I didn't—"

"I know." Jamie trusted Joe. He liked him, too, always had. If things worked out, he'd enjoy being Joe's friend. "I'm talking about Farmington Research Institute at Harrod University. The institute houses labs that study parapsychology phenomena." He smoothed a wrinkle in his jeans, then added with a shrug, "They studied me."

Joe appeared hesitant to pry, but concerned all the same. "No shit?"

"No shit." Jamie made his explanations as short as he could. "My folks died when I was real young, and I spent a lot of time in the foster-care system. I got shipped around a lot because I freaked people out."

"I can imagine."

Lost in memories, Jamie missed Joe's note of humor. "When I was sixteen, Professor Kline heard about me somehow, and he took me to the institute. I spent a hell of a lot of years there." He'd never talked much about his past with anyone, other than Faith, since he'd been a green, defensive, confused kid.

"Professor Kline?"

Jamie felt Joe's sympathy, but Joe didn't voice it, and Jamie appreciated his discretion. He hated talking about his youth because so much of it was . . . bleak.

But it was all he'd known.

Jamie nodded. "A real son of a bitch, not that I realized it at the time. I just knew that, unlike most people I'd met, Kline appreciated the things I could tell him."

"I gather you're talking about your predictions? You could do that stuff even when you were younger?"

Jamie nodded. "It doesn't take a kid long to realize he's different, especially when other kids—and even adults—are always pointing it out. And for me it was especially noticeable. Even among the gifted, I'm an anomaly. Not only am I telepathic, but my precognition and remote-viewing skills surpass any others that are known. It's unusual to excel in more than one ability, especially to the degree that I have them. But mine seem intertwined, so you can imagine how the board of directors at Farmington valued me."

Joe looked from the road to Jamie and back again. "So all that mind-reading stuff you do—"

"That's telepathy." In an odd, talkative mood, Jamie pointed out, "You do it sometimes too, only you like to call it gut instinct, shrewdness, intuition, even good judgment."

With a snort, Joe said, "There's a huge difference in what I can figure out with logic and common sense and what you just . . . know."

"Yeah, there is." He'd suffered many years for being a freak of nature. While other people went about in happy indifference, Jamie saw the world as a transparent cloud of pain. "Precognition is awareness of a future event, and remote viewing is like . . . well, seeing things as they happen, even if they're not happening anywhere near me."

Joe looked dumbfounded.

"Yeah, it's a lot to swallow, I know." Jamie turned thoughtful. "Sometimes, I get hit with so much information from so many sources, it's hard to piece everything together so that it makes sense. It's frustrating for me, because I'll know some things, but not enough to be clear on it."

"It makes you feel helpless," Joe guessed. "Not a good feeling for any man to have."

"Yeah." Jamie slowly nodded, realizing that Joe had just summed it up. "Helpless." Sharing only the most necessary details, Jamie explained about Professor Kline's, Delayna's, and Faith's roles in the experiments that had taken place in the labs. He didn't go into how wounded he'd felt, and how badly he'd needed to hide away.

"So now Faith is here." Joe chewed that over before asking, "You trust her?"

"For right now I do. It's possible that she's come to me because it's her daughter at risk." Jamie flattened his hands on his thighs and took a deep breath. "Corey's only eight years old, and she has the same ability I have."

Joe whistled through his teeth. "That's rough."

"Yeah." Jamie was a little surprised at Joe's insight, when really, he shouldn't have been. Joe had always proven to be perceptive of others. "No child should have to feel what she feels."

"What you felt." With the new information,

Joe's gaze became watchful, and he scanned the area as he drove. "Do you think she understands it?"

"I know she does." Jamie remembered how the little girl had connected with him, and he shook his head. "Faith says that Cory is especially bright for her age. I think she'd have to be to deal with the uglier reality of the world."

"A reality most people are oblivious to." Joe thought about that, then glanced at Jamie. "In case I haven't told you lately, I've been damn glad for your help. You're a good man, Jamie." He looked back at the road without giving Jamie a chance to react to that disclosure. "So no one knows for sure where this Delayna woman is?"

Jamie shook off his surprise and discomfort at Joe's compliment. "That's what Faith said, and she wasn't blocking me then, so I assume she's telling the truth."

"What does she look like?"

"Faith?"

Joe's mouth curled in a knowing grin. "I meant Delayna."

Frowning at himself, Jamie determined to keep his thoughts off Faith and on the subject at hand. "It's been a while since I've seen her."

"How long?"

"A man loses track, living in the mountains alone. But I'd say close to a decade."

Spearing him with a sharp glance, Joe said, "You've been in the mountains that long?"

"'Bout that." Sometimes it had felt like a day, sometimes a lifetime. For dozens of reasons, Jamie hadn't exactly logged the time. "When I knew her, Delayna was attractive. Tall. Slim. Green eyes. Short, dark brown hair." Jamie shrugged. "Sexy."

"This is going to be hard to get used to."

"What's that?"

"You being so verbose and using descriptions like *sexy*." Chuckling, Joe gave him a companionable slug in the arm. "Hell, I can't imagine what it's going to be like if you really do lose the beard."

"You'll find a way to cope, because I'm really losing it." Scratching at the scruffy beard he'd worn for years now, Jamie added, "I grew it to look different."

"To hide," Joe said with understanding. "But since you've shown yourself around town as a bearded caveman, being clean shaven and well groomed will be a better disguise."

"As long as too many people don't know about it."

"We'll keep it mum. Only the people you trust will know."

Trust. Such a fragile thing that had once seemed so elusive. Before Faith, Jamie hadn't even trusted himself. Now he had Joe, Bryan, Bruce, and Clint—and all their wives. And because that trust was so precious to him, worry squirreled through his conscience.

Not because of a premonition of doom and gloom, but because he cared.

"If you could be on the lookout for strangers in town that meet Delayna's description, I'd appreciate it. But it's my problem, Joe. I don't want anyone taking unnecessary chances."

Joe shrugged off his concern. "We'll be careful."

Then, with more gravity, he added, "Anything else you need, just let us know."

Deciding he'd been morose enough, Jamie nodded. "I was hoping you'd say that." Reaching into his pocket, he withdrew the list Faith had given him. "You any good at shopping?"

Joe groaned, but the groan morphed into a laugh. "Sure, why the hell not. What have you got on there?"

Jamie had known all along that he could count on Joe.

He could count on all of them. Because despite doing his best to avoid them, they were now his friends.

The noonday sun made the stupid disguise more smothering than usual. But it could be ignored. Up ahead, a young man stood alone beside his fancy car at the side of an empty field. Kyle Braeder. While in town earlier, he'd drawn attention to himself by waving around a wad of bills and bullying a group of younger boys.

Now, he'd regret showing off.

Following him had posed no challenge. But he hadn't gone home. No, he'd stopped by the field, probably waiting for someone.

This was just too damn easy.

Luckily, ripe targets that would serve the plan well flooded Visitation. Kyle would be the second. Soon, if Jamie Creed didn't put in an appearance, there'd be a third.

Leaving the concealment of trees and stalking forward drew Kyle's attention.

Laughing, Kyle asked, "What the fuck are you

supposed to be? The Lone Ranger? Batman?" And because he was ballsy as well as a punk, he strode forward.

Just perfect.

When Kyle got within reach, it took no more than a swift turn, an extended leg, and the element of surprise for a boot heel to connect solidly with his solar plexus. Hitting the submission point dead-on sent Kyle back several feet, wheezing and gasping in pain.

While struggling for breath, Kyle doubled over, and gave the perfect opportunity for a knee to the chin.

His head snapped up and he fell onto his back, landing hard, a little dazed. He shook his head to clear it, and rubbed at his jaw. "What the hell is wrong with you?"

"What are you doing here, Kyle?"

He wheezed in another pain-filled breath and gingerly sat up. "You know my name?"

"I know you have a lot of cash on you. Why?"

"That's none of your damn business."

Behind the black mask, eyes narrowed. "I don't like you, Kyle."

"And you think I give a shit?"

"You will. Get up."

Kyle's eyes glittered when he smiled. "Yeah, I'll get up, you ignorant puke." He rushed to his feet with a feral growl, plowing forward with all the momentum of a linebacker.

At the last second, one fast step to the side sent Kyle face-first into the dirt. A knee landed in Kyle's back, and with a hold on two fingers, he ended up with his arm painfully twisted back and high.

"Now do you care?"

"Go to hell—*ahh*, stop it!"

"Do you know how easily I could break your fingers, your wrist, or even your elbow?" The arm went higher—and so did Kyle's squeals of pain. "There, you see, Kyle? A good fighter knows how to use leverage in hand-to-hand combat, to make use of the natural movement of his body, which places his opponent's body in a position of *unnatural* movement."

"Fuck you," Kyle ground out between clenched teeth.

"It's not about strength, Kyle. A person half your size can defeat you by using smarts—something you seem to be missing." The knee pressed harder, making Kyle fight for every breath. "So tell me, why are you carrying so much cash and hanging out here alone?"

"I was gonna buy some dope, okay?" He groaned. "Turn me loose."

Oh-ho. Talk about unexpected news. "From who? Who's selling you drugs?"

It took a little more twisting before Kyle spilled his guts. But as promised, once he did, he got released. However, the second the pressure eased on his arm, he lurched to his feet and again tried to attack.

"Idiot." The word barely emerged before bodies collided. Knowing how to go with a fall had its advantages, as did speed and agility. They rolled, and in the process, an elbow deliberately met with Kyle's balls.

His muscles suddenly useless, Kyle went limp, groaning in pain.

Oh yeah, that hurt.

Satisfaction started to grow—and a noise intruded. Had someone else joined them? Listening hard provided only the sounds of birds and insects and a gentle breeze rustling tree leaves.

But there was no reason to take chances.

Another roll, a quick adjustment to make sure the disguise stayed in place, and it was time for a quick retreat.

Standing over Kyle made the fallen man feel more defeated, more helpless—just as intended. "You're a coward, Kyle."

"You won't get away with this," Kyle wheezed, still holding his crotch.

"I'm standing. You're on the ground crying like a baby girl. I'd say I've already gotten away with it."

Kyle tried one more surprise attack—and got knocked out cold for his effort. Damn idiot.

Time to go. And if the buzzards ate him . . . well, it was no more than he deserved.

While dodging across the street toward the concealment of trees and a hidden car, the attacker grinned.

A few more tricks, and Jamie Creed would expose himself. He wouldn't be able to resist.

Damn. Mosquitoes seemed determined to have a fine feast. But there'd be no leaving the concealing weeds until Kyle . . . oh, good. The idiot finally started to groan, then sat up. He dug a cell phone out of his pocket and made a call, then stood and walked—more steady than otherwise—to his car.

So he'd survive. And maybe, just maybe, Kyle would learn a thing or two.

The smile came unexpectedly, but this was almost fun. Of course, if things continued, a report would have to be made. But for now, it seemed safe enough to just observe.

Timing was everything.

And surely a little more time wouldn't hurt.

Jamie actually enjoyed his shopping trip. Throughout the year, there were occasions when he had to purchase things that the moonshiners couldn't provide. He'd gotten used to the stares, to feeling out of place, to hearing the thoughts of fear, pity, sometimes even disgust as shoppers moved in a wide arc around him, unwilling to get too close.

But before shopping this time, Joe had taken him to the outskirts of the adjoining town, where they visited a small barber first. Jamie now had a smooth jaw and neatly trimmed hair that curled a little over his ears and nape, but wasn't long enough for his usual ponytail.

During the rest of the drive, Joe kept peering at him in wonder. At one point he'd said, "Don't take this the wrong way, Jamie, but you're actually a good-lookin' guy."

Jamie had almost laughed, except that Joe did enough laughing for the both of them. It had felt . . . companionable. Comfortable. The same sort of camaraderie he'd often seen between Scott, Bryan, and Bruce. He'd denied any yearning then, but now he could admit how badly he'd wanted to be a part of their group.

Once they reached the town, they split Jamie's list and went separate ways. Joe would get some of the food and medicinal supplies that Jamie needed while doing his own shopping, and Jamie roamed the various shops in the mall, picking up things for Faith.

He enjoyed buying her clothes. Panties, shirts, shorts. More clothes than she'd asked for, but so what? He had money that he never spent, because there was very little he needed.

Amazing how a few small changes could make him reputable to the other shoppers. His clothes were the same, well worn and faded from age and wear. His manner was the same, aloof and wary. Yet everywhere he went, women glanced at him—but only with admiration, not out of some swooning melodrama because he reminded them of a spook. Hell, here in the bordering city, no one even knew him. They didn't know that he'd lived for years as a recluse, isolated because of a stark fear he wouldn't have admitted to anyone.

For only a moment, Jamie paused, opening his mind to the crowd around him. For the most part, people's thoughts were mundane at best, ridiculous at worst. So much silliness annoyed him, and he turned his focus back on Faith.

A big mistake, that.

Her image hit Jamie like a kick in the guts, stopping him dead in his tracks. He saw Faith clearly, standing in the shower, her face turned up, her hair slicked back, lingering just as he'd suggested.

Water ran over her throat, her breasts, and down her belly, onto her thighs.

As Jamie concentrated on her, she turned her back to the spray, and this time her head dropped forward. She covered her face with her hands. Her shoulders shook.

Shit. Was she crying?

Someone bumped into Jamie, and with a start, he recalled the here and now. The middle of a busy mall wasn't the best place to lose himself in remote viewing, but he couldn't quite force himself to leave Faith yet. He repositioned against a wall, away from the stream of human traffic, and stared off in the distance until he located her again.

She'd turned the water off and used a towel to dry herself. Jamie felt like a pervert, a damn voyeur. Hell, he'd already seen her naked. Every inch of her. From various angles. And remembering that wasn't appropriate to time and place either.

At least there weren't any tears on Faith's face, just a very sad expression, laced with worry. She flipped her hair forward to wrap in the towel, and Jamie surveyed the graceful line of her back, all the way down to that heart-shaped ass that begged to be enjoyed.

Jamie had enough packages in his arms to hide his sudden erection, but he couldn't conceal the flare of heat just under his skin, or the way his hands shook. He wanted Faith. She was willing. That would have to be enough.

With new urgency, Jamie headed for an exit to wait for Joe. His life had been forever altered. That fact both exhilarated him and scared him spitless. He wasn't sure he could handle all the changes.

But making love to Faith . . . he'd have no problem handling that at all. In fact, it was top of the list once he got back on the mountain.

There were still a lot of questions that needed answers, but Jamie would be patient. He'd gain Faith's trust, wear her out sexually, and eventually she'd tell him everything he needed to know.

Bright sunshine reflected off the blacktop parking lot when Jamie stepped outside. A second later, Joe's truck pulled up close, proof that he'd been waiting for Jamie.

Through the open window, Joe asked, "You find everything?"

"Yeah." Jamie stored the bags in the bed of the truck before getting in. He'd have a load to carry up the mountain, but he didn't mind. He'd been carrying things up that mountain for a good portion of his life.

This time, however, there'd be someone waiting for him when he got there.

After a moment, Jamie realized that Joe watched him. "What?"

Shaking his head, Joe half grinned. "I was just thinking about how the ladies are going to react when they see you now. I expect at least one of them to faint. And Jamie, keeping them away isn't going to be easy, you know that."

"Buy me as much time as you can."

"Spoken like a man who doesn't have to deal with a wife." Joe left the parking lot and merged with traffic. "Luna is already fussing, Bruce says Cyn isn't sleeping, and Shay has grand plans on organizing a posse to come after you. Only Julie, who's caught up in wedding preparations, ever lets it go for more than an hour at a time. But even she's pushing."

"I know." Jamie sighed, as lost to the workings of the female mind as any other guy.

"I'm guessing tomorrow will be the big day. If not, then the day after for sure. An elephant couldn't hold the ladies off any longer than that."

Chagrined, Jamie laid his head against the seat back. "They think Faith is going to hurt me."

Joe shrugged, and ventured cautiously, "She might."

"No. I wouldn't let that happen."

"Jamie . . ." Joe fell silent, then cleared his throat. "Damn, I hate this kind of shit."

Swiveling his head toward Joe, Jamie asked, "What kind of shit?"

"You know." He gestured helplessly. "Butting into other people's relationships. It's usually a no-win situation. But the truth is, where women are concerned, no man is immune from heartache."

Because Jamie's experiences with women had stopped after Delayna, he was curious to hear Joe's thoughts on the subject.

Of course, he could have just taken those thoughts from Joe, but their relationship had changed, and now it seemed grossly impolite to intrude into the head of a friend. Especially when no threat existed. And besides, he enjoyed talking to Joe.

On a roll, Joe continued to share his opinion on the fairer sex. "No one and nothing can twist a guy inside out like a woman can. I swear, it's a talent they're all born with. Or maybe it's a weakness in the male species. But whatever the hell you call it, I'm telling you, Jamie, even you can't avoid it."

"Faith can't hurt me."

"Yeah, I forgot. You're all-powerful, all-knowing." Joe made a disgusted face. "You're still a man, and you let it happen once with Delayna, right? So who's to say it couldn't happen again? None of us wants to see that."

Jamie stared at Joe, half insulted, half bemused. "You think I'm fragile."

"Physically, no. I imagine you could hold your own."

Male ego surfaced. "I'm a damn good fighter. I'm strong and fast, and I stay in shape." Jamie tapped his forehead. "And I always know what the other guy is going to do."

"Sure. The other *guy*. That doesn't count with a woman, though." Joe squeezed the steering wheel and again flashed Jamie a look. "Listen, all I'm saying is to take it easy. Maybe go slow."

Not likely. He'd been celibate for damn near a decade, and now Joe wanted him to go slow? *No, thank you.* Besides, making love to Faith would go a long way toward defining his ability. Jamie knew, once they were intimate, he wouldn't be able to stay indifferent to her. When he was deep inside her, when her heels dug into the small of his back and she tightened around him, then he'd see if he could still read her.

And thinking things like that weren't making the long drive back any easier. Jamie swallowed a groan, counted to ten, and then, already knowing the answer, he asked, "Did you go slow with Luna?"

Predictably enough, Joe stiffened. "That's different."

"How? You didn't want to marry her when you met her. You just . . . wanted her. And you went after her. You even followed her here just to get her in bed."

Judging by the flush of red on Joe's neck, he didn't appreciate the reminder. "Yeah, maybe. But I wasn't a damn recluse, floating down off my mountain only long enough to send the ladies into a swoon and to royally piss off the guys."

Jamie blinked at that description, and half smiled. "Floating?"

Joe's brows lifted and he grunted in surprise. "Good God. Now you're smiling, too? Incredible." He shook his head. "At least take some good advice."

"Which is?"

"Take charge. You be the one in control. That's the only way to make sure your heart won't get trampled. And hell, sometimes that doesn't even work."

"Control," Jamie repeated, intrigued by that idea. "In bed?"

"Ha! Well . . ." Joe shifted uncomfortably. "Yeah, sure. Especially in bed."

Jamie considered that for a moment, imagining Faith stretched out naked atop his mattress, following his every instruction, doing anything and everything he asked—and he'd ask for a lot, enough to make up for ten years of abstinence. It wasn't a bad fantasy. "All right."

Joe did a double take. "Why do I have the feeling you just misconstrued the point of everything I said?"

Shrugging, Jamie reached for the radio dial. "I have no idea." He tuned in to a popular station, and then spent the rest of the ride back to Visitation tapping his fingers in time to the music—and wondering if, just maybe, Joe had a valid point.

Not that he'd put off sex with Faith. He couldn't do that. Anticipation already hummed inside him. He would be alert to any deceptions—even though he expected none. He would keep his head, no matter what.

And he'd be in control—of Faith and everything she did, everything he did to her. Afterward, he'd have an answer on whether or not getting close to someone impeded his ability.

It was well after six by the time Jamie made it up the mountain, his arms laden with bags, his body damp with sweat. Even before he reached the cabin, he knew Faith dozed on the couch. Still exhausted, and probably bored out of her mind, she'd given in to healing sleep. Seclusion suited Jamie; he'd learned to embrace it. But he doubted it would appeal to many other people, especially a chatterbox like Faith.

Leaving the bags on the porch and opening the door without a single squeak, Jamie crept into his cabin—and inhaled a fragrant steam. He hadn't expected that. A cold, empty, silent cabin—that's what he usually got.

He glanced at the stovetop and realized that the delicious scents permeating the air came from simmering soup. He stared at the big cast-iron pot, bemused.

Faith had made him soup.

It was such a dumb, simple thing. Just soup, and

he'd provided all the ingredients. She'd only put them together. But no matter what argument Jamie gave himself, another piece of ice melted away from his heart.

He turned from the stove, and made note of the kitchen table, not with one chair, as usual, but now with two. Faith had apparently rummaged around outside, and she'd dragged in the chair from his porch. For as long as she visited, there'd be two at his table.

A lump formed in Jamie's throat, nearly strangling him. Instead of staring at the table, thinking on what the two chairs symbolized, he looked at Faith.

On her back with her face turned away from him, she lay on his small sofa. Her head rested on the padded arm and her legs bent slightly to the side. She now wore an old gray thermal shirt that he'd altered by shearing off the long sleeves, paired with baggy navy blue sweatpants. The pants hung low on her hips, and the shirt bunched around her ribs. He could see her belly button, the plump curves of her breasts, and her small bare feet. Her hair spread out around her, over her shoulder, off the end of the couch.

Jamie crept closer, taking in the sight of her and appreciating the way she made him feel. When he stood close enough that he could hear her breathing, he considered waking her, but changed his mind. She might yet suffer a fever, and after everything she'd been through, she needed the rest.

Forcing himself away from her, Jamie climbed the ladder to his loft and retrieved clean shorts and jeans, then went outside to the creek, where he washed. The cool water helped to calm his lust. But some other, harder-to-define emotion had taken root and dug in deep.

He concentrated on the lust because at least he understood it. It was a feeling he could embrace, one he could accept and act on. The other feelings . . . Joe's warning came back to him, and as Jamie left the rushing creek to dry off, he planned what he'd do, all the ways that he'd touch and taste Faith, how he'd sate himself with her.

Let her sleep for now—with what he planned, she'd need all the rest she could get.

Faith stirred awake slowly, then groaned as she realized she'd done it again—fallen soundly asleep. Curse the lingering lethargy from exhaustion and stress and illness. She felt mostly fine now, except that she could fall asleep at almost any time. In the normal course of her life, she never napped and had boundless energy. Which worked out well since Cory wasn't a child who did well with idle time, either physical or mental.

At least this time she was on the couch, not tucked up in bed for the night. She opened her eyes and started to sit up.

Near her feet on the couch, a large, hot male body moved, almost stopping her heart.

Good God. There was a *man* in the cabin with her? She stared at an unfamiliar profile—and screamed.

Chapter Ten

"What?" On his feet in an instant, his legs braced wide, his hands out at his sides in a combat stance, the man darted his gaze left, right, up, and down.

When no threat presented itself, he speared Faith with a querulous glare. "Damn woman."

Oh, those eyes. Faith's mouth dropped open while she did a quick once-over from his head to his toes. It . . . it couldn't be. But it was. *"Jamie?"*

He cocked a brow and waited.

"Oh my God, what have you done?" The words were little more than an awestruck squeak. Jamie . . . didn't look like Jamie anymore. Not the Jamie who'd left her that morning, not the ragtag hermit she'd uncovered in his mountain hideaway.

He looked . . . oh, man, he looked *good.*

"Thank you."

Faith was too stunned to complain about his reading her mind, but she quickly barred her thoughts from him. The fact that he *could* read her mind left her floundering. What did it mean?

Could Cory have been wrong after all? Maybe the depth of Jamie's relationships had nothing to do with his ability. Or maybe he just didn't care about her.

Then again, maybe he did.

Faith rubbed her eyes, trying to reason it all out. Cory claimed Jamie was confused, that he needed to know caring wouldn't distort his remote viewing. Faith had hoped that he was starting to care for her and that he'd then realize the truth for himself. But maybe an eight-year-old, even an eight-year-old of Cory's stunning ability, wasn't mature enough to interpret adult contradictions.

She'd also hoped that Jamie was starting to trust her, starting to care for her a little. But now she just didn't know. He'd made such a drastic change, and he knew her thoughts.

Did that mean Cory was right, and while Jamie cared, he could still get in her head?

Or could Jamie read her so easily because he didn't care at all?

"I'd love to know what you're reasoning out right now, Faith."

Mouth clamped shut, Faith shook her head in emphatic denial. She'd die if he knew how badly she wanted him to care. That wouldn't help either of them.

His annoyance palpable, Jamie ran a hand over his shorter, neatly clipped hair, then eyed her body in the clothes she'd borrowed from him.

"Let's start over." He lifted her legs and settled back onto the couch with her feet in his lap. Turning toward her, one hand curled around her ankle, he said, "Hi."

Faith tried to say hi, she really did. But Jamie wore only jeans, no shirt, and beneath his fly, her feet rested on . . . an erection. Faith jerked back so fast, her heel struck where it shouldn't, and Jamie groaned.

"I'm sorry!" Scrambling onto her knees, Faith knelt close to him and studied his new image. She could hardly take it in. Trying to figure him out would make her head explode. "How? Why? You . . ."

Jamie looked at her mouth and asked, "You're finally at a loss for words, huh?"

She nodded, but then said, "Your beard is gone."

"Yeah, I know." He rubbed a hand over his cheek and chin. "It took the barber a good hour and a lot of grumbling to get me shaved and trimmed. I think he charged me double."

Hands shaking, Faith reached out and touched his lean jaw, his firm chin. "I'd almost forgotten how beautiful you are."

His eyes warmed, and one corner of his mouth kicked up.

Seeing that smile, Faith collapsed back on her heels, as limp as a rag doll. A smile. Not a barely there hint of a smile, but an honest-to-God full-blown sign of happiness. "You're . . . you're smiling, Jamie."

His amazing eyes crinkled at the corners. "Yeah." He traced her cheekbone with one fingertip. "You infuriate me, Faith, but you also amuse me."

So much emotion welled up at one time, a churning tidal wave of feeling, that Faith couldn't contain it. She hadn't expected this, hadn't thought he'd have such an impact on her so soon. For years, she'd thought of Jamie, prayed he was okay, that he was happy and well.

Then her daughter had come to her with the wrenching news that Jamie wasn't happy at all. Cory, so articulate and wise for such a young girl, had solemnly told her of problems that had to be fixed and of a future that required Jamie's participation. Cory knew where to find Jamie, and she promised that Faith could make things better for him—and for them.

But never had Faith thought that her heart would break all over again, as badly as it had when Jamie first left the institute. When he'd first left *her.* The pain had been almost unbearable.

Even though he'd never noticed her, she'd cared for him and she hadn't thought to ever see him again. Then God had gifted her with Cory, giving her plenty of reasons to smile. But Jamie had remained alone. Unsmiling.

Big tears filled Faith's eyes and spilled over, and she gulped once, twice. Shaking her head, she rasped, "I'm sorry." She rubbed away the tears, but more fell, accompanied by a broken sob. "I'm not usually a crybaby, I swear."

Jamie sighed as he gently tugged her against his chest. "Always apologizing," he teased in a rough whisper. "You need to quit that." And his big, strong arms willingly went around her.

Afraid she'd wake up, that Jamie's acceptance of her might disappear at any moment, Faith clutched at him. Beneath her cheek, his chest was so strong and solid. And hot. Luxuriating in the wonderful scent of him, the sense of security, she locked her hands around his neck so he couldn't escape. And she sobbed.

She felt like a complete idiot, but she couldn't

seem to stem the tears or stop the awful, snuffling noises. It was humiliating.

Jamie rubbed her back, kissed her ear, and made soft, shushing sounds that sank into her bones and melted her heart. "How do you feel, Faith?" He pressed the backs of his fingers to her cheek. "I don't think you're feverish anymore."

"No." She shook her head against his shoulder and squeezed in closer. "No fever."

"And your leg?" His hand slid along her thigh. "It's not bothering you too much right now?"

Again she shook her head, amazed at how his touch electrified her, even through the thick jogging pants. She had some nasty bruising, but the discomfort could be ignored.

"You made soup," he said. "It's smells delicious. I hope you didn't tire yourself out."

By making soup? How wimpy did Jamie think she was? Faith winced at her own question. Given her sleeping jags and current crying fit, he probably considered her as frail as a fading flower.

"Making soup is no trouble, Jamie. I just hope you like it. Are you hungry now?"

Tightening his arms around her, he rasped huskily, "Yeah, real hungry."

Faith's stomach took a free fall. She'd known all along that a look from Jamie could be lethal. Now she knew his gruff whispers were just as intoxicating.

She didn't want to let him go, but she couldn't keep hanging on him like a needy child, so she suggested, "We can eat now if you want."

His lips brushed her temple. "The soup will wait. I added more water to it, and it's barely simmering."

Faith bit her bottom lip.

"The cold spell has passed through." His hand moved up her naked arm until he reached the short sleeve of the shirt she'd borrowed from him. "You're comfortable? Warm enough?"

With Jamie touching her, she started to burn. After mopping her eyes on the sleeve, Faith leaned back enough to reassure him. "I'm . . . I'm good."

"Yeah." He cuddled her cheek in his palm, using the edge of his thumb to lift away a lingering tear. His eyes warmed and his voice dropped. "Good enough to eat."

Oh. If he expected her to remain coherent, he really shouldn't say things like that to her.

Minus the beard and ponytail, the intensity of Jamie's gaze became more noticeable than ever. So dark they almost appeared black, shadowed by thick lashes and keen with intelligence, his eyes possessed an awareness that most people would never know.

And with that persuasive look fully trained on Faith, she felt shaken, hopeful, and frantic with erotic sensation. It was almost as if he'd already touched her in preparation for lovemaking.

After exhaling a shuddering breath, she curved her palm to his hard shoulder, taut with strength, his skin hot and sleek. She wanted to touch him all over. She wanted to give him incredible pleasure. But she felt so confused by such a complete turn-around. "What's happened, Jamie? Why are you doing this?"

He caught her hand and lowered it to his naked chest, holding it flat right over his heart. Faith knew that Jamie used the gesture to connect solidly with another person. It was something her daughter had learned to do, and the similarity between the two of them sent more tears to her eyes.

But with Jamie, the touch was so very different. Sparse hair tickled her palm, and Faith experienced the warm slide of desire pooling in her belly. Her breathing deepened, came faster.

"Open your mind to me, Faith." He stared at her, already invading, crowding her soul, compelling her to remove the barriers no matter how important she knew them to be. "Let me in," he commanded, sensing his triumph. "Let me have all of you."

Faith caught her breath, a little afraid of his new intensity.

"No, don't be afraid." Jamie spoke in a coercing whisper, his gaze trained on hers, unrelenting, refusing any avoidance. And then, taking her by surprise, he explained, "I'm going to make love to you, Faith."

Oh God. Everything inside her twisted with excitement. From the moment he'd left her that morning, Faith hadn't been able to think of much else. No matter how she tried to put things in perspective, how she tried to prioritize, she'd caught herself repeatedly imagining what it'd be like to love Jamie.

Satisfaction blazed from his eyes and relaxed his frown. His cheekbones darkened with desire. "I've been thinking about it, too." He put his hand to the side of her throat, slipped it under the neckline of the loose shirt, down to her shoulder. "I've seen you naked, Faith. I've touched you and had my fingers inside you."

Hearing the words sent a flood of sensation into the most sensitive areas of her body; her breasts tingled, her belly pulled tight.

Jamie watched the progress of his hand, flattening over her collarbone, then dipping to cup her breast. "But that was different."

Faith's eyes drifted shut. Against the heat of his fingers, her nipple drew tight and aching. "You didn't know me."

"I didn't trust you."

Optimism erupted, and she opened her eyes to see him. "But now you do?"

For a single heartbeat, he looked hunted. Then the emotion faded away and his eyes narrowed the tiniest bit. "Enough to want to fuck you."

That should have hurt, but with his face flushed and his breathing deep, the crude words only turned her on more.

"I'm glad." Rubbing his thumb back and forth over her jutting nipple, Jamie said, "I want you as turned on as I am."

Faith licked her lips, more than anxious. "I think I'm there."

"No." Jamie gently pressed her nipple between finger and thumb, tugged, rolled. "Not even close, Faith. Not yet."

Desperate on so many levels, she said, "Kiss me, Jamie. Please."

Going slow, so slow that Faith had a hard time waiting, Jamie released her breast and moved both hands to her shoulders. He drew her closer. His mouth brushed hers, and Faith's eyes closed. She parted her lips on a sigh.

Jamie whispered, "You want me to rush, but it's

been a hell of a long time for me, Faith. I want to touch you everywhere. And taste you everywhere. I need to savor every second."

Her heart beat so hard, it rocked her whole body. She said, "Okay," then leaned forward and took his mouth, seducing with her tongue, edging closer—

Jamie held her away, his arms unyielding. "Stand up."

Trembling, uncertain, Faith nodded and rose to her feet. Jamie looked her over, leaned forward to kiss her belly above the drooping waistline of the jogging pants, and when he leaned back, Faith realized he'd untied the drawstring.

With a simple tug, the pants fell to her ankles. Jamie held her hips between his hands and leaned forward again, this time nuzzling against her, breathing in her scent.

Faith locked her knees and tangled her fingers in his hair. Her head fell back, and when he gently bit her, she let out a vibrating moan.

"I want you to come up to my bed."

Up. To his bed? Faith mentally shook herself, looked longingly at the couch, which was right *there*, but forced herself to compliance. "Okay."

Whatever he wanted, she wanted to give to him. "That sounds promising."

Oh, she just knew her thoughts were going to be embarrassing.

That unfamiliar half grin appeared again. His hands contracted on her hips, his thumbs teasing her hipbones. "I like it that you're impatient."

Impatience hardly covered it. More like desperate. Faith wasn't altogether sure her legs were steady enough to make it up the ladder to the loft.

"Let's find out."

Jamie stood, crowding close to her, looking down at her, so male and so sexy. She swayed, then grabbed his shoulders when her feet got caught in the pants around her ankles.

"Easy," Jamie said, once again amused. He held her hand while she struggled free of the material. And since Faith had his hand, she immediately turned and tugged him toward the ladder.

He held back, forcing her to an unhurried walk. "Calm down, Faith. It's not a race."

"Who's racing?" Her laugh sounded maniacal, and she winced. "I just thought we should get this show on the road." Oh God. How dumb was that?

Stopping at the base of the ladder, her back to Jamie, Faith slapped both hands to her cheeks. She had to quit behaving like a sex-starved nympho. But for the first time in her life, she *felt* like a sex-starved nympho.

After all, this was Jamie, not any other man.

Standing close behind her, Jamie squeezed her waist. "Up you go." His warm breath drifted over the side of her neck, sending a shiver down her back.

Only then did it occur to Faith that she was bare-assed and about to climb a ladder in front of him. Hoy. Not a good visual. "Um, why don't you go first?"

"Because then I'd miss the show."

So he'd stripped her pants away on purpose?

"Yes." Jamie ran his hand down her waist to her hip. "The fewer clothes you wear, the more I like it."

"Oh."

He nipped her earlobe. "Now *I'm* getting impatient." He patted her butt. "Start climbing."

Faith nodded, put a shaking hand on the closest rung. "Right. Okay." Five steps up, she felt Jamie's hand slip beneath the shirt and settle on her naked bottom. She stopped dead in her tracks.

Voice trembling, she whispered, *"Jamie . . ."*

He moved up closer to her until his face was even with her behind. Through the shirt, his lips nuzzled against her. He held the ladder with one hand near her breasts, while the other hand curved over her belly, stroked twice, then pressed between her legs.

With a gasp, Faith locked her hands around the rungs and prayed she wouldn't fall. Why in the world would he want to do this here, when they'd left a perfectly good couch, and they could reach a bed in only a few more steps?

Fingers gently prodding, Jamie said, "I wanted to see if you're wet." He stroked along her cleft, searching through her curls, then slipped his finger inside her. Not far, just enough to tease. With satisfaction, he murmured, "And you are."

Faith knew she couldn't take it. She started to move.

"No," Jamie said. "Just let me touch you."

Her vision went hazy. "I . . . I can't do this."

Jamie took another step up, bracing his body against hers. "I won't let you fall." The promise ended on a growl as he pushed his finger deep, testing her, withdrew a little, only to slowly work it in again. "Jesus, you're tight."

Faith locked her knees, closed her eyes, and absorbed the astounding sensations. Her breath came out in a rush, then sucked in hard and fast when he pulled his finger out to touch her stiffened clitoris.

"I'd forgotten"—Jamie whispered as he played with her, rolling that one long finger over the tip of her, making her quiver—"just how fascinating a woman's body is. I thought about it, fantasized, but the reality is so much better."

Amazingly enough, Faith felt the building of a climax.

And Jamie pulled back. "Not yet. I want to be inside you when you come. I want to feel you squeezing my cock." He lightly bit her. "Climb."

Faith wanted to sob, to yell at him for being a dominating jerk, and she wanted to rush up the ladder and beg him to hurry. With all the grace of a robot, she went further up the ladder.

"I bought you some clothes in town today."

Void of any intimacy, Jamie's remark felt like a weather report, shaming Faith with his control, considering she had none. Not with him. "Thank you."

She reached the top of the ladder and gained the landing to the bedroom.

"I'm not sure I'm going to let you wear any of them, though."

It figured that after all his infuriating silence, he'd want to start conversing now, when she could barely form words. Keeping her face turned away, her eyes closed, Faith waited for him.

Jamie pulled himself up in front of her. She could feel him standing there, knew he was looking at her. The seconds passed; her tension rose until she practically hummed with it. Then he brought her chin around so that she faced him. "So this is how I keep you from being so chatty?"

"I'm sor—"

His mouth settled over hers, stealing the apology, and this time he went in for a deep, wet, tongue-twining kiss that had her groaning and clinging to him. His big hands settled on her bottom, but over the shirt so that he didn't touch bare skin. His grip was firm, lifting her to her tiptoes, holding her tight to him, so tight that she could barely move, could only rub against him in an effort to make him hurry.

The thick ridge beneath his fly pressed flush to her mound, and Faith's knees went weak. She felt him throbbing, but still he only kissed her. Never in her life had she been kissed with so much hunger or so much patience. Jamie seemed fascinated with the taste of her, his tongue stroking hers, tracing her teeth, drawing her tongue into his mouth.

Faith parted her legs a little, writhed against him, stroking herself along the length of his erection. With two big steps, Jamie backed her up to the wall and levered himself snug between her thighs, keeping her still as he fed on her mouth.

Their hot breaths mingled, coming hard and fast. Their combined body heat warmed the air around them. But Jamie only kissed her, and Faith wanted to scream with frustration. She bit his bottom lip and got a hoarse groan in return. His silky hair drew her hands and she tried to pull him away to free her mouth, but he didn't budge. A hot haze settled around her, crackling with sexual urgency. Tears again stung her eyes, tears of overwhelming need. She hadn't known that carnal need could be so strong.

She hadn't known that mere kissing could have her on the verge of a climax.

The realization came to her, and in the next second Jamie caught her waist, lifting her up and turning to lay her on the bed.

Stunned, Faith pushed up to her elbows. She started to speak, to ask Jamie why he seemed determined to drive her insane with lust. But the sight of him busily undoing his jeans stole her voice.

Breathing hard, his hands shaking, Jamie eased the zipper over a thrusting erection and shoved his jeans off in record time. Faith had only a glimpse of his incredible body, of dark, silky hair and sculpted muscles, before the bed dipped and he knelt astride her thighs. He grabbed the hem of her shirt, jerked it up and over her head, then settled back to look her over from her flushed breasts to her moist sex.

"You are so beautiful," he breathed.

Doing her own fascinated study, Faith clutched his hard, hairy thighs and moaned at the sight of his flat, washboard abdomen and the sexy line of hair leading from his navel down to his penis, which was now long and thick, pulsing with life.

She wanted to touch him, but Jamie quickly removed her hands and pinned them above her head. That position lowered him over her breasts, and before she could even assimilate his intent, his mouth closed hungrily over one nipple and he began sucking.

"Oh God." Faith squeezed her eyes shut as her control shattered.

With single-minded intent, Jamie held her immobile while he drew on her, teasing with his tongue, nibbling with his teeth, then sucking hard again, stopping only to switch to her other breast. Transferring both her wrists to one hand, he used his free hand to tease the wet nipple he'd just released. The dual assault made the pleasure so acute that Faith fought him, struggling to free herself, digging her heels into the mattress.

Jamie rose up to look at her, his chest laboring, his eyes burning. "You want me." He continued to knead her breast, shaping her, tormenting her nipple with instinctive touches that sent small tremors though her body. "You like what I'm doing."

"I like it too much."

She spoke the truth, and Jamie knew it.

Calculating, watching her closely, he caught her nipple and lightly tugged. Her back arched. "Once I get inside you, Faith, I won't last. It's been too fucking long. Damn near a decade."

Faith's heart expanded. So he had been celibate all that time. "Closer to nine years," she whispered, then bit her lip, stunned that such a telling thing had left her mouth.

But Jamie was too far gone to notice or care about the significance of the exact time frame. He left her breast to stroke up and down her body, his hand open, fingers spread wide to feel as much of her skin as he could. He traced her ribs, touched a fingertip to her navel, fondled the tops of her thighs.

He stared at her belly as he wedged his hand between her legs, cupping over her mound, the heat of his hand driving her that much closer to the end. "I want to take you in so many ways, Faith. I want to eat you until you come."

Faith twisted beneath him, almost feeling his tongue on her, in her.

Connected to her so that her thoughts became his, Jamie said, "Yeah," in a near-soundless whisper. "And I want to feel your mouth on me, too, taking me deep. Sucking." He went still, a great shudder rocking his body. "Jesus."

"Let me go," Faith urged him, "and I can do it right now."

His eyes opened and met hers. His hand tightened on her wrists, almost hurting before he caught himself and released her.

But not to let her pleasure him.

Roughly readjusting, Jamie moved between her thighs to spread her legs wide with his knees. He stroked his fingertips over her, searching, then opening her to wedge the head of his erection against her wet vulva. With a low groan, he stared at where they touched, holding her legs wider still with his hands.

"Jamie . . ." More than anything, Faith needed him to come inside her, to fill her up.

He hooked his elbows through her knees and leaned forward. Faith was open and vulnerable, completely exposed. She knotted her hands in the sheets, anchoring herself as Jamie lowered over her, his chest against her breasts, his heartbeat matching the frantic rhythm of her own.

He watched her face as he pressed in, his shoulders bunched, his biceps flexing.

Faith wanted him, but this was new to her and

she couldn't help but be a bit nervous. Her wide-spread thighs left her no way to resist him, no way to adjust as the pressure built. Her body had no choice but to accept him, and little by little she felt him sinking deeper, each slow push driving him forward and at the same time exacerbating sensitized, swollen nerve endings.

The burning intrusion excited her more, heightening her pleasure, and at the same time, frightened her.

"No," Jamie groaned, his whole body trembling as he restrained himself. "Don't be afraid of me, Faith. Just relax. Let me in."

Faith didn't want him to hold back. To let him know it was okay, that she would gladly give him anything, she opened her mouth on his shoulder and gave him a soft love bite.

Jamie froze, gasping, his eyes closed and his brows down in a private struggle. Suddenly he broke, clamping her tight to him and filling her with one savage thrust. The breath rushed out of Faith, and before she could draw another, he was driving fast, groaning long and low, and she knew he was ready to come. Her thighs strained against the unfamiliar hold and the tantalizing friction as with each glide and retreat, he rasped against her clitoris, filled her—touched deep.

Faith cried out as an orgasm crashed through her.

Jamie lifted his head, and she knew he watched her, knew he absorbed her feelings into himself. But it didn't matter. She couldn't think beyond the incredible pleasure, could focus on nothing but the intense satisfaction that gradually sparked and ebbed like a dying fire before fading away, leaving her throbbing and limp.

Realizing that Jamie still moved in her, Faith lifted heavy eyelids and saw him staring at her through barely opened eyes, fierce with concentration. She lightly touched his clenched jaw, and with a hoarse, feral growl, he came, too. His head went back, chest and shoulder muscles straining as he pressed deep, deep into her.

He collapsed to his forearms, and his head dropped forward beside hers. Sweat dampened his shoulders and chest. He labored for breath.

Faith wallowed in the wonderful moment of fulfillment. Her legs remained in the awkward position, and though she knew he'd already come, Jamie still filled her. She'd dreamed of this, of being with him, and now the dream was a reality. She tangled her fingers in his dark hair, stroked his neck, squeezed his biceps, placed her hand over his pounding heart.

She wanted a lifetime of touching him. She wanted everything.

Eventually Jamie's breathing evened out, his skin cooled, and by small degrees, he left her. Faith felt the trickle of his semen, but she didn't care. There wasn't anything she could do about it anyway, not with the restrictive way Jamie held her.

She barely formed the thought before Jamie's right shoulder knotted, and with sluggish effort, he freed first her left leg, then her right. Her bruised thigh throbbed with discomfort, and seldom-used muscles ached as Faith started to straighten her legs. But Jamie remained between her thighs, and he didn't seem to be in any hurry to move away from her. She gave up and curled her legs around him instead, trying to draw him back to her. She wanted Jamie as close as he could be, heartbeat to heartbeat, skin touching everywhere.

Jamie resisted, then propped himself on his elbows and looked down at her.

And Faith, seeing the inferno of heat still in his eyes, had a hunch that the fantasy wasn't even close to being over.

"No," Jamie assured her, bending to take her mouth. "Not yet."

Chapter Eleven

Their breakfast together hadn't afforded them a single moment of privacy, and now Alyx looked forward to getting Scott alone. Unfortunately, instead of turning toward his street, he continued down an old gravel side road. "Aren't we going to your place?"

"Not yet."

Alyx frowned at him. She wanted to burst with the anticipation of moving in with him, but Scott seemed a little grim. Was he already regretting the offer? Her hands curled into fists. If so, tough. She needed special time with him to make him see they were compatible. She'd hold him to the deal whether he had regrets or not.

"So where are we headed?"

He glanced at her, then back to the road. "I need to have a little talk with Knute first."

Surprised, Alyx drew back in her seat. "Lamar Knute? That smarmy little guy who keeps his place like a dump?"

"You know him?"

Oops. Alyx made a show of checking her nails. "Yeah, I've seen him around."

"Then you've probably seen him drunk."

Avoid eye contact . . . "Seems to be the norm for him."

The flexing of Scott's hands on the steering wheel gave away his tension. He brought his brows down in a frown and let out a long breath. "God, it's been a crazy couple of days."

She hoped their plans to live together didn't figure into the "crazy" part. Fishing for a clue to his thoughts, Alyx asked, "Has the rain caused a lot of problems?"

"That didn't help. But there's been some strange stuff going on, too."

Alyx tucked in her chin. Had he seen that blond bimbo again? "What do you mean? What strange stuff?"

Scott's mouth flattened in disgust. "One of the local kids, a real pain in the ass, got jumped the other day. He wasn't robbed, just beat up."

Not the blond bimbo. But Alyx couldn't quite relax. Surely, Scott wasn't suggesting . . . "You think *Knute* beat him up?"

"That's not what I'm saying at all." Scott sent her a chiding frown. "I wouldn't put it past Knute to be drunk enough, and dumb enough to take Kyle on. But if he did, Kyle would make mince-meat out of him."

"So then . . . why are we going to see Knute? I'm not following you."

"*I'm* going to see Knute. You're going to wait in the car. But since Knute's house isn't that far from my place, I figured I'd pick you up first to save some time, rather than backtracking."

He looked at Alyx, apparently waiting for her agreement, which she gave. "I'm glad you came by. I've missed you."

A funny expression replaced the frown. "You saw me this morning."

Trailing a finger over Scott's muscular biceps, Alyx said, "But I didn't get to touch you." She walked her fingers up to his shoulder, then to the warm, bare skin of his tanned throat. As always, touching Scott thrilled her, and her voice lowered to a husky whisper. "I didn't get to kiss you. I didn't get to—"

Scott caught her hand, brought it to his mouth for a quick kiss, and returned it to her lap. "Take it easy, babe. I still have work to do, and I can do it better without a boner."

Alyx laughed, delighted to have that effect on him. "Once we're living together, I'll be able to have my way with you every night, and that'll surely make it easier to behave during the day."

For only a second, Scott appeared almost pained. But before Alyx could be sure, the look was gone.

"So," Alyx said with false brightness, "what's the connection between Knute and Kyle?"

Her question brought his frown right back. "Some kids told me Knute's been mistreating his dog."

A rush of anger straightened Alyx's shoulders. "So are you going to shoot him?"

Scott eyed her with astonishment. "Why the hell would I shoot the dog?"

"Not the dog." Lifting her chin, Alyx said, "I meant good old Knute."

Scott half laughed and shook his head at her. "You are such a bloodthirsty woman."

"Well, you know he deserves it."

"Maybe."

"Somebody really ought to—"

"Yeah, well, hold that thought, okay?" Scott patted her thigh, acting more like his old, sweet self. "The dog is safe now. Seems someone took him from Knute and dropped him off with a neighbor known for loving animals."

Alyx barely hid her smile. "Good plan, huh?"

"I thought so. But the thing is, the people who have the dog know he belongs to Knute. They want me to make sure that Knute doesn't try to reclaim him."

Alyx snorted. "Like you'd let that happen."

Pleased by her faith in him, Scott said, "I'm not planning on it, no. Actually, I went by to see the dog, and unless Knute can come up with a good enough excuse for why the dog was so damn skinny and neglected, I might even drop a hefty fine on him."

"I still think you should shoot him." And since Alyx was only half kidding, she suggested, "Maybe just in the foot?"

Scott laughed. "All I'm going to do today is talk to Knute. And while I do that, you're going to sit in the cruiser and keep quiet."

Alyx's spine stiffened, and she arched a brow. "I am, am I?"

In a heartbeat, her humorous boyfriend disappeared beneath the rigid demeanor of the town deputy. "I mean it, Alyx. You will keep your thoughts to yourself. You will behave. You will—"

"Become deaf, dumb, and mute?" Folding her arms under her breasts and lifting her nose into the air, Alyx huffed. "Fine. I'm not even here. You can forget all about me, Deputy Royal."

That had Scott rolling his eyes. "Right. As if anyone, especially anyone male, could ever ignore you."

Now, that was more like it.

Scott squeezed her knee. "Just let me do my job, honey, okay?" And then, by way of a threat, he added, "Otherwise, I won't be able to let you ride along anymore."

Meaning she'd see him less often, and Alyx didn't want that. She promptly crossed her heart. "Okay, I'll be a nice, quiet civilian." And to loosen him up again, she added, "But at least explain to me what Knute losing his dog has to do with Kyle."

Scott seemed suspicious over her quick agreement, but he let it go. "Maybe nothing. Kyle's a real pain in the ass, always has been. I've had trouble with him for years now, so I wasn't surprised when one of the moms called to complain that he'd been picking on a couple of the younger boys. Again."

"He picks on kids younger than him?" Alyx shook her head. "Wow. What a jerk."

"No question. The thing is, when I went to see Kyle, he was the one beat up. He answered the door all bent over like an old man. Had a big bruise on his chin, and he'd been icing his..." Scott faltered.

"His what?"

After clearing his throat, Scott shrugged. "Let's just say he took a shot to a sore spot."

"Ah, I see. Well, that sort of sounds like a female move, doesn't it?" She kept her voice cavalier. "Maybe one of the moms decided to teach him a lesson."

Scott grinned at her. "Trust me, no woman did that to Kyle."

Alyx bit her tongue to keep quiet.

"Here's the real kicker though." The grin slipped away. "Kyle claims he got jumped from behind—and that the guy who attacked him was wearing a mask."

"You don't say?"

"I'm dead serious. A mask. Can you believe that?"

Yep, she believed it. "Kyle's probably making it up just because he got his tail whipped."

"I don't think so. Kyle was pretty convincing. And that means that in a matter of days, I have a mistreated dog rescued and a bully laid low."

"And you think one has something to do with the other?" Alyx couldn't hide her surprise—or her pride. Scott amazed her. He was such a good law official.

"I want to hear what Knute has to say."

Fascinated by Scott's deductive mind, Alyx asked with casual interest, "So . . . do you have any suspects?"

"I'm chewing over some ideas, yeah. But I'm not going to mention any names without proof." Scott pulled the cruiser into Knute's gravel drive and killed the engine. Knute's ten acres spread out before them, mostly weeds, except for the bare muddy spots in front of the dilapidated house.

Alyx sighed. "It's such a shame how alcohol can ruin a man's life." Scott suddenly turned to her, staring at her for so long that nervousness crawled along her spine and set the fine hairs on her nape at attention. "What?" she snapped.

With stern emphasis, Scott said, "You'll stay right here, in the car, and wait for me."

"Yeah, yeah." Relaxing again, Alyx waved him off. "Heard you the first three times you said it."

Scott caught the back of her neck and brought her face up to his. Alyx just knew he was going to start lecturing, laying it on thick about wanting to protect her, wanting to keep her safe.

She braced herself, and instead Scott kissed the tip of her nose and smiled. "Damn, Alyx, I can't resist you when you pout." His thumb rubbed her bottom lip. "Actually, I can't ever resist you."

Scott shook his head, apparently bemused over his own statement, then he opened his door and left the car.

Speechless, Alyx watched him settle his hat on his head, roll his shoulders, and start toward Knute's front door.

Staring after him, Alyx realized that she probably should have been indignant. After all, Scott had just accused her of pouting when she would never do anything so wimpy or girlie. Pouting was for passive-aggressive women, not her.

She was more of a kick-butt, take-charge type of woman.

But Scott had also said he couldn't resist her, and that was a good thing. The way he'd touched her, the suggestive tone he'd used . . . Well, she was a little turned on, just as Scott no doubt intended. He'd probably thought it was a good way to get her to comply with his wishes.

And really, she didn't even care.

*   *   *

Distracted with thoughts of Alyx and her unsatisfying plan to move in with him, Scott almost missed seeing Lamar Knute come slinking out of his side door to hobble forward in greeting. Strange, considering Knute usually spent all the daylight hours sleeping off a hangover from the drinking binge of the night before. Scott had expected to either wake him up or not find him at home.

Lamar did look hungover, with his hair dirty and hanging in his face, his slack jaw bristled with a scraggly growth of whiskers, and his slept-in, sweat-and-alcohol-stained clothes. Why Lamar would be up and about now, when he obviously wasn't alert, left Scott wondering what he might have interrupted.

As Lamar made his way forward, Scott took in his limping gait, then his ramshackle house with the front door still closed tight.

Maybe Lamar had something inside that he wanted to hide. Scott decided to check into that—discreetly, of course. It was always best to take Lamar by surprise.

"Deputy." Knute's speech was slurred as usual, but he didn't exactly seem drunk. "What're you doin' here?"

Scott crossed his arms and surveyed the shorter man. Knute held his ribs while favoring one hip. "What happened to your dog, Knute?"

He looked confused, chuckled once, then frowned. "You're here about Badger?"

"That's right." What had Lamar expected?

Slapping his knee, Lamar started chuckling and then couldn't seem to stop.

Scott glanced back to make sure Alyx remained in the car. He didn't trust her to control herself around a jackass like Lamar Knute. Outwardly, Alyx had perfected the part of a hard-nosed independent, but inside, she harbored a soft heart filled with the burning need to protect anyone or anything she thought mistreated. That included animals of all kinds.

It was something they had in common.

At that moment, Alyx had her head hanging out the window, glaring at Knute. She wore an intimidating frown and appeared ready to launch an attack if provoked. Scott gave her a warning look, then turned back to Knute.

"That's enough, Lamar."

"Right." He chuckled again, but started winding down. An odd odor came from his clothes.

Scott's suspicions solidified. "Care to share the joke?"

"Sure. Why not?" Knute grinned up at Scott, and said with a flourish, "Badger was stolen. That's right. Swiped right out from under my nose. You see, some crazy fool in a black mask came and took him."

Scott nearly gave voice to the groan burning up his throat. At the last second, he swallowed it back and managed to keep his façade of icy professionalism in place. No reason to let Lamar know how the news troubled him.

Wondering what had turned normally recalcitrant Lamar so chatty, Scott said, "A black mask, huh?"

"Yep. Covered his whole face."

"That's a little hard to believe."

Knute lifted his dingy T-shirt and showed several purpling bruises on his ribs and lower near his hip. "I'm tellin' you, some lunatic in a disguise came and beat me with a stick and then stole my dog."

Scott rocked back on his heels. The ramifications left his brain churning and his temper rising. "Why didn't you report it?"

Shrugging, Knute dropped the shirt and laughed again. "He threatened to kill me. 'Sides, I don't give a damn that the mutt is gone. Good riddance. Dog wasn't nuthin' but trouble anyhow. Always barking or howling—"

Scott stepped closer, interrupting. "Give me a description."

"I jus' told ya, he wore a mask."

"Right. But was he tall, short, thin, fat?" Scott absolutely hated mysteries. Clint might have taken over as Visitation's sheriff, much to Scott's relief, but Scott was more familiar with the town and the people in it.

He felt a responsibility toward them.

And because he felt responsible, he'd made a point of knowing everyone in his town. As he'd already told Alyx, he had his suspicions. He only hoped they proved wrong. "You said he threatened you, Lamar. Did he have an accent? Any identifying marks like a tattoo or scar?"

Lamar scratched his grizzled head, thinking about it. "I'd say tall, least taller than me."

That told Scott little, considering Lamar was a stump of a man. "As tall as me?"

"Can't say. I was busy dodging blows, not measuring the man. I know he weren't fat, no sir. But he was strong as an ox. Damn near killed me with that stick. He just kept hittin' me and hittin' me and—"

"I get the picture." Both Kyle and Knute, punished by a masked assailant capable enough to inflict physical harm, and one who didn't hesitate to do so. It sounded like something out of a cheesy comic book. "Anything distinctive about the speech?"

"Can't recall no accent or nuthin'. I think I was too scairt for my life to pay much attention."

"Did you notice the color of his eyes? And what about his hair? Ponytail, crew cut, blond, brunet?"

"Mean eyes, I can tell ya that. The kind of eyes that'd cut right through a man. And he wore a hat that covered his head, but I think I saw a peek of dark hair." Lamar lifted bony shoulders. "That's all I remember."

"So he beat you, and then you just watched him take your dog?"

"No. He beat me, and I went back inside soon as I could. He must've taken the dog after that."

Damn. Scott knew only one man in Visitation with penetrating eyes and dark hair. But Jamie Creed stayed on his mountain. At least, he used to. But maybe that was before Clint saw him carrying a naked woman up to his cabin, before Alyx confessed to seeing the woman there still.

Jamie had a lot going on, most of it unexpected and out of the norm. He always wanted to right wrongs and to help the innocent. But never before had he allowed anyone else to move into his cabin.

Shit, shit, shit.

Scott decided that he just might have to make a visit himself, to see Jamie before anyone else did.

He had no doubt he'd offend a lot of people, most especially Alyx, if he started pointing fingers at Jamie. But . . . he'd have to at least talk to Jamie about it.

Knute screwed up his face, narrowed his red-rimmed, dilated eyes, and Scott could see him conniving. He waited, and finally Knute sneered, "Why you still standing there, boy? You should be out looking for the guy that attacked me, not badgering me."

Scott stared until Lamar began to squirm. In his most serious deputy's voice, he said, "If I find out you're lying to me, Lamar, I'll be back with an arrest warrant."

Bloodshot eyes flared. "Arrest warrant? Why would you want to do that?" He giggled nervously. "I ain't broke no laws."

"Why? Because you're an abusive drunk, and I'm not about to take you at your word on anything important. So understand this. Badger is with another family now, and I expect you to leave him be."

"I said I don't want him. Dog wasn't nuthin' but trouble anyway. I'm glad he's gone."

Red anger clouded Scott's vision. "I saw Badger, Knute. He was hungry and dirty, and trust me, nothing would make me happier than to beat the hell out of you." Scott drew a calming breath. "But I'm not going to do that."

Knute snickered, secure in Scott's legal limitations.

Scott stepped closer until Knute began backing up. His reasons for crowding the smaller, older man were twofold. He wanted to intimidate him, to make sure he never touched another animal.

And he wanted a better whiff of him, which was about enough to bring up the contents of his stomach.

But it also confirmed what he thought—Knute wasn't just drunk. His clothes held the sickeningly sweet scent of marijuana. "I'll be writing up a fine for you, based on the treatment of that dog. I suggest you get it paid right away. And if you step out of line even once, I won't hesitate to toss your sorry ass in jail and leave you there until you rot."

"For what?"

Scott flexed his fists, hoping to ease his tension before he lost his temper and repeated the work of the vigilante. Nothing would make him happier than to knock some much-needed compassion into Knute.

But officials didn't take the law into their own hands, and besides, he had a feeling he'd learn more from Knute if he left the man free to bungle around. But that didn't mean he wanted the fool to end up hurting someone else. "Drunk driving, most likely." Scott looked at him with disdain. "I'm going to be watching you, Knute. If I catch you drinking and driving, that's it."

Sputtering, Knute bumped into a tree—the same tree where he usually kept the dog tied. "You *threatening* me, Deputy?"

"Just reminding you of the law—and that I enforce it." Scott glanced at Lamar's house again, then at the overgrown land surrounding it. Yep, definitely time to do some snooping. He tipped his hat and turned to leave.

When Scott got back in the car, still rigid with mind-numbing anger at Knute, and poleaxed by the possibility of Jamie's involvement, Alyx slid over next to him.

Just having her near somehow made him feel better, when he'd always preferred to stew in isolation. Being alone made it easier for him to rationalize, to think things through. With Alyx around, he tended to have a one-track mind.

"Scott?" Her voice was a soft, soothing whisper, filled with admiration. "You look ready to explode."

"Just pissed." He took a deep breath and let it out slow. He had no intention of taking his bad mood out on Alyx. Not that she'd let him anyway. "Thank you for staying in the car." It surprised Scott that she had, especially when Knute, acting so strange, had showed no remorse for the dog.

Alyx inched closer, her gaze warm, her touch warmer. "Have I ever told you how hot it makes me when you're all macho?"

God love her, the woman could make him nuts. He'd worried about offending her with his temper, and instead she claimed to be turned on by it. Scoot shook his head. In every way imaginable, Alyx was different from any other woman he'd known. Others had kept their distance when noticing his temper. But Alyx just went toe to toe with him, trusting in his control and knowing his basic nature well enough to understand that he'd never abuse a woman in any way, not even verbally. He enjoyed her confidence in him, and her fearlessness.

Much of his anger evaporated. Alyx often had that effect on him—when she wasn't the one infuriating him.

Scott started the car, wrenched it into drive, and

made a U-turn to leave Knute's property. Thinking of Alyx's fearlessness, he suddenly wished he hadn't brought her along. He meant to talk to her, to compare the pros and cons of shacking up to marriage.

Now he realized that he should have just driven back to get her after he'd finished with Knute. She'd been too docile during that confrontation, which didn't bode well at all. "Listen to me, sweetheart."

"Sweetheart?" Smiling, Alyx stroked his shoulder. "Does that mean you're a little hot and bothered, too?"

"No." What a lie. Around Alyx, he was always primed. "And put your seatbelt back on."

With a sigh, she slid back to her own seat and buckled up. "Spoilsport."

Alyx never seemed to take him seriously. "For just once, will you listen?"

"I'm all ears."

No, she was all sexy legs and female cockiness and mile-a-minute excitement. "Alyx, I want you to stay away from Knute."

She stared out the windshield. "Now, why would I want to be anywhere near him? He's disgusting."

Oh God, he could almost hear the wheels turning in her head. "Because he's mean, and you don't like mean people, that's why."

"No, I don't." She tipped her head toward him, smiling again, one brow raised. "But then, neither do you."

"It's my job to deal with those people. Not yours."

"And now we're back where we started, with me telling you what a great job you do, and how exciting I think it is."

Scott glanced at her, and she smiled.

God, she worried him.

Alyx reached for his thigh, her busy fingers teasing him while she whispered in that special, husky voice, guaranteed to push him over the edge, "How long will it take to get to your place?"

Damn. They really did have to talk. But maybe he could put that off till later. Like . . . until tomorrow morning.

With the sudden rise of an erection, Scott pressed his foot to the gas. "Ten minutes." Maybe less if he didn't see any other cars on the road. It couldn't be soon enough for Scott.

Jamie tunneled both hands into Faith's wildly tangled hair and held her still for a kiss so sweet it took even him by surprise. What she'd done to him, how she made him feel, didn't bear close scrutiny.

He cleared his throat and said by way of apology, "I forgot you hurt your thigh. Are you okay?"

Eyes vague, lips parted, Faith nodded.

That particular look turned Jamie inside out. And like any basic male animal, he wasn't immune. He wanted her again, right this second, because he knew she wanted him. He could thrust back inside her and she wouldn't voice a single complaint.

Displeasure gnawed at his insides. He had to get a grip.

Her skin was still dewy, her nipples still tight, her belly still quivering . . . Jesus. If he didn't get a handle on his lust, Faith would realize just how susceptible he was to her.

"Let me see." Moving to the side of her, Jamie leaned over her body to examine her leg.

Faith rolled toward him, her expression dreamy and turned on. "I'm fine, Jamie." Her hand touched his chest, and she sighed. "You wouldn't hurt me."

Her pose added emphasis to the deep dip of her waist, the tantalizing rise of her hip, the long, shapely length of her thigh. It also showed the bruises that marred her otherwise pale skin.

"Damn." Jamie didn't mean to do it, but he found himself bending over her, kissing her leg from the first dark bruise down to her knee.

Faith purred, stretched, and that prodded Jamie on. He kissed a path back up to her hipbone, then across her silky belly to her navel. The smell of her skin, the combined scent of sex and woman, filled his head, pushing him near the edge again.

"You didn't wear a rubber."

Jamie paused with his tongue in her navel, stunned, bemused. He pulled back to stare at Faith. Protection. It hadn't even occurred to him, and now that he did think about it, he didn't know what he could do. He didn't have any condoms, and because he'd brought Faith into his home buck naked, he knew she didn't have birth control of any kind.

"Don't worry. I won't get pregnant." She rolled to her back again, smiling in a sad, accepting way. "I can't."

Opening his hand wide on her belly, Jamie said, "I know." He'd felt the truth of her words even before she gave them.

"What do you mean, you know?" She rose up on one elbow, suddenly more alert. "You're in my head?"

Annoyed, Jamie started to reply that he didn't need to be. The look on her face had reassured him even before she'd spoken. But suddenly he felt a premonition of trouble.

Pulling back from Faith, Jamie opened his mind, seeking a source. He saw Scott in full deputy mode, and at the same time, he detected Scott's suspicions toward him. Suspicions about acts that shouldn't have been attributed to Jamie. Only that didn't cover it. No. There were other conspiracies at work, other people scheming.

Jamie frowned, disgusted that he couldn't enjoy Faith in peace, while at the same time trying to pull the various clues together to make sense of them.

Unfortunately, details remained just out of reach. Faces and motivations were blurry along the edges. He saw a woman and a man, and he saw Scott.

Worse, he saw Alyx.

What the hell was going on?

Faith groaned, shifting beside him. "God, Jamie, I hate that cold mask of distance." She started to separate herself from him, and Jamie caught her knee.

He sent the premonitions away and put thoughts of Scott from his mind. He could deal with it all later. Right now, he intended to settle some things with Faith. "It's not for you. I was thinking of something else."

"What?"

Still on one elbow, Faith presented a pretty picture. Jamie eyed her full, naked breasts, noting how rosy her nipples had gotten from his suckling. He thought of what else he wanted to do to and with her, and he started breathing hard again.

Until Faith caught his hand, and said, "Jamie, I'm confused."

He pulled his attention away from her breasts and looked into her dark blue eyes, clouded with worry. "Confused about what? You want me. I want you. It doesn't get much simpler than that."

"You're still reading me."

Jamie trailed his free hand down to her hip, then nudged her thighs slightly apart. He wanted to see her, all of her. There wasn't much on this earth prettier than a woman's body. "Your thoughts are a turn-on."

"But . . . I thought . . ."

Her hesitation struck him, and Jamie felt his guts tighten. Faith wanted declarations from him. She wanted him to expose himself. She wanted control.

But he wouldn't give in to her. "What? That I can't read people I care about?"

She nodded.

So Faith wanted to know if he cared for her? She thought one fuck and he'd be swearing undying love—just as he'd done with Delayna?

Jamie retreated, both physically and emotionally. Joe had said to stay in control, and he intended to do just that. If he admitted to Faith that in the last hour she'd become crystal clear to him, would she understand that he already cared too damn much?

What would she do with that information? Spilling his guts sure as hell wouldn't help maintain his control. Just the opposite. Even if Faith didn't plot against him, she was a woman—and women always wanted that type of information so they could use it.

Easing close to her again, Jamie put his hand high on her thigh, curling his fingers inward, near her dewy sex. He deliberately wiped all inflection from his tone. "What makes you think I'm reading you?"

Faith was so easy that already her skin flushed and her nipples tightened. She glanced down at his teasing fingers, then bit her lips. "You know what I want, even before I say it."

"Sexually, you mean?"

She met his gaze. Her chin firmed. "Yes."

Regardless of her bravado, Jamie knew her heart beat fast and her blood rushed through her veins. He felt it, the same as he felt his own.

"So you want this?" Wedging his hand between her thighs, he encountered the stickiness of his come, with the slipperiness of her release, and he breathed harder.

He easily sank in two fingers, began a slow, gentle rhythm, and felt the clamp of her body, the shudder that ran through her.

Faith closed her eyes, but Jamie said, "*No.* Look at me, Faith," and he continued to finger her as their eyes met, hers liquid, his fierce. He wanted her bad, almost as much as he had an hour ago.

Fingers tightening in the sheets, Faith moaned and arched her back, lifting her breasts toward him.

With a smile, Jamie bent to draw her nipple into his mouth, tonguing her, nipping with his teeth. "I don't need to be a mind reader to know you're turned on, Faith."

He straightened and heard her indrawn breath, saw the way her thighs parted to encourage him. "You see? It may have been a hell of a long time since I've had a woman, but some things a man doesn't forget."

Breathless, her hips beginning to lift beneath his hand, Faith asked, "What do you mean?"

With her eyes so heavy and her lips trembling, she looked beautiful to Jamie. Beautiful and sexy and ready.

"You have an expressive face and an even more expressive body. The way you move, the sounds you make, let me know what you want. And right now, you're close to coming."

He pressed his fingers deeper and heard her gasp. Pleased with her, Jamie taunted, "Aren't you, Faith?"

She bit her bottom lip, hesitated, and finally gave one jerky nod.

The flush on her face was only part embarrassment, but mostly lust. Jamie whispered, "Do you want me to make you come, Faith?"

"I don't understand you."

He counted his blessings on that one. "No, but you still want me, don't you? Tell me."

She swallowed hard and turned her face away. "You're being deliberately cruel."

"Cruel?" Jamie worked his thumb through her curls, found her clitoris, and gently pressed. "Is that what I am?"

With a broken moan, Faith's hands tightened more, until Jamie thought she might rip the sheets. Her chest rose and fell on labored breaths and her legs stiffened, her heels pressing into the mattress.

"So close." Jamie forgot about control and the repercussions of giving it up. "So beautiful." He bent to her breast again, circled her nipple with his tongue. "Will you come for me, Faith?" And then, more insistently, "Come for me."

"Jamie."

Her back arched, and he pressed his fingers deep, worked her with his thumb. "That's it." He sucked at her nipple, hungry for her, and she broke, crying out, moaning and twisting, her inner muscles clamping down hard on his fingers while the orgasm rolled through her.

Jamie waited until the climax receded, until she went limp and soft, before moving between her legs. He lifted her hips in his hands and drove into her, hard and fast.

Faith whimpered, clutching at his shoulders, holding him like a lifeline. Little aftershocks of pleasure still rippled through her.

Connected to her, falling into a deep carnal void, Jamie closed his eyes. He felt Faith's mouth on his chest, moving over his burning skin. He felt her body welcoming him, milking him.

He felt her sadness and acceptance. And he felt her love.

He doubted himself, knowing it was too damn soon for anything remotely close to love, but still it filled him up and drove him wild.

"No," Jamie groaned in denial, even as he ground his teeth together and exploded. The pleasure went on too long, until he was drained from the combination of pulsing release and tender emotion.

As his strength gave way, he collapsed onto Faith, breathing hard, trembling like a virgin, shaken to his soul.

She hugged him to her, and Jamie could do no more than accept the kiss she pressed to his shoulder and the flood of affection that she didn't even try to conceal.

Chapter Twelve

Faith didn't know what to say or think when Jamie suddenly rolled to his back, drew in two long, shaky breaths, and thrust himself away from the bed. He walked like a drunk at first, clumsy, his footfalls heavy, until he managed to straighten.

Sitting up, Faith stared after him as he headed for the ladder. "Jamie?"

"Stay put."

Hurt, Faith frowned, then flopped back on the bed and covered her face. Good God, what they did together couldn't be called mere sex. It was so much more than that. And she knew damn good and well, despite his closed expression and distant attitude, that Jamie had felt it, too.

"I did," he yelled, sounding annoyed. "Now be quiet."

Faith sat up again and resisted the urge to shake her fist at him. She took a few calming breaths, then shouted back, "I didn't say anything."

"You don't have to, damn it!"

Oh. That left her even more confused, and when she heard Jamie returning, she scrambled for the sheet and quickly covered herself. The second his head cleared the landing, she grilled him. "So you can read me still? Is that it?"

He didn't answer, but he had a damp washcloth in his hand, and that alarmed her enough that she didn't bother asking again.

Jamie stopped by the bed, frowning like a villain, and looked at the way she clutched the sheet to her chin. He rolled his eyes. "Let it go, Faith."

She shook her head. "No." Then she looked at the washcloth. "What are you going to do?"

He followed her line of vision to the washcloth. "With this? I don't know. Maybe murder you with a scrap of terrycloth. Or perform some barbaric ritual on your body using damp material. Maybe something perverted—"

"*Stop it.*"

"Then don't be ridiculous." Before she could draw another breath, Jamie ripped the sheet away and dropped it on the floor. "I'm going to clean you, and then we're going to go downstairs and eat soup and try to have a civil conversation that doesn't include me molesting you or you hiding secrets."

Faith wrapped her arms around her breasts. "I don't want to." Not until she knew what he had on his mind—which she considered only fair.

Jamie sat beside her on the bed. "Which part? Going downstairs or talking to me?"

All of it, really, but Faith nodded at the washcloth. "I can clean myself. I don't need you to do it, and I don't want you to watch."

Those awesome eyes of his sparked with annoyance. "Why so modest all of a sudden?"

"I've always been modest." And now she knew he'd read her thoughts, and she knew he knew that she cared so much for him and—

Jamie held up a hand. "That's far too convoluted for me to figure out on an empty stomach."

Her empty stomach roiled with distress. "I was blocking you, damn you!"

"Yeah, well." Smiling, Jamie bent and kissed her nose. "I don't think you can anymore, but you're welcome to try." One hand landed heavily on the inside of her thigh, and he moved her legs apart. "Now be quiet and hold still."

Frozen with mortification, Faith watched the intense concentration on Jamie's face as he visually examined her. He frowned, and gently began wiping away the residue of their lovemaking.

"Are you sore?"

Humiliation rippled through her. Faith thought about lying, but knew it'd be no use. "A little."

Jamie glanced up. "I'm sorry."

He looked remorseful, and tender. Faith's heart tripped, and then promptly softened. "Don't be. I'm not. Not about that."

Something darkened in his face. His shoulders tensed, and Jamie closed his eyes as if counting to ten. "This is ridiculous."

"What is?"

"I want you again."

Shocked, Faith looked at his lap, saw he was in fact semi-erect, and raised her objections. "I really think I need a few minutes. Maybe a shower. And I'm getting hungry, too."

Cursing, Jamie stood in a rush, his hands clamped behind his head as he paced the length of the room.

Faith watched him with no idea of what to say. She had no idea that a guy could even—

"You're right, you know." Jamie turned to stare at her. "I remember sex, and it wasn't . . ." At a loss for words, he indicated her, the bed, something, and added, "This."

Then he dropped his head forward and groaned. "Not that you'd know what I'm talking about really, because you were a virgin."

Faith gasped. Oh no. She *definitely* hadn't thought about that. She was sure of it.

Jamie looked at her over his shoulder, his expression forbidding. "How many times do I have to tell you? I'm not an ignorant man. I knew right away you hadn't given birth, but to not even have had sex? That's bizarre, Faith. It doesn't make any sense."

Faith opened her mouth, and he said, "No." He strode toward her. "Let's go downstairs first and feed our faces. I've worked up one hell of an appetite, so I imagine you have, too."

"Yes." Thankful for the reprieve, Faith gingerly swung her legs off the bed and stood. The room spun around her, and she grabbed the nightstand. "Wow." Her legs were shaky, her head muzzy, and she felt like someone had sapped all her strength.

Jamie stood close, but didn't touch her. "Yeah, I know. I felt the same way."

He didn't show it. He looked strong and confident—and determined. And that worried her.

Straightening and taking a cautious step forward, Faith said, "I'm okay now."

He nodded. "Good. Let's go."

Faith reached for the shirt she'd worn earlier, but Jamie ordered, "Leave it."

Scandalized, Faith whipped around to see him again. She sputtered before finally getting out the words. "I can't eat naked."

"Why not? I'm going to." Jamie gave her body a thorough once-over. "I enjoy looking at you, and it's not like I haven't already seen everything."

"Not while I'm eating!"

"What difference does it make?"

Faith had no idea, she just knew that it did make a difference. Scrambling for a good defense, she said, "It's cold."

Jamie lifted one shoulder. "So I'll make another fire."

He waited, expectant, and Faith gave up. If he enjoyed seeing her, what harm would it cause? She could handle it. Hadn't she handled everything else up to this point? "No. We don't need a fire. There's plenty of steam from the soup. The cabin is actually warm."

"I know."

Of course he did. He was in her head. Faith lifted her chin. "Fine, we'll eat naked like all civilized people do."

Jamie moved closer to her, and Faith held her breath. But he only tucked her hair behind her ear and said, "Thank you."

How could he melt her resistance so easily? Before coming to Jamie's cabin, she'd had a backbone. Now she felt like a jellyfish. "At least put something over the windows."

"No one ever visits me, Faith. It'll be private enough."

"What about Alyx?"

Jamie shrugged. "I always know when she's coming, and she's not going to be here tonight."

"But . . . I still feel exposed."

Jamie smiled, and this time his hand trailed over her shoulder to cup her breast, where he gently thumbed her nipple before continuing down to her waist, her hip.

Scrutinizing her body, he murmured softly, "You are exposed, just as I like you to be." He brought his attention back to her face and frowned. "But if it'll make you happy, I'll cover the windows while you serve the soup."

"Thank you."

Five minutes later, Faith sat at the table without a stitch of clothing, eating soup and buttered bread and feeling very jittery again. That had more to do with Jamie's nudity than her own. And the way he watched her, how his gaze strayed again and again to her breasts, and the heat in his eyes.

"This is good."

Faith nearly jumped out of her seat. "Thank you. It seemed a waste to use a roast for soup, but I wasn't sure when you'd be back, and if a roast cooks too long it can get tough, and—"

"So." He interrupted her rambling, and when she fell mute, he took a long drink of his tea before giving her his undivided attention. "You're a virgin."

Faith held her breath. But . . . Jamie didn't seem to be particularly upset about that, when she'd been half expecting the worst.

He shook his head. "No. Just tell me why, and how it is that you came to adopt Cory. She is adopted, isn't she?"

"Yes. In every way possible, other than by birth, Cory is mine. I got her the day she was born, and I've loved her as much as if I had given birth to her."

"I know."

Over and over again, Jamie gave the same reply. *I know.* But this time, the inflection he put on the simple retort sent warmth all through her. Why had no one ever told her how his voice could affect her?

Hands shaking, Faith leaned toward him. "I love her, Jamie."

"And you're here because you need me to protect her from someone?"

Faith sat back in her seat and drew a deep breath. "I don't really know—and that's the truth."

Eyes narrowed, Jamie said, "Go on."

"Cory sent me here. She said bad things would happen and I had to find you."

Jamie stared at her while considering that, and finally nodded in acceptance. "Sometimes it's not easy to figure things out. You get only bits and pieces of what will happen, not the whole thing. It's like putting a jigsaw puzzle together. Until enough pieces are in place, you don't know what the picture will be. It'd help if I could talk with Cory. Maybe together we could work through it."

Looking down at the table to avoid Jamie's reaction, Faith said, "I imagine you'll be meeting her very soon."

He jerked so hard, the small table shook. "How?" In the next heartbeat, he shot to his feet and planted both hands on the table to lean toward her, crowding her space. "Where is she, Faith? Who is she staying with?"

His reaction stunned her, and Faith pressed back in her chair, speechless.

In a fury, Jamie rounded the table and caught her arms just above her elbows. He lifted her to her tiptoes. "Answer me, damn it."

"It's okay, Jamie." She pressed a hand to his chest and felt the wild thumping of his heart. Fear for her daughter? Faith thought so. "Jamie, Cory is like you. She knows when bad things will happen, so she wouldn't make the trip if it wasn't safe."

"Who's she with?"

"My mother, Tracy." Faith tried to soothe him. "I love Cory, and I trust her. She's only eight, but her ability is astounding."

Jamie didn't relax one iota. "I know. I saw her."

"You did?"

He nodded, his face still hard with worry. "It was almost like she stood right there in front of me, with me. She saw me, too." Jamie released Faith and took a step away. "She . . . talked to me. But . . . not really."

Faith had no idea what to say, not that Cory's actions surprised her. "She told me you would connect with her. She knew that. But she also told me that I had to get to know you before I could explain why I was here."

Jamie turned away, and Faith eyed his broad

back, the indention of his spine framed with long muscles, the tapering angles of his hips.

He jerked back around to face her, some heated emotion blazing from his eyes. His hands flexed, and then he opened his fingers, deliberately relaxing. Two deep breaths, and seconds later, Jamie returned to his seat. "Don't tempt me, Faith."

"I wasn't—"

"Finish eating."

Concerned, Faith pulled out her chair. "Jamie, are you okay?"

"You said Cory would be here soon. When?"

"I'm not certain. Maybe tomorrow."

He gave a laugh that had nothing to do with humor. "Great. Just fucking great."

Stiffening, her maternal hackles rising, Faith said, "You don't want her here?"

Jamie jerked his head up to face her. "No! I didn't mean that." He fell back in his seat and locked his hands behind his head, his biceps knotted with frustration. "I look forward to meeting her." He returned his hands to the tabletop. "The thing is, the others are coming soon, too."

"What others?"

"All of them. Scott first, but then Joe and Bryan and their wives . . ." Jamie shook his head. "Everyone."

"Oh." Faith didn't understand. "Why?"

"To check you out, and because they have some lame idea that I need their help."

"With what?"

"You."

"Oh." She cleared her throat, tried a smile that didn't quite work. "Do you?"

"No. Maybe. Hell, I don't know." Jamie growled, scrubbed his hands over his face, and then picked up his spoon and pointed it at her. "What I do know is that I'm nowhere near done with you. So finish eating and I'll try to be patient through a shower. But that's about as much as I can promise."

Faith blinked at Jamie, but having him say it, so bold and blatant like that, made her want him again, too. Well, his nudity also helped. Seeing his body made her hand shake as she picked up her spoon. And once she looked at him, she couldn't look away long enough to get her spoon in her soup bowl. Jamie was just so gorgeous, such a fabulous model for male strength and sensitivity and—

"Faith?"

Swallowing a moan, she managed to drag her gaze to his face. "Hmm?"

"Eat. And hurry."

Squeezed into the tiny shower, Jamie held Faith from behind. But even with his hands covering her breasts, her body a mighty diversion, he finally remembered his other question. She'd thrown him with the news that Cory would visit, and made him forget. But now . . .

"Faith?" He gently squeezed her breasts, teasing the edge of her nipples with his thumbs. His cock nestled between her cheeks. He wanted her, but he wanted answers, too.

Her head moved restlessly against his chest and she made soft, sweet female sounds each time he shifted his hands or his body or both.

Jamie smiled. "Tell me how it is that you were a virgin."

Faith groaned and tried to turn to face him, but Jamie held her in place. He'd already taken a turn washing her, moving his soapy hands over her body, exploring her everywhere. And still she intrigued him. He wanted to know everything about her, physically, emotionally. He wanted to know her past and what plans she had for the future.

As weak as his discipline seemed around Faith, hers was worse. He could give her a certain look, and she started to melt. He mentioned sex, and she was immediately agreeable.

Her enthusiasm and willingness pleased him.

Pressing one hand between her legs, Jamie relished her heat and the way she quivered. "Tell me."

Her fingernails sank into his thighs, stinging in force, turning him on more. She parted her legs to encourage his touch, and Jamie didn't disappoint her.

"Tell me," he urged again while stroking her.

"I . . . I never wanted anyone but you." Her breath caught, and she moaned. "I tried dating other men, but they weren't . . . right. I had no interest in them."

"That's why you adopted? Because you didn't think you'd ever meet a guy you wanted to marry?"

She hesitated, trembling all over. "No."

Jamie knew he'd lose the fragile rein on his lust if he didn't slow things down. He released Faith and turned her to face him. The warm water hit his back, and Faith's heat warmed his front. He held her shoulders, needing to understand. "Then why?"

Faith moved up against his chest, her cheek over his heart. She rested her hands on his waist. "Cory's mother didn't want a baby. She knew she couldn't take care of her."

"So you agreed to take her?"

Nodding, Faith whispered, "I never regretted it. I fell in love with her the second I saw her. So I adopted her, gave her my name, and she's mine."

She was holding back. Jamie sensed it. But somehow her thoughts proved too elusive for him to grasp. Or maybe his thoughts were too centered on her body to free his abilities. "Have you seen her mother since then?"

"No, never. There'd be no reason. Cory is all mine, and that's the way it's going to stay."

Her ferocious tone made Jamie smile. "I wasn't questioning your devotion to her." But something in the way Faith answered didn't add up. Jamie tried to work it out, until Faith's small hand curled around him.

He stiffened, felt a surge of desire that blocked everything else, and switched places with Faith so he could lean back against the shower wall. Bracing himself, he let her have her way.

Gently stroking, her lips touching his chest, Faith whispered, "I always cared about you, Jamie. Even when I was far away from you, when I assumed I'd never see you again."

"No." That didn't make sense, but Jamie couldn't rationalize the problem, not while Faith's hand moved up and down, pushing him closer and closer to the edge.

He watched her through a red haze, aware of her caring, her excitement.

She looked up at him and licked her lips. "Once I knew you, no other man could even begin to compare. They were all . . . just men, when you were so much more."

Jamie hated that he couldn't remember her. He started to tell her so, but she sank to her knees in front of him, and seeing her like that, knowing what she would do and how he'd react to it, obliterated everything but his savage need.

He tangled his hands in her wet hair, holding her head, urging her forward. Not that Faith needed much encouragement. Her eyes were heavy. Her lips parted when she brushed them against him, teasing, butterfly soft.

Jamie groaned and his fingers tightened.

Her tongue came out, licking up the length of him.

Jerking with the unexpected, extreme pleasure of it, Jamie locked his knees and watched Faith service him. She continued to use her tongue, licking from the base of his shaft all the way to the head, over and over again.

He couldn't bear it; he didn't ever want her to stop.

His heart, already full to bursting, punched hard against his breastbone. He couldn't draw a deep enough breath. Then Faith parted her lips and he felt her tongue swirl around the head of his cock before she closed her mouth over him, sliding down, taking him deep.

He gripped her head, holding her close, turbulent with the need to come and the desire to be tender. His thumbs curved into her hollowed cheeks as she sucked, and he knew he had to pull her away.

She didn't want to leave him, and Jamie groaned, close to begging as he said, "Faith, honey, that's enough."

One hand knotted in her hair, the other cupped around her jaw, he eased her away. Faith stared up at him, her eyes dark and dazed. "I want you, Jamie. All of you."

She couldn't be faking it; forget his gift, his vulnerability. Jamie saw the truth in her eyes. *She couldn't lie to him.*

"You have me." Jamie lifted her under the arms, turned her against the shower wall and pinned her there with the press of his body. Frantic to be inside her, to let himself go, he rasped, "Put your right leg on my hip, Faith."

Holding his shoulders, she did as instructed, and Jamie sank into her with one strong thrust. It felt so right, so perfect, he gave a shuddering groan.

Faith caught her breath, whispered, "Oh."

He loved the sultry surprise on her face, the adventurous smile, the soft satisfaction. She pushed closer, moving against him.

"That's it." Going slow and deep, his feet braced on the wet floor of the shower, Jamie built a rhythm. Faith's mouth sought his, and she rocked with him, countering his thrusts, rapidly climbing toward her release.

Jamie gave her the kisses she wanted, swallowing her small moans, then her higher-pitched cries as she stiffened and her inner muscles convulsed around him.

It kept getting better. Hotter. More intense. And

each time, he felt Faith's caring. He felt her honesty.

Jamie let himself go. With Faith holding him, he didn't have much choice.

Staring at the ceiling, watching the moon shadows dance with the sway of the trees outside the window, Jamie contemplated the sleeping woman beside him. He'd known her only days, but it felt like a lifetime. She was a part of his past, aware of things he'd never told anyone else. And that meant she knew him as few ever would.

They'd slept for about four hours, and he felt refreshed. He didn't want to go back to sleep. He had an almost panicked need to make the most of his time with Faith. He didn't want to waste time sleeping, not when they could talk. When he could look at her, listen to her, touch her.

Make love to her again.

He'd spent so much of his life alone, not even wanting company, assuming he couldn't have it anyway. And now Faith was a part of his life. He wanted to relish every second.

Dismissing any guilt he felt for disturbing her rest, Jamie turned to his side and propped himself up on an elbow. For a few more minutes, he just watched Faith sleep. She wasn't quite snoring, but close, and he smiled.

Odd, how quickly he'd gotten used to smiling, to showing his pleasure.

Reaching out with one finger, he touched her pale cheekbone. Then he didn't want to stop touching her. Her skin fascinated him. Her red hair and blue eyes mesmerized him. Her laughter and her chatter amused him.

Her sexual drive thrilled him.

Leaning down, Jamie brushed his lips over the bridge of her nose and then drew back, waiting to see if she'd awaken.

She didn't.

And he realized that even the sound way she slept gave him pleasure.

Plucking up the edge of the sheet, Jamie slowly drew it off her body, unveiling her breasts to the milky moonlight in a slow tease. But that didn't suffice, so he lowered it more, until he could see her belly, and lower, until the bunched sheet rested around her knees.

She was on her back, her face turned toward him, one leg out straight, the other bent toward him.

She was his.

Jamie caged her in with his arms and leaned down to kiss her breasts, brushing his mouth above her nipples, along her cleavage, nuzzling underneath.

Faith stirred, murmuring and sighing. She started to pull her legs together, but Jamie caught her thigh, holding her until she settled again.

He kissed each rib, breathing in the subtle fragrance of warm, sleepy woman, a tantalizing scent that got stronger as he worked his way down her body.

When he nibbled on her hipbone, she shifted and her hand fluttered up to rest on his head. "Jamie?"

He gave her a soft love bite on the belly for that and asked, "Who else?"

Sleepily, she inquired, "What are you doing?"

Though it amazed even him, he had another boner. "I'm making love to you."

She groaned, more alert and now teasing. "Seriously? Again?"

Settling himself down low between her soft thighs, Jamie murmured agreement. "It's your fault, you know. You're irresistible." Very gently, he parted her labia. There was just enough murky light for him to see her, and his stomach clenched with need.

Faith shifted, and Jamie could hear her breathing. "You're . . . you're insatiable," she accused.

"I know." He leaned down and kissed her, a soft press of his lips that made her still in reaction. "I admit it. But what does that make you, Faith?"

He touched her with the tip of his tongue, gave one tiny lick, teasing her. "You've come . . . what? Five times now? And not little mewling orgasms." He rolled a shoulder forward, knowing she'd left scratches there. "You burned up and were plenty vocal about it, too."

Her hips lifted the slightest bit. "Braggart," she breathed.

Smiling, Jamie pushed one finger into her. "I felt you squeezing me, Faith. I felt every single contraction." Talking about it made him hotter. He nuzzled her, and said, "I want to feel it again." Then he closed his mouth over her.

An hour passed before Jamie had his fill, allowing Faith to nod off again. Limp as a rag doll, she curled against him, her head on his shoulder, her hand resting over his abdomen.

Temporarily sated, Jamie automatically sought out the trouble in town. Usually, he had nothing more important to do than concentrate on problems, which made them easier to decipher. But now . . . Faith kept him sidetracked in so many ways.

He kissed the top of her head and closed his eyes, trying to find the source of danger. Jamie didn't recognize the woman, but she was blond, attractive. Conniving.

And he saw Scott again, but he didn't think Scott had anything to do with the stranger.

Scott planned to come see him in the morning, but Jamie decided he'd go to Scott first. As much as he hated to lose any of his time with Faith, some vague urgency pushed him to correct Scott's misconceptions. Leaving it alone could mean a tragedy. And Jamie wouldn't let that happen.

He hugged Faith closer, already feeling the loss of their isolated time. After seeing Scott, the others would come, obliterating the privacy. Knowing it made Jamie rigid, which disturbed Faith. She mumbled in her sleep, and Jamie hugged her tight.

He felt protective. He felt . . . territorial. And then he made up his mind.

To hell with it. They could all troop in if they wanted, but Jamie wouldn't let them interfere with Faith.

Plain and simple, he wasn't ready—not to leave her, not to explain her.

Sure as hell not to give her up.

Chapter Thirteen

After her trip to the post office to pick up some computer supplies, Alyx went by the drugstore to get a soda. The pharmacist, Marshall Peterson, greeted her with a smile. "How you doing today, Alyx?"

"I'm good, Mr. Peterson."

His eyes twinkled, and he said, "Now, I don't believe that for a second."

Alyx laughed with him—until she noticed the blond bimbo browsing the magazine rack. Her eyes narrowed, and she had to fight an urge to confront the woman. Just what was good old Becky up to now?

Mr. Peterson whispered, "Tourist. She's only been here a few days."

As far as Alyx was concerned, that was a few days too many. The woman had blatantly come on to Scott, even with Alyx right there in plain sight. And that wasn't something Alyx would ever forgive or forget.

Besides, she didn't trust her. There was just something about her. . . .

Mr. Peterson ran his fingers through his thick, silver hair. "She's been in several times now. Always buys something."

Alyx scowled, remembering how Becky had asked Scott if she'd see him around town. Did that explain her frequent trips to the pharmacy, which sold everything from basic medical supplies to snacks to housewares?

Or did she have other reasons?

Alyx took Becky's measure, noting her elegant height and very feminine curves.

Unlike Scott, she wasn't fooled. Not for a second.

"Now, why are you looking like a thundercloud?" the pharmacist asked.

Unwilling to give away her thoughts, Alyx pulled herself together. "Sorry. I caught her flirting with Scott, that's all."

"Ah. And you're as territorial as that brother of yours, I reckon." Mr. Peterson nodded with approval. "It's a good thing to care that much. Don't let her bother you none. The deputy's a good man."

"I know." Alyx sighed, starting to feel like a fool. She'd gone from being a woman who never felt jealousy to putting on a jealous display in public. "How about a pink cow? I'm in the mood for sugar."

They chatted while the pharmacist moved to the ice-cream section, put two scoops of vanilla ice cream in a tall paper cup, and poured cream soda over it. He was careful that the foam didn't run over.

All the while, Alyx kept her eye on Becky—and that was probably the only reason she noticed the teenagers loitering behind Becky, near the candy aisle.

The three boys glanced around the store while whispering to each other. Suddenly, they grabbed handfuls of candy bars and stuffed them inside their shirts.

Appalled, Alyx started to protest, but she saw that Becky watched the boys too, her interest very suspect in Alyx's opinion. Why would Becky be so interested in the local youths?

Deciding not to rat the boys out—yet—Alyx alternately watched them make a hasty exit out of the store and Becky's rapt attention to them.

"Here you go. That oughta hit the spot."

"Thanks." Absently watching through the front window, Alyx saw the boys get in an old, rusted Ford Falcon, where three girls waited for them. Laughing and sharing their loot, they all drove away. She recognized them, and she had a pretty good idea where to find them later.

She glanced again at Becky, but the woman had moved on, putting more items in the small plastic basket she carried.

Giving her attention back to the pharmacist, Alyx eyed the frosty pink cow and smiled. "Just perfect, Mr. Peterson." She pulled out some singles and paid him. But Mr. Peterson was in a talkative mood, and Alyx hung around several more minutes, visiting.

Just as she prepared to leave, Scott pulled up out front. Happiness bloomed inside Alyx—until she noticed that Scott hadn't seen her yet. No, he had his eyes on Becky.

Swallowing her unease, Alyx whipped around to face the pharmacist with a false smile. "I guess I should be on my way. You have a great day, Mr. Peterson."

The pharmacist waved to her as she rushed out the door, only half hearing the chime that sounded. She intercepted Scott on the walkway. "Hey, handsome!" She went to her tiptoes and gave him a friendly smooch. "Want a drink of my soda?"

"Alyx." Scott, seeming very distracted by her sudden appearance, barely acknowledged her kiss. "What are you up to?"

"Nothing illegal." She hefted the bag in her left hand. "I had to pick up some things from the post office. What about you?"

He glanced into the pharmacy, his gaze on Becky. "I didn't see your car."

"No," Alyx said slowly, while her temper went up a notch. "I left it at the post office." And to see if he paid her any attention at all, she added, "I decided to crawl here."

Scott gave an absent smile. "I see."

That did it. She loved him like crazy, but apparently she'd been only a convenience to him. Now that another attractive female was in Visitation, Scott couldn't keep his eyes off her. Maybe it was time to do as Jamie said, and let Scott make a move.

"You know, Scott, I'm half inclined to dump my pink cow over your head, but truthfully, it tastes too good to waste that way." And Alyx pushed past him to leave.

As if he only then realized her pique, Scott snagged her from behind and pulled her back around to him. "Whoa. I'm sorry. I've got a lot on my mind." He smiled. "What were you saying?"

Damn it, why did she always end up looking foolish with Scott? Before, it hadn't mattered so much. But that was before . . . before her heart felt ready to break. "Forget it."

His brows shot up. "What's this? Withdrawal from a Winston?" Bending the few inches it took to have their gazes even, he said, "Come on, honey. Let me have it."

Alyx's eyes narrowed. "Have what?"

"The blast of your temper. You know you want to."

"No," Alyx said slowly, "actually I don't."

Scott drew back in surprise. "Why not?"

"Because truthfully, I'm tired of chasing you." And again, she started to walk away. But again, Scott brought her back around. "You're causing a scene," she hissed, and noticed Becky making her way out of the drugstore.

"Since when do you care about scenes?"

"Oh great. Here comes Blondie. Just what I *don't* need."

A knowing glint entered Scott's eyes. He leaned close to her ear and whispered, "Swallow down that jealousy, sweetheart."

A sharp breath nearly choked her. Alyx opened her mouth, ready to verbally slay him.

And he continued, saying, "I don't trust her, Alyx. Just play along, okay?"

Startled, Alyx frowned up at him, but Scott threw his arm around her shoulders and hauled her into his side, almost causing her to dump her ice-cream float.

He didn't trust Becky? Did that mean that he was onto her, too?

Becky paused, seeing the two of them cuddled so close. But not for long. "Deputy. It's so good to see you again."

Scott released Alyx to hold out a hand. "Becky, isn't it?"

Nonplussed that he might have forgotten, Becky said, "Yes. How are you?"

"Busy as always. And you?"

"Just picking up a few things."

Once again ignoring Alyx's presence, Scott peeked into Becky's bag at the magazines she'd bought. "I've seen you in town several times now. I take it our landscape doesn't appeal to you?"

Alyx wasn't a dope. It dawned on her that Scott was subtly interrogating the woman. Ready, willing, and able to help, especially since she had her own suspicions, Alyx spoke up before Becky could reply to Scott.

"Hi. I'm Alyx Winston." She didn't have a free hand to greet the woman and didn't particularly want to touch her anyway. "We sort of met that night on the road, but we weren't formally introduced."

Becky looked down her nose at Alyx. "Uh, hello."

"Where are you staying, Becky?"

Becky's gaze darted from Scott, who looked a

little stiff, to Alyx, who made a point of smiling like the village idiot.

"I rented a small cabin."

"No kidding? And you're hanging out in town?" She laughed. "You must not realize what a great lake we have here in Visitation. My brother runs it. There are always activities going on, everything from boating and swimming to fishing and sunbathing. Or you can hike one of the bird trails. Or maybe—"

"I'm not much of an outdoorswoman."

Alyx pretended great surprise. "Wow, that's weird. Doesn't make much sense to vacation in Visitation if you don't like nature. There's not much else to do here. I guess that's why you've visited the pharmacy so much, huh? Mr. Peterson, the pharmacist, says he's seen you a bunch of times."

Becky's mouth opened, but she failed to utter a single word.

Scott gave a quick glance at Alyx. With a tight smile, he said, "I think she must like the quiet time to read." And then to Becky, "I noticed you here not that long ago, and you bought some magazines then, too."

Becky actually flushed, and again, Alyx launched into speech. "Don't mind us. It's a small town, and everyone knows what everyone else is doing. That's just the way it is." She scooted closer to Scott and leaned her head against his rock-hard shoulder. "Isn't that right, Scott?"

"Pretty much."

Shaking her head as if to clear it, Becky said,

"Well, as to that, I had something to tell you." She peered around the sidewalk to ensure they had privacy, gave Alyx a dubious once-over, then whispered, "I noticed some young boys shoplifting."

That caught Scott off guard. He glared at Alyx, rightly assuming that if Becky had seen them, she had too.

Rolling one shoulder, Alyx said, "Yeah, I saw them." She took a drink of her float before explaining. "I was going to have a talk with them, make them come back in and pay for what they took."

Staring down at Alyx, Scott's eyes widened in disbelief and he flushed before he visibly got himself under control. "So you know them?" he asked with notable restraint.

"Of course." She didn't, not really. But she knew she could locate them.

"I see." Scott slid his arm around her shoulders again, and this time it felt more like confinement than a show of affection. Turning back to Becky, he affected a jovial tone. "Thanks for letting me know, Becky. I really do appreciate that. I'm sure Alyx would have given me the details anyway, but it's nice to know you're so honest and willing to get involved."

Clearing her throat, Becky said, "Yes, well . . . are there many young people in the area?"

"Same as anywhere else, I suppose."

"I'm willing to be a witness if you need one."

Scott asked, "To what?"

"The shoplifting."

Alyx laughed. "Scott won't need witnesses. He can handle it."

Scott's hand tightened on her shoulder. "She's

right, but again, I thank you." He tipped his hat. "It was nice chatting with you again, Becky. But now Alyx and I have to be going."

Uh-oh. Alyx didn't think that sounded good. And when Scott began steering her toward his cruiser, she considered refusing, then changed her mind and straightened her shoulders.

Scott opened the front passenger door and said, "Inside, sweetheart."

"Thank you." Hiding any misgivings, Alyx slid in and put her bag on the floor.

Scott stomped around the hood of the car and settled in beside her. "So."

Taking the offensive, Alyx said, "I don't like that woman."

Sidetracked, Scott said, "No, I don't either. But I don't think she fits the description of the woman Jamie is worried about."

Prepared to argue, Alyx opened her mouth— and his words sank in. He didn't like Becky, either? Did he have the same suspicions she had? She started to ask him. Then she realized the rest of what he'd said, and she frowned.

"Jamie's worried about a woman? Who? Faith?" Alyx laughed. "Let me tell you, he didn't look all that worried to me. More like hot and bothered."

"Not Faith, no. Delayna."

"Who's Delayna?"

Scott took in her confused expression and groaned in resignation. "Joe didn't tell you about her, did he?"

Anger sparking, Alyx said, "No, I've spoken to Big Brother only in passing lately." She'd been too busy snooping. "Why?"

More to himself than to her, Scott muttered, "He must have told only the men."

She'd box Joe's ears later. "Told only the men *what*, exactly?"

Scott dropped his head back. "Joe's going to be pissed, but what the hell?" He proceeded to tell her all about Jamie's getting a haircut and a shave, buying Faith clothes, and worrying that some evil woman from his past might be threatening Faith's daughter or maybe even Jamie himself.

And her brother hadn't said a word to her, the sexist pig. Why did Joe persist in thinking of her as a baby sister? "Hmmm. So you think Becky could actually be Delayna?"

"She's a stranger in town, and she's definitely female." Scott shrugged. "But Becky doesn't fit the description, and hell, she doesn't look like she could threaten a fly. It's probably just coincidence that she's here. Still, there's something about her I don't like."

So much confusion converged on Alyx that she could barely speak. Her worry for Jamie was very real. There were some strange things going on in Visitation, and she was starting to think they all had to do with Jamie.

And what about Scott? He'd actually confided in her. Alyx wanted to bust with happiness.

Joe might not want her involved, but Scott trusted her enough to tell her everything. Emotion lodged in her throat. How dumb. She *deserved* Scott's trust, but still, it felt like a concrete sign of intimacy— the kind of intimacy she craved.

Deciding to reciprocate, Alyx said, "About Becky—"

Grim, Scott interrupted her. "I don't want you involved, Alyx. From what Jamie said, this Delayna person could be very dangerous. And who knows? Maybe Becky is working with her. If you notice anything or anyone that doesn't look right to you, I expect you to call me."

He hadn't given her a chance to explain about Becky. "Of course I would, but—"

His eyes narrowed. "Just like you were going to tell me about the kids shoplifting?"

Inside, Alyx winced, but she kept her composure and spilled the truth. "Actually . . . I wasn't going to say anything about *that.*"

Scott went livid. "Yeah, I figured as much."

Alyx reached out a hand to grab his upper arm. "Listen, Scott, I could have lied to you and said I planned to tell you. But I don't ever want to lie to you. I want us to trust each other." *In everything.*

"Trust?" His laugh was hard and mean and lacking in any humor. "Right. So where's your trust for me, Alyx?"

Her mouth fell open. "I trust you completely!"

"Yeah, that's obvious in the way you hide things from me."

"I don't."

"What about visiting Jamie?"

Sighing, Alyx twisted closer to face him. "Jamie is a good friend. I care about him. That's why I want to—"

Scott interrupted her again. "And shoplifting kids? What justification would you have *not* to tell me about them?"

"I know you, Scott. If I'd told you about the boys, you'd feel obligated by law to go after them.

They're dumb kids, doing a dumb thing. But they might not be really *bad,* ya know?"

Scott didn't look convinced.

"I think they were just showing off for girls," Alyx explained. "But if they had agreed to come in and apologize to Mr. Peterson, and to pay for what they took, if I told them how close they'd gotten to serious trouble, maybe even gaining a criminal record, that might have been enough to set them back on the straight and narrow. That might have taught them a lesson that would affect the rest of their lives."

"And if it didn't?"

Alyx drew a calming breath. "If not, you could always get involved. But I didn't want it to go that far if it didn't have to."

"So you planned to confront them alone?"

She didn't like the way he said that, as if it indicated a lack of intelligence or something. "They're only teenage boys, Scott, maybe sixteen or so. Not grown men."

The contempt on Scott's face seared her. "Teenagers, Alyx? I know a lot of sixteen-year-old boys who would outweigh you, outmuscle you, and outrun you. Especially when there's more than one. At that age, they're more like wild animals than rational humans."

"Oh, for crying out loud." Alyx couldn't credit such a ridiculous comparison. Then again, she well remembered her brother at that age. . . .

Scott's teeth locked. "It's a period of raging testosterone, when guys feel the need to assert themselves. They're more confrontational, more aggressive." His voice rose in tandem with his anger. "They're boys on the verge of being men, and they're out to prove it. What the hell makes you think they'd welcome your interference with politeness?" And then in a growl, "What makes you think you could handle them on your own?"

And that, Alyx thought, seemed to be Scott's biggest complaint. Not that she might have let kids get away with trouble, but that she might have endangered herself rather than go to him.

In direct contrast to his mood, she kept her tone low and controlled. "I was going to see them in a public place, where it'd be safe. I recognized the car they drove, so I know they hang out at the lake a lot. Odds are they were going there when they left the drugstore. They all wore trunks, and the girls had on bikini tops."

"I don't believe this."

"Come on, Scott. I would have been fine. I promise."

Deflated, Scott rubbed his face. Alyx thought he looked tired as well as enraged, and that worried her.

"So tell me, Alyx. What makes you think I wouldn't have been just as sensitive to the situation as you would be?"

Alyx drew a blank. "I don't know."

"There you go. You don't know, but you automatically assume you're better able to handle it. Never mind the years I've been in law enforcement. Never mind my experience."

Guilt assailed Alyx, but Scott didn't give her a chance to apologize.

"Have you seen me tossing kids in jail? Have you seen me overreacting to situations?"

Cautiously, Alyx said, "No."

"You're right that I would have gone after them. And if they didn't have any priors—which isn't something you could check, by the way—then I probably would have done exactly as you suggested. I also would've notified their parents, so they could get involved. Parents deserve to know what their kids are doing. More than any law official, more than any meddling citizen"—he looked at Alyx, leaving no doubt whom he considered the meddling citizen to be—"parents can influence their kids."

"You're right, Scott, and I'm sorry." Feeling burdened by more than just the topic under discussion, Alyx rubbed his shoulder in a gesture of appeasement. "I guess we have a lot to get worked out once I move in, huh?"

Scott froze, then slowly raised his face. His expression guarded, he took Alyx's hand and held it tight.

"I've been meaning to talk to you about that." He drew a long, deep breath, as if preparing himself. "This morning in fact. But . . . the timing just never seemed right."

Something inside Alyx went cold and dark. "Talk to me about what?"

"Moving in." Another deep breath, then Scott's eyes gentled and his gaze became direct, almost compelling. "I'm not sure living together is the right way to go."

Alyx's heart lurched into a too-fast, too-hard, frantic beat. She'd love him forever . . . maybe he just needed more time.

Though sickness churned in her belly, she forced

a smile. "It's an ideal situation. No real commitment, no legal ties, so . . . *neither of us* will feel trapped."

Eyes closing, Scott cursed under his breath.

Oh God, the thought of losing him left Alyx panicked. "You'll be able to come and go as you please. I'll be able to come and go. What could be better?"

Scott's face darkened. "Have you thought about how that's going to look to everyone?"

Relying on pure bravado, Alyx shrugged. "Hey, these are modern times. Lots of people cohabitate."

"Alyx." He said her name in soft rebuke. "Like you told Becky, this is a small town and we do things differently here. That day I found you with Willow made me stop and consider how awkward it might be."

Awkward? Damn, it hurt. Wanting to deny his words, Alyx shook her head.

But Scott persisted. "What if Willow asks you why you're living with me? What would you tell her? That we're just shacking up? What if she decides she wants to go off with Clay, too? And I respect your brother, honey. He won't like it if we're—"

"I see." Belatedly, Alyx found her backbone. She really didn't need Scott to say any more. No matter how he explained it, the statement was clear: he didn't want her moving in after all.

Knowing she was going to lose it at any second, Alyx jerked her hand free from Scott's and wrenched at the door handle.

"Alyx, wait." Scott reached for her shoulder, but she shrugged him off and finally the door opened.

She tumbled out so fast that she nearly spilled her now-melted ice-cream float. A garbage can sat close to the curb, and Alyx tossed the drink inside. Her stomach churned too much to put anything more in it.

She heard Scott's door opening, knew he wanted to offer up more lame excuses—excuses that all amounted to a rejection that hurt more than anything she'd ever experienced in her life. *Let me have my pride,* she silently prayed.

Smiling wasn't easy, but Alyx managed it. "Hey, it's okay, Scott. No big deal." She held up a hand to halt him. "I understand. And sure, we can talk about it more later if you want." After she had a chance to regroup, to summon up her arrogance so she could get through it without tears.

Scott kept his gaze glued to her face. "I want to talk now. This is important. Just because I don't want to—"

"Can't." Alyx hustled backward, moving farther and farther away. With her façade crumbling fast, she just knew she'd die if she fell apart in front of Scott. "I've got a ton of things to do. Lots of things. Really."

Concern—and something else—showed on Scott's face. "But . . . I bought you something."

A present to soften the blow? No way. She had almost reached the corner. In three more steps, she'd be out of sight. "No need for gifts, Deputy. The sex was good, but I agree, it probably wasn't enough to warrant shared living quarters."

Raw anger flashed on his face. "It was more than sex, Alyx, and you know it."

Sure . . . more, *but not enough.* "Later, Scott." With a quick wave, Alyx ducked away, and the second she was out of sight, tears burned her throat and blurred her vision.

Determined to hide her wretched weakness, she sprinted to her car in the post-office parking lot, lumbered inside, and fumbled with her keys until she got them in the ignition.

"Stupid, stupid, stupid." Sniffing hard, Alyx tossed her bag from the post office out of her way and slipped on sunglasses to hide any signs of emotion. Her hands shook as she put the Mazda in gear and pulled out of the lot. When she turned the corner, she couldn't help but glance toward the drugstore.

Scott still stood outside by his car, one hand braced on the hood, his head down. He looked dejected, damn him. He looked hurt.

And like a lovesick idiot, she couldn't stand to see him like that.

Alyx needed a distraction and fast. She needed to vent. She needed—

Up ahead, barely visible in the roadway, Alyx spotted a recognizable car—and with a smile of mean intent, she stepped on the gas. The timing couldn't be more perfect.

Becky would give her just the distraction she needed.

Jamie carried in the bags of clothes he'd forgotten on the porch. He hoped they might serve to soften the blow when he gave Faith the news. She had just finished doing morning dishes, and Jamie dropped everything on the table to free his hands so he could hug her from behind.

"How do you feel?"

Faith laughed. "You keep asking me that, and I keep telling you, I'm fine."

"Very fine." Jamie nibbled on her nape and got a soft sigh in return. He adored Faith's sighs, just as he adored her fragrant skin, her silly chatter, her carnal nature that exploded with him.

"Okay," Faith said on a long breath. "The truth is, I'm sated. Full. Very soft in the head and the body, and my legs are like overcooked noodles, and my skin is still tingly."

"All that, huh?" Jamie grinned against her shoulder. And God, it was starting to feel natural, smiling so much. Having *reason* to smile. "You weakened my legs a little, too."

Turning her head to peer at Jamie over her shoulder, Faith raised a brow. "Only a little?"

"And good thing." He stepped away from her, and braced himself for the arguments he knew would come. "Because I need to make another trip down the mountain."

The peacefulness that had surrounded her moments before now turned to alarm. She jerked around to face him, soapsuds and water dripping from her hands. *"Why?"*

"I'm sorry. It's necessary."

Anger mixed with the alarm. "Oh, no, you don't. That is not an explanation, Jamie Creed."

"And you're not my wife. I don't have to explain myself to you." She looked wounded, making Jamie frown. What he said was true, but damn it, he didn't like seeing her disappointment.

He couldn't relent, but he could give her a partial truth. "I wouldn't go if I didn't have to. Believe me, Faith, I'd rather stay here, preferably with you naked and in bed."

Faith colored before she began drying her hands in a rush. "Fine." She tossed the dishtowel aside. "I'll go with you." She headed toward the bathroom in a militant march.

Jamie caught her shoulders, drawing her to a halt. "No."

Her chin shot up. "I'm going and that's it."

He hadn't expected this, hadn't seen it coming. But Faith in a mutinous mood was kind of cute. He wished he could accommodate her, except that wouldn't be fair to Scott.

"I said no, Faith." On the heels of that rejection, he caught her to him for a hug and gave her an explanation after all. "I'm sorry. But it's a personal matter. Not my personal matter, but someone else's. And I don't think he'd appreciate an audience."

Her hands fisted against his shirt.

"Come on, Faith. Give it up." Jamie didn't want to leave with her upset. "I shouldn't be gone long, just long enough to go down the mountain, have a talk with someone, and come back up. An hour or so at the most."

Confused, Faith tipped her head back and stared up at him. "You mean someone is down there waiting for you?"

"Not exactly, no. He thinks he's going to come

up here to see me later in the day. That's his plan."
A plan that would put Scott behind schedule on
events that demanded immediate attention. "But
what I have to tell him won't wait until later. So I'm
going down instead."

Scott had a habit of driving the deserted back
roads a couple of times a day. He liked to ensure
that all stayed secure. Jamie suspected he might
also make the drive to check up on him, although
Scott would never admit it.

Jamie kissed Faith's forehead, and wanted to go
on kissing her, everywhere. He found it impossible
to keep his hands off her, a fact that made him feel
weak and strong at the same time. "I'll be back before you can miss me."

Shaking her head, Faith said, "Not possible, because I miss you already." Then she hugged him
tight. "But I won't be a baby about it. As long as I
know you're coming back, I'll be fine."

"I live here," Jamie reminded her. "Where else
would I go?"

Shrugging, Faith moved away and kept her gaze
averted. "I don't know. But since you are coming
back, well then, it's no big deal, right?"

Jamie frowned. Before giving that cavalier retort, Faith slammed the door on her thoughts. He
hadn't been exactly reading her, but when she
shut him out, Jamie felt it like a chill down his
spine or a cutting insult. He didn't like it. Was she
up to something?

Probably. Why else deny him access to her
thoughts?

Unless she simply didn't want him to know how

much she'd miss him. Maybe Faith felt the need to protect her heart as much as Jamie did.

If he had her beneath him, if he had her aroused, she wouldn't be able to shut him out. Jamie glanced at the clock and saw there wasn't enough time for what he wanted. Once he started, he'd need at least half an hour. Maybe more. Resigned to waiting, he decided he'd seduce her later.

Or maybe he'd let her seduce him.

Faith pasted on a bright smile that made his suspicions grow. "So," she asked with annoying cheerfulness, indicating the bags on the table. "What's all this?"

Jamie spent the next few minutes showing Faith the things he'd bought her. She oohed and aahed over several feminine T-shirts, grinned over a pair of funky jeans that would fit her ass like a glove, and laughed at the sexy, barely there panties he'd chosen. To Jamie's surprise, her enjoyment, even over a pair of soft white socks and plain sneakers, seemed genuine.

Because he'd never had anyone to buy for, he'd never experienced the pleasure of giving gifts. It awed him that the gesture affected him as much as it did Faith.

While Faith shimmied into the panties and jeans, Jamie settled back in his chair to enjoy the show. "It'll all fit," he told her.

Picking up a T-shirt to go with the jeans, Faith said, "I think so."

"No," Jamie corrected, watching the jiggle of her breasts, glad that he hadn't bought her a bra. "I wasn't asking. I'm telling you—it will fit."

"Oh." Faith laughed, tugged the shirt over her head, and came to sit on his lap. Arms looped around his neck, her rounded bottom right where Jamie preferred it, she asked, "You knew my size?"

Jamie kissed her forehead. "It's here, inside you. All I had to do was take the information."

"Well, thank you. I love surprises." Laughing, she added, "I feel like a kid at Christmas."

The expression she wore prompted Jamie to place her palm flat on his chest. He wanted to see what Faith described, but she still had him blocked, denying him. "Let me in, Faith. Let me see what Christmas is like."

Faith went still, her eyes big and full of disbelief. "Oh my God. Jamie . . . you've never celebrated Christmas?"

"No." He held her wrist, keeping her hand over his heart. "Why would I have?"

Sadness filled her gaze, and her bottom lip quivered. Jamie squeezed her close. "No, baby, please don't. I don't like it when you cry." Seeing her sad hurt him, too.

Faith's hold was so tight and her feelings so strong that when she opened herself, her vivid memories slammed into Jamie, rocking his composure.

Festive lights, scents of pine and cinnamon. Brightly colored packages, swirling ribbons. Singing and laughter. Storybooks and anticipation. Jamie drew a shuddering breath, overwhelmed with it all, but determined to take in everything that he could.

He saw Cory, warm and sleepy from her bed, still dressed in a flannel gown with fuzzy slippers on her feet. He saw her hair tumbling around her small face and her eyes full of excitement. He saw Faith, sitting to the side in a yellow robe, her contentment and love tinged by melancholy. And he felt the hugs, from Faith's mother and father, from her brother and Cory, and from Faith herself.

"We have big dinners," Faith whispered against his throat. "It's not formal in any way, more like an eating frenzy with everyone talking and laughing at once. So many desserts, you feel sick afterward. We sing silly songs, like 'Rudolf' and 'Frosty the Snowman,' and religious songs, like 'Away in a Manger' and 'Silent Night.' We have snow fights and ice-skating with hot chocolate and cinnamon sticks. And there are gifts galore. Nothing too expensive, but presents full of caring. There are holiday cartoons and movies that make you laugh and cry. And lots and lots of love."

Experiencing it all through Faith, Jamie nodded. What she'd had, and what she shared with him now, contrasted sharply with the composed cycle of his life. Being honest, Jamie admitted, "I didn't know there was something so special that I'd missed."

He'd known only that isolation was necessary, so he'd accepted it. The thought of how much *living* he might have wasted made Jamie sick at heart. For only a brief moment, he indulged the impossible and wondered what it'd be like for him to share the holidays with Faith and her family.

As if she somehow knew of his cravings, Faith slid her hands up to cup his face. She kissed his chin, then his mouth. Her forehead to his, she asked, "You never thought about a family gathering for the holidays?"

Jamie shook his head, but then he did consider the various families he knew. He pictured Joe and Luna on Christmas morning with Willow and Austin—and to his surprise, his vision of Luna showed her big with child.

"Oh shit."

Faith half laughed at his strangled curse. "What is it?"

Jamie shook his head. "I just realized something." He concentrated again, this time on Shay and Bryan, and sure enough, Shay wore maternity clothes. Jamie wondered if the husbands knew, but accepted right off that they didn't. He laughed, imagining their reactions when they found out.

In the middle of that vision, a gun blast sounded, echoing through Jamie's system, chasing away the more pleasant images and jarring him back to the present.

Heart pounding, Jamie realized that the cabin was as silent as ever. The gun played into the future, the very near future, and he had to move now to ensure no one got hurt.

He lifted Faith off his lap. "I have to go."

As he went to the door and pushed his feet into his boots, Faith kept on his heels. "Is everything okay?"

"It will be. But I have to get moving." Jamie opened the door, started out, and then paused long enough to turn back to Faith, lift her up to her tiptoes, and kiss her silly. "I'll be back as quick as I can."

Her smile trembled. "All right. Be careful, please."

To Jamie's surprise, having a woman worry about him didn't feel half bad. He nodded, kissed her again, and left before he wasted too much time.

Lingering could jeopardize the people he cared about. And Jamie would never do that.

Chapter Fourteen

Driving the winding roads by rote, Scott considered his suspicions that Knute might be dealing some dope. He'd certainly been high when Scott had last visited him, and he'd been more antsy than usual about anyone getting near his house. But, Scott reasoned, Lamar couldn't grow enough marijuana in his house to make it profitable. And if he wanted only a buzz, he'd likely stick to his whisky.

Scott wanted to check out Lamar's land, but to do it right, he'd need a search warrant. He doubted he'd be able to make a good case for that, so maybe he'd do a little discreet snooping first—on the side.

Even to his own ears, that plan sounded unethical.

Damn it, sometimes his conscience was a pain in the ass. Not that he'd let his conscience stop him. Not this time. Not when he badly needed *something* to distract him.

Pushing that black thought aside, Scott mentally composed the questions he planned to ask Jamie. He'd wait until Lamar left for the bars, as he always did before dinnertime, and after he checked out Lamar's place, he'd visit with Jamie to confirm or disprove his role as a vigilante.

That plan brought his thoughts full circle, back to Alyx. In order to find Jamie's cabin, he'd probably need Alyx to give him directions. That would at least give him a good excuse to get in touch with her, to spend time with her. To . . . damn.

She'd played on his mind all day. He wanted to marry her, but she wanted freedom. He'd bought her a ring. He'd been ready to propose.

Watching her walk away from him had burned like acid in his guts.

Then iron determination had taken over.

For months, Alyx had chased after him, running him to ground, then stealing his heart. It was time for her games to end—because he was through playing.

One way or another, Alyx Winston would understand that she belonged with him.

Scott turned the bend in the road, close to where he'd found Alyx after her last trip to see Jamie. To his surprise, a stranger emerged from the trees. A thousand possibilities ran through Scott's mind, none of them pleasant. He braked hard, shoved the car into park, and reached for his gun.

Fear for Jamie sent his adrenaline surging.

Then the man lifted his hand in a gesture that seemed far too familiar. Cautiously, Scott stepped out of the cruiser. He kept the car between him and the other man, his gun in his hand, his instincts at the ready.

The stranger's gaze connected with his.

Like a kick to the lungs, realization dawned, making Scott wheeze. *Jamie?*

No way. Scott left the dubious safety of the side of the cruiser and moved forward with the numbness of a zombie. He couldn't blink. He couldn't speak.

"Don't swallow your tongue," Jamie grouched, and he ran a hand over his much shorter hair.

Scott's leaden feet finally drew him to a halt. He couldn't stop staring. "It's . . . incredible."

Full of sarcasm, the new Jamie said, "Yeah, who knew I was human under all that hair?"

Disbelief turned Scott's voice raspy. "You're a good-looking guy."

Jamie smirked. "Yeah, so Joe already told me, and he sounded about as thrilled as you do. What'd you guys think? That I'd grown the beard because I was hideous?"

"I don't know."

Jamie rolled his eyes. "Get over it, will you? We have to talk."

Finally, Scott gathered his scattered wits enough to grin. "You know, I just wasn't prepared. Even though Joe mentioned all the changes, I didn't expect—"

"Yeah, whatever," Jamie said. He folded his arms over his chest. "And the changes are why you think I might be overstepping myself."

Chagrined that Jamie already knew, Scott lost his humor and frowned. "Sorry, Jamie. I hate to ac-

cuse you of anything, but the circumstances are
such that I have to ask."

"I know."

Right. Jamie always knew. It was the part of his
personality that annoyed Scott most.

Jamie propped his hands on his hips. "It's not
me, Scott."

"Okay." Scott accepted Jamie's word on it. "How
long have you known?"

"About the *guy* who wears a mask and is attack-
ing some of Visitation's not-so-sterling citizens, all
in the hopes of luring me out?"

"So that's the motivation?"

"I think so. But I haven't known all that long. In
fact, it's still a bit confusing."

Something in Jamie's tone warned Scott that he
wouldn't be enjoying this conversation. He put his
gun away and lounged back against the hood of
the cruiser. "I suppose you know who it is?"

"I know someone who's involved." Tense and
evasive, Jamie paced away. "The thing is, I'm not
sure how you're going to react." He glanced at
Scott. "And that's strange, because normally I would
be. So maybe you don't even know how to react."

"What the hell does that mean?"

Jamie locked his gaze on Scott's. "Maybe you
know what I know, and you just don't want to
admit it to yourself."

The short hairs on the back of Scott's neck
stood on end. His stomach bottomed out. His
lungs squeezed tight.

Only one person had ever had that devastating
effect on his system.

Straightening away from the car, Scott stared at Jamie in growing horror. Praying that Jamie would deny it, Scott shook his head. "Not Alyx."

But Jamie didn't change expression.

Tall. Dark hair. Able to kick ass . . . "Ah, shit, *no.*" Tunneling all ten fingers into his hair, Scott knocked his hat to the ground. "Couldn't you be wrong?"

Jamie gave him a pitying look. "I've seen her there." He tapped his forehead. "Up here, I mean. But other than that, I haven't put it all together yet."

For the love of . . . Scott started breathing hard, on the verge of hyperventilating with fear, exploding with anger, or both.

Every muscle in his body contracted as he faced the horrible truth, a truth he hadn't even wanted to consider.

Alyx was the vigilante.

Anger won. *"What the hell is she thinking?"*

As enigmatic as ever, Jamie shrugged. "Like I said, I'm not certain yet. But maybe she wants to help you. Maybe she wants to tempt me off the mountain so that she can help me, too. Maybe she just wants to help . . . everyone." Still holding Scott's gaze, Jamie drove home his point. "Just as you and her brother have done time and again."

Scott howled. He put his head back and let out a furious animal roar of frustration that echoed around the mountains. It didn't alleviate one iota of his rage. What would he do with Alyx? When he got hold of her, should he arrest her, hug her—turn her over his knee?

"I wouldn't try that," Jamie said, half smiling.

The smile was enough to stump Scott, because it sure as hell wasn't what he usually got from Jamie.

But then Jamie pondered aloud, "Alyx respects you and her brother more than anyone. And while you both care about her, neither of you acknowledge her capability. Alyx is actually damn good at anything she does."

Scott gave him a blank stare.

"Even fighting," Jamie explained.

Scott shook his head. "She's a woman."

"Yeah, uh, I'm glad you said that to me and not her. Alyx would castrate you if you disregarded her just because of her sex."

When Jamie stepped closer, Scott had the faint suspicion he enjoyed himself. Especially when he said, "Alyx is not your ordinary female."

And this was news?

"No kidding, Jamie. I figured that out about five seconds after meeting her, when she knocked me into a pile of mud." Scott rubbed his face, angry, sick with the realization of what could have happened to her, and insulted that Alyx thought he needed help.

Jamie made a sound of disgust. "She knows you don't *need* help, Scott." He narrowed his eyes and added, "But she doesn't know that you need *her.*"

It wasn't easy to admit the truth to Jamie, but after watching Alyx walk away from him, Scott figured he could use a little help. "I love her."

"Yeah, I know." Jamie's mouth twitched with yet another smile.

"I tried to tell her, but . . . it didn't go well."

"I know."

Thinking he maybe liked Jamie better when he wasn't so damn jolly, Scott glared. "Is there any fucking thing you don't know?"

To Scott's surprise, Jamie's expression darkened, and his smile faded. Turning away, Jamie whispered, "You have no idea."

Scott realized that he'd stepped in it. And honestly, Jamie's distance had always pained him. As the deputy, Scott wanted to take care of everyone in his town, but more often than not, that duty had fallen to Jamie.

Now Jamie might need his help, and Scott wanted him to know he could count on him. Clasping Jamie's shoulder, Scott said, "I'm sorry. Alyx has me half nuts."

Jamie nodded in acknowledgement of that. "You didn't tell her you loved her."

"What?"

Locking gazes with Scott, Jamie said, "You didn't tell her. You just told her that you didn't want to live with her."

"I want to marry her."

"But you didn't tell her that."

"I . . ." Scott frowned. "She doesn't want to commit."

"No, she doesn't want to do anything to drive you away."

Scott just blinked, totally confused.

"She's chased you since she met you."

"I've always let her catch me."

"Big of you. But don't you think she'd like to be chased once? Alyx isn't used to loving anyone but family. She's feeling a little vulnerable and out of sorts. And all you did was tell her you didn't want to live with her." Jamie shrugged.

"Oh, shit."

"Yeah."

"She loves me, too?"

"Yeah."

It was an awkward moment. Scott didn't know if he should shout, laugh, or give Jamie a bear hug.

"No hugging," Jamie warned.

"Right." Fighting a smile of pure happiness, Scott said, "Thank you. I should go now. I need to find her." He hesitated. "Listen, Jamie, if there's anything, anything at all that I can do to help—"

"I know," Jamie said again.

Scott couldn't help it—he laughed.

With a crooked half smile, Jamie said, "I guess I need some new punch lines, don't I?"

"I have a feeling you'll soon have plenty."

Jamie's expression sobered Scott, sending his humor away as quickly as it had appeared.

"What is it?" Scott asked.

"Nothing. Something. I'm just not sure." Jamie dropped his head forward in thought. "I sort of feel . . . threatened." He looked up at Scott, and for once, appeared helpless, maybe even bewildered. "That's damn unusual, even though Faith said I might need her help. I'm used to sensing the menace toward others. It's different now, though."

Scott went rigid. "I'll call Clint. We'll find out what the hell is going on. We'll stick close. No one is going to get a chance to hurt you."

Visibly ill at ease, Jamie frowned. "Yeah, as to that . . . Alyx has gone to see Knute."

And just that quick, Scott's blood ran cold. *"What?"*

"She's snooping for you. She hopes to find out about the pot."

"The pot? *Shit.*" So there was marijuana, and Alyx had beat him to the draw.

"I can take care of myself," Jamie assured him. "You need to see to Alyx."

Scott had already turned away, driven by a blind urgency to protect Alyx before she got hurt. He reached the driver's door in three long strides and jerked it open.

"You have just enough time," Jamie called after him. "Go in quiet."

Go in . . . Did that mean Knute would find Alyx in her stupid disguise? *Oh God.*

Jamie said. "He'll find you both. But it should be okay. Just don't waste any time getting out there."

Through the open window, Scott shouted, "Damn it, Jamie, you could have said something sooner instead of just chewing the fat." He turned the key, and the engine roared to life.

Jamie snatched up the hat Scott had forgotten, stepped back and gave a careless wave as the spinning tires of the cruiser kicked up rock and dust before gripping the gravel road. Stepping on the gas, Scott spun the car around to head to Knute's. *If that drunken idiot hurts one hair on her head . . .*

He raced for Knute's house, all the while praying that he'd make it in time. He needed Alyx. To argue with, to make love to, to share his days and his nights.

Life wouldn't be right without her.

And once he got her safe, he'd make her understand just what she meant to him.

Jamie waited until the cruiser was out of sight. Slapping Scott's hat against his thigh, he concentrated, searching for the odd threat that he'd felt.

Before he could locate it, a twig snapped. Jamie jerked around, startled that anyone had snuck up on him but prepared to fight if necessary. His muscles bunched and his adrenaline shot into overdrive.

He came face-to-face with Faith.

Seeing him in attack mode, she froze, guilt, embarrassment, then annoyance showing clear in her blue eyes. She went on the offensive, thrusting her chin into the air and propping her hands on her hips.

"Don't you look at me like that. I know you said I should stay in the cabin, but I couldn't stand the wait. So I followed you. Sort of."

Jamie stared at Faith. What wait? She must have left the cabin seconds behind him to be down the mountain so quickly.

"I lost you back a ways," Faith continued in a grumbling tone. "But I could hear you, and so I just followed the sound of voices. I couldn't make out the conversation, so your friend's privacy is still protected. No reason for you to be angry with me. No reason at all. But I do have a few grievances with you."

Jamie drew a steadying breath, but he couldn't relieve the tension that held him in its grip. "What are you talking about, Faith?"

"I ran into some nasty bugs. One bit me."

She lifted her arm to show Jamie a raised red welt near her elbow.

The sense of foreboding increased, keeping Jamie quiet.

Making a face, Faith trudged down a few more feet, slipping once, swearing under her breath. "I've got scratches, too. Right here." As if she somehow blamed Jamie for that as well, she showed him the side of her neck, where a thorny bush had grazed her delicate skin.

Jamie flattened his mouth. That Faith might have followed on his heels had never occurred to him, proving that she'd once again been able to close him out of her thoughts. He didn't like it—but at the same time, it made her so very different from any other woman he'd known.

Whether or not that was a good thing, Jamie couldn't decide. But the facts that Faith was here now and that he had a growing sense of unease confused him. Surely, Faith wasn't the source of the unease.

She shook a finger at him. "You're not an easy man to track, Jamie Creed. I figured if I tried to follow you too closely, you'd hear me. But keeping my thoughts blocked while trying to see you and not make any noise didn't make it easy to get down that stupid mountain."

She stepped closer, and finally stood in front of Jamie, her arms crossed over her chest, her head tipped back to glare up at him. "If you'd agreed to let me come along, none of this would have happened."

The tension grew until Jamie felt ready to break

with it. He gripped Faith's shoulders. "Open yourself to me. Right now."

Alarmed, she dropped her militant stance and her mouth fell open. "What's wrong?"

"I don't know." He gently shook her. "Stop blocking me, Faith." If the threat came from Faith, Jamie would know it once she let him in.

"All right," Faith gently agreed. She smiled up at him, and her thoughts became crystal clear. Caring. Worry. Tenderness. Protectiveness . . . It was the last that threw Jamie for a loop.

"You think to protect me?"

"If I can. Don't you see? I don't know what's wrong. Just as you can't always figure things out, Cory can't either. She said I needed to be with you. She said I needed to stay close. But you keep running off on your own, and I can't bear it." Pressing closer, Faith put her arms around him and laid her head on his chest. "I'm sorry, Jamie. I know I'm rushing you, and I know you don't completely trust me. I know you can't possibly understand. But . . . I care about you. I always have." Her arms tightened. "I know I always will."

It took Jamie a few seconds to make sense of Faith's words, to absorb the depth and complexity of her feelings. But when he did, his knees weakened. The emotion in Faith's heart was unshakable, a tidal wave of sincerity that washed through Jamie, leaving him weak and yet filling him with strength.

Shaken, Jamie tangled his fingers in her hair, and his eyes closed to savor the moment.

Faith squeezed in tighter and, with the need for reassurance in her tone, whispered, "Jamie?"

The sound of a car saved Jamie from trying to form words. "Something's wrong," he told her. "I don't know what, damn it, but something is." He put Faith behind him and turned to see who approached.

Given the tumultuous mix of emotions bombarding Jamie's senses, it amazed him that he'd heard the car. On every level, he was aware of Faith curled against his back, her hands on his waist, her nose touching his spine.

Rigid and waiting, Jamie studied the bend in the road and let out a breath when Joe's truck came into view. "It's okay," he told Faith, but added, "at least for now."

Because the sense of a threat remained, stronger than ever.

Chapter Fifteen

Now that he'd alerted Clint to Jamie's predicament, Scott's thoughts were free to center solely on the situation with Alyx. It occurred to him that he hadn't questioned Jamie's prediction. Jamie said Alyx would be at Knute's, that she'd be in trouble, and he accepted it as fact.

And because Jamie told him to go in quiet, Scott kept the lights and sirens off, and pulled the cruiser into a field adjacent to Knute's overgrown acreage. Leaving the car in near silence and bending low, Scott hurried across the field until he could see the back of Knute's house.

He scanned the area, looking for Alyx or Knute or both. His gaze caught on a flash of red barely visible in the woods to the left. Alyx's red Mazda. Damn.

Almost at the same time that Scott spotted the car, Knute came out of his house. As disheveled and filthy as ever, but moving with sure-footed purpose, Knute strode toward a dilapidated shed at the outer edge of his property.

At a discreet distance, still crouching, Scott followed. As Knute went around the right side of the shed, a tall, dark-haired figure materialized on the left. And Scott's mouth tightened.

Without a disguise, Alyx flattened herself against the raw boards and peered around the corner at Knute. Apparently deciding the coast was clear, she sprinted away from the shed.

And unknowingly made a beeline toward Scott.

It amazed Scott how little noise she made, given the tall weeds, roots, and broken branches on the ground. She reached a tree and darted behind it, then glanced back again to make sure she hadn't drawn Knute's attention.

But Knute stayed busy examining a hidden growth of marijuana. Not enough to be truly alarming, but more than any one man would need. Scowling, Scott ruminated on plans to lock Lamar Knute away while somehow managing to keep Alyx uninvolved.

He wanted badly to protect her, to remove her from the situation right now. But any movement from him might give her away, and he wouldn't risk that.

Then Alyx pushed away from the tree in another mad dash. Unfortunately, her flight sent several crows screeching into the air—and Knute looked up.

She damn near stepped on Scott before he reached out and snagged her ankle. To her credit, she didn't make a sound while falling, and the second Scott's arms went around her, she went still.

Against her ear, Scott breathed, "Shhh. Knute is looking."

Alyx nodded, but otherwise didn't move a single muscle. Scott wondered which alarmed her more— Knute . . . or himself.

When enough time had passed with no noise, Scott lifted his head and surveyed the area. He didn't see a single soul. Had Knute gone back to his house? Or farther into the field?

Alyx whispered, "Coast is clear?"

"Seems to be."

"He's growing pot."

Scott looked down at the crazy, fearless woman he loved so damn much and considered throttling her. Nose to nose with her, in a whisper that matched her own, he said, "Yeah, I know." Then, his eyes narrowed, he asked, "Where's your disguise, Alyx?"

"My . . . ?" Alyx's eyes widened. "You think I'm the vigilante?"

"I'm not an idiot." Scott didn't bother explaining what Jamie had told him.

"Not about most things, no." Alyx sighed and sprawled out on her back in the itchy weeds. She stared up at the cloudless blue sky. "You want to know the truth, Scott? If I was going to attack someone, it'd be face-to-face, not hiding behind a mask."

Scott called himself ten times an idiot, but seeing Alyx on her back, hearing the husky hush of her voice, made him think of things he shouldn't. He had to keep in mind that they were presently on Lamar Knute's property without proper authorization, and Lamar was involved in growing an illegal substance.

Ignoring the rise of Alyx's breasts beneath her green blouse and the sexy length of her long legs stretched out in front of her, Scott summoned the voice of calm and reason. "You're telling me it's not you?"

She didn't look at him. "That's right."

"But Jamie said he'd seen you . . ."

"Yeah. I was there." Very smug, she said, "Following Becky."

"Becky?"

"Shhh."

"What the hell are you talking about?"

"I think she's the vigilante. She's the right height, probably the right weight." Her shoulder lifted. "And I think she has something to do with Jamie."

"Ohmigod. Jamie did say that the vigilante wanted to get him off the mountain."

Alyx pushed up on one elbow. "Maybe because she can't find him otherwise."

A flood of awful scenarios ripped through Scott. His teeth locked. "Do you mean to tell me that you suspected all this—and still you followed her?"

"Hey, I'm taking an interest in the community. If you don't like it, well, what can you do? Break things off with me?" She snorted. "Oh, wait, I forgot. You already did that."

Frustration sharpened his tone. "I did not break things off. I was trying to—"

"Ha!" In a sudden rush, Alyx pushed into a sitting position.

Scott caught her arm. The urge to tell her his

feelings, to propose, burned in his throat, but now wasn't the time. "We can talk about this later, honey. But for right now—"

"For right now, I'm outta here." Alyx shook off his hold. "Lamar's out of sight, so now's a good time for me to hit the road."

Again, Scott snagged her arm in a gentle hold. "Be reasonable, Alyx. You can't go trooping across the field."

"I didn't intend to."

Scott sighed. "Then you're going to have a long walk ahead of you. Leave with me, and I'll drive you around to your car."

"Thanks but no thanks." She didn't quite look at him. "I'd rather walk."

At her flat, emotionless tone, Scott released her.

Crouching, just as he'd done, Alyx darted away and disappeared into a line of wild brush and skinny trees.

"Damn stubborn woman." Scott didn't want to let Alyx leave before he'd explained a few things, but she was in no mood to listen to him, and hiding in the woods wasn't exactly the best place to convince her. He reasoned that by letting her go, she'd at least be safely away from the situation. Once they were both well off Lamar's land, he'd have plenty of time to start mending fences.

Determined to be patient, Scott lay low, keeping an eye on Knute's land and house while waiting for Alyx to reach her car. He waited. And waited a few minutes more.

And when he still saw no sign of Alyx, he began to worry. Where the hell had she gone? Alyx wasn't a woman who ever dawdled. She should have gotten to her car and left already. But he could see a peek of her red Mazda hidden in the woods.

Loving Alyx was likely to give him heart failure, considering how often she made his heartbeat hammer. Right now, he instinctively knew something had gone wrong.

Creeping forward, his gaze constantly scanning the area, Scott heard the voices before he saw Alyx and Lamar Knute.

"Forget it, Knute. You don't scare me."

No, Scott thought. Alyx didn't sound scared. Pissed maybe. But in no way worried.

Fury rang from Knute's tone. "You got no business snooping around on my property."

With a shrug in her tone, Alyx said, "So sue me. And then I'll just tell everyone about your little crop of pot."

"Bitch!"

"Slimeball."

A heavy silence, fraught with sudden comprehension, hung in the air. Knute bristled with accusation. "I know another fella that called me a slimeball."

"I'm not surprised," Alyx quipped. "It suits you."

Scott heard twigs and leaves crunch beneath heavy boots and knew it was Lamar's drunken stomping. Creeping closer, Scott ducked behind a large rock and a growth of wild blackberry bushes. When he peered around the rock, he saw Knute crowding near Alyx, holding what looked like a hunter's knife in his hand.

His blood ran cold. If Lamar decided to strike, he'd likely cut Alyx before she'd have a chance to escape—before he'd have a chance to reach her.

Alyx, damn her, examined a fingernail and kept her stance relaxed.

Focused and full of fury, Scott crouched, his thighs tensed, ready to launch himself at Knute. He didn't want to announce his presence for fear of startling Knute. Drunks were often dangerous enough. But a drunk with a knife . . . No, Scott wouldn't chance it.

Slow and full of menace, Knute snarled, "That son of a bitch hit me with a stick."

"Yeah?" Alyx glanced up. "Too bad he—or should I say she?—didn't break your fool neck."

"It *was* you!"

Alyx smiled. "If it was me, Knute, you wouldn't have gotten up." Taunting Knute, she leaned closer. "I could hit you, and you wouldn't even see it coming."

Knute's eyes widened.

With a silent curse at Alyx's lack of caution, Scott threw himself out of the hiding spot and toward them both. At the same time, Knute bellowed and lunged for Alyx.

To Scott's disbelief, Alyx reacted so quickly her movements were almost a blur. Stepping to the side to avoid the thrust of the sharp knife, she grabbed Knute's arm and flung him forward, using his momentum against him.

Unfortunately, Scott couldn't pull back, and Lamar crashed into him.

They both went down, Scott onto his back, Lamar atop him. The knife remained in Lamar's hand.

For the first time since knowing her, Scott heard Alyx scream. And not just any scream, but a high-pitched, girlish scream full of bloodcurdling terror.

Had Knute somehow managed to cut Alyx despite her fighting skill? Was she bleeding even now?

Dazed only for a moment, Scott snatched Knute's wrist tight in his fist and flipped to put Knute beneath him. So livid he could barely see, Scott struck Knute once, hard enough to knock him out, then launched to his feet. He kicked the knife away from Knute's lax hand and turned to Alyx.

Her face was white.

Reaching her in one long stride, Scott demanded, "Are you okay?" He looked her over from head to toe but didn't see any cuts. When he urged her to turn so he could examine the rest of her, Alyx resisted.

Hands shaking, Scott cupped her face. "Alyx, honey, are you hurt?"

Her voice was thick with regret when she gasped, "I didn't know you were right there behind me—"

Realizing that her pallor was from fear, not injury, Scott pulled her in close for a hug. "Shhh." Her trembling matched his. "I'm okay, babe."

Pushing back, Alyx ran her hands all over him, his chest, his shoulders, his face. "You're sure? He didn't cut you anywhere?"

"I'm fine, sweetheart. Calm down."

She choked on a deep breath, and for one horrifying moment, Scott thought she'd cry. Then anger flashed in her beautiful eyes and she shouted, "He could have killed you!"

Drawing back, Scott smirked. "Gee, thanks. You were plenty safe, naturally. But I was a hairbreadth away from death?"

She squeezed her eyes shut. "Damn. I didn't mean that exactly."

Scott softened. "Yeah, I know." He tipped up her chin, kissed her mouth, and tried to regulate his heartbeat. The threat was over and Alyx was fine. Better than fine. "You know that you scared ten years off my life?"

"Sorry."

"Are you?" When she didn't quite meet his gaze, Scott bent his knees to see her face. "You impressed the hell out of me. You were calm and in control. And fast. Damn, Alyx, you're fast."

Her head lifted, and her face colored with pleasure at such an enthusiastic compliment. "Really?"

Nodding, Scott tunneled his fingers into her long hair. "Should there ever be an emergency where you're forced to defend yourself, I trust you'd do fine. But honey . . ." Scott hesitated, trying to find the right words that would make her understand without insulting her.

Alyx nodded at Lamar, who was starting to show signs of renewed life. "You're not too bad, either."

Scott gave her a level stare. "It's what I do."

"Yes." Her smile never wavered. "And I've always said you do it well."

Turning away, Scott retrieved his handcuffs and knelt to restrain Lamar. "Would you like to ride to the station with me, Alyx? Once I get Knute settled, we can . . . talk."

"Depends," Alyx said, watching as Scott helped Lamar scoot into a sitting position against a tree. "What do you want to talk about?"

With Lamar taken care of, Scott rolled his shoulders and rubbed the back of his neck. This was hardly the right place, but Alyx deserved answers. He wiped the sweat off his brow and cleared his throat. Moving closer to her so that Lamar wouldn't overhear, he said, "I'd like to talk to you about . . . us."

"What about us?"

"I want you to marry me."

Alyx froze. "You . . . Why?"

He saw her expectation and her wariness. It was the wariness that cut him to the bone "You've been chasing me forever. . . ."

"I'm done chasing you," she reminded him.

And that punched up his temper. "Well, maybe *I'm* not done." Determined to do this right, Scott dug into his pocket and pulled out the small velvet-covered box to thrust toward her. "Here."

Alyx stared at it with the same fascination she'd give a snake. "What . . . what is it?"

"Open it and see."

With incredible caution, Alyx accepted the box, lifted the lid, and gasped. "Oh . . . Scott."

And then the words just tumbled out of him. "I love you."

Eyes flaring wide, Alyx took a step back. Scott followed, curling his hands over her shoulders to keep her in place. Now that he'd said it, he wanted to say it again. Loud. All over Visitation.

"I love you. But I don't want to live with you— not without marriage."

Her breasts rose on a sharp breath and she choked out, *"Marriage?"*

She sounded far from thrilled with his proposal. But so what? If she had reservations about tying herself permanently to him, he'd find a way to convince her. "Damn right. All or nothing."

She nodded, but said, "You bought me a ring."

Did she have to torture him? "Yeah, I heard you tell Willow that you'd never gotten a ring from a guy." He cleared his throat. "You like it?"

"I love it."

A good start. "Do you love me?"

Her smile bloomed, bright as the sunshine. "Yes."

Thank God. "Will you marry me?"

"I . . . yes."

She looked a little less shell-shocked now, which pleased Scott. But he wanted no misunderstandings. "I'm proud of you, Alyx. For more reasons than I have time to list right now, but I promise, later tonight, if we can get alone, I'll spell it all out. Just know that I respect your capabilities."

Her chin tucked in. "My . . . ?"

"Capabilities. I honestly believe you could do anything you set your mind to, and that includes slugging it out with a drunk." Now that he'd started, Scott couldn't seem to reign himself in. "But it was damn wrong of you to trail Becky without telling me."

"I took the dog to the neighbors after she left Knute."

"I see."

"I was going to tell you all about her, Scott. I swear. But then you told me you didn't want to live with me, and . . . I was too hurt."

He pressed a gentle kiss to her forehead. "I'll do my best never to hurt you again."

Alyx smiled.

"But even though you'll be a Royal after we marry, you were still born a Winston, so I have no doubt we'll have our fair share of fights."

"Yeah, you're probably right."

God, he adored her sass. "Do you really love me?"

"If you have to ask, then maybe I've been too subtle about my feelings."

Scott laughed out loud. From day one, Alyx had been tackling him, tormenting him, and making him insane with lust. "No one would ever call you subtle, sweetheart. Not with a straight face."

"Are you complaining?"

Scott shook his head. "Are you kidding? I adore your lack of subtlety."

"In that case, yes, I really do love you." Suddenly she blanched. "Oh, no."

"What is it?"

"It just occurred to me. I followed Becky, but when she went around a bend, I lost her. I figured she'd be here." Her eyes searched his. "But she's not."

"Shit." Scott released her and headed for the cruiser. "Jamie said he was worried. He said he felt threatened. And if Becky kept going instead of pulling in here . . ."

Alyx shot past him before Scott even realized what she intended.

"Alyx, *no.*"

With her long legs taking her quickly to her car, Alyx yelled over her shoulder, "I'm the only one who knows where he lives. Please trust me, Scott. I'll be careful." And then she was in her Mazda, gunning the motor and pulling away in a roar.

"Damn it." Scott jerked Lamar to his feet and shoved him into the cruiser, then raced around to the driver's door.

One thing was certain—being married to Alyx would keep him on his toes.

Then he, too, stepped on the gas.

Jamie had no idea why Joe insisted on detaining him. He wanted to get back to his cabin, where he could keep Faith safe. He wanted to be alone with her. The sense of time slipping away, combined with the looming threat, left Jamie unsettled.

But once Luna spotted him, Joe had no choice except to pull his truck to the side of the road and stop. It had been a very awkward half hour since then, starting with Luna's strange behavior. She'd jumped from the cab, approached Jamie wide-eyed, and circled him twice in shock.

Jamie had stood there, letting her get it out of her system. But when Luna blurted, "Good God, Jamie, you're *gorgeous*," he thought Joe would expire.

Before Jamie could react to the outrageous compliment, Joe had snatched his wife back to his side and scowled at Jamie as if he'd somehow wrung the words from Luna.

Luna laughed and excused her reaction as shock, but plenty of time had passed and she *still* kept staring. Not an impolite stare, but one of disbelief.

She introduced herself to Faith—but stared at Jamie.

She shared all the latest news—and stared at Jamie.

She apologized to Joe, who growled something about her pushing her luck, and yet she stared at Jamie.

Rubbing a hand over his face, Jamie groaned. If all the women reacted that way . . .

Faith touched his arm and said into his ear, "I told you that you were a hunk. You might as well get used to it."

But Joe heard her. "The hell he will. I'm going to buy a burlap sack to cover his mug until he can grow that damn beard again."

"Oh, no," Luna said, finally dragging her gaze away from Jamie. "That'd be a crime. Besides, I can't wait till Shay and Cyn and Julie see him." She pulled out her cell phone. "As soon as I get some reception, I'm going to call and see if one of them can bring a camera."

Heat crawled up the back of Jamie's neck. He cleared his throat. "That'll have to wait." He caught Faith's hand. "We need to get going—"

"Stupid phone." Luna said, interrupting Jamie's excuses while tossing the cell phone inside the truck. "So Faith, how long have you known Jamie?"

Faith's fingers tightened on his own. "I knew him long ago."

Luna waited, her eyebrows raised in interest.

Laughing, Joe hugged her into his side. "Let it go for now, baby. Jamie can explain all that later."

Jamie thought Joe's consideration would give him a chance to escape, but he was wrong. Undaunted, Luna launched into inane, polite conversation about the weather, about Julie's upcoming nuptials, about . . . everything under the sun.

And since Faith was a chatterbox too, the women were soon gabbing it up like old friends.

Giving Jamie an apologetic look, Joe opened the tailgate on his truck. "You ladies might as well get comfortable." He lifted Luna up to sit.

When he turned to Faith, she sidestepped him but looked at Jamie in expectation.

Thinking that social mingling was a regular pain in the ass, Jamie dutifully lifted Faith to the gate.

She smiled. "Thank you."

The sunlight on Faith's hair left a halo around her head. Long lashes shaded her dark blue eyes. Her smile was relaxed and happy.

She looked incredibly appealing, and Jamie wanted to be alone with her, damn it, not wasting time visiting on the side of the road. His body burned with a never-ending need to make love to her.

"Now that's an expression I'm familiar with," Joe said around a laugh. Both women gave him questioning looks, but Joe shook his head. "You two visit all you want. Jamie and I'll leave you to it."

He put his arm around Jamie and steered him off to the side.

"You could just leave," Jamie told him, and he didn't care if he sounded rude.

Given Joe's grin, he hadn't taken offense. "I could. Not that dragging Luna away would be easy, but hey, you know I'm always up for a challenge. It keeps me young."

Jamie said, "Great. So how soon can you leave?"

It was not an easy thing to insult the inimitable

Joe Winston. More often than not, he just laughed—
as he did now.

He also retaliated by thwacking Jamie on the
back hard enough to knock him off his feet.
"Sorry I can't accommodate you." He held out
both arms. "I'm your backup."

"My backup for *what?*"

"Scott claims you're expecting trouble."

"Scott called you?" He couldn't have mentioned
the trouble with Alyx. If Joe had even a clue, he'd
be blazing a trail to Knute's right now. "What did
he say?"

Joe shrugged. "I didn't talk with Scott. He's off
checking out some other problem. But he did call
Clint, who called me, because he's handling a
three-car mishap. No serious injuries, but plenty of
reports to fill out."

"I see."

"So what's the problem?" Joe rubbed his hands
together. "I'd prefer not to have Luna involved. Is
there time for me to take her home, or should we
stick around until the others get here?"

Jamie closed his eyes. "The others?"

With a shrug in his tone, Joe said, "Yeah, sure.
Bryan is coming. And so will Clint and Scott when
they finish up."

Jamie doubted that Scott would be done anytime soon. He started to tell Joe to leave, that he
could handle things on his own—and the sense of
menace mushroomed. Gunshots echoed in his
head, and pain exploded in his chest.

Grunting without realizing it, Jamie's brows
snapped down in a grimace and his hands fisted
over his chest.

"Jesus," Joe said. "What is it?"

Bile burning his throat, Jamie whispered, "Delayna."

"She's here? In Visitation? You're sure of it?"

Turning to stare at Faith, Jamie said, "No." Was Faith involved? Had she led Delayna to him? She'd admitted to knowing Delayna. Maybe they'd been more than employer and employee. Maybe, instead of Delayna's giving Faith his files to destroy, she'd given them to Faith for safekeeping.

No. Jamie couldn't even begin to consider that possibility.

"So what's going to happen?"

Shaking his head, Jamie said, "I don't know."

Joe drew himself up. "What the hell do you mean, you don't know? You know all kinds of shit. Every damn thing I don't want you to know, you know."

"I don't know this," Jamie snapped right back. He put his hands to his head and paced away, trying to think, to gather the information. But his gaze kept slipping back to Faith, and no matter what he wanted to tell himself, he knew she'd somehow be involved.

"Is it going to get dangerous?" Joe demanded.

Shaking his head, Jamie lied, "No." If he told Joe about the gunshot, he'd never get him to leave. "I think I have time."

"Fuck this," Joe said, and he grabbed Jamie's arm. "I'm taking you both back to my place."

Wracking his brain for a way to dissuade Joe, Jamie allowed himself to be dragged a few feet. They'd just gained the attention of the women when the sound of another car engine disturbed the air.

"Get in the cab," Joe barked to Luna, and she didn't argue. She did, however, tug Faith along with her.

The balisong knife, a weapon Joe always carried, appeared in his hand with the blade exposed. His posture changed; his gait became stealthy.

In the blink of an eye, Joe transformed from family man to warrior. No matter what happened, Joe was always prepared. Nothing intimidated him.

Which meant Jamie might have to resort to extreme measures to regain his privacy. Joe wouldn't like it. Hell, neither would Luna. But he'd do what he had to.

And when he got Faith alone, he'd tell her that Delayna was in Visitation. If she'd betrayed him . . .

Jamie shook his head. He really had no idea what he'd do. But he would never again let a woman hurt him.

Chapter Sixteen

Jamie put a hand to Joe's shoulder, relieved that he still had time. "It's only Bryan and Shay."

Joe didn't relax. "You're sure?"

"Yes." At least about some things.

Chagrined, Joe flipped the knife to cover the blade and slid it back into his jeans pocket. "Coulda said so sooner, damn it." He started toward his truck. "Give me something to work with here, Jamie. I don't want Luna at risk."

"I don't either." And using that as an opening, Jamie said, "It'd be best if you took her home."

"And leave you on your own—the way you prefer it?" Joe snorted. "Luna would have my ass."

"Don't tell her there's a problem."

"I already told her," Joe reminded him. "When I explained why you shaved and got a haircut."

"So tell her I've worked everything out."

"Yeah, right. Somehow, she always knows. I swear it's uncanny, but I can't lie to her worth a damn. The woman is almost as psychic as you."

"She's wise to you, that's all." Jamie offered a workable solution. "I'll tell her everything is fine. She'll believe me."

"Don't count on it."

At that moment, Luna rolled down the driver's window and scowled at her husband. "Is there a reason I'm cowering in the truck with Faith while you and Jamie chew the fat?"

Joe strode up to her window, leaned in, and took her mouth in a firm, lingering kiss. When he straightened away, leaving Luna a bit glazed, he said, "Yeah." He pointed to Bryan's car as it appeared. "Wasn't sure who that was." His hand cupped her cheek, gently stroking, and his voice dropped. "I don't take chances with my valuables."

Luna accepted that explanation with a dreamy smile and climbed out of the truck. "And you're worried because?"

"Because I'm the cautious sort."

Tone firm, she said, "Joe?"

Giving Jamie a didn't-I-tell-you look, Joe said, "Jamie's a little jumpy, that's all."

Luna turned big eyes on him. "You're jumpy? Like right now?" She glanced around the area. "Is something about to happen?"

"No." Unlike Joe, Jamie had no obligation for further explanations, and appeasing Luna wasn't the main thing on his mind.

Reading Faith took priority.

As she left the truck, Jamie delved into her mind, prepared for anything. He detected Faith's confusion and worry over his current mood, and her speculation on what it might represent. She feared for her daughter, and for Jamie.

But he perceived no signs of deception.

His gaze locked with Faith's, Jamie said, "We need to get going."

Luna rushed over to latch on to his arm, forcing him to take his attention away from Faith. "You can't leave yet," Luna insisted. "Shay and Bryan are here."

Jamie considered that the best reason of all for retreating. Large gatherings always made him uneasy, but more than ever before, he had reason to seek out his cabin.

It would afford more quiet time alone with Faith, and he knew they'd be in bed within minutes.

But Bryan and Shay didn't give him a chance to sneak off. They both strode to him, gaping as if he had two heads, instead of one with a clean shave and a haircut.

Faith's sympathy washed over Jamie. She understood how awkward he felt being the center of attention. To assist him, she came to his side, hugged his arm, and leaned into him. "Introduce me to your friends, Jamie."

He didn't want to. But Shay didn't wait for him anyway. She thrust out her hand and took care of the matter on her own. "It's so nice to meet you, Faith. I can't wait to hear about your history with Jamie."

Bryan laughed. "Very subtle, Shay." And he took Faith's hand. "I'm sorry, but the wives have all been bursting with curiosity."

"I don't mind sharing," Faith assured them. "I met Jamie long ago, when we both . . . worked for a parapsychology lab."

Shay indicated Jamie with a nod of her head. "And he looked like that? It's a wonder you were able to get any work done."

Bryan turned to frown at his wife. Joe commiserated with him. And Jamie just wanted to escape.

The women ignored their husbands; they even ignored Jamie finally, to crowd around Faith, befriending her. With Faith's being such a chatterbox, and with all her recent isolation, she seemed happy with the company.

Bryan turned to Joe and shook his head in disgust. "It's enough to make a man jealous."

Propping his hands on his hips, Joe eyed Jamie. "Think we should rub some mud on his face or something, so he's not so pretty?"

"Yeah. Or maybe he needs a scar or two," Bryan joked. "A broken nose would blunt those good looks a little."

Out of the blue and totally unexpected, Luna's fist connected with Joe's shoulder. "Leave him alone. Can't you tell he doesn't like teasing?"

Like a kid with his hand caught in the cookie jar, Joe blanched. "Damn, woman, I didn't think you were listening."

"I hear everything you say, Joe Winston. Remember that."

Bryan hooted, but only until Shay began tapping her foot. "What?" he said. "I didn't do anything. It was all Joe."

It wasn't easy for Jamie to witness the love and friendship they all shared. And now their open-armed acceptance included him, leaving him exposed and overwhelmed. Feeling out of control, Jamie opened his mouth to announce he was leaving despite any protests they might give—and instead he groaned.

Faith immediately moved back to his side, proving that, while she chatted with the women, she'd still been attuned to him. "What is it?"

"More people."

"Here we go again," Joe said, then demanded, "Good people or bad people?"

"Preacher people."

"My brother?" Bryan shielded his eyes with a hand, and sure enough, an aged station wagon, driven by his twin brother, Bruce, came into view.

Giving up, Jamie moved to sit on a large rock. He put his elbows on his knees, his head in his hands.

Half laughing, Faith followed him. "Poor Jamie. You're not used to crowds, are you?"

"This is more like a swarm," he said without looking up. "They can act as cavalier as they want, but they're all trying to protect me." He dropped his hands and turned his head to see Faith. "Do I really seem that damn pathetic?"

Her fingers sifted into his hair, and her face shone with admiration. "Not pathetic at all. Just well loved."

Jamie jerked upright.

"And with good reason, I'd say." Putting her hands on his shoulders, Faith knelt down to kiss him. "You're a very special man, and they all know it."

When Faith would have moved away, Jamie kept her close. "I'm on the ragged edge here, Faith. If you kiss me like that again, I'm carrying you home, and that's that."

"Home." She beamed at him. "I like the sound of that."

Jamie realized what he'd said too late to take it back. And what the hell? The cabin did feel more like home with Faith in it. Not that she could ever live there. And what about Cory . . . ?

Joe shouted, "Hey, you two. Break it up. There's a preacher present."

Shaking off ridiculous musings about any sort of future with Faith, Jamie led her back to the gathering. "Let's get this over with." He leaned down near her ear. "The sooner they get their curiosity appeased, the sooner I can get you alone."

Faith always reacted to his suggestive comments, and now was no different. She took a few deep breaths, pulled away, and went to stand by Shay and Luna—where she probably thought it'd be safer.

"It's nice that you'll get to meet most everyone at once," Luna told her. "Of course, there's still Clint and Julie, and Scott and Alyx."

"I've met Alyx," Faith explained. "She came up to the cabin for a nice visit. I like her."

Joe stiffened. "My sister's been hiking in that damn mountain again?" He rounded on Jamie. "Why the hell didn't you tell me?"

Seeing that warm flush that remained on Faith's face, Jamie considered putting her over his shoulder and just walking away. One look at Joe told him that wouldn't work. He sighed. "Alyx is an adult. If she wanted you to know, she'd tell you."

Bruce saved Joe from finding an adequate reply to that truism. "Hello." He held out a hand to Faith. "I'm Bruce Kelly, Bryan's brother."

It was Faith's turn to be stunned. "You look exactly alike."

"Luckily," Cyn said, smiling at Faith, "Shay and I can tell them apart."

Bryan sent his wife a slanted look. "Most of the time anyway." And Shay turned bright red.

In a carrying stage whisper, Cyn leaned forward to confide to Faith. "Shay got a little bit confused once and kissed the wrong man. That was before she married Bryan and before I married Bruce, but Bryan does like to tease her about it every now and then."

Fascinated, Faith said, "I can see how that could happen."

"It doesn't happen." Bryan hauled his wife close to his side. "Not anymore."

"So," Cyn said, and she faced off with Jamie. "What's going on? What's wrong?"

From the first, Jamie had recognized a special bond with Cyn. She always seemed to be one step ahead of him, making it impossible for him to separate himself from her. Fooling her wouldn't be easy. "Nothing's wrong. I'm fine."

She looked between Faith and Jamie, and then Bryan and Joe. "Uh-huh. That's why these two hulks are here, just to pass the time on the side of the road?"

Bruce lifted his shoulders in apology. "I'm sorry, Jamie. I had no idea you'd all be here. We were on our way into town."

Cyn stared up at Jamie, then began to fret. "Bruce told me everything that you shared with Joe. All about your past involvement and Faith's daughter and what happened at the Farmington

Research Institute. But I didn't realize that specific things would happen today."

"Institute?" Luna asked. "Shay, did you know anything about this?"

Shay straightened to her full, impressive height. "No, I didn't."

Sending a mean glare at Joe, Luna said, "So this is something you've kept from me?"

Perplexed, Bruce looked at Joe and Bryan. "You didn't tell your wives?"

Together they growled, *"No."*

Rather than let the men take the heat, Jamie stepped forward and gave a very brief explanation about his time at Farmington. He explained about Cory, how Faith had raised her, and how the little girl had abilities that mirrored his own.

When he finished, both Luna and Shay looked amazed.

"Wow," Shay said. "This is fascinating."

"Did Cory's mother have psychic ability?" Luna asked. "Did she inherit it, do you think?"

The innocent question brought a strange reaction from Faith. She slammed the door on her thoughts and shot a guilty look at Jamie.

What did she have to hide?

Even with her thoughts closed off to him, Jamie could see a thousand emotions in Faith's eyes. And the longer he studied her, the more ill at ease he felt. Something monumental was about to take place. He just didn't know what.

Faith licked her lips. "I don't think it's ever been proven that paranormal ability is inherited."

"But you must have known her mother," Cyn persisted. "Did she have the talent?"

"No." Faith stared down at her feet. "She didn't."

Joe grew thoughtful. "Any idea who the dad might be? Maybe he was the psychic. Or someone in his family."

Swallowing hard, Faith brought her gaze back up to Jamie, and the pleading in her eyes staggered him.

He needed a distraction and fast.

Taking a step forward, he shielded Faith with his body. Blood rushed hot through his veins, and a pulse pounded in his temple. He felt Faith knot his shirt in her hands, felt her face press into his back.

Breathing became difficult. "This isn't an inquisition." One by one, Jamie met the gazes of his friends. "You all have plenty of your own business to contend with, without butting into mine."

Bryan shot him a look of incredulity. "You've got to be kidding."

"We only want to help," Luna added, her expression worried.

Nodding, Cyn reached out to touch his forearm. "Jamie, it's easy to see that you care for Faith, and we don't want to make her uncomfortable."

"Then go home."

"Not a chance," Joe stated in flat denial. "Something's going on here. You said so yourself. I'm not accusing anyone, least of all Faith. But if you won't protect yourself, we'll do it for you."

They all nodded.

Jamie hesitated, but he saw that none of them would relent. Deciding he had no choice, he dropped an emotional bombshell. "Luna's pregnant."

Joe's eyebrows shot up, and he stumbled back a step. *"What?"*

Luna wailed, *"Ja-mie!"*

Joe jerked around to face his wife. He swallowed twice. "You're . . . ?"

With a furious glare at Jamie, Luna folded her arms and nodded. "Yes."

Joe bent his knees to look her in the eyes. "You're . . . *We're* having a baby? Really?"

A smile teased her mouth. Her voice dropped to a happy whisper. "Really."

"Holy shit." Stacking both hands on top of his head, Joe turned a circle to look at everyone, then let out a whoop and grabbed Luna into his arms, holding her high against his chest and kissing her. She laughed, hanging on to him, kissing him back. They seemed to forget about their audience.

Pleased, Jamie watched as everyone began to smile.

But not Cyn. She took a step forward. "Nice tactic, Jamie, but I still want to know—"

He gave Bryan an apologetic shrug and said, "Shay's pregnant, too."

Bryan's mouth fell open.

Startled, Shay said, "I am?"

Funny that Shay hadn't even realized it yet. But she would have soon, Jamie assured himself. Rubbing his face, he gave up his guilt and pointed first at Luna, then at Shay. "Girl, boy."

Bryan continued to stare. He looked blank-brained, ready to keel over, pale and shaken. In a rasp, he said, "We're going to have a son?"

"Yeah. In about seven months." And then to Joe, before he could ask, "Five months."

"Five!" Joe set Luna back on her feet and held her shoulders at arm's length away. "How long have you known, woman?"

Luna glared at Jamie again. "We weren't trying, so at first I thought I'd just missed a period or two. By the time I got an appointment with the doctor, I was a few months into it. I found out for sure only yesterday."

Joe looked ready to hit the roof. "So why the hell didn't you tell me?"

Eyes on Jamie, Luna growled, "I had a romantic night planned and would have told you then, if *someone* hadn't ruined it."

"Congratulations," Bruce offered.

Cyn looked like a deer caught in the headlights, and Jamie took pity on her.

"No, Cyn, neither you nor Alyx is pregnant, so you can relax."

Bruce laughed and hugged his wife. "I wasn't worried. When it happens, I'll welcome fatherhood. But it is fun to see the others."

Joe rubbed the back of his neck. "Given Alyx's . . . enthusiasm around Scott, I'm just relieved to hear she isn't pregnant, too."

"They'll have plenty of kids," Jamie told him. "After they're married."

"And that'll be . . . ?" Joe asked with some skepticism. "Last I saw, Scott was still playing hard to get."

"Not anymore." Jamie could feel Faith trembling behind him. Keeping his composure wasn't easy. He had a feeling that whoever had fathered Cory, he wasn't going to like it. But he wouldn't pin Faith down in front of everyone. "Scott proposed to Alyx today."

For the second time, surprise jolted Joe. "You don't say!"

Luna leaned into her husband. "Gee, I wonder if Alyx said yes?"

And while Joe rolled his eyes, everyone else laughed.

Jamie worked hard at keeping himself contained, at balancing the need to know the truth, while protecting Faith, with his attempts to distract the others. That probably accounted for why he jumped along with everyone else when the car horn beeped.

As one, they all turned to see who had joined them now.

The minivan pulled up behind the other vehicles. When the driver's window rolled down, an older woman—with faded red hair—stuck her head out. "Hello. Could one of you tell me how I might find Jamie Creed?"

Gasping, Faith pushed her way out from behind Jamie. "Mother!" With obvious joy, she rushed to the vehicle.

Standing where Faith had left him, Jamie mentally reeled. *Mother?* A ton of bricks couldn't have flattened him more. He was about to meet Faith's mom. Which meant he'd finally be face-to-face with Cory.

The menace that had plagued him all day darkened and thickened, swirling around him in an ominous cloud.

A small face haloed by black curls poked out the window. Dark eyes zeroed in on Faith, and a smile put dimples in rosy cheeks. "Mommy!"

And Jamie knew. Faith didn't have to tell him a damn thing.

One look at Cory, and anyone could see who had fathered her. It didn't even require psychic ability.

Jamie was a dad.

Cory was out of the car with her arms open by the time Faith reached her. Scooping her up, Faith hugged her tight, relieved, anxious, and so scared she felt ill. If Jamie hurt her daughter's feelings, she'd—

Thin arms went tight around Faith's neck, and a wet kiss landed on her cheek. "It'll be all right," Cory said, and Faith laughed.

Settling Cory back on her feet, Faith smoothed her wild tumble of dark curls away from her face and kissed her nose. "It will, huh?"

Cory nodded. "Come on, Grandma. Let's say hi." She caught the older woman's hand and urged her out of the car.

Faith's mother gave her a quick embrace. "You're okay?"

"Yes." Faith didn't want to turn to see Jamie. She couldn't bear to do that yet. "I'm fine."

Her mother didn't look convinced, but she smiled all the same. "Cory's been bouncing in her seat for the last five miles. I'm glad you were here, where she thought you'd be, so we didn't have to go any farther."

Reluctantly, they both turned and found the entire group clustered together—around Jamie. Did they already know? Probably. Cory was the spitting image of her daddy, right down to the dark eyes that could see into your soul.

Though no one looked particularly hostile, Faith held back, intimidated. Her mother also hesitated, wary.

But Cory, standing between them, one of her hands clasping Faith's, the other holding her grandmother's, showed no reserve.

Towed in the wake of an almost-eight-year-old's enthusiasm, Faith approached the group.

She cleared her throat. "Everyone, this is my mother, Tracy, and my daughter, Cory."

Tracy nodded. "Hello."

A round of reciprocal greetings followed, but few could take their eyes off Cory. Not that Cory minded. Unlike her father, she reveled in attention and adored large gatherings. Flashing a big toothy grin, she said to Faith, "They like you."

Amused at Cory's optimism, Faith smoothed her hair. "Not yet, sweetie. But I'm getting there."

Cory turned to peer at everyone and then moved away from her mother and grandmother to stand within inches of Joe. Tipping her head back, she stared up. "You're all Jamie's friends. You're worried about him, huh?"

Spellbound by this small, dark-haired psychic, everyone spoke at once, rushing to reassure her, to put her at ease.

Separating himself from the others, Joe crouched down, facing Cory. He tugged at one long, twining curl that hung over her shoulder. "You're a cute little munchkin, aren't you?"

Faith alternated between watching her daughter interact with Joe and seeing Jamie's reaction. As immobile as a statue, he stood right behind Joe. Faith couldn't tell if Jamie was angry or not, or if he felt deceived.

Luna, Shay, and Cyn crowded in close around him, with Bryan and Bruce behind the women.

Jamie didn't acknowledge any of them. All his concentration centered on Cory. When she answered Joe's question, saying "Yep" without a single speck of modesty, Jamie's mouth twitched, but the smile showed mostly in his eyes.

Cory tipped her head at Joe, making more curls bounce. Her face scrunched up as she scrutinized him. "You got a daughter, huh?"

Joe hid his surprise well. "Yes. And a son."

"Can I visit with 'em?"

"Anytime you want."

"Thanks." Turning serious, Cory put her small hand to Joe's cheek. "You like Jamie a lot, doncha?"

"He's a very, very special friend."

Satisfied, she patted his cheek. "Good. Don't go away, 'kay?"

Tugging at his earring and fighting a laugh, Joe straightened back to his full height. "Trust me, munchkin, wild horses couldn't drag me away."

Bristling with sudden impatience, Jamie nudged Joe aside and sank to one knee. He didn't say anything. He just waited, looking stern and unapproachable and as distant as Faith had ever seen him. She held her breath, anxious over how Jamie would react to the news of fatherhood. She prayed that he'd understand why she hadn't told him, that she couldn't have told him until recently, after Cory gave her directions to find him. No one had known where to find him.

Her mother's hand slipped into hers and, thankful for the support, Faith clung to her.

Cory looked around at everyone before finally settling her gaze on Jamie. Suddenly shy, she eased over next to him. Toeing the dirt, she whispered, "Hi."

Jamie swallowed hard. "Hi." He crossed his arms over his bent knee, assessing her. "I'm Jamie."

"Yep." Cory glanced up, lifted her shoulders. "It's good to meet you. In person, I mean."

"Yes."

After a nervous giggle, Cory darted a quick look back at Faith, looking for reassurance. Faith's heart beat so hard she wondered that everyone didn't hear it.

Nodding, she reminded Cory of what she'd said to Faith minutes before. "It's okay, Cory. You told me so."

"I remember." Cory drew a deep breath of contentment, turned back to Jamie, and held out her arms.

Jamie showed no hesitation. As if she were the most precious thing he'd ever seen, he gathered Cory close and held her. For once, Faith knew what he felt as he relished the small, warm body against his heart, the silky dark curls against his cheek.

Silence swelled in the air around them. Everyone seemed as absorbed as Faith, drawn into the special moment.

After a minute, Cory pushed back from him,

and Jamie finally released her. "You're squishing me," she said with a smile.

"I'm sorry." Jamie held her small hands in his. "I didn't mean to."

Sounding so much like her daddy that tears burned Faith's eyes, Cory said, "I know."

A chuckle sounded from those who watched, because they'd heard those very same words from Jamie many times.

Jamie glanced back at them with a grin. Cory tugged at his hand. "You have to be ready."

"Okay." Running his big hand over her head, Jamie pushed the wild curls away from her face—curls the same color as his own hair. "Ready for what?"

Cory bit her lip, gave her mother a guilty glance filled with apology, and shrugged. "For when they hurt her."

Faith frowned. For when they hurt whom? Apparently, Jamie wasn't the target, since Cory said "her." And it didn't sound like she wanted protection for herself.

Jamie jerked back, breathing deep. He looked at Faith, his sudden perception rolling over her like a warm breeze.

She was the target? Oh, but . . . that didn't make any sense.

Fierce with determination, Jamie lifted Cory onto his knee. "Someone is going to hurt your mother?"

Cory put her arms around Jamie and pressed her face into his shoulder, her hold desperate. "I don't want Mommy hurt."

Jamie's expression could have been carved from stone, but he rubbed Cory's back in gentle comfort. "No, sweetheart, I swear to you. I won't let anyone hurt her."

But Cory clung tighter and her voice wavered. "Please. You gotta help her."

With Cory secure in his strong arms, Jamie stood. "It's okay, baby. Can you tell me what will happen?"

Cory sniffed and rubbed at her eyes. "You have to care." She pushed back, her chin trembling. "You do, doncha, Jamie? You care 'bout us?"

"I care." His gaze met Faith's again, and for her it was a physical touch, a promise, maybe even forgiveness. "Very much."

But he didn't know it all, Faith thought with ill misgivings. And now wasn't the time to tell him. She hadn't planned on Jamie's learning any of this with a group surrounding him. She wanted time alone with him, to explain, to make certain he understood her reasons. But it appeared her time to explain had run out.

Faith had no idea what to do. Her mother put her arms around her as if she could bodily protect her, and already Joe and Bryan had moved closer, shielding her while searching the woods.

Why would anyone want to harm her? She didn't have any psychic ability. She had nothing . . . except Cory.

Oh God. Did someone plan to use her to get to her daughter? The awful possibility chased away her fear. She'd die before she'd let that happen.

Jamie gave her a long look, and said one word: "No."

But Faith would do what she had to. She closed her thoughts to him and prepared herself for any eventuality.

Angry, Jamie turned away from her and instead cupped her daughter's cheek. "Cory?" He turned her face up to his. "I need to know when it will happen."

Nodding, Cory gulped down a sob, squeezed in tight to Jamie's neck again, and whispered, "Now."

Chapter Seventeen

Remembering the gunshot he'd heard in his head earlier, Jamie blanched. He sought the scene, pulling it from the future, hearing the harsh, ugly sound as it reverberated across the still mountain air, very real and very much a threat.

A female voice yelled, "Faith Owen, come to me and no one else will get hurt."

Everyone reacted at once. Bruce pulled the women to the ground and stationed himself in front of them. Joe and Bryan dragged Faith and her mother to the side, crouching low, using the minivan as concealment.

Jamie shoved Cory behind him. Rage afforded him an eerie calm. He didn't understand everything that was about to happen. But he believed what Cory told him, and he trusted that his caring, a caring he couldn't deny, would play into keeping Faith from harm.

He'd known all along that Faith wasn't Cory's mother. Not only had she been a virgin, but eight years ago, he hadn't known Faith, much less made love to her.

Eight years ago, only one woman had known him intimately.

In the back of his mind, the truth dawned, there for Jamie to examine. But he shied away from it. Right now, the identity of Cory's mother didn't matter.

Protecting Cory and Faith did.

Two people, a woman and a man, emerged from the woods across the road. The woman yelled, "Faith Owen? Come on now. This can all be very simple if you'll just cooperate."

Lifting his head, Jamie saw them—and it all became clear. He knew what to do. He knew how to do it.

"Bruce?"

"Right here, Jamie."

Easing Cory away, Jamie said, "Stay with Mr. Kelly, baby. He'll keep you safe."

"No." Crying, Cory tried to cling to Jamie, but he pried her skinny arms loose and handed her over to Bruce.

"All of you, stay out of this."

"You can handle it?" Bruce asked.

And with utmost confidence, Jamie nodded. "Yeah. I can handle it."

Cory's big dark eyes watched Jamie, taking his measure, evaluating his promise. She sniffled, but stopped crying. She put her arms around Bruce and let him pull her close.

"We'll be fine," Bruce told Jamie. And to the women and Cory, he said, "Come on. Quiet now. Let's move over here behind these rocks."

To Jamie's relief, no one argued.

Except Faith.

She fought Joe, trying to break free, more than ready to sacrifice herself in order to protect Cory. Joe held her with one arm around her waist, his other hand clamped over her mouth. Leave it to Joe to handle things, Jamie thought. He gave his friend a nod of approval.

Appearing harassed, Joe nodded back, whispered in Faith's ear. Finally, she quieted, drowned in misery and the worry only a mother could feel.

Jamie knew her panic, the wild beating of her heart, the uncompromising love she felt for Cory. He knew she'd willingly die for her daughter and that she would entrust Jamie with Cory's care, should it come to that.

He wasn't about to let either of them be hurt. Bruce would keep Cory tucked away safe, so Faith would have no reason to be a martyr.

Jamie pushed to his feet and started toward the gravel road without a single sign of caution. "What took you so long? I was beginning to think you wouldn't show."

The woman, a blond bombshell reeking confidence and edgy with malice, laughed while waving a 9-millimeter gun. The man with her looked grim and out of his element. He was tall but slim, dressed in jeans and a faded gray T-shirt, a thick black watch on his wrist. He wore glasses, and his light brown hair was long and thin.

He tried to look as confident as the woman, but the façade didn't work. Jamie smelled his nervousness, could see the stark fear in his eyes. More the creative sort than a killer, he posed no real threat.

Knowing it would spook him more, Jamie trained his probing gaze on the man's face and smiled. "Hello, Doug."

Ready to faint, he turned to the woman, urgent and pleading. "Maybe we should—"

"Be quiet." She steadied the gun, aiming at Jamie's heart.

Sweeping his gaze over her, Jamie assessed her before giving her the full focus of his attention. "Hello, Becky."

"Nice try, Creed," the woman said. "But I'm not buying it. If you knew about us, if you expected us, then how did we take you so unawares?"

"Who says you did?" Jamie kept walking, getting closer and closer. He stopped when only the width of the road separated them. "I knew you were in town, dressed in a disguise and dark wig, torment-ing the locals."

"I wanted you off that damn mountain." She grinned. "And here you are."

"You didn't realize that Deputy Royal was on to you, did you?"

"Oh shit," Doug said. "I told you that you should have avoided him."

Her mouth pinched. "Don't be an ass, Doug. Scott has no clue who I am."

"The deputy is not a stupid man, taken in by a conniving woman. He might not have realized your identity right away, but Alyx had been follow-ing you, and she surely told him. He's alerted the sheriff, and Clint is on his way here right now."

"Shut up."

"Have you met Clint Evans?" Jamie taunted. "He eats people like you for breakfast."

Doug began breathing hard, wringing his hands.

Jamie focused on him, then shook his head in mock regret. "It's a shame, Doug."

"What is?"

The lie came from Jamie's mouth smooth as silk. "You won't live through this."

Blanching, Doug floundered back a step. "What are you talking about?"

"You're going to die." Jamie shrugged. "Not by my hand, but you'll be dead all the same."

Several deep breaths only heightened Doug's sheer terror. His voice went high and shrill. "This is insane."

"He's bluffing you," Becky insisted. "He doesn't know shit."

"He knows our names!"

"That's all he knows. Now be quiet."

Jamie took pleasure in proving her wrong. "You're Becky Kline, Professor Kline's daughter. You want the files that Delayna gave to Faith."

Doug sagged. "Oh God."

"I will have them," Becky told him. "By rights, they're mine."

"Faith destroyed them."

Savage hatred distorted the woman's beauty. "The fuck she did! Those files were important to her, because they apply to the kid, too." Gathering herself with a deeply inhaled breath, Becky smoothed her blouse and composed her features. Her anticipatory smile turned Jamie's stomach.

Stealing her thunder, Jamie said, "It's no use, Becky. Your father was wrong."

Blank surprise wiped away the smirk. "What are you talking about?"

"He told you that emotions ruined my perception, didn't he?" Easing a step nearer, hoping to get Becky—and the gun—within reach, Jamie stated, "He couldn't have been more wrong. You see, the closer I am to someone, the stronger my abilities."

She whispered, "No."

"Afraid so. Your plan is about to backfire."

Doug moaned and started looking around for a way to escape. Jamie ignored him and instead glanced at Faith. She slumped on the ground beside her mother, her balled hands pressed to her mouth, her eyes wide as she stared at Becky.

She had her thoughts blocked, but this time it didn't do her any good. Jamie didn't need to be a psychic to know that Faith would still sacrifice herself if she thought it necessary.

Becky's shoulders stiffened, and her trigger finger twitched. "So then you know who the kid's mother is? That's what you're saying?"

Unease sank into Jamie, but he kept his manner inscrutable. Convinced of what he'd find, he delved into Becky, wading through the ugliness and the malevolent spirit to steal her memories. The planned demise of her immoral father had robbed her of her heritage and her accustomed social standing. She felt cheated of a plush lifestyle and the recognition Professor Kline might have received as a great scientist.

Now she wanted retribution.

Faith had hidden Cory's talent so well, Becky didn't realize the depth of what the little girl could derive. But she knew Jamie's reputation—and she knew . . .

Jamie stiffened, accepting the inevitable.

Delayna. Of course she had to be Cory's mother; he hadn't been intimate with any other woman during that time period. Knowing it for fact didn't make it more palatable—but knowing Cory did.

"Ahhh," Becky purred. "So you didn't know? Faith didn't tell you."

Jamie narrowed his eyes at her. "She didn't have to. I can do math."

Either Becky didn't hear him or her grasp on reality slipped further away. "Her experiments with you left her knocked up, and like a stupid bitch, she gave away everything my father accomplished to birth the brat."

"Careful," Jamie warned. "Or you just might die with Doug."

"What's this? You're already playing proud papa? That's so . . . pathetic." She laughed, thrilled with the turn of events. "How does it feel, knowing two women would lose everything rather than admit that the infamous Creed had spawned a prodigy?"

Jamie wanted to seek out Cory, to tell her to ignore the nonsense spewing from Becky's mouth. But taking his attention off Becky, even for a moment, wouldn't be wise.

Cocking out a hip and waving the gun at Jamie, Becky continued. "Seems Delayna didn't mind experimenting on you, but she didn't want the same to happen to her kid."

Thank God for that, Jamie thought—and then he froze. Faith was making plans. She worried not only for Cory, *but for him.* Damn her. If she interfered now, one or both of them might be hurt, even killed.

Faith thought he would put stock in Becky's ravings.

She was wrong.

He'd fathered Cory. Faith had loved her. That's what mattered.

Later, there'd be time to sort through all the details. For now, Jamie had a promise to keep to his daughter.

He wanted to know how Becky had learned the truth. Faith wouldn't have left anything to chance, not when it came to Cory. Never would she have kept documents revealing Cory's parentage. And he knew firsthand that she wouldn't have told anyone—not even him.

Becky laughed again. "Gotcha with that one, didn't I?"

Jamie frowned in thought. "Not really, no."

"Bullshit! You hated Delayna. That has to make a difference."

Jamie locked his gaze with hers. "You're wasting your time, Becky. Your father was a madman, a sadist, and the world is a better place without him."

Anger flashed in her eyes. "You shut up! My father was a brilliant scientist. I'll publish his life's story, detailing his work, and the whole world will understand everything he accomplished."

"You're as insane as he was."

"No, I'm smart. And soon I'll be rich."

Jamie pointed out the obvious. "Someone went to great lengths to make sure your father couldn't reveal details. Do you really think you'd be dealt with any differently?"

Doug paled and folded his arms around himself. "Becky, maybe he's right."

"No!" For only a blink of time, Becky took her attention off Jamie to glare at her coconspirator. "I already told you, we're safe."

Before Jamie could react to her inattention, she swung the barrel of the gun back around. "I've made a pact with parties who'd rather stay anonymous. They know I have a contract with a publisher, and they know that if anything happens to me, their names will go public. As long as I get to write this book the way I want, I can keep their dirty little secrets."

She edged closer to Jamie—and to her own demise.

"But I need the factual accounts of your time at Farmington to make it complete."

"I don't have them," Jamie reminded her. "Faith doesn't have them."

"Maybe not." Becky glanced behind Jamie, searching the woods. Her voice dropped. "But Faith remembers plenty. And if she wants her kid to stay safe, she'll tell me what I need to know."

Absorbing the riot of Becky's memories, Jamie studied her. "You mean the way Delayna stayed safe?"

Doug hadn't moved. He now stood several steps behind Becky. Jamie addressed him, aware that he already waffled in his convictions. "You're a reporter, Doug. You think this is your big breakout story."

Doug gulped, and nodded.

"You're wrong."

Sweat ran down the other man's temples. He glanced between Becky and Jamie before deciding to explain. "I'm going to do a documentary to coincide with the release of the book. Becky gave me exclusive rights. This will make my name in the industry."

"No," Jamie said gently. "Dead men can't make documentaries. You'll die an unknown, and I doubt anyone will miss you."

"Shut up," Becky yelled, lunging forward, prodding the gun at Jamie. "Doug, don't listen to him. He's just messing with your head."

Jamie pressed his advantage. "She killed Delayna, didn't she, Doug? And you know about it, so that makes you an accessory."

"It was an accident," Doug wailed. "We went there just to get the files on you."

"To steal them, you mean?"

He nodded jerkily. "She was Kline's partner. Becky thought sure she'd have kept copies."

"Shut *up*, Doug."

But Doug was beyond hearing Becky. He babbled out the truth, maybe hoping for redemption, maybe out of a sense of guilt. "Delayna wasn't supposed to be home. But she didn't have the documents anyway. She . . . she had birth records, adoption papers." He looked up at Jamie, his eyes blank, his voice hollow. "She had Faith's address. We were ready to go—but then she came home."

"Why didn't you just leave?" Jamie asked, feeling his own measure of guilt over how Delayna had died.

"I never touched her," Doug insisted, stepping back, separating himself from Becky.

Like a film on fast-forward, that awful day flashed through Jamie's mind. The hysterical way Delayna had tried to guard Cory's identity, her blind panic at the idea of being exposed. She'd attacked, as fierce in her protectiveness as Faith would have been.

"There was a scuffle," Jamie said, regret and forgiveness burning away old resentment. Delayna had died trying to protect his daughter. How could he not forgive her? "She confronted you on the basement steps. She tried to stop you from leaving."

Doug nodded. "It was Becky. She shoved Delayna. I never touched her. But the way she fell . . . there was nothing I could do."

Refocusing on the coward in front of him, Jamie growled, "She was still alive when you left her, Doug."

"*No.*"

"If you'd called the paramedics, if you'd alerted anyone, Delayna probably would have recovered from her internal injuries. Instead, you left her there to die."

Enraged, Doug faced Becky. "You said she was dead!"

"Don't be an idiot." The gun found a new target as Becky tried circling away. Her nervous steps took her closer to Jamie. "If we'd called anyone, it would have ruined our plans."

Lifting the gun in both hands, Becky tried to fend Doug off.

He stalked her. "You said she was dead. You said he wouldn't be able to get in our heads. You said we'd both be rich and that no one would get hurt. You . . . you lied to me. You dragged me into this mess—"

A siren blared and lights flashed, delivering lots of fanfare to disrupt the drama.

Clint arrived at the scene.

He slammed the brakes of his cruiser, and the car spun sideways before coming to a halt. A second later, a rifle appeared over the top of the open door. In his deep, carrying voice, Clint shouted, "Drop the gun. Now."

Everything happened too fast.

"Nooo." Becky twisted around, taking aim at Jamie. "You can't ruin all my plans."

Doug turned to flee into the woods.

Faith screamed, racing toward Jamie. He didn't have time to stop her. He didn't have time to protect her.

Becky fired once, twice.

Jamie saw the contorted agony in Faith's expression; he heard her gasp as the echo of gunfire faded away. Anguish exploded inside him, shattering his heart. *Faith.*

Oblivious to everything and everyone except Faith, Jamie barely noticed when Becky turned to flee into the woods, only to be drawn up short when Alyx materialized like an avenging angel and, with one sharp pop in the nose, knocked Becky out.

Joe cursed, shouting his sister's name.

Clint roared orders.

Faith staggered to a halt at Jamie's side. Her

face was ravaged with visible pain, her hands
reaching for him.

Oh God, no. Faith *was* his heart. Without her,
he'd go back to being cold and alone. He'd be
empty. He couldn't bear that.

"Faith?" Jamie wrapped his arms around her,
but she fought him, rejecting his touch, his comfort. He couldn't get any words to come out. He
felt sticky blood covering his arm.

Her lips moved, and she whispered urgently,
"Jamie?"

He could barely hear her over the roar in his
head. He'd promised Cory that her mommy
wouldn't be hurt. He'd thought he could protect
them both.

He'd failed miserably. Again.

Suddenly Clint was there, taking his arm, trying
to pry him away from Faith. "Jamie, sit down. It'll
be okay. Let me take a look."

Jamie didn't want to let her go. "I'm sorry," he
said. "Jesus, Faith, I'm sorry."

"Shhh." Big tears spilled down her cheeks.
"Jamie, *please.* Let Joe and Clint help you."

Help him? Confused, Jamie stared at Faith, saw
the blood on her shirt and the whiteness of her
face. His contracted fingers wouldn't relax. "Don't
leave me, Faith."

She sobbed once, then touched his cheek.
"Never. I swear. Now please, Jamie, you're bleeding. Let me go so they can help you."

The words registered, and when they did, a sear-
ing pain pierced his consciousness. "Son of a bitch,"
Jamie said in shock. "I'm shot."

Joe chuckled. "Yeah, no kidding."

Jamie's hold abruptly loosened, and Faith stepped back. He caught the hem of her shirt. "You're okay?"

"Yes."

"You swear it?"

Her composure disintegrated, and she swiped at her eyes, talking around her tears. "Scared to death, sick in love with you—but other than that, I'm fine."

Jamie slumped, his ass making contact with the gravel road hard enough to wrench a groan from him. "Sick . . . ?"

"In *love* with you." More tears fell. "Damn you, you stubborn man. With everything you know, you hadn't figured that out yet?"

Oxygen finally filled Jamie's lungs. He shook his head. "No, I . . ." He smiled, shrugged his shoulders, then winced at the pain that caused. "Well, thank God." Then he frowned. "Where's Cory?"

Faith stared at him, dumbfounded by his reaction, before replying. "My mother has her. She says you'll be okay. Tell me she's right, Jamie."

Everything went foggy as Jamie tried to concentrate. His relief was so great, he couldn't find a single reading, but male ego had him snorting, and he said, "Of course I'll be fine."

Concentrating on the facts restored his wits. Bryan loomed over Doug. He wasn't dead, but he did have Joe's knife sticking out of his upper arm. The creep wouldn't be sneaking away anytime soon.

Becky, her nose bloody, was starting to moan. Bruce stood over her, holding her gun, unsympathetic to her injuries.

"Clint," Jamie asked, "did you shoot anyone?"

"No, I just hit the dirt, to make the woman jump and throw off her aim."

"You didn't throw it off enough," Faith grouched, and her hand slipped into Jamie's. "You should have just shot her."

Joe grinned. "Damn, she's starting to sound like my sister."

"And thank God for your sister," Faith added. "If it wasn't for her, Becky might have gotten away."

Joe rubbed his ear. "Yeah. You could be right."

Peering at his shoulder where Clint mopped at the blood and examined the wound, Jamie grunted. "Hell, it's just a graze."

Irate, Faith stared at him. "You were *shot.*"

"No, he's right," Joe said. "It's not deep. The hospital will clean and stitch it, but it's not bad at all. He'll be fine." Then Joe glared at Jamie. "So why the hell did you look like you were dying, damn it? You scared ten years off my life."

Jamie tightened his hold on Faith's hand and struggled to his feet. Joe hurried to assist him, as did Clint.

"Well?" Clint asked. "I'm a little curious about that myself."

Feeling like an idiot, Jamie confessed, "I thought Faith was the one hit."

Stunned by that confession, Faith pressed her hands to her mouth. "You couldn't feel it?"

"I felt something, all right." Jamie put his forehead to hers, and his voice lowered to a strained whisper. "I thought it was the pain of seeing you hurt."

Both Clint and Joe nodded in understanding.

As Scott joined the chaos, shouting Alyx's name, Jamie laughed. Damn, it seemed the whole of Visitation had come to his reckoning.

Forcing himself to stand on his own, he looked around. "I want to see Cory."

"Here I am." The little girl stepped out from behind him, fear still etched in her features. Her dark eyes met his, and her thoughts were so clear. *I thought you were going to leave me. I thought you were hurt bad.*

Jamie put his hand to the top of her silky hair. "I'm sorry, baby. I didn't mean to scare you."

Cory chewed her lips. "I knew you wouldn't let Mommy get hurt. But I didn't know . . ."

He nodded. "It's not always clear for me, either." A finger beneath her rounded chin, Jamie tipped her face up. "We'll work on it."

Sounding world-weary and resigned, Cory sighed. "I know."

Jamie looked at Faith, at Tracy, at his friends, and at his daughter. He chuckled, and the chuckle turned into a laugh.

"Jamie," Faith protested. "Come on. I want to get you to the hospital."

Jamie agreed, just so Faith wouldn't fret. Not that he cared about a little gunshot wound. After all, his life was looking pretty damn good.

The hospital waiting room bulged at the seams. Jamie felt like an ass, drawing so much attention, but not a single soul would be dissuaded from going along, worrying about him . . . caring.

According to Joe, who had just led Faith to him

in the sterile room, Cory sat with Bruce and Bryan, keeping them entertained while Alyx and Scott played kissy-face in the hallway and Clint paced, angry that he'd allowed Jamie to be hurt. The women, including Faith's mother, were huddled together making plans. Joe had said the last in a rather ominous way, making Jamie wonder just what type of plans they made.

Now, with his wound cleaned and dressed, Jamie looked at Faith—and reached out a hand for her. Face crumbling, she rushed to him, and Joe, being rather intuitive himself, said, "I'll, ah, wait with the others."

Jamie didn't bother to reply.

He pulled Faith close enough to kiss her. "Shhh. Please don't cry."

"I won't."

But tears tracked her cheeks, and Jamie smiled. "It's okay, you know. I understand why you couldn't tell me about Cory."

"I didn't even know where to find you!" She pressed her face into his throat, her breaths uneven. "Until Cory told me, I had no idea where to look. But she didn't tell me that I was the one who might get hurt."

Smoothing Faith's unruly hair, Jamie said, "She knew you wouldn't have sought me out just to protect yourself."

Faith shook her head. "You've had more than your fair share of heartache. I would never have deliberately brought you more."

Jamie nuzzled her cheek. Even with his arm throbbing, in a crowded hospital, Faith could turn him on.

"Why didn't you tell me that Delayna was Cory's mother?"

"Oh God, Jamie, I'm so—"

"Shhh." He pressed his fingers to her lips. "No more apologizing."

Her lips trembled, and she drew a steadying breath before nodding agreement. "I wanted to tell you. But Cory said you had to care first, so that you'd know to trust your instincts when everything happened. She said you'd know when you saw her that she was your daughter."

"You told her?"

"Yes." Faith touched his face. "She had all those abilities, and I wanted her to know that she'd gotten them from the most amazing man."

Jamie waited.

"But . . . when I told you I worked for Delayna, you were so furious. You . . . you told me—"

"That I hated that bitch and anyone associated with her."

Faith nodded. "Yes."

"I was wrong, Faith." What Jamie felt was as far from cold hatred as an emotion could get.

Very slowly, with utmost care, Faith put her arms around him. "I'm glad."

While giving her a one-arm hug, Jamie explained what had happened, now that he finally understood. "Becky was pretending to be a vigilante. She had some harebrained plan to get me off the mountain so she could grab me. She thought curiosity alone would force me to interfere."

"I'm surprised you didn't figure all that out sooner."

"Alyx had me confused." He grinned, then shook his head. "Here she was, following Becky, stealing a dog, always on the scene, but not the cause of it. And Alyx wanted me off the mountain too, so she could force me to accept them all." The grin faded. "Becky just wanted me so she could lure you in." His hug tightened with the memory of how close the bullet had come to Faith.

"She knew I was with you, then?"

"After she killed Delayna, she knew Cory would feel the threats, and she figured the only person you'd be able to go to would be me."

"Well." Faith pushed back with a shaky smile on her face. "She was right." After straightening her hair and wiping away the remnants of tears, Faith folded her hands in front of her. She looked nervous, and Jamie fought the urge to steal her thoughts.

"Are you ready to go? Your daughter is very anxious to get to know you better, and Joe said we . . . that is, he invited us to stay with him awhile. . . ."

Jamie put his good arm around her and led her to the door. "I hope you said yes, because I'm not letting you out of my sight."

Faith's smile became genuine. "I said yes."

Two weeks after that awful debacle, Julie and Clint's wedding day came with a burst of sunshine and a gentle breeze. There'd been no question of Jamie's attending the wedding, given that he, Faith, Cory, and Tracy were still ensconced in Joe's house. Not an ideal situation, but Jamie couldn't see dragging Tracy and Cory up the mountain where they'd be short on beds and entertainment.

Jamie still wore a sling on his arm, but only because Faith insisted on following the doctor's orders to the letter. He felt fine. Better than fine. More than able to make love to her without the stupid sling getting in his way.

Not that a single female seemed inclined to believe him.

Not only did he have Luna and Shay, Cyn and Julie checking on him daily, but Faith's mother had joined their ranks. And Tracy was a woman who knew how to pamper.

When Jamie tried protesting, she called him "son" and scolded him one moment, then hugged him the next.

When that unsettled him, Tracy told him she was a mom and a grandma, and she loved him by association, so he might as well get used to it.

Her generous heart left Jamie tongue-tied and with a lump in his throat the size of a grapefruit. He couldn't remember ever being mothered before.

It was the kind of thing a man could get used to.

Joe's kids were fascinated with Cory. Willow, a young lady at sixteen, took Cory under her wing. But Austin, the scamp, had her doing parlor tricks and ridiculous predictions.

Jamie discovered that his daughter had a wicked sense of humor. She got even with Austin's constant prodding by telling him outrageous things. One night, she claimed a snail would creep in and sleep in his mouth, leaving behind a pile of slime. Austin didn't sleep a wink all night, and Faith ended up scolding Cory, who gave Austin a most insincere apology, while she and Jamie shared a private moment of humor.

Joe, understanding Jamie's predicament, made sure he had plenty of time alone with Faith. It wasn't hard, given that Cory adored the lake. Even now, dressed up for the wedding, she stood at the edge of the shoreline, skipping rocks with Austin.

Joe sauntered over to the park bench where Jamie sat with Faith close to his side. "You two having fun?"

"It was a beautiful wedding," Faith said. "The lake as a backdrop is just perfect."

"We think so." He eyed Jamie, cocking one brow in blatant suggestion. "Everyone seems to want to get married here. And you can tell Luna adores organizing it all."

Jamie looked away. He knew he should have cemented things with Faith by now, but damn . . . he'd never had to spill his guts to a woman before. And even when he had privacy with her, he knew there were people looming just around the corner.

Suddenly Faith stood. Somewhat militant, she propped her hands on her hips and glared at Jamie, but spoke to Joe.

Her voice bright and cheerful, a direct contrast to her expression, she said, "Do you still have openings?"

Uh-oh. Jamie knew his time had run out. And if Joe's grin was any indication, he knew it too.

"Of course we do. In fact, last night, Luna had the calendar out, and she's marked all the available weekends."

Jamie said, "Ah—"

But Faith plopped down on his lap and wrapped her arms around his neck. The skirt of her pretty pink floral dress spread out over his jeans—jeans she'd objected to his wearing, until he'd explained he didn't own anything else.

She was so busy rehearsing what she'd say to Jamie, she left herself wide open, and he heard it all before she'd voiced a single word. He'd never tire of experiencing her love. And no way in hell would he ever let her go.

Others seemed to have sensed that something historic was about to happen, and a small crowd gathered around him.

For a man who'd had immeasurable privacy for damn near a decade, the imposition of so many people privy to his personal business should have been unsettling. But Jamie wasn't unsettled. The warmth of their caring satisfied a long-buried hunger. The only way his life could be fuller would be to make Faith his wife, and claim Cory legally.

He intended to do it, soon as he found the right words to explain. But now he wouldn't have to.

Faith gave the words to him.

When she started to speak, he kissed her, and felt her hot blush along with her stirring interest.

"Jamie," she scolded.

"You're right," he said. "We should get married."

Her eyes widened. Beautiful, stormy blue eyes that had captivated Jamie from the moment he'd found her on his mountain.

Determined to work out all the kinks, Faith cleared her throat. "Your cabin—"

"Joe thinks it'd make a great private retreat for the soon-to-be-wed and the blissfully married."

Startled, Joe said, "Yeah, I do. I was going to suggest that."

"I know." Jamie put Faith's hand to his chest and held it there. "Because I own a hundred and twenty-five acres, it should stay private."

"You own—"

"Yeah. There's enough land for us to build something closer to the road. Or we could buy something here by the lake. I'd really like to stay in Visitation—if that's okay with Tracy."

Everyone looked at Faith's mother, who preened under the attention. "It's wonderful here. It'll give me a nice place to visit."

Jamie stared at her. "You won't live with us?"

The question flustered her.

"I'd like for you to," Jamie said. "Or at least be close by if you prefer your own place." To Faith, he added, "I really do have enough money for . . . whatever."

Faith bubbled out a laugh that sounded shaky with tears of happiness. "Why don't we let my mom think about it for a little while?"

"All right." He kissed her again. "So, will you marry me?"

"Will you tell me you love me?"

His smile came slowly, unlike the emotion that had walloped him upside his head the moment Faith had invaded his life. He cupped her face. "I love you."

Laughing, Cory scampered onto the bench to sit on the other side of Jamie. "You love me, too."

"Yes."

Joe put a hand to his heart and teased, "What about me?"

Jamie scowled and said, "Even you." He looked around at the group and nodded. "All of you."

"Ah, shit," Joe complained, pretending to mop his eyes. "You're gonna make me cry."

"There's lots of love," Cory exclaimed. Then on her fingers, she counted off, "Mommy and Jamie, Alyx and Deputy Royal—"

Jamie straightened. "Hey. Where did they get off to, anyway? They haven't put on one single public display through this whole gathering."

They all looked around, and finally spotted them out on the lake in a small rowboat. Everyone could see them smooching.

"Good grief," Joe grouched.

Luna leaned against his side, laughing. "Maybe it could be a double wedding. As long as Jamie and Faith aren't waiting too long, because I heard Alyx tell Scott the sooner the better."

Cory piped up again, still holding her fingers in the air. "And Clay and Willow."

Joe jerked around to stare at his daughter in shock, before narrowing his eyes at Clay. "What's she talking about?"

Cory grinned. "He's sweet on her."

Jamie hugged Cory tight. "Sweetheart, you can't just go around telling everyone's business—"

That brought a round of guffaws from Bruce, Bryan, and Clint, because Jamie had always done just that. But Joe was still too speechless to chime in.

Willow turned bright pink. "Joe," she complained under her breath.

Taking her hand, Clay smiled. "She's special."

"She's *sixteen*."

"Yes, sir. I know."

Left with nothing brilliant to add, Joe nodded. "All right then."

And with a roll of her eyes, Willow dragged Clay off.

Luna hugged Joe. "You're learning."

Tipping her head in a thoughtful way, Cory watched them as they headed toward the lake. "Willow's embarrassed, but Clay's not. I think he's lots like Joe."

Floored by the possibility, Joe muttered, "Dear God." He started to go after them, but Luna caught him by the seat of his pants and pulled him up short.

Jamie squeezed Cory again. "You're torturing Joe." Then he added with a laugh, "But I like it."

A mischievous twinkle appeared in Cory's dark eyes. "I know."

Keeping Willow and Clay in his sights, Joe said, "She sounds just like you, Jamie Creed."

And Jamie, grinning with the thrill of a family, friends, and a brand-new life, said simply, "Yeah . . . I know."